EMPIRE

JOHN CONNOLLY
EMPIRE
JENNIFER RIDYARD

headline

First published in 2015 by
HEADLINE PUBLISHING GROUP

1

Cataloguing in Publication Data is available from the British Library

Hardback ISBN 978 1 4722 0972 6
Trade paperback ISBN 978 1 4722 0973 3

Typeset in Bembo by Avon DataSet Ltd, Bidford-on-Avon, Warwickshire

Printed and bound in Great Britain by Clays Ltd, St Ives plc

Headline's policy is to use papers that are natural, renewable and recyclable products
and made from wood grown in well-managed forests and other controlled sources.
The logging and manufacturing processes are expected to conform to the
environmental regulations of the country of origin.

HEADLINE PUBLISHING GROUP
An Hachette UK Company
338 Euston Road
London NW1 3BH

www.headline.co.uk
www.hachette.co.uk

For the other sisterhood,
Jacquie and Lucy

NAIRENE SISTERHOOD

OF THE SECOND CIVIL WAR
AND THE COMING OF SYL HELLAIS,
THE EARTHBORN

It is strange that the discovery of an advanced species – **humanity** – and the successful occupation of their planet should also have marked the beginning of the end of the Illyri Conquest, leaving the Illyri teetering on the edge of a second Civil War.

The seeds of conflict had been sown long before, of course: the **Military** and the **Diplomatic Corps** had been engaged in low-level hostilities for centuries, with neither side able to gain the upper hand. Then, in the early years of the Conquest, the Diplomats formed an **alliance** with the secretive order known as the **Nairene Sisterhood**, a union secured by the marriage of the Archmage **Syrene** – the public face of the Sisterhood – to Grand

Consul **Gradus**, the most
senior Diplomat in the
Illyri Empire. From that
moment on, the fate of
the Military appeared
sealed.

Syrene and
Gradus travelled to
Earth to confront
the most influential
Military leader on the
planet, **Lord Andrus**,
who served as something
of a lightning rod for
those who opposed the
Diplomats and their Nairene
allies. What happened next is
well documented: the capture
of Gradus by the **human
Resistance** and his death
at the Scottish castle called
Dundearg. However, this
bloodletting was overshadowed
by the human Resistance's
discovery that the Illyri were
not the only otherworldly
invaders, for there were those
among our own race who
carried an advanced **alien
organism** within themselves.

Indeed, they had welcomed
the creatures into their bodies,
for these were ancient beings,
as **old as time**, and their
knowledge was almost as
immeasurable as their hunger.

Yet everything that
occurred on Earth during the
Conquest is overshadowed by
the emergence of one of the
pivotal figures in Illyri
history: the daughter of

Lord Andrus, the child known as Syl Hellais, the Earthborn. **Syl the Destroyer.**

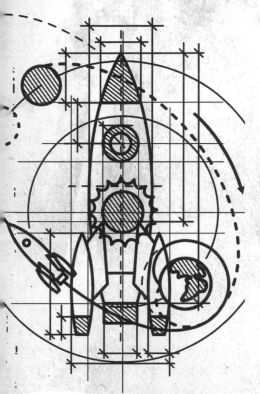

She was the first Illyri to be born on Earth, and formed a bond of deep affection with the human Resistance fighter, **Paul Kerr.** The Sisterhood succeeded in separating them, banishing Syl to the **Marque,** its sealed convent orbiting the homeworld of Illyr, and sending Kerr to fight – and, it was hoped, to die – in the **Brigades.** Finally, Lord Andrus was forcibly infected by the alien parasite, thereby depriving the **Military** of its most accomplished leader. It seemed to the Sisterhood and the Diplomats that the Empire was theirs for the taking.

But they were wrong.

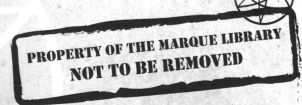

I
APART

CHAPTER 1

The predators circled, each taking a turn to snarl at her, some more vicious than others, but everyone determined to take a piece of flesh.

'Stupid, shabby thing.'

'She never learns.'

'She's too stupid to learn.'

'Why are you here?'

'You don't belong in this place.'

'Why do you even exist?'

'Elda. Even your name is ugly.'

'Look at yourself!'

'She can't. She shuns mirrors. She's afraid they'll crack at the sight of her.'

And then the leader, the alpha, came to bite, the pack parting, their faces turned admiringly upon her, her radiance reflected in their eyes.

Tanit, beautiful young Tanit: cruel, and worse than cruel.

'No, that's not the case,' said Tanit. 'She stays away from mirrors because there's nothing to see. She's so insignificant that she's barely there at all.'

It was the way that she spoke, the words tossed carelessly as though the object of her disdain were unworthy even of the effort involved in crushing her. She looked down on Elda – Tanit was tall, even for an Illyri; it was part of her power – reached out a hand, and let it slip through this lesser Novice's mop of dark hair, the strands tangling in her fingers.

'Nothing,' said Tanit. 'I feel . . . nothing.'

Her victim kept her head down, her eyes on the floor. It was better that way, easier. Perhaps Tanit and the others might grow bored if they couldn't provoke a reaction, and seek other prey to torment.

But no, not this time. Elda felt a prickling on her skin. It began at her cheeks, then slowly spread to her nose, her forehead, her ears, her neck. Warmth became heat; heat became burning pain. What Tanit was doing to her was against all the rules, but the rules did not apply to Tanit and her acolytes as they did to others. After all, this was merely practice for them. They were like disturbed children encouraged to torture insects and rodents so that they would not falter when told to inflict pain on their own.

And they had no fear of being caught. This was the Marque, the ancient lair of the Nairene Sisterhood, and held no shortage of places in which the weak could be victimised by the strong.

The burning grew more intense. Elda could feel blisters forming, her skin bubbling and lifting. She put her hand to her face in a vain effort to shield herself, but her palm immediately started blistering too, and she snatched it back in fright. She tried not to scream, determined not to give them that satisfaction, but the agony was becoming too much to bear. She opened her mouth, but it was the voice of another that spoke.

'Leave her be!'

Tanit's concentration was broken. Immediately, Elda's pain began to lessen. There would be marks, but no scars. That, at least, was something.

The Novice looked up. Syl Hellais was pushing her way through the pack – a well-placed elbow here, a knee there. Some resisted, but only passively. There was grumbling and confusion, but Tanit merely looked on and laughed, folding her arms across her chest as if settling in to see what Syl planned to do.

Now Syl stood by Elda's side.

'Elda, are you all right?'

Syl helped her to her feet, looking anxiously at the girl's face, then turning her hand over and inspecting the injury on her palm. Elda appeared badly sunburned, and her hand was red and sore, but the blisters were small and unbroken.

'Is it awful?' whispered Elda.

'It will fade,' said Syl, which wasn't quite answering the question. Anyway, there was no time for that now. They had more pressing concerns. The pack was brave when in numbers, but still only ever as strong as its leader. Tackle the leader, and the pack would slink away. In theory.

But this was Tanit, and Tanit did not back down easily. She was watching Syl closely, her face set in a mask of amusement.

'What did you do to her?' said Syl.

'I simply told her she was pretty,' said Tanit. 'I made her blush.'

'What is it to you anyway, Smelly?' said one of the braver females, bristling on Tanit's left. Her name was Sarea, and she and another Novice, Nemein, were competitors for Tanit's favour, and the floating post of her best friend. Tanit enjoyed playing them off against each other. Each would deny Tanit nothing for fear that she might turn instead to the other.

Now Syl and Tanit exchanged a look, a brief flash of ice-cold understanding between deadly rivals. Sarea was trying to score points by baiting Syl. Tanit gave Sarea a barely perceptible nod, granting permission for the entertainment to begin.

Sarea stepped forward. She was graceful and almost delicately pretty, all fine bones and sparkling eyes. However, Sarea's prettiness hid a near-psychotic lust for violence. Her particular skill was the application of pressure with the power of her mind, from the merest sensation of tightness on the skin to the breaking of bones and the crushing of skulls. She had tried it on Syl once, shortly after her arrival at the Marque; a little welcoming bruise, that was how Sarea had described it.

Syl had broken Sarea's nose in reprisal, and it hadn't required much mental effort at all on her part. It was mostly physical.

Mostly.

Now Syl smiled, though her stomach felt weak and empty, her hands shaky. She balled them into fists.

'You're brave when picking on those weaker than you, surrounded by your friends,' said Syl. 'Would you be quite so mouthy if it were just you and me?'

She could feel Sarea itching to hurt her: a little pressure and she could burst some of the blood vessels in Syl's nose, or in her eyes. Slightly more, and a finger might snap, a toe break. And then there were all those lovely internal organs: lungs, bowels, heart.

Oh, the heart! Sarea yearned to crush a heart. And already what she was envisaging was becoming real. Syl felt the faintest squeezing behind her ribs, a pressure on the beating organ, and knew that it was Sarea's work, even though Sarea was banned from using her skills out of class. However, Sarea was just a Novice too, and not completely in control of her dubious talents, not yet. Or perhaps, she merely chose not to be.

Now Sarea opened her mouth as if to reply, but then her eyes glazed over and she stood, silent but open-mouthed. She stared hard at Syl before looking to the rest of her group, bewildered. Syl watched her, her heart released again, freely pounding in her chest. She waited for the pack to attack, but then Tanit spoke once more.

'I'm sorry. We meant no harm.'

'Excuse me?' said Syl.

'It was nothing, Sister. Nothing. We're sorry. No harm.'

Tanit stepped away, turning to leave, and the others moved after her while Syl and Elda watched, slack-jawed with surprise. But one of the pack remained, staring at Syl, unmoving as the rest of Tanit's creatures melted away. She was half-obscured in the shadows, a reedy, dark-haired figure in rich blue robes. Her name was Uludess, but her friends called her Dessa. As Syl looked into that intense, furrowed face, a bead of blood slid from the older girl's nose, and she shrugged and gave a rueful little grin. Syl opened her mouth to speak, but Dessa shook her head ever so slightly then spun away, wiping the blood on her sleeve as she hurried after her friends.

A tutor in the red garments of a full Sister approached.

'What was all that about?'

It was Cale, who was responsible for the junior Novices like Syl.

She was young for a senior Nairene. Her family had died in a shuttle crash shortly after her birth, and only Cale had survived. The Sisterhood had taken her in and raised her, so Cale's progress through the ranks had started earlier than most.

Syl and Elda stared at the floor.

'Do either of you want to explain to me what was going on there?' asked Cale, but it was only for show. She knew what Tanit and her pack were like, just as she understood that Syl and Elda would tell her nothing of what had happened. Even if they did, Cale could only go to the Grandmage Oriel to complain on their behalf, and Oriel, who supervised the training of all Novices, would only ignore her. Oriel had a fondness for Tanit and her kind.

'I tripped,' said Elda. 'Syl was pulling me to my feet.'

'And the others?' said Cale.

'They were queuing up to help too,' said Syl.

Cale gave Syl a peculiar look. She seemed about to smile, but thought better of it.

'Get back to your duties, both of you,' she said.

They did as they were told. Cale watched them go, but so too did another, unseen. The Grandmage Oriel remained in the doorway for a moment, and then was gone.

CHAPTER 2

Far from the Marque, and from most civilised systems, a Military shuttle came in low across a desert, following the mounds and crevasses of the sands below, dipping, rising, shifting gently to left or right under the expert control of the pilot. Sometimes he came so close to the ground that the shuttle's thrusters kicked up clouds behind the craft, causing the proximity sensors to activate and send alarm signals pinging through the craft.

'He's going to kill us. I swear he's going to kill us.'

The voice was Private Cutler's. He was the unit's communications specialist, and resident pessimist. As far as Cutler was concerned, the only reason he wasn't already dead was because God hadn't yet come up with the worst possible way of killing him. Cutler was from Omaha, Nebraska. The first time he saw the ocean was from the window of the Illyri transport shuttle that was taking him to join the Brigades. On that day, he was convinced that he was going to drown. Since then, he'd variously believed himself to be on the verge of burning, falling, suffocating, being poisoned, or being crushed to death. Today, crashing seemed the likeliest fate, especially with Steven Kerr at the controls of the shuttle.

Beside him, Steven's older brother Paul rested his head against the back of his seat and closed his eyes. He had no concerns about Steven's abilities as a pilot. Steven was gifted: there was no other word for it. Paul believed it had something to do with all of those PlayStation games that had cluttered their shared bedroom back in Edinburgh. Paul had dabbled in games – he liked POV shoot-'em-ups, although he quickly grew out of them after his involvement in the human

Resistance movement against the Illyri invaders introduced him to the sordid reality of killing – but Steven's devotion to them was total. He could immerse himself for hours and hours, forgetting even to eat, his fingers and thumbs dancing over the controls as though he had been born to the buttons. His particular fondness was for cars, planes and helicopters – anything that could be driven or flown. When the time came for their aptitudes to be tested by the Illyri, Steven had aced all of the flight simulations. He had immediately been fast-tracked into the pilot program, spending most of his time sitting in a comfortable chair playing a glorified computer game, while his older sibling was left to muddle along with the grunts – running, jumping, falling and shooting.

Oh, Paul knew that it wasn't really like that for his brother, however much it amused him to tease Steven about it. Pilots had to be at the peak of mental alertness and physical endurance, and Paul had watched Steven stumble back bleary-eyed to their shared barrack room, his head thumping and his limbs aching from hours of increasingly difficult simulations. Fewer than one per cent of those who aspired to be Brigade pilots made it to the level that Steven had reached – command pilot – and none had ever attained it so soon. The shuttle they were now in was Steven's, the first craft over which he had sole control, and he was relishing every minute of it, even if Cutler was not.

'He's crazy, you know,' said Cutler. 'If he flies any lower, we'll be travelling underground.'

'He's not crazy,' said Paul. 'He's just happy.'

'At least one of us is.'

Paul opened his eyes. He'd been hoping to nap on the flight, but even he had to admit that Steven's manoeuvres were not going to allow anyone to rest peacefully. Not that Military shuttles were designed with comfortable sleep in mind: they were heavily weaponised and armoured transports, with individual flight seats facing one another along the length of the craft. Twin cannon hung beneath the pilots' cabin, with a second pair of cannon contained in a bubble at the rear of the craft. When required, four sets of rocket launchers could unfold from the body of the craft in an X-formation: it was a fast, ferocious weapon of war.

On this day, though, they were not at war, for theirs was an exploratory mission. In fact, of their unit only Cutler and De Souza, their lieutenant, had ever fired their weapons in anger. Even they had done so only as part of a protective mission on a moon that didn't even have a name, only a number, and their pulse weapons had been used on creatures that were just an evolutionary step above jellyfish. The truth was that the universe was mostly empty of intelligent life – in fact, empty of much life at all. So far, the human race was the most advanced species that the Illyri had encountered, and look what had happened to the people of Earth: invasion and conquest, followed by occupation. The Resistance still fought the invaders – Paul and Steven had been captured in just such a battle against their conquerors, before being forcibly conscripted into the Brigades – but their campaign was mostly just an annoyance to the Illyri.

Through the window Paul watched the arid white landscape of the planet pass below. This was Torma, and it had taken them a month to reach it. Somewhere above Torma lay the Illyri destroyer *Envion*, now undergoing repairs after a difficult trip, or 'boost', through the final wormhole. Paul was still not used to the sensation of wormhole travel – the distortion of space and time, the sickening sense that he was leaving his brain and internal organs trailing behind him. The best that could be said was that at least it was over quickly, and he was always relieved when the trip was completed, and he found himself alive and intact.

Peris, their Illyri training supervisor, now sat at the head of the craft, just behind Paul. The Illyri soldier had once been the commander of the guard at Edinburgh Castle, but had given up his comfortable existence in order to watch over Paul and Steven in the Brigades. Paul did not truly understand Peris's motives, but he had accompanied the Kerr brothers from Earth, and had been with them throughout their basic training at the Brigade base on the planet Coramal.

The training had mostly involved learning how to function as a unit, along with honing the weapons skills of the recruits, teaching them the basics of Illyri technology, and improving their command of the Illyri language, mainly through immersive techniques, including feeding them a steady stream of words and grammar while they slept. The alien tongue proved less complex than Paul had first thought, and soon he could speak it better than most, which was undoubtedly one of the reasons why he had been promoted to sergeant. The recruits had also undergone a range of medical procedures designed to prevent their bones from becoming brittle over long periods in space, and to address the increased risk of cancer due to radiation exposure.

Now Peris caught Paul looking at him, and nodded. Paul had grown to respect the old Illyri, even though he could not say if he liked him. The Illyri were the enemy, and Paul's ultimate aim was to destroy their empire. If Peris got in his way, then Paul would kill him. And yet he could not look at Peris without thinking of Edinburgh, and the castle.

And Syl.

Face it, Paul thought, not for the first time: you're in love with an Illyri. In an ideal world, you'd bring her civilisation to its knees and then run away with her through the ruins. How do you think that's going to work out? Oh, and there's also the small matter that she's millions of light years away, separated from you by countless wormholes, and imprisoned in a convent run by a bunch of weird nuns who worship knowledge as a god. You should have just dated a girl from Leith, or even Dundee, or, at a push, Inverness.

Beside Peris sat Faron. Although Peris exceeded him in age, experience and wisdom, Faron was technically the ranking Illyri officer on board, and this was his first full mission. The Brigades were used to give new and inexperienced Illyri officers like Faron a taste of command. As far as Paul was concerned, Faron was particularly useless: his arrogance concealed his uncertainty, and he was contemptuous of the humans under his command, a poor attempt to mask his fear of them. Faron had only joined them on this trip because he needed to rack up a certain number of missions before he could leave the Brigades behind.

Paul watched him sweat. Steven's piloting of the shuttle was clearly terrifying Faron as much as Cutler, but Faron didn't want to appear weak in front of the humans, or Peris.

'Are we there yet?' said Cutler.

Paul closed his eyes again, and dreamed of Syl.

CHAPTER 3

Elda muttered her vague thanks for Syl's timely intervention as she followed her from the chamber. Together they walked along in awkward silence until they reached the junction where the Twelfth Realm joined the Thirteenth, and Elda turned to go. She paused, and then touched Syl's arm briefly.

'Take care,' she said, looking at Syl directly for the first time since she'd arrived at the Marque all those months before. 'These old halls are treacherous. My friend Kosia was killed by a falling wall . . .'

She trailed off, looking uncertain, as though considering saying more, yet fearful of the consequences if she did.

'Your friend Kosia?' said Syl. Instantly she regretted the disbelief that seemed to slip unbidden into her voice as she repeated the words 'your friend', as though friendship was somehow beyond Elda.

Elda stepped away and looked down, her shoulders slumping even further.

'Yes,' she said, 'my friend. We joined together.'

'I'm sorry,' Syl started to say, but Elda was already scurrying away into the Thirteenth with not a glance behind her.

Syl couldn't decide if she wanted to shake the Novice or hug her. Elda was so uninvolved, so passive. She faded into the background, limp and washed-out, doing everything she could not to draw attention to herself, so anxious to avoid any unnecessary contact with others that the sleeves of her robes were grimy from pressing against the walls of the Marque. And yet clearly she felt sadness at the death of her friend, this Kosia, of whom Syl had never heard before. She was hurting, but who would ever know it to look at her?

Who would ever look at Elda anyway, when she hardly seemed to be there at all?

Still shaken, Syl headed back to her quarters. Despite what Cale had said, her duties for the day were done. She had spent much of the afternoon in the Scriptorium adjoining the main Library in their Realm, together with her best friend Ani, translating a series of abstract poems from English to Illyri, before Ani rushed off to her special classes, the lessons she attended with the other 'Gifted' Novices.

Syl had continued translating, but her mind had been anywhere but here, everywhere but now, and eventually the Sister in charge of the exercise sent her off early, tutting at her incompetence. Syl was relieved, for it was slow, painstaking work, and she couldn't see why they bothered anyway. What use did the Sisterhood have for the musings of long-dead poets from a distant world? But then her tutors argued that the poems represented knowledge, however ancient and alien, and knowledge was the lifeblood of the Sisterhood. No knowledge could really be described as useless; there was simply knowledge that could be applied, and knowledge that had not yet found its application.

And, of course, it was part of their training as Novices. Translating, transcribing, reading, writing – that was how the majority of Novices spent most of their first three years. In between these tasks, they studied Illyri history, universal geography, mathematics, the sciences, and much more. Syl and Ani excelled in only one subject: existential biology, which explored the zoology and botany of conquered worlds, most specifically Earth.

The subject Syl disliked most was applied diplomacy. It was a mix of Illyri etiquette, social studies, psychology and politics, with rather too much practising of polite conversation, folding of hands neatly on laps, and discreet dabbing at one's mouth to surreptitiously remove hypothetical crumbs for Syl's liking. The subject's purpose, as far as she could tell, was to train Nairene Sisters to enter the larger Illyri world and charm – or manipulate – everyone they met to further the Sisterhood's own ends. For Syl, it was only useful in teaching her how the Sisterhood operated, and how it viewed the world outside the Marque. Know your enemy: that was what her father had taught her.

Her father, Lord Andrus . . .

She swallowed hard at the memory of him, and her eyes prickled. No matter how much she tried, she could not quite resign herself to his loss, even though six months had gone, fully half an Earth-year since she had last seen him. But his loss was more than just the distance between them, for still she recalled the strange sweet smell of his breath, and the vacant look in his eyes when he had last held her and said goodbye. He was infected – his mind, his will, even his internal organs taken over by an unknown alien organism, leaving his body as just a carrier for the parasite that dwelt within it. Yet he looked and felt as warm and real as the only parent she'd ever known, and still loved with all her being.

And the public face of the Nairene Sisterhood, the Archmage Syrene, was responsible. Somehow, she had implanted that thing in Syl's father. Somehow, she had stolen him away just before Syl could say goodbye, and poisoned him from within. Syrene was in league with these entities, these alien life-forms, but to what end Syl could not say. The handful of Resistance fighters who knew of their existence called them the 'Others', and Syl had seen them with her own eyes, had borne witness to them at a remote castle in Scotland before fire and explosions destroyed the evidence, leaving only smoke and denial. Still, she knew, and so did a handful of Resistance fighters on Earth, even though what they had seen raised only more questions.

Syl had sworn to find out the truth, to avenge her father, to free him from that creature inside him if there was any way at all, though she felt consumed by a sadness so overwhelming she thought it might crush her. She had to believe there was hope, and the Nairene Sisterhood – guardians of all universal knowledge – was where hope lay.

The Marque was enormous: a series of interlinked sections, or Realms – as many as twenty in total – stretching throughout Avila Minor. Syl had first seen the Marque from above, when their shuttle was coming in to land. The boulders and sculpted cliffs that reared from the surface reminded her of Petra, the great rock-cut city in Jordan back on Earth, but now that she was inside it she knew the Marque was more like the huge, busy mounds built by termites on the African savannah.

The walls of the visible buildings were thick, but much of the Marque lay hidden below the surface. Each Realm had its own landing pad for shuttles, and its own emergency systems, stores, generators and solar farms. While the individual Realms were connected, most could be sealed off from their neighbours in an emergency, or in the event of an attack – although who would dare attack the Marque? By day any invading force would be burned to a crisp by the sun, and by night it would be devoured by the vicious creatures that hunted in the dark. The moon would take care of any hostile force long before the Marque's defences could be breached.

Since her arrival, Syl had remained imprisoned within these walls, feeling like a termite herself, digging, burrowing, going about the business of being a student, but all the time looking for clues to the Sisterhood's true aims.

Well, when she wasn't getting into trouble for protecting poor, wretched Elda.

And yet, and yet . . .

Syl was silently grateful for Elda and her submissive ways, because without Elda's example she herself would never have known how to even begin to explore those parts of the Marque that were off-limits to her. She subtly watched how Elda slunk everywhere like a beaten dog, sidestepping the other Novices as they strode confidently by, slinking unnoticed into the shadows, hanging her head so as not to make eye contact, ducking nimbly into fissures in the rock face to escape comment. It was four years since Elda had first arrived at the Marque, but in that time she'd become as much a part of the place as the furniture, and as unremarkable as a wall or chair. Syl had learned that Elda had ceased going to class in her first months as the Nairenes' expectations of her faded away to nothing, for she was so clearly born servile and ignorant, and so obviously doomed to remain that way. The Sisters had happily handed her a drudge's chores, setting her to cleaning and dusting just to keep her out of the way.

By now Elda should by rights have been a Half-Sister, clad in the proud sea-green robes of those who had all but completed their education, who were only awaiting investiture into the order as full Sisters, but still Elda trailed around dull-eyed in her threadbare butter-yellow robes, the robes the Novices wore every day in the Marque, and gradually her garments had faded to the white that the lowliest, most unpromising order of the Sisterhood – the Service Sisters – donned when they were supervising cleaning, or on kitchen duty.

And somehow, somewhere Elda became invisible to those who believed themselves her betters, just as servants often do.

Syl had realised this as she was on the verge of almost ceasing to notice Elda too, and she had quickly taken her cue from the older girl's cleaning headscarf and washed-out clothing, wrapping her own telltale bronze hair in a piece of sheet torn from her bedlinen, and even stealing one of Elda's dirty-white robes from the gymnasium when the girl had been hard at work in the showers in nothing but her underwear, scrubbing the mouldy floors clean as water splashed on her bent back. Guiltily, Syl had replaced the garment with her best robe, crisp and fresh and yellow, but Elda seemed not to notice, putting Syl's clothes on without even raising an eyebrow.

Slowly, Syl had started to explore, modelling herself on Elda as she did so, gradually moving further into the places that were off-bounds to a mere first year Novice, a bucket of cleaning utensils and dusters in her hand at all times. She did not risk venturing out often, and certainly followed no pattern, but when she did explore she hunched her shoulders, shuffled her feet and practised disappearing into the background. On the rare occasions when she was stopped or questioned she claimed to be there in place of Elda or on the orders of a Service Sister, mumbling and apologising until she was sent on her way, sometimes with a sharp word and once with a very nasty pinch to the soft flesh on the underside of her upper arm. Yet nobody seemed unduly perturbed by her presence. After all, those within the Sisterhood accepted the honour of their place here: surely there could be none inside that intended harm or serious insurrection. There were so many females crowded into this space that it was relatively easy to disappear in the throng.

So Syl dusted libraries that weren't meant for juniors; she wiped surfaces in higher Scriptoriums where the older Novices worked; she mopped floors in the Half-Sisters hallways, listening to their conversations; and she opened books that were not for her eyes. But so many corridors remained unexplored – countless warrens of rooms and chambers and private quarters, of dead ends and blank walls, and the main channels all led inevitably to the sealed door at the end of the Thirteenth: the sealed door painted with the red eye of the Sisterhood.

Too often, with her efforts frustrated, she'd lie on her bed, hatching new schemes as she dreamed of how she could make her world – indeed, all worlds – right again.

Yet sometimes she found herself dreaming of other things and other places too, dreaming of warm sunshine and the smell of roses, of dewy grass and birdsong, of an eagle soaring against heavy Scottish skies, of a deer walking beside an icy Highland stream, of fingers drawing a heart on her back . . .

Dreaming of the human boy she'd kissed on Earth.

Dreaming of Paul Kerr.

CHAPTER 4

Paul was roused from his private thoughts by Steven's voice rasping over the coms system.

'Destination in sight. Touchdown in five clicks.'

'Thank God,' said Cutler. 'Tell your brother I'll walk back.'

Faron also looked relieved at the prospect of finally landing. He swallowed his nausea for long enough to issue an order.

'Standard scan,' he said. 'Quick as you can.'

A standard scan was the minimum required for landing in possibly unsecured territory, as it searched for signs of movement, heat signatures, and carbon-based life. Peris seemed about to say something, but instead remained silent. Ahead of them loomed the exploration platform, designed to probe for mineral deposits. Torma was believed to be rich in iron ore, gold and uranium although, as with everything else, the Illyri had their own names for them. Exploration platforms were typically staffed by scientists, engineers and seismologists, who would assess the viability of mining the resources. The platform on Torma had been dropped ten weeks earlier, and was not due for retrieval until the end of its six-month assessment mission.

Unfortunately, all communication with the platform had ceased shortly after its first month so the *Envion* had been dispatched to investigate and, if necessary, perform a rescue and retrieval mission.

'Scan negative,' said Steven. 'All clear to land.'

'Circle,' said Faron.

Steven did as he was ordered. The shuttle soared over and around the exploration platform. It resembled a small fortress, with high steel walls surrounding a central courtyard of desert sand. At its northern end stood a cluster of buildings: laboratories and living quarters for the small survey team. To the south was what appeared to be a long pipe, one end buried deep in the sand. This was the hull of the primary search device, and protected a complicated mass of drilling, coring and cutting equipment. A raised walkway linked it to the laboratory complex, allowing samples to be easily transported for analysis. Lights blinked on the platform's various masts and towers. A small Civilian shuttle stood on its sole landing pad, but there were no signs of life.

'Were they armed?' asked Faron. His knowledge of drilling platforms and their operation wouldn't have occupied much time in a conversation.

'Just basic pulse weapons,' said Peris. 'The shuttle has a single seventy millimetre cannon mounted on its underside, but that's all.'

Faron detected a note of disapproval in Peris's voice.

'The planet was cleared as I-Two,' he told Peris. 'No further protection was deemed necessary.'

The Illyri classified planets according to two primary designations – I for Inhabited and U for Uninhabited. The first designation allowed for a series of numerical progressions: 1 was basically microbial life; 2, lesser unintelligent and generally unthreatening life-forms – insects, lizards, small mammals; 3 was significant life, with lower-level species of some intelligence, the equivalent of Earth's apes; and 4 was an advanced civilisation. So far, only Earth had qualified as a 5: an advanced civilisation with the potential capacity for interplanetary travel, if only within its own system.

The initial life-form survey of Torma had revealed little indication of life beyond bugs and the peculiar lizard-like creatures that fed upon them, which the Illyri had nicknamed tormals. They seemed to combine the scaled bodies and cold-blooded metabolisms of reptiles with a thick, retractable exoskeleton. This shield could be folded away like wings until the creature felt under threat, whereupon the exoskeleton was activated, sealing the lizard inside a hard black shell. Some of the scientists and engineers on Torma had begun keeping tormals as pets – despite standing orders against such practices – for the little lizards were content to spend their time eating, sleeping and playing with coloured balls, which they fetched and returned in the manner of tiny dogs. They rarely activated their protective shells in the company of the Illyri, and it remained a mystery as to why the mechanism existed at all. It was suggested that it might be a kind of evolutionary hangover, a form of protection against something that no longer existed, but which was by now so embedded in the development of the creatures – like the human appendix, as De Souza had explained to them, by way of comparison – that it had not been discarded.

Paul hadn't contradicted De Souza, even though he seemed to recall that scientists had, in fact, discovered that the purpose of the appendix was to store helpful bacteria. Besides, just because something didn't easily reveal the reason for its existence wasn't the same thing as not having one at all.

'Take us down,' said Faron. 'Land inside the perimeter, but stay at the controls and keep the shuttle primed. I want us to be able to leave here in an instant, if necessary.'

'In the blink of an eye, you might even say,' a jaded voice announced.

It was Thula, the Zulu corporal. Faron shot Thula a hateful glance, but said nothing. Like all Illyri, Faron did not have eyelids. Instead his eyes were protected by a nictitating membrane similar to that found in birds, reptiles, and some mammals. He knew that Thula had made a joke at his expense, but he wasn't about to reprimand the youth. If Faron hid a secret fear of the human troopers, he failed utterly to disguise the fact that Thula terrified him.

Thula's full name was Khethukuthula. It meant 'choose to stay quiet' in his own tongue. Cutler had once suggested to Thula that it really meant 'mouthful', at which point Thula had lifted Cutler from the ground by his neck and waited for him to start turning blue before releasing him. Thula's name was not entirely suited to him, for Paul had found him to be more open in private. His public face was serious, though, and he rarely smiled. He was slim but immensely strong, and almost as tall as the average Illyri. Like Paul and Steven, Thula had been a member of the Resistance, fighting and killing the Illyri in South Africa, and had barely escaped a death posting to the Punishment Battalions, where the Illyri sent those humans who were regarded as terrorists and criminals. It was one of the reasons why he and Paul had bonded. Thula's intelligence and strength marked him out: even the Illyri were not inclined to waste the potential of such a fighter.

Thula winked at Paul. Paul just shook his head in amusement. Faron was only a few months into his command. They could be stuck with him for many more. It made sense to try and find a way to live with him as best they could, and antagonise him as little as necessary.

But, then again, Faron really was a jackass.

Steven slowly brought the shuttle down. Without being ordered, the twelve troopers on board began checking their weapons. All Illyri weapons issued to humans or other species were fitted with sensors that prevented them from being fired at an Illyri target, so that the Brigades could not rebel against their Illyri commanders. Brigade troops received pulse weapons as standard issue, but few really liked carrying them, for the pulse weapons were designed for use in conjunction with the Illyri's own implanted neural Chips. This meant that the force of the pulse blast was decided in the split-second inter-action between the user's brain and the Chip, and transmitted instantly to the rifle: a stun, a kill, or a full force shot that could blow a hole in a wall.

Humans, though, were not permitted to be chipped – supposedly because the functioning of the human and Illyri brains differed, but mostly because the Illyri did not want to implant subject races with such cutting-edge technology. But the truth, as Paul had quickly come to learn during basic training, was that the Chips had made the Illyri slightly lazy: they had come to depend upon them so much that some of their natural responses had been dulled. For instance, Paul's brother might not have been as technically proficient a pilot as some of the Illyri, but he was a more adaptive one, relying on his wits, not just technology.

Without Chips, the only way for humans to use pulse weapons was to adjust them manually or rely on a neural 'net' worn as part of a helmet. Even then, reaction times were slower, and a blow to the helmet could result in the net malfunctioning, leaving a trooper holding a useless weapon. In addition, pulse rifles occasionally failed to identify the DNA of their human users, rendering them unusable. In the event of such a failure, a message would appear on the weapon's digital display: URD, for 'User Recognition Denial', or, as the Brigades renamed it, 'U R Dead'.

Where possible, therefore, humans preferred conventional weaponry. Thus it was that Paul checked the depleted uranium loads in his Illyri Military-issue SR automatic rifle: 300 rounds to a load, and he carried five loads as standard, enough to start a small war. His webbing belt also contained five grenades – three incendiary, two gas – a seven-inch knife with a serrated edge, and a Colt pistol.

The Colt was technically illegal, but many of the humans complemented their Illyri-issue weaponry with some lethal additions from Earth: pistols, handguns and even sawn-off shotguns. Machetes and the odd sword or axe were also not uncommon. Officially, the Illyri frowned on such Earth armaments because, unlike pulse rifles or other Illyri arms, they could be used on the Illyri themselves. Gradually, though, the Illyri came to realise that any risk of rebellion was relatively low. Those who had, in the early years, turned against their Illyri officers had been hunted down within days, and footage of their unhappy deaths – tossed from airlocks and freezing in the blackness, or wasting away of radiation poisoning in a Punishment Battalion mine – was shown to new recruits, just to remind them of the consequences of rebellion. So Earth weapons incapable of automatic fire – shotguns, semi-automatic pistols – were reluctantly permitted. Their familiarity was found to make the troopers more effective fighters, and psychological tests had revealed that humans with Earth weapons as backup were more willing to enter dangerous combat situations that those without.

The shuttle touched down. Peris was the first to his feet.

'Gentlemen, you're up.'

He nodded to De Souza, who took over. De Souza was Brazilian, and one of the smallest men in the troop, but he radiated a confidence and authority that inspired respect.

'Sergeant Kerr, Thula, you have point. Cutler, Olver, you have the rear. The rest of you keep in the middle. Baudin and Rizzo, you stay with the ship. Any questions?'

'No, sir!' their voices shouted in unison. Cutler was the only exception.

'Hey, Lieutenant, do Baudin and Rizzo get to stay here because they're chicks?'

Baudin, a muscular French girl who carried a crossbow as her additional weapon, gave Cutler the finger. Rizzo, a tiny dark Italian, flicked her right hand, and a throwing star headed straight for Cutler's groin. It buried itself in Cutler's helmet, which, fortunately for him, he happened to be holding on his lap. Cutler lifted the helmet and stared at the little silver weapon.

'Not fair,' he said. 'Like, that could really have caused me some damage.'

'Cut it out, all of you,' said De Souza. 'Let's try to pretend we're professionals.'

He pointed at Baudin and Rizzo.

'You know what to do: we come running, and you start shooting.'

The two young women nodded. They were the best shots in the unit. If something went wrong at the platform, De Souza wanted them to provide covering fire. At least he could be certain that Baudin and Rizzo would hit whatever was chasing them. Cutler couldn't hit a barn door if it was lying on top of him.

'Steady,' said De Souza.

A red light flashed. The shuttle doors began to open.

'Go!' said De Souza. 'Go, go, go!'

CHAPTER 5

Syl's enforced stay with the Nairene Sisterhood was conducted entirely in the Twelfth Realm of the Marque, which was one of the more recent additions to the home of the order, rebuilt some years earlier after the collapse of its main tunnel system.

However, it was still a place of stone and rock, its classrooms starkly lit and hard-edged, while the rest was dim and thinly coated in a layer of dust. The Twelfth Realm was used to house and train the Novices – those in their first, second and third years – for it was thought to be beneficial for older and younger Novices to mingle easily, although Elda, had anyone cared to ask her, might have had something to say about that.

The Twelfth Realm was directly connected to the Thirteenth. The senior Novices lived in the Thirteenth for the final two years of their education – or rather their indoctrination, as Syl preferred to think of it. The seniors were known as Half-Sisters.

These two sections were the only Realms that could not easily be sealed off from each other. Beside them was the Fourteenth Realm, which contained the living quarters for those Sisters directly involved in the training and education of Novices, shielded from prying recruits by that wretched door.

Syl walked past the kitchens, past the gymnasium, past the doors that led to greenhouses and lecture rooms, and into the small yet adequate quarters that she had initially kept with her governess Althea, and Ani. Each had her own bedroom, but they shared a living area, a kitchen and a bathroom. They had settled into these close confines easily enough, and Althea had arranged a cleaning roster, but first she showed them how to use the communal laundry to wash their robes and sheets, because the highborn castle girls had never stared down at a pile of grubby washing before. Indeed, they'd never scoured a pot either, or swept a floor. Althea forced such domesticity on them, settled them in, ensured their basic needs were met, and then only last month she'd asked to speak to Syl in private.

'Would you mind excusing us, Ani?' Althea had said, but it wasn't so much a question as an instruction.

Ani raised an eyebrow of sympathy at Syl before leaving them be, for over the years it had fallen to Althea to admonish Syl when she had misbehaved and her father wasn't present, and countless times Ani had been sent on her way before the grand telling-off. But Syl knew her relationship with Althea had changed since their adventures on Earth: Althea no longer treated her as a child to be protected, nor did she defer to her as a hired nanny might. Instead, she viewed her charge as her equal, and an ally in the fight against the darkness that shrouded the Illyri Conquest. Like a mother acknowledging that her daughter was a woman now, Althea advised Syl, and warned her to take care, and fretted about her, but she avoided giving orders and instruction, and also refrained from mollycoddling the girl.

To outsiders she appeared to be nothing more than a doting nursemaid, but in private she was a force to be reckoned with.

'Now, my dear,' Althea had said when they were alone, and there was a firmness to her voice that made Syl anxious over what would come next. 'I need to go back to Earth. At least for a while.'

'What? Why?'

Syl felt childish tears welling in her throat.

'I am incapacitated here and of no use at all to anyone,' replied Althea.

'You're of use to me!'

'What? To pick up your discarded underwear? To make sure you have laundered robes? To soothe your ego when they call you names? You don't need a maid, Syl.'

'But you came to be my maid,' Syl had said nastily, words she later remembered with shame.

'Oh Syl, don't be churlish. You know very well it was a ruse so that I could accompany you and Ani, so that you would not be alone. But you told me what happened on Earth after I last saw your father – you told me he might be infected. In Edinburgh I am able to do what I can to help, and at least I am better informed there. Meanwhile here I must play the role of simpering nursemaid, forbidden from entering the Nairene libraries, or reading their precious books, or even looking the Sisters in the eye.'

'You can't leave me here alone!' Syl had sobbed, but Althea merely hugged her tightly, breathing in the scent of her near-daughter's hair.

'You're not alone; you have Ani. You have each other. And you have a mission to fulfil, as do I,' said Althea. 'I know you're both safe here; I know Syrene has no intention of harming you – at least not physically. I can't guarantee she won't try to play with your emotions, but I have faith in your ability to handle that kind of nastiness. Meanwhile, I have my own business to attend to.'

'What business?' asked Syl, although she remembered all too clearly what Ani said about seeing Althea kiss a human. *Passionately*, Ani had said, but Syl was sure she'd been imagining any lust. Althea wasn't the sort for such things, surely.

'Oh, my little one' – and Althea laughed drily as she looked up at her charge, so much taller than herself these days – 'you know it's best if I keep my own business to myself. Then you can't tell, or be forced to tell.'

'When will you go?'

'Well, that's the thing. As your supposed maid' – she looked at Syl archly – 'the request for my removal from the planet needs to come from you, as my mistress. I need you to inform the Sisterhood that you no longer want me here.'

Syl looked at her, shaking her head. 'How . . . ?'

'Tell them you're tired of having me hovering over you. Tell them you feel like a child tripping over your nursemaid constantly, and that you'd be able to fit in better without me here, and make friends if I'm not hanging around. Tell them you want independence. Tell them I'm annoying – I really don't care. They'll be delighted to be shot of me though, so it hardly matters. Please, will you just do it, Syl?'

Syl stared at her feet.

'Of course I will.'

'Thank you.'

'But when will you return, Althea?'

'I'll return if you summon me. Being your lowly governess prevents me from making such decisions for myself.'

'So you'll come if I call?'

Althea laughed again. 'As fast as the nearest wormhole will allow. But promise me you'll be safe, Syl. Be careful. Look after Ani. Take care of each other.'

Syl had done as Althea requested, and her governess had left smartly on the next ship off Avila Minor, but not without more tears, for they had never been apart for more than a few days before. Syl had also implored her to try to find out what she could about Paul Kerr and his brother Steven, and whether they were safe. Althea had frowned disapprovingly but, seeing Syl's distress, had finally nodded her assent: she would try.

Now Althea's room waited for her return, neat and strangely sterile. She'd changed her bedlinen before she'd left, but some of her clothes hung like a promise in her modest wardrobe, and her favourite volume of poetry lay bookmarked on her desk. It was a small comfort. Otherwise, the living arrangements were companionable – or had been until it became clear that Ani and Syl were to be treated differently by the Sisterhood.

The Sisters, through Syrene, had become aware of Ani's abilities. She was a natural psychic, and those with any sort of mind powers were of great interest to the Sisterhood, for such individuals were very rare. This was why Tanit and her gang, with their assorted mind tricks and tortures, were given so much leeway. Ani's own skill appeared less harmful, for hers was an ability to merely cloud minds, a minor gift as far as Tanit's hellcats were concerned. But it was a gift Dessa also had, and one in which she had proved to be most adept.

Syl grimaced in confusion as she pondered the motive behind what could only have been Dessa's intervention earlier – her conspiratorial nod as Syl and Elda had hurried away had confirmed as much.

Perhaps Tanit and her gang had forgotten that deep, dark Dessa could make others see what she wanted them to see – a full Sister where a Novice stood, for instance – and perhaps they were careless about shielding themselves from her. And indeed, why should they be on their guard with Dessa when she was one of the inner circle, one of their own?

Yes, it was definitely unsettling.

As for Syl, as far as the Sisterhood was aware, she was not special like Ani, for Syl had no powers at all. Yes, Syl and Ani had been seized together by the Sisterhood, tricked into becoming Novices by the Archmage Syrene, but only Ani had a gift that could be developed and used by the order. As for Syl, her father was a great Military leader and the Military were known to distrust the Sisterhood, so securing the daughter of Lord Andrus was something of a coup for the Nairenes. She was treated as a trophy, for display only, and that was where her usefulness began and ended.

The Sisterhood was wrong, though. Syl had power beyond its imagining, and she was being very careful to keep it hidden. Not even Ani guessed, nor did Althea. Syl was a psychic with depths of potential that she barely comprehended herself.

But Syl knew she had to hone her strengths, so she routinely cross-questioned Ani about her extra lessons, and Ani was always eager to chat because her own psychic awakening was at once exciting and terrifying, so what she was learning – or trying to learn – spilled out of her in a stream of words. Ani had never considered herself exceptional before, and her gift had always been a source of unease. She had kept it hidden for most of her life, fearful of what might happen if it were discovered, afraid that she was, as she put it, 'a freak'. But the Sisterhood embraced her, and told her that her abilities made her special, made her extraordinary. Ani was encouraged, celebrated even, and she revelled in the special attention she received as one of the Gifted.

So Syl listened to her friend rambling on excitedly, drinking in every breathless word, and privately she practised all that Ani was being taught about focusing her powers, about control, repeating the exercises over and over while the Marque rested, building up inner protective walls so that her abilities wouldn't be detected by the Nairenes.

The grizzled Sister who was in charge of all the Novices, Grand-mage Oriel, was particularly sensitive to psychic ability. Syl had felt Oriel testing her when she and Ani had first arrived at the Marque, probing for any signs of power. It had been all that Syl could do to remain passive, but she believed that Oriel had been fooled, for the old crone appeared to have shown no further interest in Syrene's latest acquisition. It was Ani who interested Oriel, and that was fine with Syl. Well, kind of fine, because it meant Ani spent many hours with Tanit and the Gifted, and many hours away from her.

A distance was growing between them and it frightened Syl, for without Ani she stood alone and friendless in the Marque.

CHAPTER 6

The Tormic atmosphere was a reasonably sweet mix of mostly oxygen and carbon dioxide, but the heat of it still scorched Paul's nose and throat as he left the shuttle. His thermally regulated suit instantly began cooling his body, but the system didn't work as well with helmets and sweat was already leaking into his eyes. A breeze created ghosts from the sand, as though the grains were fleeing from him. Thula stood at Paul's back, each mirroring the movements of the other, turning, scanning, their eyes fixed to the sights of their weapons. Both had activated the lens over their right eye, the small circle offering details of wind speed, distances, sources of movement – anything that might give them an advantage if it came to trouble.

Now, with the weight of the gun in his hands, Paul felt as though every nerve in his body, every synapse in his brain, was functioning at its highest level. They had no way of knowing what, if anything, had happened at the drilling platform. It was possible, Paul supposed, that they might find the entire research team treating themselves to a long lie-in, or hiding in closets and behind curtains, waiting to pop out and surprise the visitors. Possible, but unlikely. Something had gone very wrong here. He could feel it.

What he and Thula also understood was that, as point men, they were potentially sacrificial lambs. Whatever was responsible for silencing an entire research team and turning a drilling platform into a ghost town could conceivably still be present, watching and waiting . . .

Paul risked a glance behind him. The rest of the unit had left the shuttle, carefully following in the footsteps of the advance guard.

Rizzo and Baudin had taken up positions at either side of the shuttle door, Rizzo standing, Baudin kneeling, their guns raised and ready to provide covering fire in the event of a retreat.

A door stood open ahead, leading into the small living and laboratory quarters – a single-level building set against the northern defensive wall of the platform. A series of circular windows ran along its length, each set at roughly the height of an Illyri head, which made them slightly too high for any human other than Thula – and, at a stretch, Paul – to look through with ease. Peering inside wasn't an option, though, as the windows were shaded to protect those within from the blazing Tormic sun. From outside, they looked like black glass, reflecting the exterior and nothing more.

Paul and Thula took up positions at the door and Paul signalled his intention to move in first and go left. Thula would follow and go right. The lights were still on inside and Paul could see the edge of a chair and a table, on which stood some plates and drinking beakers, all covered with a coating of white sand. Sand on the table, sand on the floor, sand everywhere.

Paul took another scorching breath, tightened his grip on his assault rifle, and risked a quick glance around the door frame. He saw a rest area with functional chairs and a couch that didn't look much more comfortable than the floor itself, and beyond it the kitchen. One of the chairs lay on its back on the floor. It was the only sign of disturbance. His lens bombarded him with information about the room – its length, width, height, temperature, and the results of a scan for movement and body heat signatures, which came up negative. There was nowhere anyone could hide, but Paul conducted a careful search nonetheless, even going so far as to check the interior of an oven and a couple of cupboards that turned out to contain nothing more interesting than rations. He spoke softly into his helmet's microphone, his speech relayed to the entire unit.

'Thula?'

'It's clear.'

Paul turned and saw Thula finishing his own search of the small mess hall. Five plates stood on the two tables, from which the chairs had been untidily pushed back. One beaker had fallen to the floor. Thula shrugged at Paul, who was just about to give the all-clear to the rest of his unit when marks on the interior wall of the mess hall caught his eye.

'I have pulse strikes to the wall,' said Paul. 'Weapons discharged.' He tried to assess the power of the pulse blasts: too weak to penetrate the shell of the building but powerful enough to put an end to any average-sized life-form that took its full force. Whatever the pulse rifle had been aimed at was big enough for the blast to be set at more than regular killing power, but Paul could see no blood, and no remains.

'There's a panel loose on the floor,' said Thula.

They both approached it. Paul nodded, and Thula kicked the panel away. Beneath it was only sand. Thula shrugged, and they moved on.

The sound of swearing came over the coms system. It was Cutler's voice, quickly followed by the rattle of depleted uranium rounds being fired. Immediately Paul and Thula returned to the door, but by then the action was over.

'Cease fire, damn it!' shouted De Souza. 'Cease fire!'

Carefully, Paul and Thula peered out of the doorway. Cutler was staring at a small black object by his right foot, as if mortally offended by it.

'It's a tormal,' said Olver. He was an Australian, and had it not been for Thula's presence in the unit he would have been the quietest among them. 'It's just a tormal.'

The little lizard had reacted to the noise of gunfire and the impact of the shells on the sand around it by activating its carapace. It looked, thought Paul, like a resin model of itself.

'You're a moron, Cutler,' said De Souza. 'You nearly blew my foot off.'

Cutler poked at the tormal with the muzzle of his rifle.

'It came out of nowhere,' he said, wonder in his voice. 'I must have hit it with half a dozen rounds, and they just bounced off.'

'Yeah?' said De Souza. 'Well, if you fire your weapon again without cause I'll make you wish you had skin that thick.'

He looked at Paul.

'Pulse blasts apart, we okay in there?'

'Yes, Lieutenant. We have a closed door to the left. Layout of the platform says that's where the labs and living quarters are.'

'Well, they're not going to search themselves, are they? Let's keep moving. Cutler, you stay out here. You're making me nervous.'

Cutler did as he was told. The tormal, having decided that it was no longer in imminent danger, stored away its shell and scuttled across the sand. Its movement seemed to signal to others that it was okay to emerge, for suddenly Paul could see at least ten of the lizards on the sand. They had probably been dozing away beneath it before being roused by the arrival of the soldiers.

With Cutler outside, the rest of the unit completed the exploration of the living quarters without incident. They found no sign of the research team, although more pulse marks were found in the sleeping quarters – a heavy concentration of fire, as though a last stand of some kind had been made there.

'Look at this,' said Cady, who was the only member of the unit with any real scientific knowledge. Before she was conscripted into the Brigades, she had been preparing her application to study Chemical Physics at the University of Edinburgh. She was standing in the lab area, staring at a screen. On it was a resonance image of the drilling equipment, its drill head – or what was left of it – buried deep in the sand and rock below their feet. From the image, it looked as though the drill head had exploded.

'That's impossible,' said Faron. 'Those heads are practically indestructible. They have to be.'

'I think we found a design flaw in this one,' said Cady. 'Somebody should sue.'

'Cady,' said Peris. 'Run a scan for the research team's beacons.'

'We already did that,' said Olver. 'We got nothing.'

'Humour me,' said Peris, 'but target below ground, not above.'

Cady did as she was ordered, utilising the research team's own seismic scanners. Instantly, the screen lit up with fifteen flashing lights, scattered across an area of about half a square mile under the drilling platform, and in some cases as deep as a hundred metres beneath the ground.

'What the hell are they doing down there?' said De Souza.

'Being dead,' said Paul.

'I think we should get out of here,' Peris told Faron. 'Now.'

Faron might have been green, but he was nobody's fool.

'Agreed,' he said.

De Souza didn't need to be told twice. 'You heard what the captain said: back to the shuttle. Disposition remains the same as before. Kerr and Thula to lead. Go! De Souza to shuttle: we're getting out of here.'

'Understood,' came Steven's voice. 'Engines ready.'

They moved out fast, and reached the door to find Cutler walking towards something that had caught his attention near the wall.

'Cutler!' called De Souza. 'Where are you going?'

Paul adjusted the magnification on his lens with repeated blinks of his eye. He saw what had attracted Cutler's attention: a red protective helmet, the kind used by miners. It lay on the sand, looking disturbingly clean. It hadn't been there when they arrived; Paul was certain of it. He would have noticed, just as he now saw that the sand was scattered with the dark shapes of tormals huddled in their protective shells.

'Cutler,' he cried. 'Don't touch it.'

But it was too late. Cutler reached for the helmet, lifting it from the sand, and it was as though the sand came with it, and then the grains fell away to reveal a disturbance in the air, a shimmering like glass, and Paul had a vague impression of claws and teeth and hard angles. It enveloped Cutler, dragging him beneath the sand before he even had a chance to scream.

And then all was gunfire.

Gunfire, and dying.

CHAPTER 7

Later, all that Paul could remember – or, perhaps, would allow himself to remember – was chaos. Despite their training, despite their weapons, despite their veneer of arrogance and world weariness, they were still just young men and women far from home, thrust into an alien environment, and now they were panicking, and the panicked and frightened would always be easy prey.

A gush of blood rose from the patch of sand into which Cutler had vanished, fountaining like a red geyser. It reached its highest point before commencing an almost elegant descent towards the ground, but its impact was disturbed by another nearly transparent shape erupting from below, and Cutler's blood splashed over it, giving it a kind of definition. Its jaws, so massive as to appear to be in a state of dislocation, became a crimson maw in which jagged shards of teeth were visible. Its head was flat and its body elongated, evolved to move swiftly and smoothly through sand, but there was a hardness to it as well. It reminded Paul of a great diamond drill carved into the form of a demon. This thing could cut through rock as easily as sand.

Olver was the first to react, spraying the creature with a burst of fire. Fragments of it exploded from its body like splinters, and a spiked appendage shot from its torso like a glass thorn, spearing Olver through the chest and killing him instantly. Cady went down next, but this time there was no blood. The sand simply swallowed her, and she was gone.

A shiny metal object flew through the air and Paul heard Thula's warning cry of 'Grenade!' He turned his face away just as the device exploded, and with it the creature, shattering like crystal, the air suddenly alive with lethal splinters. Most of them impacted on Paul's body armour, but some struck his exposed right arm. The pain was intense, and almost spurred him to react, but he felt frozen in place. He couldn't take his eyes from Olver's body, now lying on its back with the shimmering spike that had killed him protruding from his chest, the rest of the beast reduced to fragments by the grenade. Thula made for the shuttle while De Souza and Peris provided covering fire, aided by Rizzo and Baudin. Someone grabbed Paul's left arm. It was Faron.

'Move!' he ordered. 'We have to get to the shuttle.'

But even as Paul stood he saw the shuttle begin to shake, and it rolled enough on its right axis to send Baudin tumbling from the doorway and on to the sand. A flat head rose next to her, and its jaws closed upon her. Baudin struggled against it, but only for seconds, and Paul heard the snap as her neck broke.

The door of the shuttle closed suddenly as it plunged even further right, until the craft was standing on its side, partly buried in the sand. Slowly, it began to be pulled under.

'Get off the ground!' cried Peris. 'Head for the walls!'

A railed walkway ran around the interior of the platform's walls, accessed by a system of ladders. They were a standard feature of such facilities, enabling a watch to be posted, or a defence to be mounted in the event of an attack from outside. Unfortunately, this particular attack was coming from inside, but they could serve a defensive purpose nonetheless.

Two figures appeared on the fuselage of the upturned shuttle: Steven and Rizzo had exited using the port door. As Paul watched, they jumped to the sand and made for the walls, and then Paul was running too, running for his life, trying and failing to keep pace with the longer strides of his Illyri captain. Thirty feet to go. Twenty. Ten. The ladder was almost within Faron's reach.

Paul's slowness saved his life. As Faron made a leap for the ladder one of the creatures exploded from the sand to meet him, catching Faron in its jaws as soon as his feet left the ground and virtually biting him in two before dragging his remains below ground. Paul was almost blinded by the spray of Illyri blood but he kept running. He reached the ladder and felt strong arms hauling him up. He had a vague awareness of jaws snapping barely inches from his boot, but then he was on the walkway and safe.

For now.

He dropped to his knees. His lungs and throat were aching from the exertion, for drawing deep breaths of the Tormic air had scalded his insides as surely as if he had swallowed boiling coffee. He could barely speak. He fumbled for his water bottle and tipped half of its contents into his mouth, trying to ease the pain.

Another hand forced the bottle away from his throat. It was Steven.

'You might be glad of that water later,' he warned.

Paul nodded. He desperately wanted to drink more, but his brother was right. Water was probably the most valuable commodity they had, more valuable even than ammunition.

Only now did Paul notice De Souza. He was huddled into himself on the platform, his face grey, his left fist clenched while Thula worked on what remained of his right arm. It looked as though it had been bitten off just above the elbow, and Thula was trying to stop the flow of blood from the stump. De Souza screamed. Thula reached into the med pack, found a sedative shot, and injected De Souza in his left thigh. De Souza stopped screaming. His head sagged, and he was rendered mercifully unconscious.

Six of them remained alive. That was all, and it wasn't even certain that De Souza would survive for long, not unless he received proper medical care. In fact, the odds on any of them living very long didn't look good.

Peris activated his coms link.

'Peris to *Envion*. Come in *Envion*.'

All of them heard the response in their helmet links.

'This is *Envion*, Supervisor Peris. What is your status?'

Paul recognised the voice of Galton, the big Geordie who was the ship's Chief Officer and therefore the second-highest ranking officer on board next to its Illyri commander, Morev.

'We have sustained casualties. Five dead or missing, one severely injured. Shuttle destroyed. We need a rescue, and fast.'

Paul could only imagine the consternation that this news was causing on board the *Envion*. Their unit was one of two on board the ship, and despite the rivalries, and even hatred, that existed between certain Brigade members – inevitable when young men and women were thrust into close proximity for long periods – they were still intensely loyal to one another.

'Can you give us more details?'

Names: Galton wanted names.

'Captain Faron dead. Privates Olver and Cutler dead. Privates Baudin and Cady dead or missing. Lieutenant De Souza injured.'

Peris paused.

'I'm sorry, Galton – sorry about Cady.'

Cady and Galton had been in a relationship. They had been close for only a couple of months, but it had been clear to all that they were smitten with each other.

'Understood, Supervisor.'

Paul heard the words catch in Galton's throat, and then his grief was pushed aside. Galton would mourn later. This was the time to worry about the living.

'Nature of threat?' said Galton. He might have been a robot for all of the emotion that his voice now held.

'Unknown alien life-forms.'

'Is your position secure?'

'For now. We're on the walls.' Peris peered over the railing. 'If they can climb ladders, we're in trouble, but there's no sign of that yet.'

Another voice came over the coms. It was Commander Morev. He was a veteran of the Brigades and, like Peris, was one of the rare Illyri who didn't seem to resent serving alongside humans.

'Peris,' said Morev, 'you're going to have to hold out. Repairs are still being completed. The second shuttle has a busted thruster and won't be ready to fly for at least another six hours, and the *Envion* is in no condition to attempt a landing on Torma after being shaken up in the wormhole. We're still running tests on the damage to the hull.'

'Then it doesn't seem like we have much choice but to wait,' said

Peris. 'I'd be grateful if you could keep us updated on progress, Commander.'

'Affirmative. We'll work as fast as we can. Hold on, and good luck.'

The coms link was broken. The survivors sat on the walls and watched as the shuttle, now almost completely submerged beneath the sand, was finally pulled under. Steven slumped down beside his brother.

'That was my first command,' said Steven. 'My first ship.'

'It could have gone better,' Paul admitted, and he was shocked by his own capacity for gallows humour, even as the blood of his comrades stained the sands below. But he couldn't think of them, not now. Like Galton, he would store away his grief until there was time to mourn.

Peris ordered an ammunition count. Between them they had a dozen grenades, a couple of pulse rifles, two semi-automatic weapons and more than a thousand rounds of depleted uranium ammunition, one pistol, and various knives. De Souza's sawn-off shotgun lay on the sand, along with its accompanying belt of twenty shells. Yet water was the real issue. Out here on the walls they were exposed to the Tormic sun, and they would grow thirsty very, very fast. Altogether they had about four gallons of water. The rest had gone down with the shuttle.

'It's not a lot,' said Peris, 'but it's enough. From now on, we're rationing. I'll tell you when, and how much. Otherwise, if you touch your water, I'll cut your hand off.'

Paul looked down on the sands below. There was no sign of the creatures, but the little tormals remained cocooned in their protective shells.

'Now we know what they need their armour for,' said Paul.

'We scanned for life,' said Steven. 'There was nothing bigger than those lizards.'

'We scanned for *carbon-based* life,' Peris corrected him. He joined them in watching the sands. So, too, did Rizzo and Thula. He had done what he could for De Souza, who remained unconscious. If he was lucky, De Souza would wake up back on the *Envion*. Otherwise it was unlikely that he'd ever wake up at all.

'So what are those things?' asked Paul.

'I'm guessing silicon-based,' said Peris. 'A theoretical possibility – until now.'

'You mean we've discovered a new kind of alien life?' said Paul.

'Maybe they'll name it after you,' said Thula, 'if you ask nicely.'

'You think?' said Paul.

'It could have been the drilling,' said Peris, ignoring them. 'Perhaps the drill reached a certain level and these things felt threatened by it. It would fit with a silicon life-form. The atmosphere here is part oxygen, which means that a silicon-based creature would produce silicon dioxide as a by-product of breathing. But that silicon dioxide would be a solid, which would choke the respiratory systems of the creatures with sand . . . Unless they lived in temperatures of several hundred degrees, closer to the core, where the silicon dioxide would be a liquid.'

'Man, it's like being back in school,' said Thula.

'So they broke the drill head,' said Paul, 'then came to find out who'd sent it down there in the first place.'

'It seems the likeliest scenario,' said Peris.

Steven got to his feet and began moving away. Rizzo watched him go. She was amusing herself by sharpening her throwing stars on a whetting stone. Rizzo, thought Paul, was very odd.

'Where are you going?' asked Paul, but he understood quickly enough when Steven stopped and stared at the research team's shuttle, marooned on its pad in the centre of the station. It was too far away to be reached by jumping. Steven's right hand instinctively stretched out to it, as though he could draw the craft to him by force of will alone. Paul joined him at the railing.

'I should have run to the shuttle, not the wall,' said Steven. 'I panicked.'

'You weren't alone. Don't—'

Paul didn't get to finish his sentence. The walkway shook beneath their feet, and for a moment Paul was sure that they were both going to be tipped to the sands below. He and Steven clung to the rails for dear life. The whole station seemed to be vibrating.

'What is it?' cried Steven. 'An earthquake?'

But Paul didn't think so. Whatever those creatures were, they could burrow through sand, and possibly rock as well. They weren't about to let some ladders and walkways keep them from hunting. If they couldn't climb up to attack then they'd settle for the next best thing.

They'd bring the walls down, and their prey with them.

CHAPTER 8

Ani's nose was bleeding again. It always gushed when she pushed her abilities to the limit, and her training with the Gifted Novices required her to do it so often that she no longer had a single garment unstained by her own dark blood. She was the only one who displayed her weakness so dramatically, although others had their own ways of revealing the strain they were under: a facial tic here, an uncontrollable trembling there.

But Ani bled.

She felt the blood running over her lips – left nostril first, then right – but she did not try to wipe it away, or stifle the flow. Instead she concentrated on the face of the tutor seated across the table from her. It was a simple test, but one that Ani had so far consistently failed. The tutor, whose name was Thona, was resting the palm of her right hand upon a small plate. Ani's task was to convince Thona that the plate was growing hotter and hotter, until eventually the perception of heat would force Thona to snatch her hand away to avoid being burned. So far, after many attempts, the plate had remained determinedly cool, apart from the natural warmth of Thona's own hand.

Ani tried to relax. Relaxing, focusing, that was the secret. You couldn't force it. You had to clear your mind and control your breathing. You had to forget the plate. The plate didn't matter; it was never going to be hot. What was required was a gentle manipulation of Thona's perceptions. But Thona was strong. She was three times Ani's age, and although she was supportive and tolerant of the Gifted Novices under her tutelage, it didn't take a mind reader to see that she was growing increasingly impatient with Ani's lack of progress.

Ani tasted the blood on her lips. She breathed in, and caught the saltiness of it on her tongue. Her concentration slipped, and in her frustration she pushed herself too far. The flow became a spray. It spattered the front of Ani's robes, the table . . .

And Thona.

Ani leapt from her chair, mortified. She put her hand to her nose but the blood wouldn't stop. She tried to sniff it in, and it caught in the back of her throat. She coughed, and more blood sprayed. She started panicking, feeling lightheaded, and the room began to spin around her.

'I'm – ' she said, but got no further. All went black, but not before she caught a last glimpse of Thona's face, dark with anger and spilled blood.

When Ani regained consciousness, she was lying on a couch in the corner. A Half-Sister from the medical wing was wiping the blood from Ani's face with a damp cloth and offering her water to drink. Thona stood to one side in a gaggle of the Gifted, who were all staring down at Ani. The tutor had cleaned most of the blood from her own face, but some still speckled her red robes with darker patches, and a single smear of it lay beneath her right eye like a forgotten tear.

'I'm so sorry,' said Ani.

'There's no need to be,' said Thona, but her face gave the lie to her words. Ani had failed. Again.

Sarea gave a spiteful little giggle, but Tanit jabbed her with a sharp elbow.

'It's not what I do,' Ani tried to explain, blushing with shame. 'It's not my strength. I can cloud. I can convince you that you're seeing something that isn't there, but I can't make you *feel* what isn't real.'

But even that wasn't entirely true. She had used the word 'you', but in truth she had never been able to cloud Thona's mind. Oh, she could trick her fellow Novices, or at least those with no psychic abilities at all, but when it came to those with their own well-honed skills, those like Thona and Tanit, she might as well have been trying to change darkness into light. She had tried repeatedly under Thona's instruction as various members of the Gifted sat before her, cold-eyed and unyielding, immune to her probing. No wonder Sarea and Nemein dismissed her so casually.

Meanwhile they could manipulate her as easily as a doll, although they did so only under the supervision of their tutors, for even seemingly weak psychics like Ani were deemed precious, and they looked out for one another. The Gifted were the elite, and it was understood that they were all still nurturing their talents, even if some made progress so much faster than the rest. Ani found this deeply frustrating, for she was acutely aware of the honour conferred by her flowing blue robes. Now she pulled at them anxiously.

'Clouding is simply the manifestation of your gifts with which you have become most comfortable,' said Thona, not for the first time. 'You've just grown into the habit of using it, while failing to develop your potential in other areas. But Dessa can cloud too, and look at her! Dessa?'

She turned to Dessa, and so did the others, but it was several long seconds before the girl spoke.

'If you can convince someone to see what isn't there, it requires only a minor adjustment for you to make that same individual feel something that isn't real,' Dessa said evenly. 'You simply haven't found the mechanism for that adjustment yet.'

Thona nodded in satisfaction, but not at Ani.

'Quite,' she added, 'but we will.'

Ani remained unconvinced: perhaps clouding was all that she had, like an athlete who could only kick with a right foot, or throw with a left hand. Sometimes a degree of ability simply made one's other failings all the more obvious.

And, hovering at Tanit's other elbow, it seemed Nemein was unconvinced too, for now she pointed a taunting finger at the small, sad figure of Ani on the couch.

'Are you sure, Sister Thona, that she has any real talent at all?' said Nemein, and cast a sidelong glance at Tanit, seeking approval. 'Perhaps we're wasting time trying to improve something that's destined to remain basic, when that energy could be better spent working on something more important?'

The implication was clear: Nemein would rather that they focused on her own more interesting talents, for her specialty was disease, and she was anxious to move on from curable illnesses to her own variations on cancer and plague. But Tanit replied before Thona could.

'Nemein,' she said in her clear, carrying voice. 'Do you not recall when you first began, and all you could muster was that ridiculous pimple on Sarea's face? These things take time, and poor Ani has only been here a few months.'

She smiled, warm as the sun, and Ani found herself grinning gratefully back at her. Like Syl, Ani was wary of Tanit, but still she couldn't help but be drawn by the young Novice's charisma. She might have been dangerous, but that made her approval somehow more significant.

'How do you feel now?' Tanit asked, almost gently.

'Okay,' said Ani. 'A little dizzy, but it will pass.'

Tanit nodded at her encouragingly, holding her gaze.

Now the medic looked to Thona. 'I would suggest that the Novice's training be suspended for today.'

'Really?' said Thona. 'Three years of medical training, and you tell me what I already know? Go and make yourself useful elsewhere.'

The medic took the insult without flinching and left the room. The Sisterhood operated a strict hierarchy, and seniors tolerated no dissent from mere Half-Sisters.

'Go to one of the meditation rooms,' Thona told Ani. 'Read. Think. Clear your mind. Tomorrow we shall try something new.'

Ani nodded. Something new would be good. If she were forced to look at that plate again, her brain would surely explode. She stood. The room tilted slightly, and congealed blood slid down the back of her throat like slime, but she swallowed it and made her wobbly way to the door. Tanit gave her a kindly pat on the shoulder as she passed, and the fleeting touch of another made Ani pause briefly, yearning desperately for her mother, for her home.

She stumbled down the hallway and into the first unoccupied meditation chamber. It was less austere than the training room –

fragrant, faintly lit, and piled with seductive tapestry cushions. Artificial intelligence systems meant she could call up art, books and music from Illyr, Earth, and the handful of other worlds that had so far yielded significant signs of culture, but Ani accessed none of them. Instead she collapsed in a corner and cried and cried.

Thona stood before Grandmage Oriel. The old Sister's quarters – the largest in the Fourteenth Realm – were illuminated by rainbows thrown by fluorescent crystals, and the crevices and carved nooks on the rock walls contained artefacts from hundreds of worlds: art, fossils, specimens in jars. Such displays were not uncommon among the most senior of the Sisterhood. Each was a physical manifestation of a piece of knowledge gathered and treasured.

'You have blood on your face,' said Oriel. Even in the dim light, her eyesight was uncannily sharp.

'Ani,' said Thona. 'She bled again, badly. She even lost consciousness for a time.'

'But you will persevere.'

It was an order, not a question.

'Yes. She has a gift, but I fear the extent of it may be more limited than Syrene hoped.'

'No matter. Some ability is better than none at all, and we have known Novices in the past who have required time to develop their capabilities. Does she still consider herself to be a hostage?'

'I hardly think she considers the question at all,' said Thona. 'She's very anxious to please.'

'And what of Syl Hellais?' said Oriel.

'What of her?' said Thona, who cared little for ungifted Novices.

Oriel's face remained impassive, but inwardly she could barely contain her impatience. Thona was so blinkered, so unambitious in her thinking that her definition of 'gifted' extended only to psychic abilities. But there were other strengths, other talents. Oriel saw much potential in Syl Hellais – potential, and more, for there was something about Syl that troubled the old Sister, a blandness to Syl's character that did not chime with her natural intelligence. It suggested the possibility of concealment, and Oriel was most curious to learn what it was that Syl might be hiding. But Syl had so far proved unreadable, even to one as talented as Oriel.

'Syrene is most anxious that Syl should find her place in the Marque,' said Oriel. 'She has high hopes for the daughter of Lord Andrus and his dead Lady. She could be a great ambassador for the Sisterhood.'

Syrene had not stayed long at the Marque before returning to Earth, her journey back to the planet made more rapid than ever by the discovery of a series of new wormholes. Officially Syrene remained in mourning for her husband, Gradus, and she partly blamed Syl and Ani for his death, but Syrene was nothing if not practical, and the Sisterhood was her first love. If the Earth hostages could be put to use in the advancement of the Nairenes, then so be it.

And doubtless Syrene had other secret aims in mind, for such was her nature.

'We should never have admitted Syl Hellais to the Marque,' said Thona, still wittering on. 'The mother turned her back on us, and now we give shelter to the daughter? She does not want to be here and I, for one, do not want her here either.'

This time, Oriel sighed aloud. How many times did they have to go over this?

'She requested admission to the Sisterhood,' said Oriel. 'We cannot turn down one who offers herself to us.'

'She requested admission to save herself from death, or the near certainty of it,' said Thona. 'That is not a genuine calling.'

'And Ani? Did she not join us for the same reason?'

'But she has a gift!'

Arguing with Thona, Oriel realised, was a fruitless exercise.

'And,' Thona added, 'we do not need her as a hostage to use against her father. That problem has been solved.'

Ah, thought Oriel, that much at least was true. Governor Andrus was now Syl's father in name only. Syrene had seen to that.

Syrene, and what dwelt within her.

CHAPTER 9

The sands of Torma were alive, both inside and outside the platform. The survivors watched as they churned and roiled, buffeted by the unseen creatures that moved beneath them. Occasionally one of them would break through, its back curved and catching the sunlight, shining like cut glass. They were almost beautiful.

Almost.

The walls of the drilling platform were constructed from sheets of heavy alloy, each riveted to the next, and specially designed to be resistant to the heat of the Tormic sun. Otherwise, to touch them would have been to risk scorching one's skin. Their foundations were sunk into the sand, but only to a distance of ten feet or so, and that was largely a result of their sheer weight. Whatever the creatures were doing underground, it was not only causing a degree of vibration capable of loosening the rivets but also distorting the shape of the walls themselves, buckling them slowly so that eventually they would put so much pressure on the joins between the plates that they must eventually collapse.

'We won't last six hours up here,' said Steven. 'And we won't last six seconds once we hit that sand.'

'We need to get to the shuttle,' said Paul. 'It's the only way.'

'But how?'

'A line. We can run a cable from the walls to the edge of the platform, and rappel down.'

'But where do we get the cable?'

'There,' said Paul. He pointed to a coil of wire that lay on top of a jumble of barrels, crates and unidentifiable pieces of mining equipment. It stood just beneath the walkway, some twenty feet from where they were. Twenty feet away, but also at least nine or ten feet below.

'Were you planning on walking over to get it?' asked Steven. They had all surmised by now that, whatever the nature of their enemy, the creatures must be acutely sensitive to the slightest of vibrations and the shifting of the sands. After all, the unit had seen no evidence of eyes on their heads, and there would be little need for them below ground. Setting foot on the desert floor would be like ringing a dinner bell.

'Nope. You and Thula are going to take a leg each and lower me down.'

Thula wandered over to where they stood.

'Did I hear my name being taken in vain?'

'I have a plan,' said Paul.

'Is it dangerous?'

'Almost certainly.'

Thula permitted himself a grin. 'Those are always the best kind.'

Paul swayed. The blood was going to his head, and he felt as though his brain was about to explode in his skull.

'Easy,' he said. 'Easy!'

The fingers of his outstretched right hand brushed against the coil of cable. He couldn't quite reach it. Just a little further. He twisted his body slightly so that he was looking up between his own legs at Thula and Steven.

'Let me down another few inches,' he called.

'We can't,' said Steven. 'We're at full stretch as it is.'

Paul tried again, but it was no good. The cable was just too far away. He was also growing increasingly nauseous. The creatures were now hammering ceaselessly away at the walls, and the vibrations were passing through Thula and Steven and into Paul. He was swaying slightly, like a man who had somehow found himself upside down while on a ship rocking at sea.

He felt a shift in the grip on his legs. He looked up again and saw that Thula was now holding both of his legs, and Steven and Peris were holding on to Thula, easing him gently over the edge of the walkway until eventually the entire upper part of his body was suspended in the air. Paul felt himself dropping lower. His hand closed on the cable.

'I have it!' he cried.

He began dragging it towards him. It made a soft metallic grinding sound against the crates.

Sound.

Vibration.

'Oh hell,' said Paul.

The ground was sky, the sky sand. Clouds disturbed it – clouds, and a shimmering like glass.

'Pull me up!' he shouted. 'Now!'

But Thula's belt had caught on the edge of the walkway. He tried to free himself by wriggling against it, which caused Paul to shift precariously in his grip.

'I'm serious!' said Paul. 'Get me out of here.'

'We're trying,' said Steven.

'Try harder!'

From his left came a clanging sound. He twisted his head to see Rizzo standing on one of the lowest rungs of the nearest ladder, banging the edge of a grenade launcher against the metal. Her more insistent vibrations caused the creature to change course, diverting its attention from Paul towards her. Paul could see that she had one leg hooked around a rung of the ladder, and another around the frame. She raised the launcher to her shoulder.

'Come to momma,' she said.

The creature emerged from the sand, its jaws agape. The grenade, set to explode seconds after impact, shot into its gullet, just as Rizzo dropped the launcher and turned her back to protect her face.

The beast exploded, showering Rizzo with fragments. Paul instinctively closed his eyes. When he opened them again, Rizzo looked like a glass porcupine, her armour and the skin on the back of her neck embedded with shiny spines. Slowly she began to climb back up the ladder. For a moment she stumbled and seemed set to lose her grip, but somehow she kept climbing. Paul rose with her as Thula's belt was freed and they were both pulled back up to the walkway. Once Thula was safely in place, Steven helped him to drag Paul up while Peris went to see to Rizzo.

'How is she?' asked Paul, once he had secured the lightweight cable, draping it over his right shoulder. He and the others stood over Peris, who was kneeling beside Rizzo. She lay on her stomach. Her face was contorted in a grimace of pain.

'Get her armour off,' ordered Peris.

Steven hit the release straps at Rizzo's shoulders and waist, and lifted off the rear panel of her armour. It had absorbed most of the impact of the shards, but some had still penetrated her body. There were smaller splinters in her neck, arms and skull. The wounds in her back were bleeding through her shirt.

'Can you move your legs, Rizzo?' said Thula.

Rizzo's feet tapped against the metal of the walkway.

'No spinal damage,' said Thula. 'That's good.'

He knelt alongside Peris and gently tested the splinters in her skin. There were no spurts of blood, which meant no arteries were damaged, and none of the splinters looked like they'd gone in more than half an inch.

Peris turned to Paul.

'Why don't you see about hooking that cable to the platform? Thula will look after Rizzo.'

Thula was already searching in his kit for antiseptic and a blade with which to work on the splinters, if necessary. Paul and Steven left him to it and set about figuring out a way to secure a line to the shuttle.

Paul found a loose strut on the walkway's support rail and tied one end of the wire securely around it. The shuttle platform was a single sheet of metal, with no holes or slats into which a weighted cable might jam, so their best bet seemed to be to aim the strut for the shuttle itself. It stood on raised landing pegs, not dissimilar to those of a helicopter, so Paul tried for the nearest of those. The first time he missed entirely, and the second and third times he managed only to hit the shuttle itself, even knocking something from its body with the final impact.

'Was that bit important?' he asked Steven.

'I'd prefer not to be up in the air when we find out,' said Steven. 'Maybe you could try not to reduce the shuttle to scrap metal before we even manage to board it.'

After each attempt Paul had to draw the strut carefully back across the sand. The last thing he wanted was for one of those creatures to pull it underground, and perhaps him along with it.

Paul threw again. This time the strut caught beneath one of the pegs. Paul gave it an experimental tug. It held. He leaned back and hauled as hard as he could. Still the strut did not move.

'That may be as good as we're going to get,' he said. He fixed the other end of the cable to the walkway.

'Somebody is going to have to be the first to try it,' said Steven.

'That would be me.'

'I'm lighter.'

'You're the pilot. If you fall, we're stuck here.'

'Peris can fly a shuttle.'

'Not like you can. Look, I did the throwing, and I'll take the chance. Once I've made certain that the line is secure, you can follow me down. We'll take the shuttle to the wall and pick everyone else up from the air.'

De Souza would have to be helped on board, but Rizzo looked like she could make it herself. Thula had removed most of the silicon shards from her flesh, although smaller fragments probably remained, and she was now sitting up and taking water. The back of her shirt was now dark with blood.

Paul was wearing his combat gloves. They'd give him a pretty secure grip on the cable. In an ideal world he'd have a clip to attach to the line, but the world in which they found themselves was far from ideal. Instead he fashioned a support harness from his bandolier. It wouldn't be much help to him if the line didn't hold, but if he lost his grip it might prevent him from falling to the sand. In the end, it was a psychological comfort, if nothing more.

Peris and Thula came over as Paul, seated on the walkway rail, was hooking his makeshift harness over the line.

'Are you sure about this?' said Peris.

'No,' said Paul. 'Not that it makes much difference.'

At that moment the wall shook and a section nearby came loose and tumbled to the ground, leaving a massive gap in the wall. Had the wall weakened on the other side, it might well have landed on the shuttle, dooming them.

'On your way, then,' said Peris. 'We don't have all day. And if you need further encouragement, take a look over there.'

He pointed north, to where the fierce blue skies of Torma had vanished.

'What is that?' said Steven.

'A sandstorm,' said Peris. 'It'll sweep us from the walls, if they don't collapse first.'

Paul said a silent prayer, curled his legs over the wire at the ankles, gave the line one final tug, and began his descent. He moved quickly, wanting to spend as little time as possible suspended over the rippling sands. He tried not to think about falling, to concentrate only on dragging himself along the line. His arms were aching already, and he was not even halfway there. His own body, his exhaustion, the heat, all conspired against him. The line sagged above him, dragged down by his weight. He had a vision of the strut shifting, its perilous hold on the shuttle's peg weakened by the drag of the human being on the wire. Faster now, faster. He could see the shuttle platform ahead. It seemed as if he could already touch it with his toes, although he estimated that he had another ten feet to go.

And then the strut shifted. He felt it move, and the wire dropped him towards the sand. He waited for the impact, but it didn't come. He was still hanging in the air, but he was at least a foot closer to the ground. Paul was afraid to move. If he moved, the strut might finally be pulled from its position. But what was the other option – to remain hanging from a line until tiredness took him, or the strut inevitably came loose, regardless of whether he was moving or not?

He inched forward.

The strut, held against the shuttle's peg by only the barest of margins, came away, and Paul tumbled to the sand.

CHAPTER 10

Paul's first thought upon falling was: I am going to die.

His second thought was: I don't want to die.

He rolled as he hit the sand, and was on his feet almost before he registered the impulse that caused him to react so quickly. It was as though his limbs were working faster than his thoughts, realising what was required of them before his mind could spur them into action. He was aware of sand churning behind him, but he did not look back. The shuttle pad was only a few feet ahead of him, with its ramp raised. It stood about six feet off the ground, so that the pad was slightly lower than Paul's head. He sprang, gripped the edge, and used his back muscles to raise himself, grateful for the long hours spent performing pull-ups as part of basic training. He heard gunfire as the survivors on the ramparts tried to hit whatever was pursuing him, but by then he had flung himself flat on the pad. He turned on his back, drew his Colt, and prepared to shoot between his knees, but nothing appeared.

'It's too short!' shouted Steven. 'The creature – it can't raise itself high enough to reach the pad.'

Paul sank back on the metal. He tried to swallow, but he had no moisture in his mouth. His head ached from thirst and, he knew, barely suppressed panic and fear. It was all that he could do not to curl into a ball and wait for someone to rescue him, but he knew that *he* was the rescuer, and his comrades were depending on him, coward or not.

He forced himself to rise, and saw that Steven was already hurriedly drawing the cable back. One of the creatures made an ineffectual snap at it, but it didn't seem as interested in the metal as in the humans. Once he had the end in his hands, Steven flung it towards the pad, and Paul caught it before it could slip off the edge. He wound it tightly around the shuttle's landing, looping the cable back on itself so that it held the anchoring strut in place.

'All right,' he called to Steven. 'Down you come.'

Steven slid off the rampart, curling his feet over the wire and moving hand over hand down its length. He moved fast – faster than Paul had done. Not for the first time, Paul noticed how his brother's baby fat had fallen from his body in recent months, leaving him lithe and rangy. He would be taller than Paul when he was fully grown.

Suddenly the landing pad shuddered. The impact was so strong that it sent Paul stumbling against the hull of the shuttle. The vibration travelled up the wire, but Steven managed to retain his hold on it and keep going. The creatures had felt movement on the pad but were unable to reach Paul. Just as with the walls, they were opting instead to bring him down to them. The beasts were smart, he had to give them that. He'd still happily have seen them wiped out of existence, but there was no denying their intelligence. From somewhere below the sands came a grinding, and the pad canted about five degrees to the right. The creatures were buckling the central support. It wouldn't be long before they sent the shuttle sliding to the sand.

Steven dropped down beside his brother.

'You took your time,' said Paul.

'Well, let's just hope they didn't lock the doors.'

The blood drained from Paul's face at the thought that, after all his efforts, they might be undone by some security-conscious scientists, but Steven simply winked at him and hit the door release with his fist. The door opened with a hiss, and Paul permitted himself a ragged breath of relief.

'That wasn't funny,' said Paul.

The pad juddered again. This time, the shuttle seemed to slide slightly to the right.

'Just get in and fly the damn thing,' said Paul.

Steven disappeared into the shuttle. Paul followed him. It was much smaller than the Military craft that was now lost somewhere beneath the sand. It could take six passengers and crew at a push, and even then they'd be crammed inside. Paul tried not to think about what might have happened if they'd all survived the initial attack by the creatures. Would they have been forced to draw lots for their lives?

Steven started the engines, and prepared for a vertical take-off. As he did so, the shuttle began to slide in earnest, and it didn't stop. Paul lost his footing, and banged his head painfully against the shuttle's hull.

'Hold tight!' said Steven. 'This will be a rocky one.'

He hit the thrusters, boosting the starboard thruster to compensate for the angle. The shuttle seemed to stagger into the air, but Steven kept it under control. Paul looked out of the window nearest to him to see the pad collapse and silicate alien forms thrusting at it in the vain hope that their prey might not have escaped.

'Not this time,' said Paul, and the faces of the dead flashed before him. 'You've taken enough of us today . . .'

They got De Souza on board first with the help of Thula and Peris. Still, Paul had to haul him up, and despite his drug-induced sleep De Souza moaned as his butchered arm struck the door. Rizzo climbed in mostly under her own steam and only reluctantly accepted Paul's help at the last. Finally, it was the turn of Thula and Peris, the latter barely getting on board before their section of the wall finally collapsed. Paul closed the shuttle door, and the craft did one final circuit of the platform. Far below, the creatures rose up in frustration, their eyeless heads turned to the sky, their jaws snapping at vibrations in the air.

But now the storm was almost upon them. It would engulf them if they didn't find shelter from it. They couldn't outrun it – there wasn't enough time. Paul joined his brother, taking the co-pilot's seat to give the others more room in the shuttle bay. Steven took them up, then hovered in the face of the approaching wall of sand.

'What are you doing?' asked Paul.

'Thinking. Supervisor Peris, sir?'

Peris came forward.

'What is it?'

Steven removed a small cylinder from the inside pocket of his flight overalls. He pressed down hard on the top, and the cylinder clicked open at the other end, revealing a red button.

'What is it?' asked Paul.

'It's the self-destruct mechanism for my lost shuttle,' said Steven. 'Permission to activate, sir?'

Peris looked at him.

'That's an expensive facility,' he said.

'They killed five of us,' said Steven, and Paul noticed that he counted Faron among the 'us'. Whatever his faults, Faron had been one of them when it mattered.

'Yes, they did,' said Peris. He nodded. 'Permission granted.'

Steven hit the button, and held it down for ten seconds as he ascended to a safe altitude. Even then, the explosion rocked the little craft, and the blast was like a new sun being born at their backs.

Paul closed his eyes.

Vengeance, he thought. Always vengeance.

To the south stood one of the massive rock formations that dotted the Tormic landscape like the spires of great, primitive cathedrals. If they could find a place to land on its southern aspect, they could wait out the sandstorm under its protection. Steven steered them towards the rock, the storm a maelstrom of impending destruction at their backs.

'Inform *Envion* that we're going to seek shelter from the storm, and then we'll be on our way,' Peris ordered.

But the *Envion* had troubles of its own.

CHAPTER 11

One of the reasons why the Illyri had looked upon Torma as a promising source of mineral wealth, in addition to its breathable atmosphere and its apparent absence of hostile indigenous life-forms – now, alas, revealed to be a fatally flawed assumption – was its proximity to the nearest wormhole. The best wormholes were those that opened close to star systems – although far from the dangers of asteroid belts or collapsing suns – and with easily reachable worlds that could be explored and, where possible, exploited.

It was now clear, though, that the wormhole near Torma was less gravitationally stable than might have been wished. The exploration vessel that dropped the drilling platform and research team on Torma had sustained minor damage both entering and leaving the system, while the lighter, faster *Envion* had endured even more of a pounding. Torma, it appeared, would not willingly give up its treasures. While the repairs on his vessel continued, Commander Morev reflected that, when something appears too good to be true, it usually is.

He watched while Galton, his Chief Officer, coordinated the ongoing work, his voice and manner never once betraying his torment at the loss of his lover. The truth was that, with the *Envion* virtually crippled and the remains of a unit marooned on Torma, there was simply no time for grief. In the end, it might be for the best: the gravity of their situation meant that Galton was forced to keep going, and in doing so perhaps he would realise that he was stronger than he thought.

The commander noticed that, like so many humans, Galton wore religious tokens around his neck, in his case a medal of Saint Jude, the Catholic patron saint of lost causes, and Saint Sebastian, the patron

saint of soldiers. Some among the Illyri hierarchy – mostly the Diplomats – disapproved of such displays of belief, but Morev, being of the
Military, knew that all soldiers have their talismans, even among the
Illyri. Now he wondered if Galton took comfort from the thought
that Cady might continue to exist in another form, instead of accepting
that her atoms were merely being scattered and recycled by the
cosmos. If so, good luck to him: let him find comfort where he could.

And now it was Galton who was breaking into Morev's musings,
Galton who was informing him of activity at the mouth of the
wormhole.

'Sir, we have a ship emerging,' said Galton.

'A ship?'

Morev couldn't keep the relief from his voice, or the surprise. An
exploratory drone had been sent back through the wormhole to
inform Military Command of their situation, but even with the system
of relay stations to boost its signal, any help would have taken time to
reach them. Perhaps an Illyri vessel had been in the vicinity of the
wormhole when the drone emerged, although Morev had not been
aware of any activity scheduled for that sector. Still, any aid that could
be offered would be gratefully accepted, especially if it meant that
they could mount a rescue on the Tormic surface. If the arriving ship
had a shuttle, or its commander was willing to enter the atmosphere
of Torma . . .

The *Envion*'s scanners identified the ship from its contact signal as
soon as it came within range: the *Dendra*, smaller even than the *Envion*,
and with a crew of no more than six. It must, thought Morev, have
endured an unpleasant trip through the wormhole. It was a wonder
that it was still in one piece.

'What's a Civilian vessel doing out here?' wondered Morev.

Civilian ships were rarely found far from the vicinity of Illyr. The
great Illyri Conquest of the universe was in the hands of the Military
and its rivals, the Diplomatic Corps. The Civilians merely represented
the masses in the Illyri Council, siding with the Military or the
Diplomats as the need arose.

Galton pointed at the screen.

'Sir, take a look at that scan. She's a wreck.'

The *Dendra* was fortunate to still be in one piece. It had not been designed for long distance travel, and the wormhole had taken its toll. The ship was barely functioning. An adjustment to the scan revealed further damage to the starboard hull.

'Wormhole?' asked Morev.

'No, those look like weapon blasts, and recent too. She's been attacked.'

'Hail her,' said Morev.

'This is the Military destroyer *Envion* calling Civilian transport *Dendra*,' Galton transmitted. 'Respond, *Dendra*.'

'This is Alis, pilot of the *Dendra*,' came the reply. 'We're very glad to see you, *Envion*.'

'And we're surprised to see you, Alis,' interrupted Commander Morev. 'We had no notification of your intended use of the wormhole.'

'We came under attack. It was a last resort.'

'Attack from whom?'

'Unknown vessels. I think we shook them off, but it was a close thing.'

'What is your mission, Alis?'

This time, it was not Alis who answered. Another voice came over the speakers. It sounded unusually calm, despite the aftermath of an attack and an unanticipated wormhole trip.

'*I* am the mission, commander. My name is Councillor Tiray, Civilian representative on the Illyri Council of Government, and I request sanctuary on board the *Envion*.'

Certain rules of behaviour governed the Illyri, particularly when it came to vessels in deep space. One was that a request for sanctuary, or for assistance from a troubled ship, could not be ignored. To do so was regarded as a serious crime, and led inevitably to imprisonment. Under the circumstances, Morev had no option but to reply as he did.

'Your request is granted, Councillor,' he said. 'Approach at will.'

★ ★ ★

Morev and Galton watched the *Dendra* draw closer. The *Envion*'s docking bay had been cleared, and the *Dendra* would land in the space that had once been occupied by the shuttle lost on Torma. The ship was close enough for the cockpit lights to be visible. Galton could almost make out the pilot's face.

An alarm sounded through the ship, and a voice from the command deck came through to Morev's receiver.

'Commander, we have two more ships emerging from the wormhole. Scans reveal no identifying markers, but they're armed.'

The *Envion*'s artificial intelligence system immediately produced an image of the approaching vessels. They looked battered and old, and even less capable of boosts than the *Dendra*. They should not have been able to come through the wormhole, but the scan revealed that their appearance was deceptive. Beneath their exteriors, they were heavily shielded, and boasted massive engine power.

'They look like Nomads,' said Morev.

Nomads: those who had rejected Illyri society, either out of idealism or, more typically, because they were outlaws, or deserters. They had bases – little more than temporary communities hidden in forests and mountains – on some of the outlying worlds of the Illyr system, although for the most part they preferred to keep on the move, for the Illyri authorities always raided their settlements when they were found. Nomads scavenged for parts and supplies, their ships resembling floating scrap heaps, but the most daring were not above attacking lone freighters. On Earth, the worst of them would have been termed 'pirates'.

'But Nomads wouldn't dare—' Galton began to say.

Morev was no longer listening. His soldier's instincts had kicked in.

'Battle stations!' he ordered, his voice ringing through the ship. 'Prepare for combat!'

CHAPTER 12

A ni wasn't sure what to do about her friend Syl. Yes, they'd come here together, joining the Sisterhood to escape certain death, and yes, they knew something wasn't right about Syrene. But they'd barely seen the Red Witch since they'd arrived, and even then she'd been surprisingly pleasant once they'd landed on the rock over which she reigned. Syrene herself showed them to their quarters, pointing out the fine Egyptian cotton sheets that she personally had supplied, direct from Earth, 'so that you'll feel at home', and the soaps that were in the bathroom, scented with real French lavender. She'd even placed a mounted photograph of Andrus beside Syl's bed, and another of Ani's parents beside her own, but Syl had turned the antique silver frame face down for the first few weeks, until finally Althea had wrapped it in tissue and put it away.

No, Syrene wasn't all bad, even if Syl couldn't see it.

The rest of them were only trying to help, to educate them in the Sisterhood's ways. Yes, even Tanit. Honestly, if only Syl could see how gentle Tanit had been earlier, how kind, or how hard the tutors were trying to teach them everything that they knew; if only she could see how much being here could benefit them both, but Syl seemed determined to hate everyone and everything that was the Sisterhood. Sure, it didn't help that there were those who insisted on calling Syl 'Smelly', but it was a childish slight, and Ani felt worn down by Syl's constant suspicion and negativity.

Did Syl not listen in history class? Why would she not acknowledge the great bravery and immense sacrifice the Sisters had made in the name of all that was good about the Illyri?

In the early days, the Nairene Sisterhood had been based on the homeworld, Illyr, where the order had started as something of an asylum for women who did not fit in, a refuge for unmarriageable females, awkward females, the argumentative, the opinionated, and all who caused unrest in a gender-segregated society. The Sisterhood quietly provided a shelter and a home, and thus troublesome females were safely shut away from their world, where they could not question its ways or sow their dissent.

But the Sisters were not content with seeing out their days idly, and so they read. They read *everything*. (And Syl loved books, reasoned Ani; she loved learning, just like the Sisterhood. So why couldn't she fit in?)

Those crones and shrews of old had collected manuscripts, memoirs and histories, and catalogued and filed them; then they'd gathered more words still before finally writing their own. They drew intimate family trees, and studied bloodlines, ancestry, genetics and heredity.

They mapped the stars and the orbits of the moons above them, and they analysed the soil and stones beneath their feet. They nurtured plants in the extensive gardens of the original Convent of Arain, and dissected them until they understood their workings, and then dissected in turn the creatures that made their homes among the roots and leaves. In time the Sisters extended their expertise to the plants of other worlds, growing, reaping, learning, creating miniature alien environments crafted from crystal and quartz. The Sisters built, they experimented, they explored ideas, they made extensive notes, and gradually the convent grew into a library, and the library grew into a repository, and the Sisters could ask any price for access to their vast store of information. Scribes, leaders and philosophers came to them for their wisdom, and the Sisters and their growing network of convents became essential to the world that once shunned them.

In time, the Sisterhood's beginnings as a cloister for burdensome females was forgotten, and it became revered. Its convents attracted only the most brilliant Illyri girls, and while the Sisters were willing to offer advice and access to their records, they preferred to have as little as possible to do with outsiders.

And yes, Ani was happy to admit that bad elements may have crept in, but surely they could be eradicated, given time, and there was still so much to marvel at, so much to admire. After all, look at what the Nairenes had already achieved; look at the troubles they'd overcome!

After what became known as The Fall, when tyranny overtook the Illyri, everything had changed for the Sisters. At the time it was decreed that all knowledge was to be eradicated – books, recordings, moving images, art, music – and the Illyri Empire rebuilt from fire and ash. Academics, writers, musicians and artists were all executed. Anyone with an education beyond the most basic was imprisoned, exiled, or killed. Many were worked to death. Families were torn apart. Whole cities burned.

The Sisterhood, by their very nature, became targets for the Fallen. Their sanctuaries were sacked, the Sisters raped and killed, and their beautiful old volumes and carefully preserved documents were used as fuel for their funeral pyres.

It was then that the seven most senior Sisters decided to leave. They filled seven shuttles with the most valuable items from their collection, and digital copies and downloads of everything else. They had no room for any of the Novices or the other Sisters, but none complained, not even the youngest of them, for they understood the necessity of their sacrifice.

The shuttles blasted off from Illyr as the Fallen stormed the gates of the Convent of Arain, and headed for Avila Minor. One was shot down before it could leave the Illyri atmosphere, and another crashed on the moon and was utterly destroyed. The other five landed just as the sky was fading to dusk. The moon was cooling after the scorching heat of the day and the night creatures had not yet begun to feed. The Sisters, who had studied the geography of the moon, hid themselves in an ancient cave system. They survived on rations and by hunting, and thus began the Marque. Of course, the Fallen sent troops to find them, but they had not studied Avila Minor as the Sisterhood had. The sun burned them to blackened bones by day, and at night the creatures that lived below ground came out and fed on the remains.

In class, when the Novices were told of the Sisters' triumph, spontaneous applause had broken out, and even Syl had joined in the cheering.

But it had quickly died down when they had learned that two of the First Five also perished in that first year.

The remaining three planted seeds and cultivated the seedlings, growing them beneath the ground in the small ecosystems they'd perfected on Illyr. They scavenged their shuttles for equipment, and slowly they created a home for themselves.

The Fall could not last. The Fallen's primitivism did not spread to the outlying colonies, and in time those colonies came to the aid of the homeworld, but the Fallen refused to surrender, and even in captivity they vowed to keep fighting. Mass executions followed, and some still believed this final bloodletting, while ending the war, had scarred the Illyri soul forever.

Eventually a shuttle was sent to rescue the Sisters and return them to Illyr, but they refused to leave, knowing full well that what happened once could happen again, for history repeats itself. So they sold the land on which their ruined convents once stood. They demanded compensation for their losses from the new Illyri government, and received it. They poured all of their wealth into extending and fortifying the Marque, utilising the complex system of caves and underground passages that riddled their moon's rocky strata like a honeycomb. The First Realm was duly constructed, housing the earliest library, along with living quarters for the Sisters. This was said to be where the five most senior Sisters, successors to the First Five, still lived to this day, led by Ezil, the oldest of them all. They had become hermits, devoted to learning, and nobody had seen Ezil or the other four leaders in public in many years.

Still, Ani thought about them often, and sometimes she felt their presence in her dreams, and wondered about the fantastical knowledge they must possess and the things they could teach her. But while Ani wondered, Syl scoffed and sneered. Syl's attitude made Ani feel lonely and isolated, and forced her to turn to the other Gifted for company and support.

Had she been a little older, and a little more mature, Ani might have realised that this was precisely the Sisterhood's intention.

CHAPTER 13

Night fell. Outside the Marque, the scorched red desert of Avila Minor came to life as the sands cooled. The moon was utterly dark. Only the Marque held light, glittering in the windows of the buildings and towers above the surface and, in the older Realms, shining from mountains and hills that had been transformed within, hollowed out in the earliest years of its construction.

In the blackness, the hunting began.

The shuttle descending towards the moon was heavily shielded, its technology so advanced that even the majority of those at the highest levels in the Military – and certainly those in the Diplomatic Corps – had no idea of its existence. It came in low, invisible to the radars of the Marque, and landed within sight of the Twelfth Realm.

From the sands nearby, drawn by the vibrations of the vessel, emerged a heavily armoured arthropod known as a cascid. It was the size of a large dog, the tracheae through which it breathed fed by the oxygen-rich atmosphere of the low-gravity moon, thus enabling it to grow bigger than comparable species on Illyr or, indeed, Earth. Its mandibles were large enough to crush the head of a full-grown Illyri, and sharp enough to cut through bone and metal. It approached the shuttle curiously. It had no conception of fear. There was only hunger.

But the shuttle was too large for the cascid to attack alone. It released chemical secretions, summoning others of its kind to overwhelm the prey, and soon the desert around the shuttle was alive with the creatures, each releasing its own secretions in turn until the whole swarm was driven into a frenzy. Finally, seemingly in unison, they moved in to attack the shuttle.

A series of small vents opened in the shuttle's underbelly. A low hissing emerged from them, followed by jets of white gas expelled at high pressure. Within seconds the approaching swarm was enveloped in clouds of liquid nitrogen, freezing them in place, creating a bizarre arthropod sculpture, as though the creatures had been hacked from ice. The panicked secretions of their dying were enough to discourage others from approaching.

The gas dispersed.

The shuttle waited.

Elda's quarters were among the smallest and most basic in the Marque, as befitted a Novice who was little better than a servant. She had a bedroom, an adjoining bathroom that was barely larger than an upright coffin, a single crate that served as a rough table, one unsteady chair, and a bed that was more comfortable without its mattress than with it. A closet for her possessions took up so much of the remaining space that she had to turn sideways to move between it and her bed.

Elda had lived in that room for four years, but she would live there no longer. The backboard from her closet lay on the floor. From the space behind it she had retrieved a small locked box, and now its contents were spread out on the bed. They included an ultra-thin darksuit that had been squeezed into a cylinder little bigger than her thumb; a short, sharp killing blade; and a pulse weapon disguised as a pen, with an electronic beacon built into it.

Elda caught sight of herself in the mirror above her table. *Oh Tanit,* she thought, *if only you could see me now.* The Elda who had haunted the tunnels and corridors of the Marque – cleaning, scrubbing, watching, and listening – was no more. The young female in the mirror stood tall. The look of perpetual fear that she wore as a mask was gone, and in its place was only grim determination. Four years, now about to end. Four years of making herself so inconsequential, so unambitious, so mundane, that the Sisterhood had virtually ceased to notice her. And because she was entrusted with the filthiest, most boring of tasks, the kind given to only a handful of others apparently like her – the slow, the clumsy, the talentless, the ones who, in a different age, would have been painlessly killed for failing to live up to the Sisterhood's high standards – she had been allowed access to areas of the Marque forbidden to other Novices. Elda possessed keys and codes shared only with the ordained Red Sisters, and she had used them wisely. True, she had failed in one of her tasks – to discover the precise whereabouts of Ezil and the other four senior Sisters, or even if they were still alive at all – but she would bring from the Marque other information of value and importance. Most of all, she now knew that Syrene was working to develop the psychic abilities of young female Illyri, something previously unsuspected outside the Marque. Elda also believed that she understood the reason why Syrene had initiated this program.

Finally, she had succeeded in mapping most of the Marque, and also possessed the details of its security systems and the disarm codes for the shields. For the first time in centuries, some of the Marque's deepest secrets would be revealed, and the great labyrinth would be vulnerable to its enemies. All this, achieved by a female who had known only contempt in that place.

Her true name was not even Elda, although she wore Elda's face. The real Elda had died seven years before, taken from her loving parents by a weak heart. But before her death could be announced, Elda's parents received visitors in the form of a pair of senior Military advisers. Elda's father and mother were both loyal members of the Military who had watched the rise of the Diplomatic Corps with unease. Even in their grief, they lived only to serve. They agreed to hide the fact of their daughter's death, and to accept another in her place: a young Illyri female who looked exactly like their lost child thanks to the wonders of ProGen skin; whose genetic profile had been manipulated to pass even the most sensitive of tests; and who spoke and acted just as their own Elda had done. In fact, so brilliant was the replication that, in time, they almost forgot she was not their own child, and when at last she was accepted into the Sisterhood they mourned their daughter for a second time.

Elda: the female in that bare room in the depths of the Marque, who had worn an identity for so long that she had almost forgotten her own. No matter. Who knew what form she would take once she was gone from the Marque? The Sisterhood and their tame Diplomats would be hunting for someone who looked like Elda, so Elda would have to disappear. The process would be painful, but necessary.

She stripped and put on the darksuit over her naked body, then dressed herself again in her Novice's robes. She would leave them forever at the door of the Twelfth Realm through which she had chosen to escape. The darksuit would disguise her from most of the desert creatures. In general, they had poor eyesight and relied on heat, movement and sound to track prey. The darksuit would take care of the first two issues, but she would have to rely on her own stealth for the third. As for those animals that could see well in the dark, her pulse weapon might have been small, but it packed a huge charge. Anything that tried to eat her would end up as a spray of blood and gore on the desert sands.

She put her blade in the wide pocket of her robes, checked her belt and pouch, and took one last look around the room. She felt no emotion at all. Already she was done with this existence. Yet even in this moment of departure and escape, Elda had recognised the possibility of failure. There was only one person in the Marque for whom she felt any affection, only one who had ever given any sign that she, like Elda, was no friend of the Sisterhood: Syl Hellais. With that in mind, Elda had taken a moment to ask a final favour of Syl. It was in Syl's locker at the gymnasium: an amulet containing an engraving of Elda's mother, or the woman whom everyone believed to be her mother, along with a note requesting that Syl find a way to get it back to her on Illyr. If Elda managed to safely escape the Marque, the amulet would be an additional record of her discovery. If Syl did not manage to return it to Illyr, nothing would be lost.

But if Elda did not make it out of the Marque . . .

Elda closed the door behind her, disabled the lock using a low pulse from her weapon, and then slipped the pulser up her sleeve. The more time that went by before her absence was discovered, the better. A Sister's quarters, even those of a Novice, were considered her private realm – a realm within a Realm, as the older Sisters liked to put it – and any intrusion was frowned upon. The sealed door would cause delay and confusion, and breaking it down would require the consent of two senior Sisters. It was all valuable time that would enable her to get farther from the Marque.

The Marque was always busy, even at night. While it quieted down during darkness, it never completely slept. The accumulation of knowledge could not, would not stop. So it was that few glances were cast at Elda – silly, dispensable Elda – as she moved along the walls, her head down, her dull eyes barely shining in the reflected glow of the lights.

It did not take her long to reach the service exit. Few Sisters – apart from those responsible for engineering and maintenance – ever ventured down to the lower levels. After all, what reason would they have to leave the Marque and wander out on to the sands? The service exits were only used by those carrying out repairs, and even then only rarely, for the Marque was built of the finest, strongest materials. Elda had discovered that some of the older service exits were not even fitted with alarms. Heavy doors and rather dated locks were considered security enough, although it had still taken Elda three years to gain access to the keys to two doors in particular.

Now, standing before the door marked L4, she cast off her robes, removed one of those slim silver keys from her belt pouch, and inserted it into the lock. She had to trust that the shuttle would be waiting, just as they had promised. Activate the beacon, they had told her all those years ago, and a shuttle will be waiting for you at the agreed spot within two hours. It will stay there for a further two hours, then leave. If you are not on it when it departs, we'll assume that you're dead.

Elda waited for the key to unlock the door. Nothing happened. She wiggled it, but still there was no satisfying click as the bolt undid itself. She took it out and examined it. It was definitely the right key. She had marked it just to be doubly certain. She had even performed a dry run the night before, and the door had opened easily. Yes, she could head for the second exit, but it would delay her. She could still make it to the shuttle, but it would be close – uncomfortably so. She tried the key one more time, but with no result.

'Damn,' she said to the darkness.

And the darkness replied in the voice of Tanit.

'I think you mean "damned".'

Elda spun, the pulser slipping easily into the palm of her hand as she raised it to fire. Tanit's face hovered in the gloom, but before Elda could activate her weapon, her hand erupted in pain. She looked at her fist and watched in horror as an unseen force crushed it, the fragile bones breaking, the knuckles splintering into shards inside her flesh until her right hand was reduced to a jointless, useless thing, packed inside a glove of skin. She screamed in agony and sank to her knees, but the pain did not stop. She both felt and heard the twin snaps as the radius and ulna in her lower arm began to fracture, then the humeral bones at her elbow, and finally the big humerus in her upper arm. Pressure followed on her scapula and clavicle, until Tanit shouted: 'Stop!'

Through her tears, Elda watched as Sarea joined Tanit. Sarea looked disappointed that Tanit had put an end to her game so quickly. Nemein followed, and then the others – Iria, Dessa, and the siblings Mila and Xaron – all staring down pitilessly at the wounded Elda, her right arm hanging useless by her side, the thin fabric of the darksuit like a vice against the shattered limb.

'Search her,' ordered Tanit.

It was Nemein who did it. She found the blade, and the second key. More importantly, she discovered the small stick drive containing all of the secrets that Elda had unearthed over the past four years. Needlessly, Nemein brushed Elda's wounded arm, causing her to scream again. Even then, as she faced her tormentors for the last time, Elda was amazed at Nemein's casual, senseless cruelty.

'I suppose you think that we're going to interrogate you,' said Tanit. 'You know, ask who sent you, who you really are, that kind of thing, but we're not.'

She squatted so that she could look Elda in the eyes. She spoke without hatred, without passion, only pity.

'You see, we don't care. Even now, at the end, you don't matter. You've failed, just like your little friend Kosia before you. She told us everything right before we killed her – everything but your name. Unfortunately, she died before she could share that with us. But all that she revealed led us to believe that she had an accomplice, that there was another spy in the Marque. So we watched, and we waited, and we discovered you. I have to confess that I was surprised. You disguised yourself well. But now, like Kosia, you're going to die.'

She turned to Nemein.

'Give me the knife.'

Nemein handed the blade to her. Elda waited for it to pierce her flesh, but it did not. Instead Tanit used it to cut away the darksuit from Elda's upper body, stripping her to the waist. She wielded the blade carefully, almost tenderly, so that the knife did not cut Elda's skin but left only slight red marks upon it. Tanit even avoided touching Elda's wounded arm, content to leave the remains of the darksuit upon it. When she was done she examined her handiwork, and nodded approvingly.

'Much better,' she said. 'And you have a cute figure. It's a shame that you had to hide it away for so long.'

Tanit reached into a pocket of her own robes, and produced a new key, shining and needle thin.

'I think this is what you were looking for,' she said. 'The locks have been changed – as have all the security codes – but you've probably figured that out by now. Actually, we were concerned that you might have tried to leave last night. Yes, we were watching you even then. We could have taken you earlier, I suppose, but it was more fun to wait until you thought you were free. Oh, and about our most recent little encounter: consider your burns a farewell gift from us.'

Sarea and Xaron stepped forward, and forced Elda to her feet. Tanit handed the key to Nemein, who unlocked the door but did not open it, not yet.

'Any last words?' said Tanit.

Elda drew herself up to her full height. She glared at Tanit, defiant despite her fear and pain.

'I may not be the first,' she said, 'but nor will I be the last. And I shall be avenged. Tell that to your Red Witch.'

'You know', said Tanit admiringly, 'I never liked you until now.'

'You know,' said Elda, 'I still don't like you.'

Tanit shrugged.

'You wanted to leave,' she said. 'So leave.'

Nemein yanked the door open, and with a swift push Elda was expelled through the gap. The youngsters inside had a brief glimpse of a rocky embrasure leading down to the desert, and Elda falling to her knees on the stones, before Nemein closed the door again and locked it.

'Time for bed,' said Tanit. 'It's been a *long* day.'

And she reached to turn off the exterior light.

Elda knelt on the desert stones in a cone of light. The night was freezing, and the pain in her ruined arm was fierce. She heard movement all around her as unseen creatures were drawn by the heat of her exposed body, and the smell of her fear. The light kept them away, though. They hated it. It hurt their eyes. Perhaps if she could survive until the sun rose . . .

Then the light was gone. The memory of it burned in Elda's eyes as something hard and sharp closed around her neck. She opened her mouth to scream, but no sound emerged, for her head was already separating from her body.

And the feeding began.

CHAPTER 14

They called it the City of Spires. Tannis: the jewel of Illyr, the largest, most glamorous, and most populous metropolis on the planet. It was the seat of government, the centre of power. It took its name from its architecture, the great slivers of glass and metal that extended like stalagmites into the air, seemingly scraping the very heavens above.

Tannis, the City of Spires.

Tannis, the City of Spies.

The building was known as the Tree of Lights. It housed five thousand of the most wealthy and powerful citizens of Illyr, all of them Diplomats or individuals with connections – professional or personal – to the Diplomatic Corps. Its level of security was exceeded only by that of the Parliament, with whom it shared a significant number of residents. In a city of tall slim structures, the Tree of Lights was notable for its unusual design: a tall central support column that housed offices and essential systems and then, spreading above it, a great crown of luxurious apartments connected by branches containing moving walkways and discreet elevators; hanging gardens that formed their own ecosystems within the building; and landing pads for the shuttles and skimmers used by its residents. The Tree of Lights was not uncontroversial. Some felt that its shape was not in keeping with Tannis's architectural character, but since they lacked the power, money and influence of those who had approved the design, funded its construction, and now lived in it, their views went largely unheeded. Anyway, as far as the residents of the Tree of Lights were concerned, they had not disturbed the cityscape of Tannis at all, for they were able to look out of their windows and see only gilded spires. It was for others to look upon the Tree of Lights, and envy those who lived among its branches.

In one of the topmost suites, a Diplomat named Radis stared at himself in the bathroom mirror. His bald skull was beaded with sweat, even though the room had instantly cooled to his preferred temperature as soon as he set foot inside. He ran the water again, delaying the moment when he would have to leave. He had already showered for so long that his skin had wrinkled, and his wife – his Nairene wife, for Radis had taken a newly ordained Sister called Paylea as his bride – would by now be wondering what was keeping him. They had only been married for a few months. Their betrothal had come as something of a surprise to Radis, but it was an honour that could not be refused. And Paylea was beautiful. Radis could still not quite bring himself to believe that she was his.

Indeed, sometimes he doubted if she truly was.

A tiny communicator lay by the sink. It was the reason why Radis was in the bathroom. After all, he could hardly tear himself from the arms of his wife to look at a message from a communicator of whose existence she was unaware. Soon, though, he would have to abandon it. He could hear Paylea in the bedroom. She had already asked him once if he was okay, and he had no desire to arouse her suspicions.

'Please,' Radis whispered, 'please.'

The communicator blinked into life, and projected a message on the mirror: the shuttle had left Avila Minor without its cargo. The message remained in place for only a few seconds, then vanished. Radis immediately placed the communicator in the sink and turned on the hot water. He watched as the communicator disintegrated and the pieces swept away like ash. He closed his eyes in despair. After so many years of waiting . . .

When he opened his eyes again, Paylea was reflected in the mirror. She stepped behind him, her right hand rose, and the thin blade entered at the base of her husband's skull. His last thought before he died was:

We are betrayed.

CHAPTER 15

They were fortunate, thought Paul, but perhaps they had been due a little good luck. About halfway down the huge rock formation was a narrow ledge, barely wide enough to accommodate the exploration shuttle. Again, Paul marvelled at his brother's skill as a pilot. Here he was in an unfamiliar vessel, a sandstorm threatening to tear it apart and scatter its occupants' remains across an alien desert, and somehow he managed to descend safely to the outcrop, the rock face so close that, had the windows been open, Paul could have reached out and touched it.

The fury of the storm was astonishing, as though it were a living, breathing thing that was aware of their presence and frustrated by its inability to reach them. Even sheltered by tons of stone, they could feel the shuddering of the ancient tor as the storm flung itself against it. At its fiercest, Paul was convinced that their shelter would finally crumble under the onslaught, burying them under rubble and crushing the shuttle like a tin can.

But eventually the storm passed, and they found themselves still alive.

'I don't think I want to do that again,' said Thula.

'Agreed,' said Paul.

Steven started the engines and took them up. Paul was staring out of the window, taking in the edifice that had saved their lives, offering up a prayer of silent thanks to it, when something caught his eye. He actually forced himself to blink, so strange did it seem, so impossible to comprehend.

'Steven, take us back.'

'What? Why?'

'Because that isn't just a rock.'

Steven brought them around again, and allowed the shuttle to hover before the face of the formation. All but the still-unconscious De Souza came forward to look.

The sand had scoured the face of the formation, causing sections of it to tumble to the sands below. Revealed in the spaces were the remains of intricate carvings: doors, windows, even hints of figurative sculptures – an eye here, what might have been a limb there. The doors and windows were huge, many times larger than those that might have been found in an Illyri or human abode. With these constructions exposed, the rock now reminded Paul of a ruined steeple of one of the great cathedrals back on Earth. There was a grandeur to it, even in the small sections visible to them. But age, and the damage caused by the storm – and doubtless many storms before – made it difficult to gain any full conception of the nature of its creators, if they had indeed depicted themselves on its walls.

None of them spoke. They could only gaze. Peris alone, it seemed, was not as shocked as the rest of them. Paul could tell from the Illyri's face.

And Paul knew.

'You've seen something like this before,' he said.

Peris nodded.

'Who built it?'

'We don't know,' said Peris. 'We've found traces of another civilisation scattered throughout galaxies in this region. This looks old, even by the standards of what we've already discovered. Some are more recent than this one.'

'Maybe those silicon creatures ate them,' said Rizzo.

'If they did, they took their time,' said Paul. 'They left them alone for long enough to let them carve out a home, or a temple, in the centre of a rock.'

'Perhaps there are more,' said Thula. 'After all, it is not the only such rock on this planet.'

Yet, Paul thought, this one was different. He recalled the

formations that they had passed over, and between, on their journey to the drilling platform. They were more angled, sometimes lying at a forty-five degree incline to the desert floor. This rock was perfectly vertical. It made him wonder if it was less a building carved into a rock, and more a building disguised to look like one.

'Why weren't we told?' he asked Peris.

'About a dead civilisation? What does it matter?'

'But where did they go? What happened to them?'

'War. Disease. Who knows?' said Peris. 'Civilisations rise and fall. Some day, the Illyri may well be no more than a series of decaying cities on dead worlds. Humanity, too. Remember that had the Illyri not come to Earth, you would have destroyed yourselves within a millennium or less. Your climate was changing. Storms, floods, typhoons were annihilating cities. Whole nations were starving. We bought you more time. The Illyri Conquest saved humanity.'

Paul didn't bother arguing. He'd heard this over and over. He'd been listening to it ever since he was a child. It was standard Illyri propaganda, but it was also the language of every conqueror to the conquered. *The worst is over. If you will just stop fighting us, then the business of peaceful rule can begin. We will build new roads. We will keep you safe from your enemies. Your life will be better under us. But if you continue to resist . . .*

But Peris hadn't been threatened with execution by hanging. Peris hadn't seen entire villages wiped out. Peris's generation hadn't been conscripted into the Illyri armies and forced to serve, and sometimes die, on distant worlds against their will.

Peris didn't know of the alien parasites living inside the heads of Illyri.

Or perhaps he did. Paul could never be sure. There were times when he wanted to trust Peris more than he did, wanted to accept that Peris really did have the best interests of Paul, Steven and the rest of the unit at heart, wanted to believe that Peris was somehow different from the rest of the Illyri. But then Peris would say something about Earth, something dismissive or patronising, and Paul would realise that Peris, despite his willingness to serve alongside humans, really wasn't very different at all.

It was probably for the best. Paul needed his hatred.

He stared out at the half-hidden ruins and felt cold unease as Steven brought the shuttle up, causing it once more to rise vertically, the face of the rock passing before them as they ascended. He had a strange sense that whatever race had built this place – as a temple, a research base, a dwelling – was still present, somewhere. It came to him so strongly that the force of it was almost physical, as though something deep inside the stone had reached out to communicate with him.

They had not died out. They had not destroyed themselves. They had simply departed.

But to where?

There are mechanisms so old that they barely resemble manufactured objects at all, and ancient inventions that, even millennia later, are still more advanced than anything we might imagine or construct ourselves. Deep in the rock formation on Torma, one such mechanism registered the presence of the shuttle, and those inside it. Unknown to Paul and the others, it scanned their thoughts and memories, their physiology and their form.

And it began to transmit.

CHAPTER 16

Elda: where on this wretched rock was Elda? Syl trawled the hallways looking for her, occasionally calling her name in case anyone was in doubt as to her purpose. Cale had demanded Elda's presence, for there had been a spill in the chemistry laboratory, and Elda had the keys to the cupboard where the necessary hazardous cleaning products were stored.

'Damn that stupid Novice,' snapped Cale. 'She still hasn't returned my keys. Go and find her, Syl.'

'But I haven't seen her for days,' said Syl, and as the words left her lips she realised, surprised, that it was true.

'Precisely. Yet she is apparently your friend, so go. *Now.*'

The other Novices sniggered as Syl stomped from the classroom, and she felt her cheeks redden. As if she wasn't already outcast enough in this dry, stale place, now she was lumped together with Elda: pathetic, sad, weak Elda. Syl walked past Ani, who gave her a sympathetic look, but Syl just strode on as if she hadn't noticed, for Ani was sitting with Tanit and the Gifted in their swathe of superior blue silk, just as she had been instructed to on their first day of lectures, just as she had every day since. She'd hardly put up a fight though, and sometimes Syl heard her friend giggling a little too heartily at the other girls' whispered chatter. It tugged at something inside her chest, making her feel even more alone, especially now that Althea had left.

Syl, meanwhile, sat with the other Novices in their unremarkable yellow robes, according to the order of things. However, they were all eager and bright-eyed, all desperate to be noticed and anxious for approval from both the Gifted and the teachers, and all utterly passionate about the Sisterhood because they had actually *chosen* to come to this place. It was like a cult, Syl had decided, and she opted to keep her equally passionate feelings deep inside, hidden. Outwardly she was cool and untouchable, while inside she burned.

The only Novice who ever matched her in apparent disinterest was Elda. It was little wonder that she was now pooled with the dull creature. Saving her from the bullying of Tanit and the others had only strengthened that wisp of a bond.

So Syl traipsed the pathways that Elda had before her, going first to the laundry, then to the storehouse, and on to the small room where Elda polished crystal and utensils. She glanced into the gym, and popped through the canteen where the Service Sisters on duty shrugged at her questions uncaringly, but finally someone directed her towards Elda's quarters, right at the dingy end of a corridor lined with supply cupboards. Syl almost laughed for, during her own exploring, she'd assumed the small door to Elda's room hid nothing but a janitorial closet.

Now she knocked, but was met with only silence.

'Elda,' she called sharply, tapping again, and the quiet seemed to offer an answer in itself, so Syl tentatively tried the door. It was locked. Now she felt the beginnings of concern. Suppose Elda had fallen, or was ill? She could be lying unconscious on the floor. It would take time to get permission to open the lock. She looked around, making sure that nobody was nearby, then closed her eyes. Her mind found the mechanism, worked on the lock, and seconds later she heard the door spring open. A light came on automatically and Syl took in the neatest bedroom she'd ever seen. It was as much of a blank page as Elda: all that it contained was a plain bed, stripped of all linen, a wardrobe no bigger than a locker, a worn chair, and a scrubbed crate set on its side next to the bed, atop which rested a new candle in a holder. The wick was white, having never been lit.

'Elda?' Syl called, just to be sure, before stepping through the door, flinching as it squeaked. She had to nearly close it again to enter the tiny shower cubicle and toilet, and that too was completely bare. There wasn't so much as a tub of cream or bar of soap to break the grim lines, and the entire measly cell of a room whiffed of bleach. It was as if no one had lived here at all.

The wardrobe was the biggest surprise though, for Syl opened it to find precisely nothing. It was utterly empty, without so much as a robe, or gown, or discarded piece of underwear. It was lined only with bare wire hooks, like a cheap motel. Althea would never have stood for hooks such as those, for they'd stretch the shape out of even the hardiest of robes.

But where was Elda, and where was her stuff?

'What are you doing, girl?'

Syl all but jumped into the wardrobe in fright. Right behind her stood Oriel, breathing the words into her ear softly, like a stale wind.

'Oh!' said Syl, turning, her face inches from the Nairene. 'Grandmage Oriel. Good morning.'

Oriel raised an old, wise eyebrow in question.

'Erm,' Syl stammered, trying to remember exactly what she had been doing, but her head felt odd for she could feel the tendrils of Oriel's fluid mind probing her own, searching, knocking seductively at the chambers of secrets she kept. Syl gave her head a little shake and smiled brightly at the Sister. It was Ani's trick, but it didn't sit well on Syl's serious face, and Oriel looked a little taken aback at the row of teeth that appeared before her, lips drawn back tightly to reveal pink gums. Still, this gave Syl a chance to focus, mentally propping up the walls in her brain.

'I was looking for Elda, Your Eminence. Sister Cale sent me to find her – she has some keys . . .'

'As you can see, she is not here,' said Oriel, 'Or did you imagine she'd be hiding in her own closet?'

Syl shook her head but said nothing, looking down at her feet as if ashamed.

'Well?'

'I was just being nosey, Grandmage,' said Syl, still not looking up.

Oriel gave a low-pitched little laugh, and it seemed to come from a much younger woman.

'Oh, you cunning child! You think you're so terribly smart. You presume you can outwit us by acting like an idiot. Elda presumed much the same, the stupid creature.'

'Where is Elda?' said Syl.

'Perhaps she has chosen to leave us.' Oriel frowned as if the possibility pained her, but her eyes sparkled strangely. 'Anyway, these are the keys Sister Cale requires. Take them to her immediately. Do not tarry.'

Oriel dropped a lightweight clutch of metal pins into Syl's hand, and as Syl slipped them absently into the cavernous pocket of her robe she felt suddenly nauseous, and it seemed that barbs were catching inside her skull, hooked thorns snagging on her brain matter, rending tiny holes in her thoughts. Oriel was trying to read her.

'Interesting,' whispered Oriel, staring intently at Syl, who stood immobile before her, like prey frozen before a predator. 'You're aware that I'm looking inside your head, which might suggest some basic skill on your part. But I can also sense that you have so much that you're hiding. Show me, little one. Reveal yourself to me.'

Each word drove the hooks in deeper – probing, testing. Syl knew she had to fight back, but how? She honed in on the barbs, mentally picking them out one by one as the voice went on, almost singing the words, and she couldn't tell any longer if Oriel was speaking aloud or inside her head.

'I know that sooner or later the dam you've created inside you will rupture, and the waters will flow free, and then I'll be there to drink in that flood. Every drop of it will be mine. Every drop of it will be *ours*. Every secret you hold in that arrogant head of yours. All of it. All ours.'

Oriel smiled coldly: 'Just like your father is all ours.'

Her father – what did Oriel know about her father? Syl jerked upright angrily, a flare of red-hot rage coursing through her, colouring her vision as her heart pumped blood faster and faster. She stood to her full height, but still she had to look up at the imposing old woman before her.

'What did you say?'

The barbs were barely a tickle now, their effect dulled by the force of Syl's own fury. She felt it as rising heat, as an all–consuming darkness, a black pool of anger swirling faster and faster, seeking an outlet, and suddenly Oriel winced, putting her hand up to her temple. Her legs seemed to weaken and she took two steps back, feeling blindly for the bed behind her, before sitting down heavily.

Oh, what had Syl done? She'd gone too far – the witch would know, would rumble her, but not now, please not yet, it was too soon – and immediately the rage flowed from Syl, her face becoming a blank mask. She took a deep breath and moved over to the bed, kneeling on the floor at Oriel's feet, carefully arranging her features into feigned concern.

'Grandmage, what is it? Are you not well?' she said.

For several long seconds all was silent. Oriel sat utterly still, her face hidden in her palms. Syl's brain remained undisturbed, inviolate.

'Grandmage?'

There was a long pause.

'Oriel?'

Oriel's hands snapped open and clasped Syl's upturned face, and she smiled triumphantly.

'You! You do have something. You must have, or why . . . ?'

Syl tried to free herself, genuinely terrified now as Oriel's sharp fingers dug into her hairline. She felt the probes pushing against her cerebrum again, and the barbs attempting to trace a backwards route up her spine into her brainstem, and it was all she could do to stop Oriel's scrutiny as it spilled beneath the mental doors that she kept closed in her mind, seeping through the cracks in the walls she'd built up. Airlocks, she thought, I need airlocks, and she started visualising them, thinking of submarines and spacecraft, and doors with wheels that operated them, wheels that she mentally smashed so that they could not be undone as each door closed, and all the while Oriel forced her to look into her contorted face.

'Maybe,' squeaked Syl desperately, 'maybe you're having a stroke, Sister.'

And with a mighty effort – part mental, part physical – she threw herself backwards, out of Oriel's clutches. The old Sister sighed heavily and slid to the floor, her skull banging against the stone. Her eyes rolled backwards in her head revealing the whites as veins burst, and they filled up with blood.

'Let me get help,' Syl said, and she scrambled for the door. Then she paused for a moment, and returned to the fallen Sister. Kneeling beside Oriel, she put her hands to the witch's temples and tried to erase from her memory any record of what had just occurred in Elda's room. Perhaps it couldn't be done, but trying was better than not doing anything at all. Then she hurried from the airless cell and went for help. As she ran, Oriel's liquid thoughts trickled away to nothing as the Grandmage lost her grip on reality and consciousness, but the fear she had implanted in Syl's mind still remained.

Syl stumbled back into the science room, breathless, and all turned to stare at her.

'And?' said Cale, frowning.

'Oriel!'

'What about Grandmage Oriel?'

Syl was shaken, overwhelmed, but it fed into her story.

'She's taken ill. She's fallen. I think she's having a stroke. In Elda's quarters.'

Cale gasped and rushed from the room and, as one, the Gifted leapt up to follow her like the blue tail of a comet. The yellow-robed Novices were soon clattering from their chairs and pushing past too, clustering uncertainly at the door; some filtered out, untethered, trailing after the action. Syl stood there alone, panting. Well, nearly alone, for now kind hands took her by the shoulders and guided her to a seat.

'Sit,' said Ani. 'Breathe. You're okay, Syl.'

Syl looked up into her friend's face and couldn't help but smile.

'You're still here?'

'Of course I am. You're my best friend, Syl, or did you forget that?'

Syl sighed.

'I thought you had forgotten, Ani. I thought that you preferred them.'

Ani looked at her hard, then turned and closed the door. It was just the two of them like it always had been, except it was different, so very different.

'You know, Syl, at the moment I don't actually *like* you very much. You never smile. We never laugh anymore. You hate everything and everyone, and you're horrible and rude all the time, while I'm just trying to fit in a bit, to make friends. Is that so bad?'

'But, Ani, how can you stand it? After all we've been through, after what Syrene did? How can you stand playing happy families with the Sisters when you know what they are?'

'That's the thing though, Syl – we don't know what they are. But I don't think they're all bad, any more than the human Resistance are all bad. Is Paul bad? Is Steven?'

'Oh, no, of course not,' breathed Syl, and she felt her stomach knot at the mention of Paul – her Paul – the human boy with the pillowy lips that she'd kissed, the memory of which still made her tingle, made her hot and sweaty as she lay alone in bed at night, wanting him with the very core of her being.

'Exactly. Now, we're going to be here until they let us go, and that could be never – never ever – if we don't try to find a way to fit in. And you volunteered us for this,' continued Ani. 'I really don't want every moment of my foreseeable future to be grim, but you seem hell-bent on making sure yours is.'

'Listen, Ani—'

'No, you listen to me. We know that there is something rotten in Syrene, and some of the Sisterhood may well be affected too, but we're here, and there is so much we could learn, and by learning maybe we can change things. There are brilliant Illyri here who actually want to teach us, to make us wiser and stronger.'

'To make you wiser and stronger, maybe,' said Syl.

'Well, you're hardly being kept from learning, you dumbass,' said Ani. 'But you're so busy sneaking about trying to find your big conspiracy that you seem to have lost sight of the little, everyday facts. This is an opportunity, and I for one intend to take everything I can from it. I wish you would too, Syl. I wish you'd try harder to get along with the others. Some of them are okay, like Tanit for instance, although I know you'll refuse to believe it, and Dessa seems genuine too. And we're stuck here. We may as well make it as pleasant an experience as possible. If we make friends we're more likely to be included, you know, to be told things directly. The Gifted know so much. And they have so many other connections.'

'But they hate me,' said Syl, staring at her slippers, feeling hot with shame.

'Well, it's because they think you're an uppity bitch. And you are.'

Syl looked up at her friend, stricken, and Ani laughed but it was not unkind.

'But you're also really smart and funny and loyal and determined, too. Very determined! You just need to relax a bit, Syl. Take it down a notch.'

'But there's so much to be done, so much to find out!'

'Well, how do you think you'll find out anything if you're putting their backs up all the time? If you open up, maybe they will too.'

Syl felt tears start to slip from her eyes. Ani shook her head and squatted down on the ground, taking Syl's hands in her own.

'Please tell me you'll think about it, Syl. Just think about what I've said.'

Syl grunted her assent, not trusting herself to speak without sobbing like a child. Ani looked steadily into her eyes, and Syl saw that her friend was crying, too.

'Like I said, I may not like you very much at the moment, Syl, but I love you with all my heart. I always have, I always will. You're my true sister, for always. Right?'

Syl nodded.

'Of course,' she said. 'And I love you. For always.'

CHAPTER 17

The small research shuttle commandeered by Paul and the others was built for surface exploration. While it had the capacity to travel beyond the atmosphere, it was a function really only to be used in the event of an emergency, when no other option was available and a larger craft stood ready and waiting to scoop it up. Its fuel supply was limited, and its off-world navigation systems were little better than peering through the cockpit window and judging direction by the stars. Steven piloted the shuttle towards the *Envion* largely by circumnavigating the small planet, relying on his memory of the destroyer's original coordinates to bring the shuttle home.

'There's still no reply from the *Envion*,' said Paul.

'Keep trying,' said Peris. 'It's out there somewhere.'

He was worried, but trying not to show it.

'We should be in sight within minutes,' said Steven.

The shuttle's scanners were strictly short range, and the *Envion* had not yet shown up on them. What Steven was seeing on the screen was debris, which was odd. No such debris had been apparent on the trip down to Torma.

'What's that?' asked Paul, noticing the blips on the screen.

'Could be anything,' said Steven. 'Meteor fragments, maybe.'

They were drawing closer to the objects now. Paul thought he could even see some of them floating towards the shuttle.

'They don't look like meteors,' he said.

'No,' Steven replied, 'they don't.'

Peris was standing between them. His Illyri eyesight was keener than theirs, and they heard him draw a breath of shock, even pain.

And then they saw it too.

A body, spinning in space.

A second corpse struck the shuttle while they were still trying to avoid the first. It came from the port side, and slammed against the cockpit window. Paul caught a brief glimpse of a face frozen in its last scream. It wore the uniform of the Brigades, a pair of red parallel stripes at the collar of its fatigues. Even in death, Paul recognised the soldier. It was Lambert, the corporal of the second unit. He and Paul had never really got along. Lambert was a fanatic, a devotee of the Illyri cause. There were some humans like him, men and women who felt that their own race had let them down, and were happy to throw in their lot with a new one. Lambert had not been bright enough to progress higher than corporal, though, and because of his fondness for the Illyri most of his own unit barely tolerated him at best. This had served only to increase Lambert's rage at humanity. He was always bitter, always angry. Now his fury was at an end.

Rizzo and Thula stood alongside Peris, and all five of them took in the aftermath of whatever disaster had befallen the *Envion*. The other body, the first one they had glimpsed, was female, but when it spun towards them Paul saw that most of its face was missing. The hair looked dark, though, which meant that it was either Stanton or Kotto. Stanton, probably. Kotto was bigger, broader. Paul had liked them both.

But suddenly there was no time left to worry about the identities of corpses. Bigger chunks of debris appeared, some larger than the shuttle itself. The shuttle's screens revealed the position of the *Envion* moments before she came in sight, but did not yet show the two ships standing off the *Envion*'s port bow. Those on the shuttle saw them before the scanners confirmed their presence.

The *Envion*'s command deck had been completely destroyed, disabling the ship entirely. There were also breaches to the fore and aft crew quarters, but otherwise the *Envion* remained more or less intact: it had not been completely finished off by its attackers.

Instantly Steven killed the shuttle's engines. They might not have produced much of a heat signature, but it would still be enough to draw attention to them if the area was being monitored. Instead,

Steven guided the shuttle towards the *Envion* by releasing small bursts of air from the cabin, minutely adjusting course each time, trying to hide among the bodies and wreckage ripped from the larger ship.

'Who are they?' asked Paul.

'Nomads,' said Peris.

But Nomads had never targeted a Military or Diplomatic mission before. To do so would be to risk utter destruction, even if they somehow succeeded in escaping with their lives at first. The Illyri would have hunted them to the ends of the universe in reprisal. And neither did Nomads tend to use the wormholes; their scavenged ships would have been torn apart. Yet here, it seemed, were two Nomad vessels – presumably newly arrived through the wormhole for there was no other way to get to Torma from even the outlying Illyri systems without travelling for centuries – standing watch over a crippled Military destroyer.

'The deck doors are sealed,' said Paul.

'I can see that,' said Steven. 'I'm going to bring us in under the UDC.'

Every Illyri vessel was equipped with at least one Universal Docking Connector, essentially a sealed hole in the hull to which another ship could attach itself when a hangar deck landing was not possible.

Nobody needed to ask why Steven was docking with the *Envion*. Basically, he had no choice. The shuttle's fuel and air would not last for much longer, especially with Steven using the reserve air to steer. For now, the *Envion* was their best bet because it was clear that the Nomad attackers had not set out to destroy it. If they had, they would have done so already. They had targeted certain sections of it in an effort to dispose of the crew and any Brigade units. The next step would be to board, wipe out any remaining opposition, and –

What? Paul wondered. What did the Nomads hope to do with a Military destroyer? There were easier targets. And what were they doing out here, so far from Illyr?

The *Envion* filled the cockpit window, the angle of the smaller ship's approach constantly altering as Steven steered both to avoid debris and to make their trajectory appear less direct, less artificial. They were close now, so close that Paul could see the UDC on the *Envion*'s underside. There was a second on top of the hull, but to use that would have been to leave them exposed to the Nomads. Also, the lower UDC was close to the damaged crew quarters, which made it easier for them to hide amid the debris.

Thula removed a ceiling panel from the shuttle, exposing the lock of their own UDC link, then pulled down the telescopic ladder that would enable them to climb through. With luck, they'd make it on board the *Envion* without the shuttle's presence being noted. Otherwise, one of the Nomad vessels could probably blow the shuttle apart without doing any further damage to the *Envion*, like someone swatting a fly from a table.

Steven carefully positioned the shuttle beneath the dock, watching their progress on the shuttle's screens, shifting the smaller craft left, right, down, until the two circles on the screen overlapped, then adjusted the thrusters and briefly hit the engines, giving them just enough of a kick to bring them straight up. With luck, to anyone watching from the Nomad ships, the quick heat signature would appear to be nothing more than fire damage.

As soon as docking was completed, Paul used the neural network in his helmet to communicate with the *Envion*'s systems, and watched as a situation report was downloaded to his lens.

'We have air,' he said. 'Crew quarters, command centre, and the mess have all been sealed off from the rest of the ship.'

In the event of a hull breach, the *Envion*'s systems would automatically have isolated the damaged sections to prevent further loss of life.

'Life signs?'

'Just one. He's activated his distress beacon. It's Galton. He's holed up in the officers' quarters.'

The *Envion* had arrived at Torma with twenty human Brigade soldiers, two Illyri officers, and its own crew of thirty. Now only seven were left alive.

'Anything else we should know?' said Peris.

'There are two ships in the hangar,' said Paul.

'Two?'

'One of ours, and a Civilian vessel, the *Dendra*. I'm getting two life signs.'

Paul looked at Peris.

'Maybe the Nomads didn't come for the *Envion*,' said Paul. 'Maybe it's the *Dendra* they're after.'

'Well,' said Peris, 'they're not going to get either, not without a fight.' He gestured at Thula. 'Open her up.'

While Thula unlocked the connector, Peris addressed Paul.

'Well?' he said.

'Well what?' replied Paul, genuinely puzzled.

'With De Souza out cold, you're the senior human officer on board,' said Peris.

'Sir, I'm just a sergeant.'

'You're a lieutenant now. I'm promoting you in the field.' Peris leaned in closer. 'You're an officer. Start acting like one. I can issue orders to members of a human Brigade, and they'll obey them, but they won't *follow* me. Very shortly, we may all be fighting for our lives. They need a leader. Right now, that's you.'

Paul noticed that the others had gone quiet. They were watching him, curious to see how he responded, waiting to see if he was worthy of being followed.

'What are your orders, Lieutenant?' asked Peris.

Just as he had back on Torma, Paul felt himself reacting instinctively to a situation, his words seemingly ahead of his thoughts.

'Thula, get everyone safely on board, then seal the UDC. I want it inoperable. When they dock, they'll have to do it through the forward link. Rizzo, put De Souza somewhere safe and comfortable, then go and find Galton. I want to see if we can get any of the *Envion*'s systems back online.'

'And what about me?' asked Peris. He gave no indication of whether or not he approved of Paul's decisions. Peris had ordered the young man to take command, and he had done so. He would not undermine Paul now.

'We need terrestrial weapons,' said Paul. 'Pistols, shotguns, whatever's in the armoury. We can't use Illyri weapons against Illyri, not even Nomads. If they board, we'll have to fight them the old-fashioned way.'

Peris nodded and went to help Rizzo with De Souza. Paul turned to Steven.

'As soon as everyone's safely out of the dock, let the shuttle drift, okay? We don't want them to catch sight of it.'

'Yes,' said Steven. 'One question?'

'Go on.'

'Why are we letting the Nomads dock at all? Why not seal off both connectors?'

'Because,' said Paul, 'if they can't get on board, then they may just destroy us, and that wouldn't be good. If we let them board, but dictate where they enter, and how, then we have the advantage. That's the first reason.'

'And the second?'

'Because I want one of their ships.'

CHAPTER 18

Things immediately felt a bit better between Syl and Ani following their confrontation in the classroom. The old friends had were perhaps a little stiffer and more formal with each other than they'd once been, as if something had shifted and then realigned, slightly off-kilter, since their arrival at the Marque. Still, they once again bumped along pleasantly in their shared rooms, and they were gentle with each other, careful to leave the bathroom as they'd like to find it, and considerate about offering tea, or sharing the little vials of cremos liqueur that some of the other girls received in care packages from their families and then resold at vastly inflated prices. On that score, at least, Syrene had been proved correct: the wine of Illyr was truly otherworldly.

Illyr . . . Sometimes Syl would see the homeworld rising through a window, bright as a jewel, while at other times it was bisected like an exotic fruit by the eclipsing shadow of Avila Minor. Illyr was golden, but pooled with green, and swirled with blue, and through the telescope in the astronomy laboratory she could occasionally make out the bright flashes of wild lightning that occurred high in the planet's atmosphere, but still it might as well have been a million miles away. She gazed at Illyr in pictures, and called it up on screens, and read all she could about the stars and planets in this galaxy, yet still the shining orb remained a mystery, like a waking dream that she could not touch.

'I wonder,' she said to Ani, 'if we will ever get off this rock, and get to see the place we came from.'

They were sharing the last of the cremos, as though toasting their new truce.

'Earth?' said Ani, teasing her friend.

'No, stupid. Illyr.'

Ani wandered over and stared out of the window too. She gave Syl a sly, sidelong glance.

'You never know,' she said. 'Play our cards right and it could happen sooner than you think. Tanit says there's a great ball on Illyr every annum, and the best of the Novices get to attend. It wasn't always that way, but Tanit told me that everything has changed since the Sisterhood starting permitting Sisters to marry.'

Syl said nothing, but inwardly she squirmed at the very mention of Tanit's name. Tanit hated Syl, and the feeling was completely and obviously mutual, although Ani acted determinedly oblivious. On the subject of the beautiful, regal, vicious Tanit, it seemed destined that the Earthborn friends were doomed to disagree. Ani appeared mesmerised by the girl, blushing when Tanit smiled at her, or going still as a statue when Tanit absently stroked her hair on the precious occasions when she shared a task with her in class. Yes, the young Illyri was an unwitting moth to Tanit's dangerous flame.

Generally Syl tried to avoid Tanit and her gang as much as possible. Still, Tanit felt nothing of jostling Syl as she carried her tray across the canteen, slopping juice onto her food, or sneering quietly at her nakedness beside the showers after gym classes, so much so that Syl had taken to changing out of her sweaty gear in the privacy of her quarters instead of in the locker room. In lectures, Tanit whispered with Sarea and Nemein when Syl answered a question, mocking her Earthly accent, for Syl's language was peppered with inflections from the world on which she was born, and from the gently Scottish brogue that came so naturally to her. The fact that Ani's speech was similarly affected seemed barely to register with Tanit and her acolytes. Syl was the one whom they despised, not Ani. Now Syl, for the sake of her friendship with Ani, had agreed to back down before a vicious pack of spoiled brats with very sharp teeth.

Oblivious, Ani chatted on.

'. . . and for the ball – it's called the Genesis Ball – each debutante is given exquisite robes and precious jewels to wear, for the Genesis

Ball is patronised by only the finest of Illyri society. The *very* finest,' she stressed.

The words that came from Ani's lips were clearly Tanit's, repeated verbatim, for they sounded nothing like Ani at all. Still, Ani's elfin face was shiny with excitement.

'Syl, if we're very lucky, we may be selected too.'

Syl frowned: 'Why? Who chooses?'

'Syrene, of course. Duh.'

'Duh, yourself. I mean – Syrene! Really, Ani? Please tell me why she would ever, *ever* choose us?'

Ani paused as if to consider this, and she looked embarrassed as she replied.

'Syl, I'm not trying to rub it in your face, but I *am* actually one of the Gifted, you know. Tanit says that of all the first year Novices, Mila and I are most likely to be chosen, because we're Blue Novices. Tanit and the other Gifted went last year of course, but Xaron got to go too and she was only new then, and the others went the year before, when they were just fresh Novices like I am, so there's a very real chance for me.'

And her eyes spoke silently to Syl, imploring her: *Don't ruin it for me*.

'Nice for you, dear heart, but there's still zero hope for me,' said Syl sourly, trying to swallow down her frustration. All her life she'd fantasised about walking on the homeworld, breathing the air for which her lungs had been created, feeling the legendary lightness of the gravity that allowed the plants and creatures of her planet to grow tall and graceful. She'd seen pictures and immersed herself in virtual recreations, but that was different from touching it, feeling it, being enveloped in its balmy atmosphere with her feet on its sands and her eyes drinking in its exotic horizons.

And, of course, a high profile function on Illyr would be such a good opportunity to dig deeper. She would get to meet the cream of Illyri society, and perhaps work out who was who, and who knew what. She could speak to people who mattered, putting all her 'Applied Diplomacy' skills to work in connecting Illyri with real power, to those who might have an inkling of what was going on. Maybe she could find out about the battles on other worlds; maybe she would receive news of Earth and her father; maybe someone could tell her where Peris was, and by extension she could then learn something of Paul – Steven too, of course, but the memories of Paul clawed at her heart. Sometimes she fretted that he was dead, slaughtered in a war not his own, far away from his beloved home in Scotland, and at other times she imagined he'd forgotten her, or fallen for another, a human being like himself. And she was ashamed to acknowledge that in the darkest hours of night, as she slipped into her flustered, mortifying dreams of him, she didn't know which would be worse.

'You never know,' said Ani, unaware of Syl's brooding as they sipped down the last drops of their tiny vials of cremos.

There was a time when Ani had been better able to sense Syl's feelings, but that was before they had both realised the extent of Ani's psychic powers, and before Syl had discovered her own secret strength and learned how to close her mind to those who would know her thoughts. Funny how Ani hadn't even noticed the disconnection.

Together they looked through the glass as Illyr dipped away behind the horizon, leaving only a sky filled with the dark sparkle of a million faraway suns.

'Hmmm,' said Syl.

'Honestly Syl, it is possible. Why shouldn't you come to the ball? Tanit has some sway with Syrene, and I'm one of the Gifted, and you're my closest friend. Maybe Tanit could help swing it for you if I asked her. You'd really have to be nice to her though. Properly nice.'

Syl laughed despite herself.

'Ani,' she said, 'if Tanit really has any sway with Syrene, and if Tanit knows I want to go to the Genesis Ball, then you can be certain that I'll be the last person in all the worlds to be invited. No, I shall remain here by the hearth, hugging my pumpkin and polishing my glass slippers, and you can tell me all about it when your carriage brings you home.'

Ani laughed too: 'Oh, poor Cinderella. So am I an ugly stepsister then?'

'Well, not that ugly . . .'

'Thanks. I think.'

'Maybe just a rather homely one. Plain, even.'

'Shut up, Syl.'

'I will if you've got any more cremos.'

'Lord, I wish. You never know though. A fairy godmother may wave her wand yet.'

Syl smiled, but she had to admit to herself that Ani had planted a seed. Maybe she had been going about things the wrong way, and the time had come to try and pretend that she wanted to be here, and make some new friends. Or at least fewer enemies.

But not Tanit. No, she'd rot before she sucked up to that bitch.

CHAPTER 19

Galton, trapped on the *Envion* and firmly convinced that he was going to die alone, was relieved to see Paul and the others, once Rizzo had managed to convince him not to shoot as he heard their approach. He also managed to clarify to some extent the situation regarding the *Dendra*: its occupants had not even been given time to disembark before the Nomads appeared, and Commander Morev had ordered that they remain in their craft until it was safe to emerge. In order to ensure that they obeyed, he had sealed all exits from the hangar.

The survivors on board the *Envion* had one advantage over the Nomads: all Military and Diplomatic vessels employed heavy interior shielding designed to repel scans, so the Nomads would be unable to tell how many individuals were still alive on the *Envion*. If the attackers were smart – and the fact that they had, until now, kept their distance from the wounded ship suggested they were both clever and cautious – they would assume that hostile forces remained on the vessel, and any attempt to board it would involve a fight. They would be expecting trouble. They just wouldn't be able to anticipate the extent of it.

But Paul knew that, even without one docking port disabled, the Nomads would still probably have concentrated their efforts to board on the upper port nearest the stern, because that was not only closest to the hangar bay but also to the Secondary Control Centre. With the main cockpit destroyed, all systems would revert to the SCC. From there, anyone remaining alive on board the *Envion* could manage the environmental controls, and any functioning weapons. The *Envion* would not belong to the Nomads until the SCC was secured.

Paul watched as Peris opened the armoury, for only Illyri were permitted to have unrestricted access to terrestrial weapons.

'You know,' said Peris, 'I appear to be the only Illyri left alive on board this ship.'

'And?'

'It would be easy, in the heat of battle, for me to lose my life. If you managed to seize one of those Nomad vessels, you could try to flee.'

Paul held Peris's gaze.

'I'm not going to kill you, Peris. None of the others will either. And we're not going to try to escape. The Illyri would never stop hunting us.'

'The Illyri wouldn't know. There are bodies floating in space. By the time a team comes to investigate what has happened, establishing who died – and how – will be virtually impossible.'

'You sound almost as if you want us to run.'

'I'm trying to think as you would.'

'With respect, you have no idea how I think.'

Their communicators buzzed into life. It was Steven.

'One of the Nomad ships has commenced its approach. It's heading straight for the upper port, just like you said. ETA: seven minutes.'

'And the other?'

'It's started circling.'

'It'll be monitoring our weapons systems,' said Peris. 'At the first sign of our heavy cannon or torpedoes powering up, it'll target us with a blast.'

'That's why we'll keep away from the ship's weapons. Just gather up those guns and as much ammunition as you can carry.'

Paul hit his communicator again. 'Galton, are you in position?'

'Yes, I'm ready.'

Galton was in the SCC. He had one task to carry out as soon as the Nomads were on board, and then he would join the fight.

'Steven, Rizzo?'

Two voices confirmed that they were standing by.

'Remember,' said Paul. 'Let them come. We know where they're headed.'

Because of the damage to the ship, and the sealed-off sections, the Nomads would be forced to turn right when they landed, moving towards the stern. That would suit the Nomads' purposes anyway, if they wanted to get to the hangars and the SCC. The longest single corridor ran straight towards the stern for almost one hundred metres. That was where the trap would be sprung.

'Thula?' Thula's task was the most dangerous. His job was to seize the Nomad ship.

'Ready, *Lieutenant*,' came Thula's voice over the coms link.

Paul thought that he detected just a hint of mockery in Thula's use of the new rank, but he didn't take it personally.

'That's "Lieutenant, sir" to you.'

'I shall try to remember that, Lieutenant, *sir*.'

Peris appeared from the armoury, loaded down with as much weaponry and ammunition as he could carry. Paul took two shotguns from him, inserted a ten-round magazine into one, and jacked a shell. He added four more magazines, along with a box of .38 rounds for his Colt.

'You sure you're not planning to start a war?' asked Peris.

He had a sly look in his eyes and Paul wondered if, after all, Peris did know more of Paul's thoughts than either of them wanted to admit.

'If I do, you'll be the first to know.'

'As I've already suggested, that's what worries me.'

Peris looked down at his feet. He had discarded his uniform footwear, on Paul's orders, and was now wearing heavy antigrav boots, just like all the others.

'It's quite a plan,' said Peris.

'If it works.'

'And if it doesn't, no one will ever know. Good luck.'

'You too.'

They parted at the main corridor, Paul moving right, Peris heading left. Steven's voice crackled in Paul's ear.

'ETA: two minutes.'

'We'll hear them when they connect,' said Paul. 'Radio silence.'

His earpiece went quiet. He ran to take up his position. Rizzo had lowered an overhead ladder for him. He climbed it, pulled it up after him, and loosely replaced the ceiling panel. Through its grille, he could see the corridor below. The ceiling measured three panels across. Paul moved to the extreme right leaving Rizzo at the left. When it came to the fight, he didn't want either of them getting in the other's way. Paul tossed Rizzo a shotgun and two magazines.

'I've never killed an Illyri before,' said Rizzo.

'No?'

'You have, right?'

'Yes.'

'Did you enjoy it?'

'I don't recall.'

Rizzo laughed.

'Liar,' she said. 'But I know I will.'

A metallic sound echoed through the ship, silencing her. It had an ominous tone, like a great door closing, sealing the fates of all those trapped within.

The Nomads had docked.

Thula saw them first. Like the rest, he was hiding in the ceiling, staring down through one of the panels. They were dressed like Nomads, in clothing scavenged from Military, Diplomats and Civilians alike, their faces concealed by heavily scarred blast masks overwrapped with scarves and turbans, but they moved with the precision of expert soldiers, and their weapons looked clean and well maintained. Perhaps it wasn't so surprising that they were disciplined – after all, the Nomads numbered Military deserters among their bands, and they might well have entrusted the final capture of the *Envion* to those with training. Yet the sight of them communicating silently through hand signals, and moving carefully through the ship, overlapping so that one group – or 'stick', as they had learned to call it in training – provided cover while the next advanced, caused Thula unease. Thula had spent most of his life fighting – hunting and killing both the Illyri invaders and the human predators who roved in gangs through his country, raping and murdering at will. He knew amateurs from professionals, and he sensed that these intruders were Nomads in name only.

Twelve, thirteen, fourteen: Thula counted them, and waited, but no more emerged from the docking bridge. One of them opened the control panel for the nearest door, cut a pair of the interior wires, and rerouted them through a small black box.

Clever, thought Thula: they were overriding the door systems to ensure that they could not be trapped, just in case there was anyone left alive on board. But Paul had anticipated just such a move. It wouldn't save them.

Now all but two of them proceeded towards the stern of the ship, with the remaining pair staying behind to guard the dock. How many more on board, Thula wondered? The Nomad vessel was unfamiliar to him, but there would be at least one pilot, and perhaps a co-pilot too. Four, then, in total. He would have to move fast once the shooting began. The Nomad ship could not be allowed to uncouple if, by any chance, the Nomads managed to get to the SCC. The last thing Paul and the others wanted was to have Nomads holding the SCC and their ship safely orbiting the *Envion*.

Thula slipped the fingers of his left hand through the grille and gripped the metal. In his right hand he held his pistol. A bead of sweat dripped from his brow and trickled down his nose. He caught it on his tongue and tasted its saltiness. It reminded him of the taste of blood. He breathed in deeply, calming himself.

Four.

Four to neutralise.

The Nomads entered the section of corridor that Paul had marked as the killing box. Paul saw them before he heard them, and he was surprised at how quietly they were moving, but he was reassured too. It meant that they were wearing regular boots and not the antigravs with which he had equipped his small force.

Come on, he thought, come on.

The Nomads paused, as though sensing some kind of trap. So far they had encountered no opposition, and it must have been tempting for them to assume that the *Envion*'s entire crew, along with any Brigade troops, were now dead.

But the Nomads had made no such assumptions. The care they were taking with their approach was proof of that. Paul counted twelve Nomads. Eight were now in the killing box, and four outside it, but Paul wanted them all. Then: a hand raised, the signal to advance given. The first line of four moved forward, the second four covering them, the final four at last entering the box.

Nearly there, nearly there . . .

Another pause. They were now in the box, but Paul needed the last four to move farther away from the doorway.

The final overlap: the second four advanced, the last four followed on.

They were in.

'Now!' said Paul, activating his communicator, and they all heard him.

Thula, by the dock.

Steven and Peris, at one end of the killing box.

Rizzo, by Paul's side, at the other.

Galton, seated in the small secondary control room, hunched over the main console.

And the Nomads: they heard him too, for their own communicators were scanning all frequencies, alert to any transmissions from inside the ship. They were already preparing for the attack, their responses honed by years of training, as Galton whispered a small prayer and hit a switch.

And the *Envion*'s artificial gravity ceased functioning.

When the shooting was over, Paul would think of it as less of an ambush than a slaughter. It didn't matter that the Nomads would almost certainly have murdered them without a second thought. It didn't matter that men and women whom he had known as friends, rivals, and comrades-in-arms had been left floating dead in space by the actions of these intruders. What he and the others visited on the Nomads was a massacre, pure and simple.

But that was after. For now, all Paul thought about was killing.

Killing.

Surviving.

Avenging.

As soon as the artificial gravity system was deactivated, the Nomads found themselves floating in the corridor, bumping against one another and the hull, upside down and back-to-front. Two had already lost their weapons when the grilles were pulled back from the ceiling and four figures in full body armour landed heavily on the floor, two at each end of the corridor, their antigrav boots attaching them magnetically to the floor panels.

The firing began. Paul felt the recoil as the first explosive round left his shotgun, a sphere of smoke expanding from the barrel. It should have bounced him back at a speed of about one metre per second, but the boots kept him anchored, and instead it was only his upper body that responded to the firing of the shotgun, and he had anticipated it. The blast hit the torso of the nearest Nomad, and globules of Illyri blood floated like bubbles from the wound. Paul jacked another round and fired again, this time hitting a Nomad in the right leg. He was aware of the noise of other guns firing, the injuries that they inflicted blossoming like great red flowers, scattering dark petals. One of the Nomads began shooting random pulses from his weapon, but the first struck the ceiling, and the next hit one of his own comrades, and then he was dead and he shot no more.

Paul had stopped thinking. There was only shooting – shooting, and killing.

And he was very good at both.

CHAPTER 20

Thula's job was to get past the two guards, enter the dock, and secure the Nomad vessel. Once inside the ship, he would be unable to use his shotgun: the risk of damaging vital equipment was too great, and they needed the ship intact. He would also have to move fast, for the boarding party of Nomads would undoubtedly be monitoring any communications on the *Envion*, and when Paul gave the order to attack the Nomads would hear it, along with those at whom it was directed.

For that reason, Thula was already moving when the order came. Instead of lifting the ceiling grille he had merely to drop it, for he had removed it earlier and was holding it in place until the time came to act. He shot the first guard just as the Nomad's feet left the ground. The second Nomad found himself upside down but face-to-face with Thula as he died. Thula could see his own reflection in the Nomad's blast mask before his gun spoke and the image was lost in a flash of fire and smoke.

As soon as he dropped down, Thula dispensed with his antigrav boots. He would be able to move faster without them, and speed would determine his success or failure. He pushed one of the floating bodies aside, bubbles of blood breaking on his skin, and pulled himself into the docking bridge. It was a circular tunnel, at the end of which he could see the open door of the Nomad vessel.

The Nomad ship was at a disadvantage. Once another vessel docked with a Military ship, the Military systems overrode its own. This was to ensure that all dock doors were sealed before a linked ship disengaged, as the last thing any ship's commander wanted was to have his crew sucked out of an airlock door because someone had unmoored a docked vessel incorrectly. Only by reaching the secondary control room could the Nomads unlock their vessel, so even if the Nomad crew had tried to flee upon hearing Paul's order, and the firing that followed, they could not have done so. Thula had them.

He was halfway along the bridge when a Nomad appeared at the door of his vessel. He, too, was floating, but had found a handle to cling to. The Nomad was wearing a helmet but no body armour, and had a pulse pistol in his hand. He raised it to fire, but his reactions were too slow. By the time the pistol was aimed, Thula's bullet was already buried in the Nomad's chest.

He moved faster, until he was at the door. This was the most dangerous moment, the point at which all might be lost. But Thula was ready: he slipped the small grenade from his pocket, armed it, and threw it inside. It floated almost daintily into the cockpit of the Nomad vessel, spinning in the air. Thula turned his face away, closed his eyes, and used his arms to cover his ears.

Seconds later the flash-bang grenade exploded, temporarily blinding and deafening anyone inside the Nomad cockpit without damaging its equipment. Thula's own ears were ringing as he pro-pelled himself backwards through the doorway, a blade in his hand. He saw only one Nomad, his body lodged behind the pilot's chair. Thula advanced on him and the Nomad moved, launching himself upwards, a pulser in his hand. He fired. The shot missed Thula, but he could feel the vibration of the pulse as it passed his left ear. The charge must have been set low, for Thula heard no explosion behind him from the missed shot. A pulser on full charge might have torn a hole in the hull: like Thula, the Nomad did not want to risk damaging the ship.

Thula was on him before he could fire a second shot. He knocked the Nomad's weapon away, and the two of them twisted and fought in the narrow confines of the cockpit, like dancers engaged in a series of movements that could only have one end. The initial advantage was with Thula, for he had a blade, but the Nomad fought hard. Thula would have preferred to take him alive for interrogation, but the Nomad was intent on killing his opponent. Thula could see it in his eyes, and feel it in the force of the kicks that the Nomad aimed at him while their hands were locked together. The Nomad was immensely strong, his skin a deep gold, the flesh at his neck scarred and burned. Even with the blade, Thula felt himself losing his advantage. He was as tall and strong as many ordinary Illyri, but this, he knew, was a trained fighter. Close up, and hand-to-hand, an Illyri like this one would beat him.

There was one chance, and Thula took it on instinct. He released his grip on the knife, and let it float off. Instinctively, the Nomad reached for it. As he did so, Thula pushed himself away. The Nomad caught the knife by the blade and prepared to use it, but by then Thula had the Illyri's pulser. His finger was already pulling the trigger when he realised that the pulser would be DNA locked. It could not be fired at an Illyri.

Thula was dead.

But Thula did not die. The pulser fired, and the pulse struck the Nomad full in the chest, destroying his internal organs. Great bubbles of blood burst from his mouth and floated into the air.

And Thula watched in surprise as the Nomad's life left him.

The secondary command deck was like a nightmare vision of a slaughterhouse. Bodies floated, bumping gently against the hull and one another, globules of blood from the dead coming together and then separating like amoebae, their biological identities seeming to combine even as their empty shells spun in uneasy orbits.

'Galton,' said Paul.

'I hear you.'

'Restore gravity.'

'Restoring gravity.'

The bodies fell, and blood rained upon the deck.

Steven ran as soon as Paul gave the order to restore gravity, sealing the bulkhead doors as he went, leaving the carnage behind. Steven had fought the Illyri back on Earth, killing Securitats during the final bitter defence of Dundearg Castle, but it had been different then, almost like a computer game. He had fired, and targets had dropped, the blood largely invisible to him. But the trap they had sprung on the Nomads . . . Steven had never seen so much blood, and the whole scene was rendered more awful, more macabre, by the floating bodies. Yet he had been excited during the fight, pumped by blood lust, and had felt little fear.

But there was more killing to be done.

Within minutes he was at the docking port, stepping over the bodies of the Nomads Thula had killed. He sealed the final door.

'Galton,' he said. 'Stand by for release.'

'Standing by.'

Steven reached the door of the Nomad vessel just as Thula was dragging out the second of the dead pilots, the one with whom he had fought hand-to-hand.

'You okay?' asked Steven.

'I think so. But I killed him with a pulser,' said Thula.

'How? All pulsers are supposed to be locked.'

Thula showed Steven the weapon.

'I've never seen one like that before,' said Steven. 'It's sleeker, more modern.'

'Then wait until you see their ship.'

Steven entered the cockpit and took in the shining consoles, the gleaming instrumentation. This vessel was more advanced, and better equipped, than even the newest of the Military craft that he had flown. The only Nomads that the Brigade had ever encountered before flew rust-buckets, kept functioning with cannibalised parts. They could only dream of acquiring vessels like this one.

'What the hell is this?' said Steven.

A crackle of communication came from the console. The voice spoke Illyri, but Steven wasn't wearing his helmet with its inbuilt translator. Unlike Paul he wasn't yet adept enough at the language to be able to understand all that was being said. Still, it didn't take a genius to catch the drift of it. Someone on the other Nomad vessel was anxious to know what was happening. If a response wasn't received soon, there was a chance that the other ship might cut its losses and run or, worse, correctly conclude that the raiding party had failed in its mission and start opening fire.

Thula stepped into the cockpit.

'Can you fly it?' he asked Steven.

'I don't have to fly it. I just have to turn it and shoot.'

'Well, can you do that?'

'I don't know. We'll soon find out, won't we?'

Steven took the pilot's seat and hit the button that activated the neural net. All Illyri ships had one, just in case of damage to an embedded Chip. The net, which resembled a white skullcap, flipped up and came to rest on Steven's head. It was unsecured, which was fortunate. Otherwise, Steven would have been forced to hack into the weapons system, and they didn't have time for that.

'Galton?'

'Ready.'

'Okay, we're closing the cockpit door. On my count: three, two, one. Release!'

In the secondary control room, Galton made a final check of the doors to make sure all were fully sealed, then powered down the locking mechanism that bound the Nomad craft to the *Envion*. The vessel lurched away and Steven took the controls. His first touch was too heavy and it turned so sharply that Thula was thrown to the floor.

'If we live, I'm going to kick your ass for that,' he told Steven.

'Do you want to fly it?'

'I could do a better job.'

Steven ignored him and called up a full display from the neural net. It appeared on the cockpit window. The movements of his pupils brought him into the weapons systems just as the second Nomad vessel appeared in the distance. It was moving slowly, circling the *Envion*, its crew uncertain how to react to the sudden undocking of the raiding ship. They were still attempting to communicate with it, but even with the neural net in place Steven was no wiser about what exactly was being said. Like Illyri Chips, neural nets needed to be uploaded with languages for the translation tool to function, and most Illyri ships didn't bother with an Illyri upload, for obvious reasons. Only equipment used by Brigade fighters and the other conquered races, like the Agrons or the Galateans, was programmed with an Illyri language upload.

'It won't be long before they figure out what's happening,' said Thula, taking the co-pilot's chair and belting himself in, just to be safe.

Steven was taking in his ship's armaments: forward, side, and rear cannon, and forty-eight torpedoes, the launchers at either side of the cockpit. The Nomad vessel might have been built to brave wormholes, but it was first and foremost an instrument of war.

'I think they've already figured it out,' said Steven.

The second Nomad ship was turning in their direction so that it would present a smaller target while enabling the aiming of its massive forward cannon. But Steven, apart from some minute adjustments to the controls, allowed their ship simply to drift.

'Come on,' he whispered. 'Come on . . .'

The Nomad ship was a glowing silhouette on his lens, shrinking into itself as it turned. They would still be uncertain, Steven reasoned, wondering if, by any chance, some of the raiding party had survived and managed to free the ship; wondering if they were injured, or their communication system was down; wondering if what was clearly a very expensive craft could somehow be saved . . .

If, if, if.

'Now!' said Steven.

He hit the ship's thrusters. It accelerated so suddenly that he was pressed back into his seat, and he heard Thula shout a prayer to some unnamed god. Steven brought them parallel to the other ship, so their port sides were facing each other, and then turned swiftly to port himself. The manoeuvre took the Nomad by surprise, suddenly exposing its entire length to Steven's cannon. Steven didn't even wait until he was fully in position before he started firing. His first shots went wide of the Nomad's stern, but the next barrage tore into it, ripping through its hull as Steven came perpendicular to it. Now the

Nomad was returning fire, but the damage it had already incurred meant that it was shooting wildly while Steven was entirely focused. He allowed his ship to continue turning to port, and as the Nomad's cockpit came into his sights he fired two torpedoes. He and Thula watched as they honed in on the Nomad, and struck home.

The bow of the Nomad disintegrated, the stern separating and becoming almost vertical. Steven saw shapes amid the debris.

Bodies. More bodies.

And then the Nomad's engines exploded, and the ship was just a memory.

'For our friends,' he said.

'For our friends,' echoed Thula.

Steven hit the thrusters, and they headed back to the *Envion*.

CHAPTER 21

Once the Nomad vessel had docked safely with the *Envion* again, Paul instructed his unit – he was already thinking of it as 'his unit' – to meet by the hangar, where the mysterious *Dendra* waited. Rizzo was the last to arrive. She had fresh blood on her hands, and some of it had streaked her face. Paul thought that she might have been crying, but he could not recall ever seeing Rizzo cry before. It didn't seem likely, somehow, or even possible.

'De Souza's dead,' she said. 'He must have passed away during the fight.'

Paul heard Steven swear, and an image of his mother's disapproving face flashed through his mind. Oh, how he hoped the gentle, upright Mrs Kerr would never have to hear of any of this killing and dying. Then her youngest son's deteriorating language would be the least of her worries. And Paul swore too, for they had all liked and respected De Souza. He'd looked out for them and never played favourites. Paul wished that someone had been with him when he died. De Souza had deserved better than to die alone.

Paul turned towards the hangar doors and hailed Galton, who was still in the secondary control centre. With so many of the *Envion*'s systems down, the only way to be certain that anything would work was to leave it in Galton's hands.

'Do you have an atmosphere reading from the hangar, Galton?'

'It's clean – or as clean as it ever is.'

That was something, at least. It meant that the integrity of the hangar's hull section had not been compromised, and the atmosphere was breathable. They could enter without suiting up. Unfortunately,

the surveillance cameras across the entire ship were no longer functioning, and the screen beside the entry door, which would usually
have displayed an image of what lay behind it, was blank. When they
entered the hangar, they would be going in without any foreknowledge
of what might be waiting for them.

'What about lighting?' asked Paul.

'It looks like most of it went down with the cameras. I think you'll
have emergency illumination, but it'll still be pretty dark in there.'

Bad. The last thing Paul wanted was to open those doors and come
under fire from unknown assailants who could see them but who
couldn't be seen in turn.

'Can you patch me into their comms system?'

'I can try.'

While Paul waited, he tried to figure out how what had begun as
a simple mission to check up on some scientists and engineers with a
broken radio had somehow ended up with a crippled destroyer, the
loss of the best part of two units, a gunfight, the destruction of one
Nomad vessel and the capture of another, and the appearance of a
previously unknown, and certainly hostile, silicon-based species. Oh,
and not to forget the discovery of a tower left behind by another alien
civilisation, about which nobody had bothered to tell the dumb
human recruits. It was possible that events could still take a turn for
the worse, but – aside from the death of everyone else on board the
Envion – it was hard to see how.

Paul heard a crackle in his ear.

'I've got a channel open and their systems have responded,' said
Galton. 'You can talk to them now.'

'Hailing the craft in our hangar,' said Paul. 'This is Lieutenant Paul
Kerr, ranking Military officer on board the *Envion*. This ship is now
under Brigade control. I order all occupants of your craft to disembark
– *unarmed* – and lie face down on the deck. You are being monitored.
Failure to obey will be interpreted as a hostile action. Respond.'

The answer came back almost immediately.

'This is Councillor Baldus Tiray of the Illyri Council of Government. How can we be sure that this isn't a trap?'

Peris looked at Paul.

'May I?' he said.

'Go ahead,' said Paul, noting once again how Peris was determined not to undermine his authority.

'Councillor Tiray,' said Peris. 'I am Peris of House Gault, formerly of the general staff of Lord Andrus. We met once, a long time ago.'

There was a pause.

'I remember. You are far from Earth, Peris.'

'And you are far from Illyr. How many of you are there?'

'Two. Just my aide, Alis, and me.'

'Then I wish to confirm the truth of Lieutenant Kerr's statement to you. The *Envion* is under Military control, but it is badly damaged, and an evacuation will be necessary. For security purposes, I would advise you to follow the lieutenant's order: disarm, disembark, and make yourselves as comfortable as possible on the deck.'

Another pause. Paul could almost picture Tiray and Alis conferring. In their position, he might well have been cautious too. It didn't take much imagination to picture Paul and Peris with a group of Nomads holding guns to their heads as they were forced to lure the survivors from the shuttle.

'We submit,' said Tiray at last. 'We're coming out. You'll see that we're unarmed, and we'll keep our hands in the air until we're on the deck.'

'We'll be watching,' said Paul.

'Watching a blank screen,' Thula muttered.

'When did you get so surly?' said Paul.

'Sometime between waking up this morning and now.'

'You need to have more faith in people. Just to help you find it, you can be first into the hangar bay with me.'

Thula sighed deeply.

'I don't think that I want you as my lieutenant anymore.'

'Noted.'

Paul addressed Steven and Rizzo.

'We go in. You cover us from here. You see anything you don't like, and you have my permission to fire at it.'

'I don't like you,' said Thula to Paul, as he loaded his shotgun. 'Does that mean I can fire at you?'

'You love and respect me like a brother,' said Paul. 'Ready?'

He held his finger above the door-release button.

'I can't stand my brother,' said Thula. 'Ready.'

Paul hit it, and the door opened. He and Thula peered through the gap and saw two figures lying flat on the deck in a shaft of illumination from the open shuttle. Orange emergency lighting flashed from the walls.

'You keep your gun on them,' said Paul. 'I'll take the shuttle.'

They came in fast, Thula moving to a standing position over the two prostrate forms while Paul inched his way along the hull of the shuttle. He could see that the pilot's and co-pilot's seats were empty, but the angle prevented him from viewing the lower part of the shuttle's interior. He would be exposed while he passed the open door but he had no choice. He backed up, the shotgun at his shoulder ready to fire.

The shuttle was empty.

Paul relaxed, perhaps for the first time since they had come in sight of the crippled *Envion*. His shoulders and back ached. He wanted to slough off his uniform and wash away the blood and filth, but the possibility of a shower was limited.

'Steven, Rizzo,' he said. 'The shuttle is clear, but help me search the hangar.'

Paul was taking no chances, not when they were so close to safety, however relative.

Steven and Rizzo entered, and together the three young humans made sure that no one was hiding in the shadows of the dock. When they were done, they returned to where Thula continued to hold a gun over the two Illyri on the deck. They were still lying face down in loose-fitting flight suits, their hands clasped over the backs of their heads. Paul ordered Steven to frisk them. He patted the first one down, found nothing, then moved on to the second. He was about halfway through the search when he paused and looked puzzled.

'They're called breasts,' said a female voice from the floor, 'and I'd appreciate it if you'd take your hands off them.'

Steven jumped back as though he'd been scalded. Thula looked at him with amusement.

'I could ask you if you found anything,' said Thula, 'but I think we already know the answer.'

'You can get up,' Paul told the Illyri.

Peris stepped forward to help the male, the one called Tiray. Paul offered his hand to the female, Alis. He saw that she was small for an Illyri, with narrow golden eyes. She looked at his outstretched palm.

'Do you want to touch me inappropriately as well?' she asked.

Paul wasn't sure if this was a trick question, but decided very quickly that the correct answer was 'No', so that was the one he gave. Alis accepted his hand and he pulled her to her feet.

'Councillor Tiray,' said Peris, 'this is Lieutenant Kerr.'

'We have a lot of questions for you—' said Paul, but a voice from his comms unit prevented him from saying more.

'They'll have to wait, Lieutenant,' said Galton. 'We're losing all remaining systems rapidly. It's a wonder the *Envion* has held together for as long as she has. I should just have time to send a distress drone into the wormhole before we start the evacuation.'

'No!' said Tiray. 'You mustn't do that.'

'We're on a dying ship, far from home,' said Paul. 'Regulations require that we inform the Military authorities of what's happened here.'

'If you do, you'll bring more of them down on us,' said Tiray.

'He's right,' said Alis. 'They'll come.'

'Who, the Nomads?' asked Paul.

'I don't believe that we were attacked by Nomads,' said Tiray. 'And somehow, I don't think you do either.'

There was a loud groan from deep in the ship, as though the *Envion* were crying out in agony.

'Lieutenant.' It was Galton again. 'I wasn't joking when I used the word "rapidly". We're in real trouble. The hull is coming apart.'

'Please, Lieutenant,' said Tiray. 'I'm asking you not to send a distress call, not yet. If I must, I'll *order* you not to.'

'Order me?' said Paul. 'Under what authority?'

'Under the authority of the Council of Government of Illyr, which requires all Civilian representatives to be offered every courtesy by Military and Consular personnel, up to and including the use of ships, equipment and any resources deemed necessary for the successful pursuit of a governmental mission. Article 15.21, I believe.'

Paul glanced at Peris.

'He is correct,' said Peris, although he had the decency not to look happy about it.

'But I don't want to use Article 15.21,' continued Tiray. 'So I'm pleading with you, Lieutenant: get us off this ship, hear me out, and then decide upon the best course of action to take. For now, though, I guarantee that if a distress message is sent through the wormhole, the response will not be a rescue.'

Paul ran his fingers through his hair. Okay, so they weren't dead, but their situation had somehow still managed to worsen. He wouldn't have believed it if he hadn't been there to see it.

'All right,' he said. 'Galton, how long have we got?'

'Twenty minutes, but I'd be happier if we were gone in fifteen.'

Paul instructed Rizzo and Steven to gather as much food and water and as many medical supplies as they could lay their hands on, and take them to the Nomad ship, while he and Thula returned to the armoury. Peris was left to take care of Tiray and Alis.

'We leave in ten,' Paul told them all. 'Galton, do what you have to do, then get to that ship.'

'Understood, Lieutenant.'

Paul and Thula headed for the armoury, but when they were out of sight of the others, Thula took Paul aside and showed him the pulser that he'd found on the Nomad vessel.

'It's not locked,' he said. 'I used it to kill one of those Nomads, or whatever they were.'

Paul took the pulser from him, set it to its lowest charge, and fired. The blast struck one of the dead bodies on the deck, causing it to shudder slightly.

'Who knows about this?'

'Only Steven, and I told him to say nothing.'

'Help me to gather as many of these weapons as we can from the dead, both pistols and rifles, then find a crate to put them in. We'll seal the crate, store it with the other ordnance, and hide it in the cargo bay of the Nomad ship. You share this with no one else, you understand? And whatever you do, don't let Peris see it.'

Paul left Thula to his work. From all of this chaos and bloodshed, something useful had emerged.

They had moved one small step closer to retaliation against the Illyri.

Chapter 22

A s they often did, Ani and Syl sank into peaceful silence, picking up their books as if they were of the same mind. Syl smiled to herself as she watched her friend frowning over a dense tome entitled *The Science of the Mind, Volume 1*. The other five in the series were piled next to the sofa, gathering dust mockingly. Ani had never been particularly interested in reading until they'd come to this knowledge-infused place, but her lack of fingertip facts in their first classes had shamed her, particularly as the Gifted were watching – they were always watching – so she'd set herself the task of remedying the gaps in her education, plugging them with as many details as she could.

Syl herself was reading a dated but oddly alluring memoir she'd found in the largest library in the Twelfth Realm a few days before. It was called *The Interplanetary Pioneers*. The fat little volume had been crammed behind a pile of hand-tooled, leather-bound books she'd been instructed to alphabetise during her work duties. As with any library, even a repository as rarefied as the Marque suffered from the carelessness of its users, who would yank out volumes in haste and then haphazardly shove them back onto the shelves with scant regard for their order. Syl had pulled the tattered book from its hiding place, shaking her head at the carelessness of whoever had discarded it there. Absently she opened it and flicked to the first page but soon she was sucked in, lost to those working around her, for it read like an adventure story, though it was in fact a true-life account of the Illyri's first exploratory missions beyond their homeworld, which were either brave or foolhardy given the clunky, dangerous craft they appeared to have set out in. It was just the sort of thing she was interested in, for surely the organism she'd encountered on Earth, the parasitic dweller in an Illyri skull, was not of this world, was not of *her* world.

She'd stood there reading until a Sister had clucked at her, nodding meaningfully at the disordered shelves. Reluctantly Syl had set the book to one side, but she'd taken it with her when she was dismissed from her duties, along with some other books about the early explorations. That was one thing that she actually did approve of on the grim old Marque: there was a seemingly unlimited supply of books, even here in the Novice libraries. Knowledge was prized, and the students were encouraged to read even more in their own time.

In this, at least, Syl was happy to oblige.

After a bit Ani slammed her book closed meaningfully.

'Hungry?' she said.

'Yeah, I guess.'

'Should we go get dinner?'

'I'll meet you there. I just need to take a load to the laundry or I'll have nothing to wear tomorrow. I've already worn this robe twice.'

'Slob. Imagine what Althea would say.'

They both looked towards the tiny kitchen with its sink piled with dirty cups and giggled.

'Maybe one of us had better do that tonight,' said Ani.

'Help yourself,' said Syl.

'Or maybe not,' said Ani. 'Anyway. See you there.'

The laundry room was empty, the silent machinery set neatly into the carved rock. The only other furnishings were a pair of hard stools, and a lone sock lay forgotten and forlorn on the floor. Syl went to the largest machine and was hauling all the pale yellow and white washing from her bag, when there was a clatter on the floor.

Something sharp bounced off her soft slipper.

'What the . . . ?' She cast the pile to one side and looked down. At her feet rested an elegant set of keys, slim and shiny as dropped pins. Baffled, she bent to pick them up. Where had they come from? Clearly from within her dirty washing, but neither she nor Ani had the need for a clutch of keys such as this.

It took her a moment to place them, and then like the proverbial lightning bolt she understood: these were Cale's keys, the keys she'd been sent to fetch from Elda. The memory drifted back to Syl woozily, a poor copy of reality. Yes, there had been keys, of course there had: Oriel had handed Syl a bunch of keys to return to Cale, and then she'd tried to open Syl's mind.

And Cale had asked her if she'd found them the next day, while Oriel still lay unconscious in the sickbay, but the entire altercation had had a strange fuzziness to it, soft-focus and liquid after the mind duelling, and Syl had not been able to recall any keys. The issue of the keys was just one of the many troubling factors about Elda's disappearance. From whispers she had overheard, Syl knew that Cale and many of the Sisters believed Elda to be hiding somewhere in the older sections of the Marque. It would not be the first time that a Novice – or, indeed, a more senior Sister – had retreated into its depths, for whatever reason: a fight with another Sister, perhaps, or bullying, or even madness. There was no shortage of hiding places in the old labyrinth. That was one of the reasons secure doors had been installed.

So Cale had decided Elda must have taken the keys with her when she went off – 'damned stupid girl' – and that had been the end of it. But now here they were, lying on the floor.

Syl snatched them up, her heart thumping with excitement and fear. She glanced around nervously to make sure nobody had witnessed what happened, her hand tight around the bunch as she slipped them into her pocket, then she leaned back against the wall, taking slow measured breaths to calm herself as she considered what she'd nearly done, the chance she'd nearly lost, for a wash cycle would surely have destroyed the electronic key codes embedded within each pin.

Time and again, Althea had drummed into her the importance of checking her pockets before washing her clothes, but since her governess had gone she'd fallen out of the habit. Now Syl sank weakly onto the nearest stool and bowed her head, running her fingers through her hair and licking the sweat from her lips. The keys might only open cupboards, but even drawers and cupboards could hold secrets, especially if they were locked.

And secrets were exactly what Syl was looking for.

'My God,' she said in English, just as the human staff at the castle in Edinburgh sometimes did, and she smiled to herself and thought now of Earth. She thought of her father, of his security adviser Meia, who had proved to be so much more to him than that, of Althea, and of Paul, always Paul, and everything that had gone wrong and everything she had sworn to do.

And she also remembered the humans fighting in the Resistance, and the earthly gods, the old gods that the Illyri defector Fremd had spoken of, the gods he claimed were part of the soil and the sky and all the natural world. Normally she would have laughed off such superstitions, but right now she felt she had to thank somebody – or some*thing* – for she had just been very lucky indeed. She shook her head in wonder, her heart still thumping as she bent to finish loading the laundry, running her hand carefully through all the other pockets first.

While her clothes sloshed around in the laundry room, Syl went to the dining hall. Ani was at a table in the far corner with the nasty little blue Novice Mila, but Syl wanted to be alone, to think, so she quietly filled a plate then sat by herself as inconspicuously as she could, eating a perfectly palatable stew made from some of the vegetables that were native to Illyr. The food in the Novice dining hall was typically Nairene: nutritious and healthy, but also bland because food was viewed primarily as fuel on the Marque – functional and necessary but nothing more, nothing less – so it tended to look worryingly like two-day-old roadkill. Most mealtimes Syl found herself fantasising about the most ridiculous things: chips drowning in salt and vinegar, battered sausages from the café off the Royal Mile, a crunchy red apple, HobNobs eaten with a sweet boy in a kitchen, a glass of milk from a cow, just a plain, earthly cow, the very notion of which would have sent the Novices around her into paroxysms of disgust. Again.

'Imagine!' one of them had squealed when Syl had requested milk for her tea when she'd first arrived. 'Just imagine drinking juices pumped from the teats of an alien!'

They'd gathered around asking what else Syl and Ani ate on Earth, wide-eyed and all too ready to be revolted as they learned of hamburgers, cheese, sushi, and even haggis. Ani threw the haggis in as a joke though the pair of them had never even tried the stuff, and it elicited just the reaction she hoped for. She elbowed Syl, amused.

'What does it taste like?'

'How can you even swallow it?'

'A burger is mashed cow? No!'

'Cheese is fermented cow juices?'

'Milk – gross!'

'What does milk smell like?'

Mila had appeared and stepped between Syl and Ani, leaning in close and sniffing Syl theatrically.

'Ooh, you smell weird,' she said. 'Maybe it's the milk.'

She was speaking Illyri and her pronunciation of the English 'milk' was completely wrong – she said 'mil-*ik*' – but that didn't deter the other girls, who gathered around, sniffing Syl and wrinkling their noses. Ani was squeezed out until she stood to one side with Mila, bemused as the sea of yellow robes made an island of her best friend.

'Oh, you do smell curious.'

'Come smell her. It's odd.'

'Is *that* what milk smells like then?'

Xaron had appeared at Ani's other side – startlingly like a stretched version of her stouter younger sister – and had smiled nastily at Syl over the throng of Novice heads, nodding approvingly.

'Yes. She's smelly all right,' said Mila loudly, glancing at her older sibling for blessing.

'Very smelly,' agreed Xaron.

'No she isn't,' protested Ani, 'and if she is, then I must be too.'

But the other blue-robed girls silently gathered as well, forming a barrier around Ani, shielding her from the slur. In this, Syl would stand alone.

Unfortunately, the epithet had stuck – Smelly Syl – and it was still occasionally whispered or giggled in her presence even though the faint Earth odours that seemed so strange to the others had long since faded away. This evening it didn't matter though, and she didn't even notice the lazy, unimaginative murmurs of 'Smelly' from the others at the table when she plopped herself down at the end, for Syl could feel the treasure that was in her pocket, the clutch of keys that had the potential to open a whole new world of exploration and discovery; feather-light yet weighted with all her hopes. Where would she begin? When? How?

She ate the rest of her food quickly, barely tasting it, then all but skipped to the laundry, hauling her clean clothes from the big machine and bundling the warm, sweet-smelling robes and sheets together messily.

She couldn't act rashly. She had to think about it, consider her options and make smart decisions. She would begin her search on another day, a better day, and then she'd see how far these keys could get her beyond the Twelfth and Thirteenth Realms.

Soon she would tackle the Sisterhood afresh.

CHAPTER 23

It was clear now that the raiders who had arrived through the wormhole were something more than Nomads. Paul and Thula took the time to search the dead in an effort to find any identifying marks or papers, but they came up entirely empty. Like soldiers everywhere, the Illyri had a fondness for adorning their skin, often with details of campaigns or unit names, but the bodies that had fallen aboard the *Envion* were as devoid of such markings as they had been on the day they were born.

'Here,' said Thula, pointing a finger at a series of tiny scars on the head of one of the dead Illyri. The Nomad was female, her scalp almost entirely shaved except for a tuft of hair at the crown arranged in a kind of ponytail. She had been strong and muscular. It hadn't saved her from a bullet, though.

'What is it?' asked Paul.

'Laser scarring, I believe. I would bet a lot of money that, until recently, this Illyri had a tattooed scalp.'

Paul examined the marks, and realised that he had passed over similar scars on some of the others.

'They were wiped clean, just in case any of them were caught or killed,' he said.

'Exactly.'

Thula reached into a pack at his feet and drew from it a hand scanner, which was used to diagnose internal injuries.

'What are you going to do with that?' asked Paul.

'Make another bet with you.'

'Which is?'

'That they've all had their Chips removed.'

Thula activated the scanner. He didn't need to scan all of the dead to win his bet: after three came up negative, Paul conceded. Chips both carried and transmitted essential data about their carriers. They were as individual as fingerprints; there would be little point in erasing all other identifying marks while leaving Chips in place.

'You want to hazard a guess as to who they were?'

'You first,' said Thula. 'You're the officer.'

'Forces of the Diplomatic Corps, not the Military. It's hard to get soldiers to turn on their own.'

'But we're not Illyri Military. We're Brigade troops – human cannon fodder.'

'Even so, the *Envion* was a Military vessel, with Military crew.'

'Okay, accepted,' said Thula. 'I'll see your Corps, though, and raise you Securitats.'

'Explain.'

'A feeling, and no more than that. But the Corps always uses Securitats for its dirty work. If it's torture, deception, murder, it will have Securitat prints on it somewhere.'

'Okay, then: Securitats, but not their A-team. We took them too easily.'

'They weren't expecting to have to deal with the Military, human or otherwise,' said Thula. 'They were just hunting a politician. You don't need hardened fighters to kill politicians. And they were working without Chips. After years of relying on their input, they were probably a little rusty.'

It made sense, but then most things Thula said made sense.

'Are you sure you wouldn't like to be the lieutenant around here?' asked Paul.

'It's above my pay grade. Also, I like to be in a position to blame someone else when things go to hell.'

'So you're just a grunt?'

'That's me.'

The *Envion* groaned again, but this time there was also a grinding sound from deep in its bowels as metal began to separate from metal. The ship was in its death throes.

'Well, grunt, get those unlocked pulse weapons stored away before we both end up floating home.'

Thula piled the crate of pulsers on to a transport platform, along with the other guns, grenades and ammunition gathered by Paul, and directed it towards the Nomad ship. Paul took one last look at the dead Illyri, all of them now stripped of their blast masks and a good deal of their clothing. If they were Securitats, there was no telling what kind of vengeance their superiors might try to visit on those responsible for their deaths, justified or not. Paul was now glad that he had listened to Councillor Tiray and had refrained from sending a distress message through the wormhole. He could only hope that the two Nomad ships had not managed to send back any messages of their own.

By the time Paul reached the Nomad vessel, Galton was seated beside Rizzo, both of them lost in their own thoughts. Rizzo had been fond of De Souza, and maybe more than that. Paul didn't know if they'd ever had a relationship, but he believed that Rizzo might have been a little in love with their dead lieutenant. As for Galton, now that the fighting was over and they were about to leave the *Envion*, he had time to think about Cady. His expression was unreadable as he stared down from the window at Torma, the world on which his lover now lay buried. Paul gently laid a hand on his shoulder, an attempt at comfort that Galton barely acknowledged. His cheeks were wet. Paul left him to his grief.

Meanwhile Peris and Tiray were locked in loud discussions with Steven about the Nomad ship's technology.

'Gentlemen,' said Paul, interrupting them, 'perhaps we could continue the debate after we've freed ourselves from the *Envion*.'

Steven glanced up at his brother as Peris and Tiray moved away without complaint. Paul's tone, although polite, had brooked no opposition. He was changing, inhabiting his new role as lieutenant. Back on Earth, fighting the Illyri, Paul had been groomed for leadership by the Resistance's commanders, and had accepted every responsibility that was given to him. But this was different. They were far from home, conscripts in an alien army and barely out of basic training, yet when they had been at their weakest – their comrades dead or dying, their ship crippled, a superior force preparing to attack – Paul had rallied them, forging them into a new fighting unit, and all those who would have killed them were dead. Steven was sorry that De Souza was gone, but he was also grateful that his injuries had led to Paul's promotion, for Steven did not believe that De Souza could have handled the situation as well as his brother.

His eyes moved past Paul to Alis, Tiray's aide. There was something familiar about her, something he could not quite place. She looked very young, but she was beautiful in a hard way, like a statue made of gold. He had tried apologising for touching her, but the apology had been almost as awkward and embarrassing as the original offence. As Steven stumbled over his words, Alis had simply watched him with her unblinking Illyri gaze, her head turned slightly to one side like a bird listening to a worm trying to talk its way out of being eaten.

The Nomad vessel shook as something ignited in the heart of the *Envion*. Fire bloomed briefly on one of the lower decks before the hull ruptured and the flames were smothered. The blast distracted Steven from Alis.

'Get us out of here,' ordered Paul.

'Yes, sir,' Steven answered instinctively, then realised that he was talking to his brother. 'I mean—'

Steven paused, and thought.

'Yes, sir,' he repeated, and in the reflection on the cockpit glass, he thought that he caught Paul smiling.

But just as he prepared to unlock the Nomad ship, it rang with an alarm sound. Paul turned to see that Galton, unnoticed by anyone else, had risen from his seat, and had opened the connector door.

'Galton!' cried Paul. 'What are you doing?'

'I'm sorry,' said Galton. 'I can't leave here.'

He stepped through the door and into the connector. Before Paul could react, the door had closed again, and seconds later he both felt and heard the shuttle detaching itself from the *Envion*.

'It's Galton,' said Steven. 'He's decoupled us from inside. Do you want me to try to dock us again?'

And in that moment, Paul made his most difficult decision yet.

'No,' he said. 'Let him go.'

Sometimes, he thought, grief was just too much for a person to bear.

He stepped to the one of the hull windows and saw Galton looking back at him from an observation bay. Paul raised his hand in farewell and thought that he saw Galton respond, before he turned away. The Nomad distanced itself from the *Envion*, the larger ship growing smaller and smaller through the windows, the great yellow mass of Torma lying behind it. Paul felt a terrible pang of sadness as he watched the final moments of the *Envion*, his last sight of Galton still fresh in his mind. He remembered the faces of those who had served upon the destroyer, losing their lives in doing so, and how the ship had held itself together for long enough to allow them to escape safely, as though it had wanted them to live. But he hoped, too, that the memory of the raiders' slaughter might die with the vessel.

A massive explosion ripped through the destroyer, instantly tearing it asunder. Its two halves separated and, as if in slow motion, the wreckage began to drop towards the surface of Torma, shedding debris as it went, the shards turning to bright stars in the planet's atmosphere, and among them was Galton, descending to join his lost love.

They watched the death of the *Envion* in silence. Only when it was gone from sight did Alis approach Paul and ask if she could take the co-pilot's seat. Paul gave his consent. It seemed like a good idea for Steven to have some help.

'Set a course?' asked Steven.

'Just take us away from that wormhole,' said Paul, 'while I try to get someone to tell me how we ended up in this mess.'

The *Nomad* – for, in the absence of a better name, that was what they chose to christen their new vessel – was a technological wonder. As Paul made his way to the rear, passing from the flight deck through a series of crew compartments and into engineering, he could hear Peris and Tiray marvelling at it while simultaneously trying to figure out where it had been constructed, and by whom. Four or five virtual screens overlapped in front of the two Illyri as they examined weapons systems, flight controls and engines. Paul watched them in silence for a time until finally he grew tired of hearing them compliment a vessel that had been partly responsible for reducing a destroyer to wreckage, and its crew to ash and floating bodies, and coughed loudly.

'Lieutenant,' said Peris, his eyes bright, 'it's astonishing. We are decades away from producing a craft like this.'

'By "we",' said Paul, 'I take it you mean the Military?'

Both Illyri grasped his implication immediately, for the same thought had already struck them.

'Absolutely,' said Peris. 'This must be the work of the Diplomatic Corps, but where did this technology come from? I mean, we have our own research divisions working on advanced propulsion and construction systems, but even if the rumours are true, we still haven't come close to developing a fusion engine of this sophistication. The *Nomad* is barely one-tenth the size of the *Envion* but its engine is at least three times more powerful. This thing is fast, resilient, and armed with weapons capable of taking down a Military destroyer. It shouldn't exist, but it does.'

'And it came hunting for Councillor Tiray,' said Paul.

Thula came back to join him. There were now two humans, and two Illyri. Paul stole a glance at Peris, still shoulder-to-shoulder with Tiray, both gazing around them in wonder. It remained to be seen where precisely Peris's loyalties might lie if he had to choose between the Illyri and the unit.

'We need answers,' Paul continued. 'Thula and I examined the bodies of the raiders on the *Envion*. All identifying marks had been surgically removed from their skin, and their Chips had been pulled from their skulls. That's not an easy piece of surgery, is it, Thula?'

Thula nodded. 'From what I've heard, true Nomads deactivate their Chips, but they don't go cutting into skulls to pull them from the cerebral cortex.'

'Right,' said Paul. 'Now, putting all these pieces together, what we have is some kind of secret Corps vessel disguised to look like a piece of Nomad junk, carrying trained raiders – we reckon Securitats, given the dirty nature of the work – who targeted an Illyri politician, and wanted him badly enough to be prepared to take on a Military destroyer and kill everyone on board.'

Tiray looked pained.

'Lieutenant,' he said, 'you are not alone in losing friends and colleagues. Do you know what lies on the other side of that wormhole? I'll tell you: the wreckage of a ship called the *Desilus*, with a crew of twenty, among them my own stepson. The *Desilus* was to have been my mission ship, but by the time I reached it everyone on board was dead, and the *Desilus* itself resembled the *Envion* in its final moments. It was only a miracle that brought me and Alis safely through the wormhole.'

Paul looked at him coldly, for it was the arrival of Tiray that had been the *Envion*'s undoing.

'You'll have to forgive us for not regarding your coming as a miracle,' said Paul. 'The last I heard, miracles involved raising the dead, not sending the living to join them. Your miraculous escape drew the raiders down on us instead, which brings us back to the main question: what makes you so important? What did they want from you?'

Tiray looked to Peris. Clearly he was uncomfortable with being interrogated by a human – resentful, even. Paul wondered how many humans Tiray had even encountered until now: a few Brigade troopers seen at a distance, perhaps, but no more than that. Tiray clearly expected Peris to intervene on his behalf. Now we come down to it, thought Paul. Now we will see.

'Councillor Tiray, please answer the lieutenant,' said Peris.

In happier circumstances, Paul might have cheered: Peris was a soldier, and soldiers stuck together, especially when confronted by politicians.

'This is a very delicate situation,' said Tiray. 'Many lives may be at stake, maybe even the future of the empire.'

He had been talking to Peris, but now he turned and directed his attention to Paul.

'I mean no offence, Lieutenant, but you are human, and I am Illyri. You fight in the Illyri Brigades, but we are not on the same side.'

Before Paul could reply, Peris intervened.

'I would suggest that, given recent events, we are now very much on the same side,' he said. 'As for the lieutenant, I suspect that he is aware of far more about the Illyri and our Conquest than he has chosen to reveal, even to me.'

He caught Paul's eye and, not for the first time, Paul understood just how clever and sharp the old Illyri fighter was. What had Peris learned back on Earth? How much did Peris know? After all, he had fought alongside Lord Andrus's head of security, the deadly, inscrutable Meia, and Meia appeared to know pretty much everything.

'And the other?' said Tiray now, gesturing at Thula.

'He's my sergeant,' said Paul. 'I trust him completely.'

'I'm your sergeant?' said Thula. 'Since when?'

'Since now.'

'And you trust me completely?'

'Almost.'

'I'm touched.'

Tiray watched their exchange with puzzlement. Clearly this wasn't how Illyri officers behaved with their noncoms. But Tiray now seemed resigned to answering Paul's question. In the end, he had little choice, not if he wanted Paul's help. Tiray could quote all of the Illyri regulations he liked, but he knew that, if they chose to do so, the humans could push him out of an airlock door – Peris too, if it came to that – and nobody would be any wiser. He didn't know Paul well enough to be able to trust him not to commit such an act.

Tiray reached into the folds of his robes and produced a small USB drive. The Illyri rarely used such primitive methods of storage. In fact, Paul hadn't seen one since he'd left Earth.

'This is what the hunters seek,' said Tiray. 'And they will not stop until they secure it.'

CHAPTER 24

Syl was anxious to finish her book, for she was still reading the gripping little wedge of a volume about the early Illyri explorations, and was close to the conclusion: just one more world to discover. Yet then, abruptly, the book stopped. Syl turned the page and that was it: from the cliffhanger final line of one chapter to absolutely nothing – just the inside of the back cover intricately decorated in the old style, and perhaps remarkable in its own right, but without further words. No end was given to the tale, despite the promises in the earlier chapters of this last world, unexplored, spinning like a small, fat opal in space, distant and unknowable. Yet it had water, it had a stable atmosphere: it was alive with possibilities, and the potential for life.

She peered closer and saw that somebody had actually defaced the book. No, 'defaced' was the wrong word: the final pages had been carefully sliced out right at the book's spine.

Annoyed, Syl threw the book across the room.

She must have dozed off, for her friend clattering through the door startled her awake.

'Syl! I did it! I did it!'

Ani was beaming, and she bent down and kissed Syl hard on the top of her sleepy head.

'I finally did it!'

'Did what?'

'Oh Syl, it was amazing! I wish you could have seen it.' Ani glanced back at the open door as if expecting someone to appear behind her. 'Anyway, I wanted to tell you. I wanted you to know.'

She gave a joyous little squeak and spun in a circle of sheer excitement.

'Oh Syl! I can't believe it.'

'You still haven't told me what happened, you idiot,' said Syl, smiling as she sat up.

Ani glanced at the door once more and took a deep breath. Her smile seemed likely to split her face as she spoke.

'I burned Thona! I made the plate hot!'

'Oh Ani — that's brilliant.'

Syl stood up and hugged her friend, which proved difficult because Ani was jigging about on the spot with the utter delight of her breakthrough.

'She shouted in fright. Everyone dropped what they were doing and turned around, and Thona looked at me in total silence for the longest time and I thought I was in trouble, but then she started laughing. And everyone began applauding — Tanit, all of the Gifted, and some of the other full Sisters. For me!'

Syl laughed, clapping her hands too.

'And it wasn't even a one-off, because Thona said I should try again, and I got it right. Again, Syl! I did it twice, and the second time it felt kind of natural.'

Syl opened her mouth to congratulate her friend, but before she could they heard voices approaching in the hall outside.

'Oh, it's them,' said Ani, looking fretful. 'Syl, Tanit and the other girls are coming over to celebrate. I'm sorry. They insisted: they said they always celebrate big achievements.'

She stopped, for Tanit had appeared in the doorway, tall and beautiful, glowing with health and privilege, but with a face carved from ice. The others clustered behind her, peering over her lean shoulders as she blocked their entry.

'Ah,' said Tanit. Her eyes travelled from Ani to Syl and her pretty lips curled. 'I thought I smelled something. Don't worry. We'll go.'

'No, please stay,' said Ani, and Syl watched the panic flit across her friend's face, the despair of loyalties being torn as she glanced from

Tanit to Syl then back to Tanit once more. Tanit managed to look a little disappointed, and turned as if to leave.

'Later, Ani.'

'Tanit . . . Don't go. I—'

Ani spun back to Syl, imploring, and with a tug in her chest Syl took the hint.

'I'll go to my room,' she said loudly.

'Thank you,' whispered Ani, looking stricken.

Tanit spun back again, smiling triumphantly.

'Wonderful,' she said, not even glancing at Syl now. 'And Ani, look what I've got! We brought cremos!'

With a girlish squeal she rushed over to Ani, brandishing a start-lingly large crystal decanter of the precious wine, draping her other arm around the younger Novice, who smiled back at her as if she'd been handed the stars from the sky. The others followed, screeching and giggling, and Ani was swamped, lost to view in a flood of blue.

Syl stalked into her bedroom and banged the door shut, but nobody seemed to notice.

Syl lay listless on her bed, studiously ignoring, or trying to ignore, what was clearly turning into quite the party on the other side of the door. It had begun with the others entreating Ani to try out her newfound skill on them, and clearly she'd been successful because there'd been cries of 'ouch' followed by cheers and applause. Syl grunted to herself, for surely Ani realised that they'd lowered their guards, and were merely allowing her to play with their minds.

Finally it had all descended into teasing, joking and gossip, and rather a lot of shouting over each other, and bawdy laughter, and sometimes the voices would disappear into whispers, punctuated by peals of merriment. Above the celebration, Syl regularly heard the voice of Tanit, ringing clear as a knife against glass, commanding and imperious, until finally Syl stuck her head under her pillow and screamed mutely into the mattress.

Eventually Syl took out Cale's keys and studied them carefully, yet again. She had already decided that they certainly weren't all cupboard keys, as she had briefly feared they might be. At least two of them were larger, similar to the ones Ani and Syl had been issued for their own quarters, but one had a thin red band around the tip. Syl had never seen a key like it before. She touched it lightly. One of the bigger keys might well be for Cale's private quarters, but this other one must be important too. The red band said as much, the violent red hue of the Sisterhood.

Still playing over the possibilities in her mind, Syl hid the bunch away and lit her candles, as it had grown dark and she loathed the stark overhead lighting of the Marque. Many of the girls used glowing crystals instead of candles, gifts from loving families on Illyr, and the stones cast soft rainbows of iridescence across the walls. Someone – one of the Gifted? Tanit? – had given such a rock to Ani, who placed it lovingly in their little lounge so that they could both enjoy its radiance. Syl rather wished she hadn't. Yes, it was attractive, but then so was Tanit, and Syl didn't want anything that called her to mind in their quarters if she could help it, although tonight was apparently out of her hands.

Anyway, candles reminded her of home, of Edinburgh, where her father had always lit tapers at formal dinners. She pictured him now, wondering if he ever thought about her, if something of the Illyri whom she loved still remained within him. She flipped on to her back and watched the pools of shadow that flickered on the ceiling. Soon. She would have to try the keys soon. Nervous butterflies fluttered in her gut. Maybe she couldn't change the world, but perhaps she could find out what Syrene had done to her father. All she needed was courage, and a plan.

After a while there was a knocking on her door, so gentle that at first Syl thought she'd misheard, but there it was again, polite yet insistent, rap–rap–rap.

'Hello?' she called softly.

The door opened a crack, letting the noise from the sitting room spill in at full power. Dessa's dark eyes peered through the gap.

'Syl?' she said.

'What?'

Syl tried to force every ounce of her displeasure into that single word, and Dessa bit her lip.

'May I come in?'

'Why?'

'I have this for you.'

Dessa opened the door a little wider and slipped inside, shutting it quietly behind her again. Syl stiffened, but in Dessa's hands were balanced two crystal goblets of garnet-coloured wine. She could smell its rich headiness from where she lay.

'Here. For you,' said Dessa, smiling uncertainly as she stepped nearer, placing the glass on Syl's bedside table.

'It's cremos,' she added unnecessarily, 'the very best cremos. But then Tanit always has the best.'

Syl stared up at her, then slowly twisted herself into a seated position, turning so that her back was against the wall, her long legs stretched across the width of her bed, making sure her eyes never left Dessa. Dessa returned her gaze, unwavering.

'Why would you give me anything, especially cremos?' said Syl.

Dessa glanced out of Syl's tiny window and sighed rather tragically, making it clear she felt misjudged.

'Because I thought you'd be feeling left out,' she said. 'And I thought you might want a friend.'

'Don't be ridiculous. You all hate me.'

'No, we don't,' Dessa protested. 'I don't hate you. I don't even know you, and you don't know me either. It would be foolish to hate each other.'

'Well, I have enough friends already,' said Syl, but her words sounded farcical even to her own ears. Dessa smiled graciously.

'Oh Syl,' she said, and plonked herself down on the bed as if it was already decided: they would be friends. Syl wriggled away uncomfortably, but Dessa didn't seem to notice. 'I've really wanted to talk to you. Sometimes you look so sad and lost, and I'm sure you've noticed that nowadays Ani spends more time with us than she does with you.'

Syl puffed air into her cheeks crossly. That was a bit close to home.

'Not that she intends to, of course,' said Dessa, leaping in anxiously to undo any offence she may have caused, 'but it's in the nature of her daily routine. The Blue Novices spend so much time together in extra tuition. It's the pattern of Ani's life now. She's one of us. You must miss her terribly though.'

Syl didn't answer. The room went quiet, and they sat in silence listening to the party beyond the doors. Dessa sipped her cremos. Syl ignored her, staring at the wall. After some time, Dessa picked up the extra glass and held it out to Syl. The candlelight caught it, and a starburst of rubies cascaded across the ceiling.

'Won't they miss you?' said Syl, ignoring the offering.

Dessa shrugged ruefully. 'I doubt it. They have Ani now, and she can do what I can do. Clouding isn't that special, you know, and I've never really mattered much to them anyway. It's what you can do for them that matters.'

Now Syl turned and looked at the girl curiously, taking in her hair, which was the colour of liquid lead, and her eyes as dark and purple as the cremos she held. Dessa looked back and smiled sadly.

'So why did you stop them that day, with Elda?' said Syl. 'It was you. Please don't deny it.'

There was a long pause before Dessa replied.

'Here,' she said finally, pushing the extra glass into Syl's hands. 'You'll have to hold this for a moment – I need to show you something. Maybe then you'll understand.'

Syl watched as Dessa pulled up the sleeve of her robe, revealing a wide cream bangle on her wrist. She took it off, holding it up in the candlelight, and Syl gasped, for carved on the ivory cuff was a row of elephants each holding in its trunk the tail of the one before it.

'From Earth?' she said, touching it reverentially, despite herself. Syrene had taken all her personal belongings before they'd arrived at the Marque. The only earthly items permitted to Syl and Ani were the ones the Red Witch herself had given to them: soap and sheets, which were hardly representative of the planet at its rawest and most real.

'Of course.'

'But how? Were you there?'

'No,' said Dessa. 'I wish. But when I was younger and still at school on Illyr there was a girl in my class called Galai. I know – it's an ugly name, but poor Galai was not exactly pretty to look at either.'

She watched Syl, waiting.

'A rose by any other name would smell as sweet,' said Syl lamely, for want of any other response.

'Pardon?' said Dessa.

Syl shook her head: 'Only Shakespeare. Never mind. You were saying?'

'Yes, dear Galai: I'd known her since we were children because our parents were friends, and I thought her to be a bit of a dullard, but she was also a good and loyal creature, although no one else knew that. They never even took the time to find out. Anyway, this bracelet was hers. Her uncle served on Earth and brought it back for her. She was so terribly proud of it—'

She stopped, her eyes faraway, her bottom lip trembling.

Syl coughed, embarrassed, and Dessa took this as a prompt to continue.

'Galai is dead, Syl. She killed herself. Some of the others in our class bullied her so badly that she took her own life. And I didn't stop them from upsetting her, from hurting her. I was scared they wouldn't like me, so I didn't even try.'

There were tears in those deep purple eyes now, and Syl looked away.

'I'm sorry,' she said, and she meant it.

'Me too,' said Dessa, slipping the bracelet back on to her wrist and twirling it fondly. 'Her mother gave me this after the funeral. She said I was Galai's only friend and that she would have wanted me to have it. But the thing is, I wasn't a friend to Galai at all. I looked away, but I have sworn that I will never look away again.'

Her voice ended in a squeak and she shook her head angrily, then took a gulp of her drink as if to oil her vocal cords.

'I see,' said Syl. She didn't know what else to say so she took a sip from her own glass, the liquid slipping like sweet velvet down her throat as Dessa picked up the threads of the story.

'Anyway I wear this all the time now, to remind me of Galai, and of my promise. And that's why I helped Elda, that's—'

With a crash, the door flew open and Tanit stood before them.

'Dessa!' she cried. 'What are you doing here? And why are you talking to *her*?'

The pair on the bed stared back at her, speechless with surprise. Then Tanit saw what Syl held in her hand.

'And why have you given her *my* cremos?' she shouted.

She reared towards Syl and snatched the goblet from her startled hands, snapping the stem off as she did so and splashing the contents across the white bedding and Syl's arm, like bright splashes of blood.

'Come back to the party, Dessa,' Tanit ordered. 'Immediately.'

She waved the broken glass at Dessa, who obediently got up and trotted from the room, guilty as a dog caught stealing from its master's plate. But before the door banged shut behind her she gave Syl a funny little grin over her shoulder, and Syl was left staring after them, confused, her sticky fingers still wrapped around the stem of the broken glass.

CHAPTER 25

The USB drive Tiray had been protecting could have been inserted into one of the *Nomad*'s ports in order to access its information, but he was reluctant to allow this. If he used its computer system then any information on the drive would automatically be stored there, and that meant others could access it, either directly or remotely. Instead, Tiray summoned Alis, who produced a portable display unit from her pack, and Tiray used that to open the contents of the drive.

What appeared before them looked at first like an image of tubular microorganisms – *E.coli*, perhaps, the kind of nasty little creatures that could make a person very sick indeed. It was only as figures and coordinates appeared alongside them, and the image began to rotate, that Paul saw them for what they were.

'Wormholes,' he said.

Paul was aware that the Illyri had discovered a lot of wormholes, and more were being mapped all the time, but he had no idea just how many had already been recorded. Now thousands upon thousands of them were being revealed to him, some so close to each other, at least in terms of the vastness of the universe, that they were almost overlapping. With this level of information to hand, it would take only moments for a ship's navigation system to calculate the swiftest way to get from one galaxy or solar system to another – however remote – using a combination of wormholes. In Earth terms, it would be like travelling from Edinburgh to London via Shanghai and Alaska, and arriving before someone in a car had even managed to reverse from his driveway.

'But isn't this common knowledge?' asked Peris.

'Some of it,' said Tiray, 'although even I was not aware of just how widespread the network was. But one wormhole in particular was a revelation.'

He waved his hand and a star system in the upper right hand corner of the map was illuminated.

'This is the Archaeon system.'

'I've never heard of it,' said Peris, 'and I've been studying the Conquest for most of my life.'

'That's because Archaeon doesn't appear in the general record, or on any of the existing wormhole charts.'

'On whose orders?'

'The Geographic Division of the Diplomatic Corps is responsible for all maps and charts,' said Tiray. 'I suspect, though, that few of them even know of Archaeon. This is the most advanced map we could access, but if I were to delete all but the oldest of wormholes, and the charted systems accessed through them . . .'

Another wave of his hands, his fingers manipulating images, and then:

Nearly all of the wormholes vanished, leaving only twelve displayed. By a circuitous route, they connected the Illyri galaxy to Archaeon.

'These are the first wormholes,' said Tiray, 'revealed by the Sisterhood to Meus, the Unifier of Worlds, only days before his death, their location believed lost in the Civil War that followed.'

The death of Meus had led to the Civil War, a century-long clash between the Military and the Diplomats, the scars of which had never fully healed. The circumstances of Meus's death remained unclear. The official version held that Meus died in an accidental fire at his home, but some said he was dead – murdered – before the blaze even started. And Meus had been no friend of the Diplomatic Corps: he came from a Military family, and under his rule the power of the Diplomats had been severely curbed.

'But it seems they were not lost after all,' said Peris.

'No,' said Tiray. 'They were hidden.'

'Where did you get this map?' asked Paul.

'I can't tell you that,' said Tiray. 'Suffice to say, there are those even among the Diplomatic Corps who believe that a darkness lies at the heart of the Illyri Empire, and it must be rooted out. The source of that darkness may lie in the Archaeon system, or why else would its existence have been hidden for so long?'

Paul waved his own right hand, restoring the multiplicity of wormholes to the map. He stepped forward so that he was standing in the midst of them. Bladelike Illyri numbers and letters floated over his head, and planets orbited around suns before his eyes. Instinctively he reached up to his throat and touched the silver cross that hung there. Perhaps this what it was like to be God, he thought, a roving consciousness moving through the universe, before whose eyes suns were no bigger than tiny gemstones, and entire systems resembled merely a sprinkling of dust.

'How did the Sisterhood discover all these wormholes?' he asked.

'They have not said,' replied Tiray, 'and they will not say. They claim only that it comes from many years of intense study.'

'But the study of *what*?'

Paul looked at Tiray, but Tiray just shrugged.

'You are not the first to have asked. But Archaeon may hold a clue.'

Paul returned to his study of the star map. He read the names of the systems to himself: Faledon, Tamia, Graxis . . .

'What's this?' he said.

A blackness at the end of one of the wormholes had attracted his attention. The Illyri had begun the mammoth task of mapping each system revealed to them by a wormhole, all except this one. It was marked only by a single word: *Derith*, the Illyri for 'Unknown'.

'The Geographic Division has not been able to map it,' said Tiray. 'Drones go in, but they don't return.'

'Have you any idea why?'

'Who knows?' said Tiray. 'There may be an asteroid field at the mouth of the wormhole, or a collapsing star. We've only mapped the tiniest fraction of the universe, but we've discovered that it is both emptier and more dangerous than we could ever have imagined.

We're finding anomalies that we can't even explain, let alone name.'

Tiray pointed a long finger at Paul's throat, where he was still gently touching his cross with the fingertips of his right hand.

'I see you wear a symbol of faith.'

'I do.'

'Well, if something – a god, for want of a better term – created the universe, then he neglected to finish it. He left empty worlds, both uninhabited and uninhabitable, and he booby-trapped space to kill the unwary.'

'Or the curious,' said Paul.

He spoke without thinking, his gaze fixed on that final wormhole. *Derith*. Unknown.

Tiray spoke again, pulling him back from his thoughts.

'Lieutenant,' he said, 'I want you to take me to Archaeon. I want to see what lies there.'

Derith. The word echoed deep within Paul. He did not know why, but that empty space on the star chart seemed almost to be calling to him. It was only with great difficulty that he turned his gaze back towards Archaeon. What was it that Tiray had said, something about a darkness at the heart of the Illyri Empire? Yes, that much was certainly true, but perhaps it wasn't so much at the heart, but instead within its very consciousness, for part of it took the form of an alien organism curled around a brain stem. He knew this much from his final days on Earth. Paul turned slowly until he found Illyr, and he reached out to trace his finger through the image of the planet, the source of his enemy, the source of his love.

His Syl.

God, thought Paul, *how had things become quite this complicated?*

Peris was watching him, waiting for Paul to make his decision. If the Sisterhood had found the Archaeon system, and they and their allies in the Diplomatic Corps had conspired to keep it hidden, then it was worth investigating. The other option was simply to head for the nearest Illyri base in order to deliver Tiray and his strange aide back to their people. But if Tiray was right, they'd have to fight their way there, because waiting on the other side of the nearest wormhole might be more hunters concealed as Nomads. So they couldn't go back, but neither could they stay where they were. Eventually somebody was going to come looking to find out what had happened to the two Nomad ships, just as at some point the Military would start to wonder why there had been no communication drones sent by the *Envion*, except Paul was willing to bet good money that whoever had sent those Nomads would be first through the wormhole.

Paul turned to Thula.

'Copy this map and share it with the Steven,' he said. 'Tell him to chart a course for the Archaeon system.'

CHAPTER 26

As soon as Paul had made his decision, he felt a wave of exhaustion crash and break upon him. He could see it in the others too: they had hardly stopped fighting for their lives since the landing on Torma, and those who were still on their feet could barely keep their eyes open. Rizzo was already fast asleep in a chair, and even the strange gecko-like eyes of the Illyri betrayed their tiredness, the nictitating membranes visible as sleep momentarily overcame them.

Thula took a seat next to Rizzo, closed his eyes, and zoned out, but Paul fought the urge to join them. Instead he went over to his brother at the ship's controls. Steven and Alis appeared to have overcome some of the initial awkwardness caused by the boy's original body search, and were now conducting a full check of the *Nomad*'s capabilities. Steven's face was alight with the joy of discovery, and Alis's fascination with the craft seemed almost to match his own. Out of all of them, only these two did not appear to be weary.

'How are you doing?' asked Paul.

'This ship is incredible, just incredible,' said Steven.

'Yes, so I've been hearing. My question is, how long can you keep going before you need to rest?'

'*Rest?*' said Steven, as though Paul had just suggested that they trade in the *Nomad* for a used Toyota with one careful owner. 'Look, I was thrilled when they gave me my own shuttle to fly – '

Yes, thought Paul, and look what happened there.

' – but this baby is something else entirely. You'll have to wrest control of it from my cold, dead hands.'

'Well, let's hope it doesn't come to that,' said Paul drily. 'How long to the first wormhole?'

'If I increase velocity, a matter of twenty hours. After that, there are two more virtually on our doorstep. Are you still worried about a pursuit?'

'They're coming,' said Paul, 'and they'll be riding in at least one of these.'

'May I make a suggestion?' said Alis, speaking for the first time.

Paul cocked an eyebrow. 'Go ahead.'

'The initial course we plotted for Archaeon was the most direct, but if we took a slightly more circuitous route we might be able to shake off any pursuers.'

Paul considered for a moment, then shook his head.

'We have to assume that they know you're aware of Archaeon's existence, otherwise why would they have targeted you and Councillor Tiray to begin with? If we take too long to get to Archaeon, then we may give them a chance to beat us there, and we could exit the final wormhole just in time to be blown to pieces. No, we have a head start, and we need to hold on to it. Just put your foot down, or whatever it is you do with these things, and get us there fast.'

Alis didn't argue. That was good. Paul wasn't in the mood for arguing, especially not with this little Illyri.

'What about you?' he asked her. 'Are you feeling okay?'

'I'm fine,' said Alis.

'Well, since you're the only ones on board properly equipped to fly this thing, I need at least one of you fresh and alert at all times. Steven, in thirty minutes I want you to sleep, whether you think you need to or not. Take four hours, then Alis, you do the same. Understand?'

'Yes, sir,' said Steven. Paul thought that he sounded like a sulky schoolboy whose dad had told him to go to bed just as the movie he was watching was getting good. In another life, of course, that's just what Steven would have been: a teenage boy in school, studying for exams, eating meals at the kitchen table with his brother and his mum, and thinking about girls, money, gaming and his future, but the arrival of the Illyri had changed all that. Instead, although not yet even sixteen, he was fighting and killing light years from home. What concerned Paul was that Steven seemed to be showing no signs of trauma or regret about what he had been forced to do. Oh, he still missed their mother, Paul knew that. He had heard Steven crying often enough in those first months, and a deep sadness still overcame him whenever her name was mentioned, but he was hardening. According to Peris, he had exhibited barely a flicker of emotion as the trap was sprung on the raiders, and he had fired on them without mercy. It struck Paul that his brother might be turning into a better killer than he was.

He left Steven and Alis to their work, passed by Thula and Rizzo quietly, and saw that Tiray was stretched out across two chairs, his eyes slightly clouded as he slept. Once upon a time, those eyes would not have failed to give Paul the creeps, but Syl had changed all that. Syl was lovely to him, and something of his appreciation of her alien beauty had transferred itself to the rest of her kind. He could not hate them quite as much as he once did.

Still, he could try.

Peris was waiting for him back in the meeting room.

'You need to sleep soon,' he told Paul. 'You have to be sharp. They're relying on their lieutenant.'

'What about you?'

'I will sleep too, once we've finished talking.'

Paul was tempted to lean against the hull, or even take a seat, but he was afraid that, if he did so, he would not be able to stay awake. He chose to remain standing.

'What is it you know?' he asked Peris.

'I might ask you the same thing.'

'Seriously, Captain,' said Paul, for that had been Peris's rank when he left Earth, 'why did you really leave the governor's service for the Brigades? Why did you choose to stay close to my brother and me?'

In all of their months together, through induction, training, and now on this, their first mission, Paul had never yet found the correct moment, or the courage, to ask Peris this question.

'Because Meia asked me to protect you. Because she told me that the fate of the Illyri might well be linked to yours, and my first loyalty is to my own kind, even above Governor Andrus himself.'

'Is that all she said?'

'Yes.'

'And you believed her?'

'Yes.'

'Why?'

'I trusted her, and . . .'

For the first time, Peris looked away.

'And?'

'After I made my decision, I must confess that I had doubts. I regretted it. It would have been easier to stay in Edinburgh. I was concerned for Governor Andrus, because he was surrounded by enemies. I almost considered going to him and asking him to take me back. I even went so far as to visit him in his quarters but—'

He paused. Paul had never seen such puzzlement, such hurt, on Peris's face before. The old soldier always appeared so sure, so confident in himself. But not now, not as he spoke of the Illyri governor who he had served loyally for so long.

'The governor was no longer the same,' Peris continued, finally. 'He had changed. I cannot explain how I knew, or even the nature of his transformation – except that he seemed ridiculously content for one who was about to lose his daughter to his enemy. He was not the Lord Andrus to whom I had sworn loyalty, and he was not alone in his chambers. The Nairene witch Syrene stood at his right hand, and it seemed that something of what burned darkly in her now burned also in him. That's the only way I can describe it. And so I left, and I did not look back.'

It was Paul's turn to speak. He chose his words carefully. He believed Peris, but he did not want to put at risk any of those members of the Resistance who knew what had happened in the depths of Dundearg Castle, so he did not name names. He simply told Peris some of the truth: that certain members of the Diplomatic Corps appeared to be carrying an alien organism in their skulls, a parasite of unknown origin, and it seemed that they were doing so willingly; that Meia had found evidence of experiments being conducted on humans by the Diplomats' sinister Scientific Development Division, including the implantation of similar organisms not just into humans but also into other animal species, but those implantations appeared to have failed. Finally, he said that Meia had seen the bodies of human beings split open like grow-bags of fertiliser, and anemone-like tendrils sprouting from their insides.

Paul stopped talking but Peris remained silent, taking in all that he had learned. He seemed shocked at the revelations of his own race's capacity for cruelty.

'Do you think Tiray knows?' Paul asked.

'Tiray is a politician,' Peris replied. 'They live for secrets, even more than most Illyri. My guess is that he does not, at least not for sure, or else he would not have risked a mission to Archaeon. But Paul – '

Paul was startled by Peris's use of his first name. Until now, Peris had only ever referred to him by his rank or his surname.

' – what you know places you at great risk. Is Steven also aware of this?'

Paul nodded.

'Be careful around Tiray,' Peris warned. 'I have no personal experience of dealing with him, but Lord Andrus always respected him. Nevertheless, Tiray has his own reasons for pursuing his investigation, and who knows where all this may lead? Tiray might not be happy to know that a human is privy to the dirtiest secrets of the Corps and, by extension, the Illyri. Murders have been committed for less.'

'And what about you?' said Paul. 'You said yourself that your first loyalty is to the Illyri. Would you kill to keep such secrets?'

'No,' said Peris. 'But I would kill to reveal them.'

'So we'll have to trust each other.'

'Yes,' said Peris. 'You will trust me not to betray you because of what you know, and I will trust you not to use on me any of those pulse weapons that you have hidden in the cargo hold.'

Now it was Paul's turn to be taken aback. But Peris said nothing more. He simply lay down on a couch, turned his face to the hull, and went to sleep.

CHAPTER 27

Ani's Gifted cohort seemed to be around rather too much after that first evening, gadding about in the lounge while Syl took refuge in her room. Dessa made it her business to smile warmly at Syl as they crowded in and she slid away. On their third visit, after Syl slunk from her room to visit the toilet, Dessa was waiting for her outside the door.

'Hi Syl,' she said, almost shyly, when the younger girl emerged.

'Hey,' said Syl.

'How are you?'

Syl looked pointedly at the visitors. 'Just fabulous, thanks. Positively peachy.'

'Sorry we keep invading your space,' said Dessa. Her purple eyes were wide and mournful.

'Why are you all here again?' said Syl.

'Well, it's a bit of a tradition we have really. Every time one of the Blue Novices has a major breakthrough, we celebrate with them at their quarters.'

'Are you telling me Ani has had three major breakthroughs?'

Syl had not known, and was surprised and hurt that Ani had not shared the news with her.

'Well, she's just had the two really. The second one was today: she clouded two minds at once. She made two tutors think plates were hot at exactly the same time. Not many clouders get that right so soon.'

Syl smiled to herself, for this was hardly a breakthrough as far as she was concerned. In what now seemed like another life, when she and Ani had rescued the human boys from the cells at Edinburgh Castle, Ani had convinced two guards that Syl was none other than Vena – Vena the Skunk, the vicious, silver-streaked Securitat whom they hated most of all. In retrospect it had been the high point of several rather horrible days.

Dessa smiled back at her, clearly believing they had made a connection.

'It's awesome, isn't it?'

'Yes. But you've been here three times, not two,' said Syl.

'Well, last time was Mila.' She had the grace to look embarrassed. 'I know, I know: Mila and Xaron have nice big rooms too, just like yours – we really should have gone there. But the thing is, Mila's governess came with her when she joined the Sisterhood. A bit like yours did. Only yours has gone, so lucky you! Freedom! And extra room.'

'Yes. Lucky me.'

'And frankly, Mila's nanny is a pain in the backside.'

'I see. Well, enjoy yourselves.'

Dessa followed Syl back to her room.

'I'm a bit fed up actually. Fancy some company?' she said.

'I'm busy.'

'Maybe next time?'

Syl felt a little guilty as she looked into Dessa's earnest, hurt face, and she recalled her vow to Ani, her promise that she'd try to be friendlier. Anyway, Dessa didn't seem that bad.

'Maybe next time. See you, Dessa. Thanks,' she said.

Dessa's smile blazed like a flashbulb as Syl shut the bedroom door.

Time dragged on that evening, and Syl grew bored locked away in her dull little room. She couldn't settle. Briefly she thought of heading out to explore, but doing so after lectures seemed foolish, for all the teachers would be back in the Fourteenth Realm, and it was to it that she hoped to gain access. No, going during class would be preferable.

Still, pins and needles prickled up her legs, and the precious sanctity of her room started to close in on her like a prison cell, its tight little window letting in the promise of a million other realities, but none that she could reach, and none that could possibly be as claustrophobic as this life she was now forced to lead in the cloistered domain of the Nairene Sisterhood. She needed to stretch her legs, to run, to escape. To be free.

And still the celebrations in the room next door continued. Would Tanit and her acolytes ever go away?

Syl got up and stretched, pacing her quarters, imagining striding across the Highlands again, scrabbling up the steep hillsides in wind and rain, leaping squealing into an ice-cold loch then warming herself by a smoking fire afterwards; cooking bits of fish on a stick as her back stayed cold and her wet hair dripped down her spine, while her front was toasty-warm, her cheeks pink from the heat.

Here, in this wretched warren, there was no change of climate, no sudden weather madness: all was faultlessly temperature-controlled by hidden monitors that made minute adjustments throughout the day and night. When you went to bed, sensors read your body temperature and adjusted the conditions in the room accordingly for maximum comfort, adding humidity, taking it away, cooling, warming. The common areas had just one setting: pleasant. All was a bubble of pleasantness: perfect weather without the inconvenience of having to take a coat. Even the showers selected the water temperature automatically. The sensors decided what was best, what would make a young Illyri's body most comfortable, yet they knew nothing of a young Illyri's spirit.

When they had first arrived, Syl had longed to feel the elements on her face again, and as the months crept by she found her yearning only grew stronger for the burning cold wind she'd so loathed in Edinburgh as it whipped around the castle in winter, cracking her lips and splitting her fingers open like swollen fruit. She thought often of the gentle sunshine of April, of the November rain on her upturned face, of snowflakes sliding down her collar and catching in her hair in January. She'd do anything to feel that brittle lake biting into her skin again as she splashed Paul, his skin slipping wet beside hers, to feel once again the goosebumps of pain and pleasure.

That was when Syl had a minor revelation. It was night-time now, and that meant the gymnasium would be empty too. During exercise classes they occasionally swam in the beautiful kidney of a pool set under a fortified crystal dome, but during the day the water that engulfed them was always tepid, its soothing droplets enveloping the bathers as gently as a womb. Syl had grown to loathe it.

Yet by night, when the gym was closed, all power would be cut, just as it was to the lecture halls, because energy was a precious commodity on the barren moon that was Avila Minor. Surely that would mean the swimming bath's cosy, cloying waters would be losing heat right now? And she'd have the place to herself. She could swim naked, and dry herself with the towel in her locker before coming back, and no one would ever know. Maybe, as a bonus, Tanit and the others would have gone by the time she returned.

She dug in her drawer for her locker key and a small glowstick – for the gymnasium would be dark, and the locker room more so – and with these tucked in her pocket, safe and invisible, Syl took a deep breath and strode out.

Nobody even acknowledged the stony-faced Syl as she sailed past, her nose in the air. Tanit, Sarea and Nemein had draped themselves across cushions on the floor, gossiping with Ani, ignoring the interloper. At least Ani had her back turned so there wasn't the mortification of being snubbed by her best friend or, worse, pitied. Syl would rather have had another showdown with Tanit than see that stricken, apologetic expression on Ani's face ever again. Meanwhile, on the far side of the room, Dessa was engaged in lively discussion with the sisters Xaron and Mila. She was leaning against the doorway of the kitchenette, and she didn't notice Syl.

Only Iria saw her leave, her features cool and unreadable. Iria had never hassled Syl, but then she'd never helped her either, for Iria just watched and waited, her eyes shrewd. Ani said Iria was clairvoyant, but had gone into a sulk and refused to elaborate further when Syl had wondered – okay, scoffed – why, then, did Iria always ask what was for dinner while standing in the canteen queue, and then complain about it every time?

★ ★ ★

True to Syl's expectations, the night-time gymnasium was cooler than
the hallways outside, low underwater lighting casting a blue glow
around the deserted cavern. The pool was dark and still as Syl slipped
her hand into the water to test it, and it, too, was colder than usual,
although still some way off the freezing waters of the freshwater lake
of her memories. Still, it felt rather heavenly to have this entire place
to herself, and she quickly slipped her robe over her head, dumping it
on the ground, then slid into the water. Goose pimples tingled briefly
across her body and she smiled, delighted by the sensations, enjoying
the surprise of cool water between her thighs, against her belly, under
her armpits. She took a deep breath and plunged to the bottom, sitting
on the floor of the pool, staring up through the rippling water at the
distorted sky. Everything was utterly silent, which was a rarity for the
Marque, for the libraries and corridors still echoed with padded
footfalls and hushed voices even in the darkest hours of the night.

Why, wondered Syl, had she not thought to do this before?

Afterwards, she scuttled dripping to the changing rooms. She was
shivering and had forgotten to fetch her towel – now she remembered
that being chilly wasn't very nice at all.

It was dark beside the lockers. Water pooled around her feet as she
fumbled with the lock, flinging the door open to be met with a funk
of dampness and unwashed garments. She grabbed her musty towel,
but as she did, something unfamiliar slid off it, settling atop the junk at
the bottom of her locker. It looked like a small parcel of some sort.
Syl bent to retrieve it, turning it over carefully in her fingers. It was an
envelope, lightweight, but there was something hard pressing against
the parchment, and her name was written in neat, curling script
on the front.

Curious, she sat on a bench and opened the packet, removing a
folded letter from inside, but the words on the notepaper were even
more vague than those on the envelope, as if written in a whisper.
Baffled, Syl activated the glowstick, bathing the message in warm, soft
light.

Dear Syl Hellais, it read, old-fashioned in its formality.

Soon I shall be leaving here, and I thank you for your kindness to me. I know your consideration did not make you any friends, but it meant much to one such as myself.

At the risk of stretching the boundaries of our acquaintance, may I request of you one final kindness?

I entreat you to safeguard the enclosed amulet and, as soon as you are able, to deliver it to my mother. Her image is engraved on the piece. Her name is Berlot Mallori, and she resides in Lower Tannis. I beg of you not to entrust the amulet to another. My mother values it highly.

I am most grateful.

I wish you a long life, Syl Hellais.

Sincerely yours,

Elda Mallori

Elda's disappearance remained unexplained. But any questions about her possible whereabouts were discouraged by Oriel and the other full Sisters. Some Novices whispered that she had been quietly returned to her family on Illyr because of her unsuitability for the Sisterhood. Now, if the contents of the letter were to be believed, it seemed that Elda had indeed somehow managed to leave the Marque, but clearly not to return to her family on Illyr. Syl reread the note, perplexed, then shook the contents of the package into her palm. A very ordinary locket fell out, lacklustre and brown, fastened on to a thong of thin, hard leather.

What a strange, ugly piece of jewellery it was, though, flat and cold and completely lacking in ornamentation or notable craftsmanship. Laser-carved on the dull metal surface was an engraving of a woman, presumably Elda's mother, sharp-faced and angry-eyed. The engraving was nothing special, nothing that any half-baked jeweller couldn't have made using an existing image and dated computer technology. Frowning, Syl slipped her fingernail into the slit that opened the locket, sure that its true worth would be revealed inside, but it opened easily like a clam on a hinge, and gave her nothing except smooth, brown metal. There wasn't as much as a memento, a lock of hair, an image, or even a love carving. Syl shut it again and turned the piece over in her hand. There were several scratchings on the back. She held the glowstick closer.

'A–R–C–H . . . arch what? Archaeon? Well, that means absolutely nothing,' she muttered to herself.

But nor did any of this. Yet there had to be some reason why Elda wanted to get this cheap, unattractive trinket back to her mother so desperately. She was such a weird girl.

None the wiser, Syl popped Elda's note and the amulet back into the envelope, dressed, towel-dried her hair, slid the slim parcel into her pocket and headed back to her rooms.

Tanit and her crew appeared to have left at last and only Ani remained, humming cheerfully to herself as she tidied up the glasses and threw the cushions back on the couch. She smiled pleasantly as her friend came in.

'Thank you so much, Syl. I can't tell you how much I appreciate you letting Tanit and the others visit. I know they appreciate it too.'

'Really?' Syl laughed, and dumped her damp towel on the table, waving a hand dismissively. 'No worries, Ani – it's nothing. But something much more curious has come up.'

Ani looked at her guardedly, then raised a finger to her lips. Syl frowned and Ani gestured towards the bathroom. Immediately Syl understood.

'So what has come up, Syl?' said Ani brightly, her voice singsong and false, all the while looking at the closed door.

'Oh, um, nothing actually.'

There was a rustling from within the bathroom, then the lock turned quickly and Tanit appeared. She studied the pair of them for several long seconds, taking in Syl's water-marked robe and dripping tangle of hair, and clucked her tongue.

'My darling Ani, you sweet creature,' she said, though it was Syl at whom she stared, gauging the impact of her words. 'I believe your continuing loyalty to your friend demonstrates your own goodness, but enough is enough. She is not like us, and I fear she is going to be your downfall. You are destined to progress higher in the ranks of the Sisterhood than she can ever hope to, and you will be forced to leave her behind sooner or later. Better to do it now than to drag it out. Think of it as doing her a favour. '

'Oh, drop dead, Tanit,' said Syl before she could stop herself, yet immediately she regretted it, for something like triumph briefly flowered in the older girl's face. Then she merely smiled sympathetically at Ani and, with a farewell twiddle of her graceful fingers, she took her leave. Ani looked after her mournfully before turning to Syl, clearly irritated.

'Drop dead? Really? You told the most important Novice in this place to drop dead? You're just making things worse.' She shook her head in disappointment and frustration. 'Anyway, what was it you wanted to tell me? And where've you been – and why are you all wet?'

Syl stared at Ani for a few moments, contemplating her options while Elda's amulet burned hot in her pocket.

'It's nothing that matters,' she said finally. 'I'm wrecking your life anyway, remember?'

'Oh Syl, I'm sorry, she shouldn't have said that,' said Ani. 'Seriously. I'm sorry. Tell me what you were going to say. Please.'

'It's nothing.'

'It can't be nothing.'

Syl thought about the cheap piece of jewellery and what it told her, or hadn't told her. Archaeon: it sounded like a promise.

'Well, I just went swimming, that's all,' she said, irritated. 'It reminded me of Scotland. It reminded me of that time we went swimming in the loch. With our friends. Do you remember our friends at all? Anyway, I don't care. I'm tired. I'm going to bed. Sleep well, Ani.'

She left, closing her door firmly before putting the envelope containing Elda's locket and letter at the bottom of her drawer, rearranging the mess so that it was hidden from the casual snooper. The last thing she needed was another link yoking her to Elda to become general knowledge.

★ ★ ★

Ani watched as Syl went into her little bedroom, her hair gleaming like knots of copper wire, her shoulders straight and unyielding, and she found herself torn and twisted inside, full of frustration and angry love. How could Syl even think Ani had forgotten what had gone before? But they were no longer on Earth, and they might never see the blue planet again. Quite simply, they had to make the most of where they were.

And hadn't Ani begged Syl to try harder? Now here it was, Ani's second major breakthrough. It was an occasion that should surely be one of joy and celebration – and Tanit in particular had made Ani feel like a queen following her success, embracing her, kissing her forehead like a blessing – and yet Syl, her oldest friend, had cast a pall over it. Somehow Syl had made it all about her.

'Bloody typical,' muttered Ani, and she went to her own bed determined not to cry.

CHAPTER 28

In the darkness above Torma, the wormhole bloomed.

The ship that emerged was many times larger than the two vessels that had pursued Tiray, but similarly disguised, like a rich man dressed in a poor man's clothes. It entered orbit above Torma, and dispatched from its underside a trio of spherical drones, two of which immediately descended to the surface of the planet while the third commenced a scan of the floating debris that was too far away to have been drawn in by its gravitational pull. The drone found metals, glass and bodies, details of which it transmitted back to the mothership before returning.

Meanwhile its two cousins soared above the Tormic landscape, searching, scanning. They found what was left of the *Envion* scattered across the sands, and farther away the remains of a second vessel that was more advanced in construction. Now the drones slowed their progress and began calling electronically – signalling, listening, signalling again. Finally, from beneath a dune in which lay buried a fragment of hull, came the response they were seeking. One drone landed and began to dig, and a casual observer might almost have thought that it gestured in triumph when one of its claws emerged from the sand holding a block of shining metal the size of a cigarette packet.

It had found the flight recorder from the Nomad ship.

The drone headed back to the mothership, the recorder stored carefully inside its main compartment, but the last drone continued its exploration of Torma. It located the former site of the drilling platform, now just a massive crater in the ground that was already filling with drifting sand. It commenced a methodical exploration of the surrounding area, covering it grid by grid, until it came at last to the great rock — half natural formation, half ancient construct — that rose up from the dunes. There the drone picked up the burn marks from a shuttle's engines. It paused before the face of the rock and scanned it from top to base, then hovered, as though awaiting instructions. A signal was transmitted to the drone's mainframe, the last that it would ever receive, and just as its fellow drone had radiated a sense of triumph at its unearthing of the flight recorder, so too it seemed that this one moved slowly, perhaps reluctantly, to fulfil its final command. It entered through an oval in the rock face, its red signal lights blinking forlornly in the darkness, until they, and it, were lost from sight.

Seconds later, the drone exploded, and the great stone column was no more.

CHAPTER 29

Illyri Biology was a class that was always of particular interest to the Earthborn girls, for while they recognised some of the better-known creatures from the homeworld, there was so much that was new and awe-inspiring to be discovered. The Sisterhood prided itself on the quality of its lectures, and so Biology occasionally meant an animal that had once walked or swum or flown on Illyr, and then died there, would be transported all the way from the planet below. It would then be brought into the laboratories for the dissecting pleasure and education of the elite young Illyri who hoped one day to be accepted into the order.

Today, the Biology tutor, Amera, stood before the Novices looking most pleased with herself. She was a youthful Nairene, her dyed hair chopped short just as full Sisters preferred it, sprouting artlessly like pink frosting from her scalp. She wore a red laboratory jumpsuit fitted with all manner of equipment and sensors, which she wielded deftly and with great enthusiasm. Amera was a firm favourite with most of the Novices, for there was something eminently likeable about her, and even Syl couldn't help but warm to her.

'Little Sisters,' Amera said, for that was her term of endearment for the youngsters whom she taught. 'On this day I have a great treat for you — great and yet terrifying.'

She gave a mock shiver and the Novices laughed as she waved a scalpel towards the bench in front of her. Upon it rested a lumpen heap roughly the size of a sheep, all swaddled in plastic sheeting.

'Oh, do hush,' Amera said. 'Don't you wake it now. But what might it be? Who would like to do the honours?'

She looked around and several students jostled for her attention, anxious to please. She pointed at Mila, chuckling, and said: 'Disrobe our subject, please.'

Mila bustled forward and cast the sheeting to one side, but she wasn't fast or cool enough to prevent the horrified 'Oh!' that escaped from her lips. She stepped back quickly, going a little pale, for on the table lay the intact remains of what appeared to be an impossibly large, obscenely ugly arthropod, complete with razor-sharp pincers and a wide, gaping jaw. It looked like a great centipede, but infinitely more terrifying.

'You don't like it?' teased Amera. 'It's only a little baby cascid: one of the unique creatures found, right outside on our own doorstep on dear old Avila Minor.'

'It's disgusting,' someone said.

Amera whirled round, affronted.

'That,' she said, 'is lazy thinking. Do you not understand the significance of this beast? You should be grateful that the cascid lives, for its very existence was crucial to the survival of the Marque on this moon in the early years, and to this day its fearsome reputation, its unrivalled adaption, and its insatiable carnivorous appetite keeps at bay those who would come here and undermine us. This, little Sisters, is our own formidable guard dog: it doesn't bark but it has a very, *very* nasty bite.'

She pointed out its outsized mandibles, its knobbled, chitin-like armour plating, its jointed, insectile legs, and the brush of incongruously delicate feelers across its head.

'The cascid cannot see. Why is this?'

'Because it feeds at night,' said one Novice.

'Precisely. As we know, nothing feeds by daylight on our barren rock. Any creature venturing out into that heat would burn up and die. No, the cascid is highly evolved to survive in inhospitable terrain in the impenetrable blackness of night.'

She spoke passionately of its other evolutionary features, pointing admiringly at various quirks of its anatomy, opening its mouth, lifting its legs to expose its softer underbelly and its excretory organs, and gradually her students drew nearer, repulsion turning to fascination.

'But most amazing of all, the cascid has no known natural lifespan. Some of those on Avila Minor are believed to pre-date the creation of the Marque. Indeed, it is presumed that several of the older cascids walking beyond our walls to this very day include those that inadvertently protected the First Five when they escaped here.'

This caused a flurry of excited chatter. Amera smiled, clearly in her element. She allowed them to babble for a few moments then held up her hands, and the students quietened down.

'Study of the organism in its habitat has understandably been curtailed by the harshness of its home, and its tendency to eat anyone foolish enough to get within reach of its jaws. It is rare, too, that one is found expired and still whole, for its own kind would usually quickly consume the remains. Yet this one was found dead near one of our service doors: dead, yet untouched. That, little Sisters, is why we are so blessed today, for we have been granted special permission to dissect this remarkable cascid right here, right now, and due to the rarity of such an occurrence, we are to be graced by the presence of the Half-Sisters.'

On cue, the door opened and Half-Sisters flooded into the room, a swirling wave of sea-green robes and superiority, smiling graciously at the young Novices. Among them Syl noted a handful with twinkling blue piping on their gowns, and she wondered if this meant that some of the Half-Sisters also had psychic abilities, if they too were among the Gifted. As if to confirm her suspicions, these select few were allowed to slip unchallenged into prime position, even when that meant a smaller Illyri's view was blocked, or a slippered toe was trodden on, a squawk of complaint stifled. The older of the blue-robed Novices – Tanit, Sarea, Nemein and Dessa – pushed closer to their higher ilk, and the Half-Sisters who stood nearby stepped aside almost indulgently, allowing the younger Gifted to join the others. Gradually everyone reshuffled and then settled, though many of the yellow-robed Novices kept glancing covertly at the serene Half-Sisters in what could only be described as awe.

'Welcome, Half-Sisters,' said Amera, smiling warmly. 'It seems like only yesterday I had you in my class, but here you are again, on the cusp of full Sisterhood. I could not be prouder. I know the Novices feel deeply honoured to have you among us. Now, let us proceed. We are here to dissect this noble cascid, and we hope too that we shall be able to ascertain the cause of its untimely demise.'

With brute force and rather a lot of grunting, Amera turned the cascid on to its back, its legs in the air like a stranded beetle. One by one Novices were selected and invited forward to make various cuts into its body: through its joints, into its sinewy heart and its reproductive parts.

'It's a boy!' cried Amera, and they all laughed.

Syl was allowed to breach the creature's respiratory system, which released a foul puff of fetid gas into her face. This was greeted by nasty sniggers, and she looked accusingly at Amera, sure she'd been selected for the task on purpose, but the tutor looked appalled.

'I'm so terribly sorry, child. I did not anticipate that,' said Amera, and she put her arm around Syl.

'What is your name? Syl, you say?' – vague recognition flickered in her eyes, but she seemed undeterred – 'Ah yes, one of the Earthborn. Come, stand here beside me. Have a front-row position for your troubles.'

Gradually the cascid was dismembered until its bloated, blackened gut could be seen, swollen and hard as a large balloon.

'Ah-hah! It is as I thought,' said Amera, prodding the stomach with her gloved finger. 'Look at that distension, that dark colouring. I suspect this poor fellow ate something that he shouldn't have, and poisoned himself. Usually cascids are smarter than that: they only consume the parts of their kills that are safe to eat and leave the toxic residue for bacterial organisms to dispose of. Isn't biology just so clever? Not this cascid though, apparently. And poisoning would be precisely why he wasn't consumed by scavengers, for cascids have a strong sense of self-preservation, and would be averse to ingesting toxic matter.'

She nodded happily and reached for a mask.

'You may want to take a step back, my dears. I shall make the next incision myself, for I anticipate putrefaction with its associated odours and discharge. Ready?'

Syl shuffled to the side as Amera made a clean incision into the cascid's belly, clearly relishing the task. Yellow slime, black jelly, and unidentifiable chunks of organic matter spilled across the table, kept from slopping to the floor by the deep reservoir of the metal work-bench. A collective shudder of distaste went around the room, but Amera was unperturbed, now sticking her hand into the fissure, grasping around for the source of the poisoning.

'Got it,' she said, slowly extracting her gloved hand again, but then something stuck within the beast and she was forced to give a final hard yank to release whatever it was she'd found. Her arm shot upwards with the effort, and there was a moment's shocked silence. Then the screaming started, for what Amera had pulled out was undeniably, unmistakably an Illyri hand, ending in the mangled stump of a lower arm. Its fingers flopped loosely as if the phalangeal bones had somehow been destroyed, but its skin was otherwise unblemished and smoothly perfect, save for a coating of clear ooze, which only seemed to magnify the horror of it all.

Syl stood frozen to the spot, watching in shock as Amera realised what she held, then dropped it, appalled, on the table beside the disembowelled cascid. The arm landed with a dull thud right in front of Syl and still she found herself immobile, unable to look away from what she knew she could never unsee. She took in the slim wrist cuffed in snug, gossamer-thin black fabric, and the pulverised joint where the limb had been severed from the body. The hand was golden and ladylike, yet it was also pounded out of shape and unnaturally twisted. Syl could make out the ragged nails on those rubbery fingers, digits that sagged inwards as if begging, or trying to grasp something. She saw the dirt beneath the pale half-moons where she imagined the victim had clawed terrified at the ground of the world she was being ripped from, and she saw a row of little unpopped blisters crossing a red mark on the palm, an injury that looked very much like a burn, a burn remarkably similar to the one she'd witnessed Tanit inflict on the hand of a Novice drudge.

Then she knew.

She turned away, at last understanding how Elda had disappeared so completely, for poor Elda had slipped forever into the jaws of this foul creature of the night.

And she understood too that the amulet Elda had entrusted to Syl's safekeeping must be more than just a sentimental trinket.

CHAPTER 30

The horror of the find was all anyone could speak of. Amera disappeared from her duties, presumably too traumatised to teach. Classes were cancelled, gossip flew, and stories became increasingly ridiculous and elaborate, sometimes even fantastical: the hand had only three fingers and belonged to an alien; the hand was merely a joke made of rubber; the hand belonged to Syrene, who had been absent for longer than anyone could previously recall. Others besides Syl started wondering if it was Elda's hand – and, if indeed they were Elda's remains, why had she gone outside alone and unprotected? Was it suicide?

But Cale finally put a stop to the rumours. She called an impromptu meeting of all Novices and Half-Sisters. They were gathered together in the examination hall, for it was the largest chamber in the Twelfth Realm, a hollowed-out moon mountain with elevated windows that drank in the blackness and the stars beyond. Nobody had called for the main lighting to be activated, so the meeting was held by candlelight, and shadows pooled the walls. It seemed somehow appropriate to Syl, as though they were holding a vigil for their dead Sister.

'Silence,' said Cale. Her voice echoed throughout the cavern, and there was no disguising her fury.

'I speak to you now with the voice of Grandmage Oriel, who is still recovering following her recent illness,' she continued. 'And yet when she should be recuperating, in perfect tranquillity, still the mutterings of these two Realms find her and disturb her peace. That is why you are here. I'm sure you have guessed that I have called you together about the incident in the Biology laboratory. Frankly, we are ashamed of your conduct, Novices and Half-Sisters. Ashamed.'

The whispering turned to silence as the students took this in.

'In the Nairene Sisterhood – this esteemed order into which you all hope one day to be inducted – we pride ourselves on facts, not gossip, on truth and knowledge and the dogged pursuit thereof, not on unfounded speculation. Yet it has come to our attention that the hallways are awash with the sort of idle talk and scandalising that we abhor. It will stop immediately. I shall now put an end to your unseemly speculation with the truth.'

The room rustled, but Cale ignored it.

'Our scientific division has analysed the limb found in the belly of the cascid and, through genetic identification, we have determined that it is the remains of an insurgent from among our own kind – yes, from among the Illyri, though obviously not from within our beloved Sisterhood. This serves to remind us of what we must never forget: that there are those in the outside world – indeed, the outside *worlds* – of who seek to bring about the downfall of our honourable order.'

There were cries of indignation, but Cale silenced them with a look and an impatient wave of her hands.

'The insurgent came to Avila Minor by night in an attempt to infiltrate the Marque: signs of an unauthorised landing were logged by our automated systems some time ago. The insurgent's nefarious intentions are demonstrated by the fact that she – yes, she, for our enemy was female – wore a darksuit to hide her heat signature: some of you may even have seen the remains of the fabric on the dismembered limb. The insurgent was torn apart by the Marque's natural protectors, the ancient cascids, before she even made it to our doors. For this we are grateful. Unfortunately, one of the younger cascids also swallowed a piece of the darksuit, and the chemicals within the fabric poisoned it. Further remains of the darksuit have been found on our moon's surface and are currently being analysed in the hope of identifying the source of this act of terrorism. That is the end of the matter. May it be a lesson to our enemies.'

Her eyes swept towards Syl, though Syl wasn't sure if this was intentional.

'As for the ridiculous rumours that the limb belonged to Elda Mallori, rest assured that she is safe and well. Most of you must have realised that she was not suited to our order. Thus it was no surprise when she was found hiding in the inner realms of the Marque, and so she was quietly returned to Illyr. Unfortunately, her dismissal brought some disgrace on her family, and Elda subsequently chose to go to one of the offworld colonies. We can only hope that she finds happiness and contentment there. Frankly, Novices, I expect more intellectual rigour from you: where would poor Elda source a darksuit anyway, and why would she even be wearing such a thing?'

Why indeed, thought Syl, as Cale brought the meeting to an end. Why indeed?

Syl sat on her bed in her locked room and took out Elda's amulet yet again, just as she had for the past few nights. She weighed it in her hands, feeling the roughness of the engraving. She prodded at the hinge and gave the thing a little shake, but there was no give, no secret compartment, nothing. She looked again at the odd scratchings on the back – Archaeon? She stroked the letters, wondering anew what they had meant to Elda, then, carefully, studied the severe face of Elda's mother, as if she could read Berlot Mallori's thoughts, or unravel the secrets she might hold behind those hard eyes. After a while, Syl put Elda's locket around her neck where it settled against her skin. Then she wrote out a list of questions by hand – she could have used her tablet, but she knew that the Sisterhood's IT system could access anything recorded on a Novice's device, and she preferred to keep her thoughts private – yet each question just seemed to raise more.

Issues re Elda

1) Who was Elda really?
   A spy? But for whom? And if she was against the Sisterhood, was she on the same side as me? Are other Illyri investigating the Sisterhood too? Who are they?

2) Archaeon? Is it a person? A place? A thing? Is it important?
   It must be, for clearly it was important to Elda, and Elda is dead.
   But why? Check libraries.
3) Where did Elda source a darksuit?
   Presumably from whoever she was working for. But she'd been here
   four years — was she a plant all along? Were there other plants?
4) What was Elda doing outside the Marque?
   Leaving? Relaying information? Having a cigarette, ha-ha-ha . . .
5) Why didn't the darksuit hide her from the cascids?
   ???
6) Why were the bones of her fingers so badly crushed that her
   hand appeared to be made from rubber?
   ???

It was these last two questions that caused Syl the most distress, as darksuits concealed heat signatures, and with it movement, and she knew firsthand how efficiently they worked, for hadn't darksuits hidden her so well when she was on the run in the Scottish Highlands? She recalled with a pang how Paul had handed her a darksuit, and how it had tightened to fit her as if she were being enveloped by snakes, and she remembered how he had given her an old sweater and waterproofs to wear over the suit, how gentle he'd been with her when the other humans had been callous, even cruel. And then as they fled, even the cutting-edge technology in the Diplomatic ships hunting them hadn't been able to detect them . . .

So if Elda had been wearing a darksuit, how then would a primitive cascid have tracked her as she sneaked across the night-time surface of the moon? Perhaps she'd been extraordinarily noisy, but that hardly seemed likely given the trouble she'd obviously taken to leave the Marque in secret. Anyway, the Elda that Syl had known was masterful at slipping by silent and unnoticed. Syl now found herself rather in awe of Elda, or of this new notion of Elda and the ruse she must have pulled off for so long. Nevertheless, clearly the plan hadn't ended as she'd hoped.

She looked again at the fifth question, tapping her finger on it: so why didn't the darksuit hide Elda from the cascids? The only explanation that made any sense was that it must have been damaged or compromised. Perhaps she'd torn it as she fled. That had to be it. But what was she fleeing?

And that led Syl to the question that played on her mind most of all. Why were Elda's finger bones crushed, yet the skin on the hand was unbroken? The image was seared on to her memory: the golden skin, the fingers floppy and pliable as caramel. It was as if the skeleton had turned to rubble, each digit pounded to a series of joints and breaks where there should be none, then stuffed back inside a glove of skin. Then there was the torn wound where the limb was ripped from the body, the bones like white splinters spiking from the skin, as if someone had shoved handfuls of toothpicks into the forearm. Yet cascids had sharp cutting pincers and strong, machete-like mandibles that would surely slice neatly through bone, not reduce it to shards no thicker than straws. The incongruity nagged at her, a tickle in her brain, something she needed to remember.

She hid her notes with the keys again and went to dinner.

That night, just as Syl was drifting off to sleep, a thought came to her.
'Oh!'

She sat upright, switched on her lamp, took out her hidden list and added one more question:

7) If Elda was spying here for four years, WHAT DID SHE FIND OUT?

As she replaced the list, Elda's amulet swung free and bumped against her arm. She touched it like a talisman before shutting her growing collection of secrets safely away again.

That night she dreamed of dark worlds, and to each she gave the name 'Archaeon'.

CHAPTER 31

'I'm going to the library,' Syl told Ani as she came out of her bedroom the next morning. Ani was sleepy-eyed and still in her pyjamas, but she stopped short, horrified.

'Oh no! I didn't forget a project, did I?' she said.

'No. I just want to look something up.'

'Oh, thank goodness! You're very dedicated. What is it?'

Syl looked around the room, then shut the door to the hallway outside.

'Those were Elda's remains inside that cascid, Ani. I have no doubt. I recognised that last burn Tanit gave her.'

Ani winced. She hated to be reminded of the violence the blue-robed Novices could so casually dish out.

'No, Syl. It's not possible. Cale said so.'

'And what else would Cale say: that a Novice had somehow been attacked and killed by a cascid? That would raise questions about what Elda was doing outside the Marque to begin with. I think Elda was much cleverer than anyone suspected – too clever simply to walk into the wilderness and hope for the best. She had planned her escape. Look: she left this in my locker, with a note.'

She scooped the locket and the note from under her robes and placed both in Ani's hand.

'Elda asked me if I could get the locket to her mother back on Illyr.'

Ani read the note, then turned the locket over in her hand, opening it and tracing the markings on the back, just as Syl had done so many times before her.

'Archaeon?' she read aloud. 'Is that a thing?'

'I don't know, but now Elda's dead, and that locket was important to her. That's why I'm going to the library. I want to find out what Archaeon is.'

'But I still don't understand why Elda would have been outside? Cale said it was a spy that was found. She was even wearing a darksuit . . .'

'Ani! Elda *was* the spy, and I think they know it. All that stuff about her going back to Illyr and then being sent off to one of the outlying colonies, it's just lies.'

'But why would they be lying?'

'I don't know! I only have suspicions, but no proof.'

Syl rubbed her head, frustrated.

'Well, tell me what you think you know then,' replied Ani, and she sat down and patted the couch beside her encouragingly.

'All right then,' said Syl, throwing herself onto a cushion, 'but you're not going to like it.'

And she told Ani what she believed: that, far from being a simple Novice, and an incompetent one, Elda had been much more complex. Elda was a spy, planted in the Marque to find out the secrets of the Sisterhood, but when her time came to flee, something had gone wrong. As a precaution in case she was caught, or something worse, Elda had left the locket for Syl, the only Illyri in the Marque whom she believed she could trust.

But Syl kept from Ani the fact that she also had a set of keys: Cale's keys. After all, the Gifted might well be able to read Ani's mind when she opened it to them during their special lessons. It was dangerous enough to have shared so much with her already.

'And Ani, I'm sorry it upsets you, but you do know how cruel Tanit and her gang were to Elda. They bullied and persecuted her. They torment anyone who crosses them. They practise their skills on the other Novices – no, don't interrupt! You know it's true. The little burns, the rashes, the unexplained pains, the bleeding, the things that fall at strange angles and hurt those that offend the Gifted. They'd love to torment me too, but' – she almost said that she could protect herself, but Ani knew nothing of her skills so she corrected her words at the last moment – 'well, you know that Syrene told them off for bothering me when we first arrived. She sees me as a trophy, a sign that Lord Andrus of the Military does the Sisterhood's bidding. I mean, what a coup, giving them his own daughter!'

He had even waved her goodbye, smiling as if his heart would burst with pride. Syl swallowed hard, fighting back sorrow, but still tears filled her eyes. Ani reached out a hand and squeezed her oldest friend's fingers, and Syl squeezed back.

'The Gifted were always hurting Elda, Ani. Nemein gave her spots and boils; Mila and Xaron definitely used their powers to throw things at her without ever lifting a finger. And Tanit burned Elda. She burned her face and her right palm. I know because I was there, and Elda showed me. There was a burn just like it on the hand they took out of the cascid's stomach. It was a right hand: it was Elda's hand. It was Elda who died out there . . . Perhaps, in the end, they killed her.'

Ani looked stricken. Mila and Xaron liked to show off their telekinetic talents, and who could forget the day in the canteen when Elda's tray of food had suddenly lurched upwards and slammed the girl in the face, the hot stew in her eyes and nostrils making the usually silent Novice scream in pain? But she didn't know if she dared tell Syl about their other talent, the combined one, because together Mila and Xaron had the ability to burst blood vessels and puncture organs, their needle-like minds pricking holes and popping veins as if they were balloons.

Ani bit her lip, shaking her head.

'Poor Elda. But I don't believe that they would have killed her, Syl. You're wrong about them. Yes, they can be cruel, but they're not murderers.'

'Are you sure about that? Did you notice how the bones in her fingers had been crushed, Ani, yet the skin was unbroken? How could a cascid do that? You saw its mouth, its pincers. It's just not possible. A cascid couldn't inflict that kind of damage, but I think a mind could. A dark, vicious mind.'

And Ani knew the truth of it.

'Sarea,' she said softly, sadly. 'I think Sarea could do that.'

Syl turned to face her friend on the couch, then swung her legs round and tucked her feet under Ani's bottom just as she used to on chilly evenings at Edinburgh Castle. She listened in silence as Ani told her everything she'd seen in her private classes with the other blue-robed Novices, all the things that she was sworn to secrecy about under threat of punishment or banishment. It was like a floodgate opening as she explained in more detail about the powers the Gifted had, the psychic skills and mind tricks they were encouraged to practise over and over. She told how Nemein was taken to hone her disease-causing talents in private on live laboratory animals, for how else could the progress of the maladies she created be monitored? The seclusion meant the others wouldn't be upset by the squeals of the unfortunate creatures as disease devoured their flesh, chewed through their organs, and snuffed out their vitality, but records were kept by proud tutors charting their protracted demise, and they were only too happy to encourage the other Blue Novices with tales of Nemein's growing prowess.

Sarea was routinely given dead animals to play with – both those killed by Nemein, and then others specially freighted in – and she shrieked with amusement as they crumpled to pulp before her, until they resembled nothing more than bags of skin and fur stuffed with flakes of bone and gore. Yes, she could make the bones pierce through the skin, but this hidden, highly controlled shattering – the breaking of bones without damaging the skin – was a new mastery of her skills, and one of which she was most proud.

And then Tanit would be set loose on the remains, making them burn, smiling peacefully as flames of many colours licked at the flesh, ultimately turning it all to ash, including the fragments of bone.

These, then, were the Gifted.

'What about Dessa?' asked Syl.

'I don't think Dessa's quite as powerful. She's like me, really. Just a clouder, only more advanced – she often has lessons alone with a tutor too. And you know about Xaron and Mila – they move things with their minds – but they have another skill too, when they stand together, touching each other.'

She told Syl about the bloody pinpricks, but Syl couldn't look more horrified than she already did. She merely shook her head, dazed.

'And Iria?'

'Well, Iria is clairvoyant. That's a bit of a game we play in class, actually: we'll give her something that belongs to another Novice, and she'll tell us whose it is, and all their little secrets. It can be embarrassing, which is why we only do it now with possessions belonging to non-Gifteds.'

'Have you given her anything of mine?' asked Syl.

'No!' said Ani. 'I wouldn't do that to you, ever.'

But Syl carefully logged this piece of information and determined to lock her room when she was away from it. She didn't want Iria nosing around, not if she could sniff out secrets merely by touching an item owned by another.

'How good is Iria?'

'Generally very good, but she struggles with Tanit. Like I said, though, she is talented with objects. If she could be trusted, she might be able to tell us something by touching Elda's locket.'

'But she *can't* be trusted, can she?' said Syl. 'None of them can.'

Ani handed the locket back to Syl, who slipped the cord over her head.

'But I don't understand *why*, Syl,' said Ani. 'Why would Sarea do something like that to Elda? She's banned from hurting anyone within the order. All of the Gifted are.'

'A ban?' Syl laughed. 'Fat lot of good it does. I watched them hurt Elda, and they tried to do the same to me.'

'You know what I mean. The odd rash or minor burn is hardly on the same scale as crushing bones, and it's a big step from bullying to murder.'

'Is it?' asked Syl. 'Is it really?'

Ani didn't answer.

'Look,' said Syl, 'all I can think is that Sarea – and I guess Tanit too, because there's no way Sarea would do anything so extreme without Tanit's approval – found out that Elda was a spy. Maybe they were torturing her and, I don't know, perhaps she tried to escape and ran out into the darkness.'

'No, don't you see? If Tanit found out Elda was a spy she'd go straight to Thona, or even Oriel,' protested Ani. 'Tanit's devoted to the Sisterhood, Syl. They all are. They worship Syrene. Tanit would report it so that the Sisters could take appropriate action. She wouldn't act alone. She's not like that.'

And suddenly it started to make sense.

'Maybe she did report it,' said Syl. 'Maybe this was what the Sisters deemed to be appropriate action, Ani. Maybe it was one of the Senior Sisters who issued the order.'

Ani opened her mouth to speak, but Syl cut across her, stabbing at the air with a pointed finger, her voice growing more strident with each word, her breath catching in her throat as the pieces fell into place.

'Do you really think the Nairene Sisterhood is training you all up in some great act of philanthropy? Don't forget who is behind the project: Syrene, always Syrene. Thona answers to Oriel and Oriel answers to Syrene. Syrene is the one who was so interested in you and your powers. Syrene singled you out, and now you're honing your skills, along with those other bitches, on her orders. You're all Syrene's "special project". But what does she plan to do with you all? Whatever it is, it isn't pretty, not from where I'm standing.'

Ani was crying now.

'Please, Syl, stop! Okay, so some of the Gifted might have hurt Elda, but you hate *all* of the Sisterhood. You hated them even before this happened. You're just using this as an excuse to turn me against them. There's goodness in the Sisterhood too.'

'Oh, you think so?' said Syl. 'Yet don't you find it strange that they never try to teach you anything good or kind? They want you to crush bones, to burn, to cause disease. They encourage that, but surely, *surely* your powers could work the other way too?'

This had only just occurred to Syl, and she ran with it: 'Couldn't they teach you to make people feel better, to cure illness, to mend bones, to take pain away instead of inflicting it? No, they have no interest in making you compassionate, Ani, just dangerous.'

Ani sniffed unhappily.

'Stop it!' snapped Syl. 'Don't you dare cry any more. Just don't. They're training you so they can use you, and clearly what they intend to use you for isn't exactly peace, love and harmony, now is it?'

'No.' One small word, one small shake of the head.

'I think Syrene's building her own private army, Ani; an army no one will see coming. Just girls in robes. Can you imagine what you could all do together, if let loose? Can you imagine the destruction you could cause?'

Syl wanted to vomit just thinking about it.

Now Ani spoke, and her voice trembled, but her words were strong, her face fierce.

'But I'm not a puppet, Syl. I may not be as clever as you, but I do have a mind of my own. Have you forgotten who I am? I'm your friend, I'm still Ani. I would never be part of that. Never. I'll die before that happens.'

They sat on the couch in silence. The words had run dry. Each was lost in her own thoughts until the cold of Illyr's second sun dazzled them through the window.

'Right then,' said Syl. 'You know as much as I do now' – well, almost, she thought to herself, guiltily remembering the keys – 'so I'd better get going to the library.'

'No, don't go yet, Syl,' said Ani, holding Syl's arm. 'It'll be too obvious at this time of day. The libraries will be empty this early on, and you'll be the only one logged in searching for one weird word. If it does mean anything, they'll be on to you. Let's do it after classes. We'll do it together.'

Syl had to smile despite her friend's tear-stained face.

'I never, ever thought that Ani Cienda would be offering to help me with my homework,' she said. 'It's a miracle.'

'Shut up, Syl, before I change my mind.'

CHAPTER 32

The many libraries in the Marque were as daunting as they were inspiring, with shelves of books stretching as high as the vaulted ceilings in the hollowed rocks and stone cathedrals of Avila Minor, the ceilings themselves often covered in even more shelving, hanging above like square bells attached to chains in the rafters. The least-used volumes stored up here could be winched down on request via an ancient pulley system. It was rare that they were asked for, though, for the chains screamed and rattled, and those waiting below feared the entire system might collapse on them at any moment. As much as the Sisterhood revered books, they still had no desire to be crushed to death by an avalanche of them.

Even the main Novice library in the Twelfth Realm was a thing to behold, serving not just as a small but impressive museum of literature from across the known universe, but also a prime example of design genius. Behind the visible shelves on the walls were hidden more shelves, and behind these even more shelves, opening up like the pages of a huge, solid book.

On the main floor, towers of glass-doored cabinets held volumes that couldn't be shelved: words carved on stones and tablets, written on scrolls of papyrus, scratched on to chunks of carefully marked bark; documents chiselled into crystals as long as an arm, and forged on to sheets of metal; records tooled on to rolls of tough hide and the softest leather; and even words almost invisibly imprinted on fragile, clear membranes from distant planets, only making any sense when held up to the light so that the shadows of the lettering stretched on to the floor.

One of Syl and Ani's favourite cabinets was filled with the jewel-like remains of long-dead insects from a distant world, balanced delicately on pinheads, their sparkling wings splayed open to reveal the mysterious, minuscule messages set down like a sprinkling of talc on the tiny glittering scales, and only readable through the high-powered magnifying glass that hung on a chain from the locked doors. Even then, they made no sense at all, and the civilisation that had created them was long gone.

'Spells,' said the old librarian Onwyn, when Syl had asked. 'It's all superstition, hocus-pocus and spells, but still in the Nairene Sisterhood we understand that all knowledge is illuminating. Yes, young ones? Even such primitive notions merely serve to cast the perfect truth in better relief.'

Syl had pressed her on what this might mean but, instead of answers, Onwyn had simply swept her frail arms wide, indicating the books.

'Inside books you will find all the answers,' she declared.

'But what if we don't know the questions?' Syl had responded, and Onwyn had looked at her oddly, her head cocked to one side, and thereafter a cautious friendship had begun between the old Sister and the reluctant Novice.

Today Syl and Ani bypassed the otherworldly butterflies, the skins and the crystals, for they were looking for just one thing: a reference to Archaeon. First they typed it into the computerised index system, hoping to find a cross-reference, but that drew a blank. This was hardly surprising since the constant influx of material meant the catalogues were always somewhat out of date, especially here in the Novice library where it fell to the youngest and least experienced to maintain them.

Of course, Onwyn would have known where to look, but Syl wasn't willing to entrust Elda's secret to anyone from the Sisterhood, not even the doddering Onwyn.

Instead, Syl and Ani moved to the rear of the library where they pored over the big old reference books – the Illyri equivalent of encyclopaedias – that dated back many centuries, and were as heavy and unwieldy as boulders. Some covered geography, both the terrestrial study of various explored planets and the mapping of the heavens above. Vast volumes catalogued notable Illyri, or famous battles, or the botany of the known worlds in microscopic detail, or the sciences, or history since the beginning of time. The lists were alphabetical, which made the task somewhat easier, but still the volumes piled up round them like a fortress. Nobody asked what the Earthborn Novices were searching for, or why. Here the pursuit of knowledge was expected, and classes had finished so the library was flooded with eager Novices anxious to prove their worthiness and dedication. Asking why a Nairene Novice might be reading would be like asking a trainee chef why she was studying a recipe: because it would be poor form not to.

Hours later, Ani closed her latest book – a plodding tome on the bacteria, fungi and algae of the Galatean planetary system – with a determined thump.

'Syl,' she said, 'this is not working. We don't even know what we're looking for, or if it even exists. I'm fed up.'

Syl mumbled something inaudible and continued studying her own bulky book, entitled *Celestial Geography*, which listed all the asteroids, planets, stars, systems, nebulae and galaxies in the known universe, along with a short description of each. It was the latest imprint, so thick that she had to stand up to see it comfortably.

'Ani, could you pass me an earlier edition of this please?' she said, still not looking up. With a small wail, Ani flopped face-first on to the table, waving her arms dramatically.

'Why, Syl? Can't we just *go* now?'

'Please. It'll take just a second.'

Ani stomped over to the shelf, clattered up the ladder and took down an older edition of *Celestial Geography*. She dumped it in front of Syl then sat down again, folding her arms across her chest defiantly. Syl leafed quickly through it, then she stopped and jabbed at an entry.

'There!' she said.

Ani sat up. 'Did you find it?'

'No – but here's *Ashkyll-2*. I knew it!'

'What? Actually, forget it – I'm not even going to ask what you're talking about.'

Syl ignored her and carefully marked the page before dragging down another volume, which was older still. She opened that one too, flipped through the alphabetised list, and then looked up, grinning.

'Right. Let me explain,' she said, pretending she hadn't heard Ani's theatrical sigh. 'In the latest edition of *Celestial Geography*, they mention a planet known as *Ashkyll-3*. But there's no *Ashkyll-2* or *Ashkyll-1*, which seems a bit odd.'

'How so?'

'Because why would they name a planet number three, if there was no two or one? Anyway, I looked in the older edition you gave me, and, surprise-surprise, there it is' – she opened the book to her marker – '*Ashkyll-2*! Why would it be in an earlier edition, and not a later one?'

Ani shrugged. 'Maybe it died?'

'Planets don't die, Ani – they're not stars. And then in the earlier edition there actually *is* a listing for *Ashkyll-1*, and for both the other *Ashkylls* as well.'

'I don't get it. What are you trying to say?'

'There's a page missing, Ani, I'm sure of it. In every volume. Look – the older volume goes from *Arbia* to *Ashkyll-1*, yet this newer one goes from *Arbia* to *Ashkyll-2*, with no mention at all of *Ashkyll-1*. Then this third one has both *Arbia* and a planet that's not in the others at all, called *Arcdarrit*, and then it leaps straight to *Ashkyll-3*.'

'But what has that got to do with Archaeon?' asked Ani, baffled.

'Well, think about it: they're the planets that would be listed on either side of *Archaeon* in alphabetical order, if *Archaeon* was originally included in these books. So if you took out the page referring to *Archaeon*, chances are you'd also lose a few references that were on the same page, or overlapped, like *Arcdarrit*, and *Ashkyll-1*. You see?'

Ani looked at the page, flipping it backwards and forwards lightly, then she glanced up, pursing her lips as she considered it. Frowning, she turned to the other books on the shelf beside them, climbing even higher up the ladder and taking down the oldest volume she could find. Syl watched in silence as Ani thumbed through it.

'*A* for *Arbia*, *A* for *Arcdarritt* . . .'

She looked at the next page then back again. Then she spoke in a whisper.

'And then *A* for *Ashkyll-3*. Oh my . . .'

'Exactly!' said Syl. 'And we'd never have noticed that those planets were missing if we hadn't seen them in the other volumes. *Archaeon* would fit right between *Arcdarritt* and *Ashkyll-1*!'

The friends stared at each other, wide-eyed. Ani bit her lip.

'What now?' she said in a whisper.

'I don't know but, just to add to the weirdness, you remember that book I was reading, *The Interplanetary Pioneers* – the one about the early explorations?'

'Vaguely.'

'The last chapter of that is missing entirely. When I looked next to the spine I could just make out where the pages had been sliced out.'

'Why would someone do that?'

'Well, at first I thought someone was just too lazy to copy them down so tore them out, that it was just stupid vandalism, but now looking at these books' – she waved a hand at the volumes splayed before them – 'I'm wondering if it's more than that, if there's some sort of censorship going on.'

Ani nodded thoughtfully.

'So what we need to do to test this theory of yours is get hold of another copy of that book, *Inter*-whatever-it's-called. If both are missing the same pages, then we know there's something very odd happening.'

'Good thinking. And we know the Marque has lots of libraries, and lots of books, and that there are multiple copies of the non-rare books. I found *The Interplanetary Pioneers* forgotten behind a shelf where it shouldn't be, but maybe there are more, perhaps even right here. So what if we were to ask . . .'

'Onwyn,' they both said together.

★ ★ ★

After they'd replaced the reference books Ani went to find Onwyn alone, for Syl was worried that if she asked and the old librarian checked on the computer system, she'd see that it was Syl who had withdrawn the book in the first place.

'I beg your pardon, Sister Onwyn,' said Ani, all big-eyed innocence and old-fashioned manners, while Syl watched from a distance.

'Yes, Novice?' said Onwyn, not unkindly.

'I'm looking for a book and I was hoping you could help me?'

'Of course. What is it you seek?'

'Why, a volume that was recommended to me by a friend: *The Interplanetary Pioneers*, I think it was.'

Onwyn's face split into a wide smile, revealing her old, peg-like teeth yellowed between her thin lips.

'Now that's a title I haven't thought about in years!' she said. 'Excellent choice, my dear. It's a wonderful book, but I'm afraid it rather fell out of fashion when the explorations moved further afield. I'm most delighted it's being sought out again.'

She hobbled over to the computer, talking partly to herself: 'Now, at one stage we had four copies, I believe, but we gave one of everything to the new library in the Seventh Realm. Well, hardly new anymore. Why, it must be sixty years since it was constructed. So that would leave three . . .'

She tapped slowly at the screen, clearly not entirely at ease with the modern system.

'Yes,' she said finally, 'we have three but one has been checked out by a, er, Syl Hellais, so there should be two remaining.'

'Syl is the friend who recommended it, Sister,' said Ani.

'I know Syl. She has excellent taste,' beamed Onwyn, 'but do tell her it's overdue. Right, follow me.'

She took Ani over to one of the chains that hung from the ceiling above, cordoned off by a rope barrier, and gave the thickest one a mighty yank, putting all of her frail form behind it. There was a faint squeak and Ani stared upwards in horror, but nothing moved.

'Oh dear. I'm afraid you'll have to help me,' said Onwyn, pushing

Ani gently towards the chain. Ani took it in her hands, her face contorted with worry, and gave a tiny jerk.

'It won't bite you – just give it your hardest tug! Put your back into it.'

Looking like she might throw up, Ani did as instructed. There was a piercing screech from high above them and a cloud of dust puffed down. Everyone turned to watch, squealing and stepping to the corners and out of danger when they saw what was happening, until Ani and Onwyn stood in the middle of the floor all alone.

'Again,' said Onwyn. Ani pulled, and there was another screech. This time a lone book plummeted down, narrowly missing a glass cabinet before it landed with a sharp crack on the floor, exploding pages and more dust. Several onlookers yelped in fright.

'Fear not. That always happens – just keep pulling!'

Ani yanked again and again, and slowly, loudly, a massive old-fashioned shelf was lowered to the floor, teetering a little wildly, shedding another book or four on its way.

'They're meant to have netting on them to keep the books in place, but it rotted away over the ages. I suppose we should replace it,' said Onwyn to nobody in particular, though the entire room was listening.

Finally the shelf came to rest on the floor beside Ani, and a collective sigh of relief went up, as another cloud of dust came down. Gradually, everyone went back to what they were doing as Onwyn began fingering the books lovingly, blowing dirt off them. She moved around, peering in close, her lips moving as she read the titles, occasionally stroking one affectionately. After a few minutes she pulled two books from the shelf.

'Here we are. *The Interplanetary Pioneers* – two copies, as I thought. Would you like to withdraw one?'

'Yes please.'

'Superb,' she said, moving to put the final copy back in place, but then she changed her mind. She smiled at Ani once more, all the pegs glistening, her tongue peeping through.

'And you know what? I think I might just take this copy for myself.

It must be the best part of a century since I last read it, and I remember it being such a favourite of mine when I was a Novice.'

Ani turned to follow her back to the computer but Onwyn pointed at the shelf.

'Pull that thing up first, please. We don't want anyone getting hurt.'

Syl hid her laughter behind a cough.

They were barely out of the library when Syl snatched *The Interplanetary Pioneers* from Ani's hands.

'I can't wait a moment longer,' she said, as she turned quickly to the back of the book.

As before, the final chapter was missing.

CHAPTER 33

Paul woke to find the *Nomad* silent. He passed Steven and Rizzo, and then Peris and Thula, all fast asleep. Only Alis was still awake, seated silently in the co-pilot's chair as they headed for Archaeon, her face lit by the readings on the cockpit glass before her. Paul became part of them as he approached her from behind, reflected so that his features appeared tattooed with figures and graphs.

'I was going to ask if you ever sleep,' he said, 'but I suspect that it might be a silly question. You're a Mech.'

Alis showed no emotion, but Paul was aware of a sudden tension in her body.

'How long have you known?'

'I've been watching you, and I finally figured it out.'

'How?'

'You remind me of someone.'

'Who?'

'Her name was Meia.'

Alis's face betrayed itself with a flicker at the mention of the name. '"Was"?'

'Is, if you prefer. She was alive when last I saw her, for what it's worth. Does Tiray know?'

'Of course.'

Paul took the pilot's chair. He yawned. Somewhere among the supplies that he and Thula had taken from the *Envion* was coffee, but he was too weary to go looking for it. He'd let Rizzo sleep for a while longer, then tell her to go and find it. After all, what was the point of being in charge if you couldn't order people to do things for you?

Then again, Rizzo would likely tell him to go and look for it himself. He suspected that her respect for his new rank only went so far.

Paul looked at Alis. The ProGen skin really was remarkable, and it would have been impossible to tell that she was an artificial life-form – a Mech – from appearance alone. It helped that the golden skin of the Illyri tended towards a kind of smoothness that even the most perfect of human features seemed to lack.

'You're staring,' said Alis.

'Sorry.'

'Your brother stares at me too.'

'For different reasons, I think.'

Her head tilted in puzzlement.

'What do you mean?'

'I think he likes you.'

'As in . . . ?'

'Exactly.'

'Oh.'

'Yes, "oh".'

'Does he know about me as well?'

'I don't think so. If he suspects, then he hasn't said anything to me.'

'Will you tell him?'

'Not unless you want me to.'

He watched her consider the problem.

'I will tell him myself,' said Alis, 'when the time is right.'

'Good. Be careful with him – with his feelings. He's young.'

Alis opened her mouth to reply, but couldn't seem to form the right words. Her brow furrowed briefly in confusion. Paul managed to hold back a smile. It didn't matter if you were human, Illyri or Mech: emotions were tricky to handle.

'I have a question for you,' said Paul.

'Ask it.'

'I heard that all the Mechs were destroyed, but I've now met two. It suggests that tales of your destruction may have been exaggerated.'

'What did Meia tell you?'

'Nothing.'

This was true, just about. What he'd learned had come directly from Syl and Ani: the Mechs were all supposed to have been destroyed, their fates sealed when they began to show signs of 'system mal-functions' – emotions, in other words – along with a growing faith in the existence of a creator, a god. It led the Mechs to believe that they had souls, a development which senior Illyri found so disturbing and dangerous that they advocated the Mechs' destruction. But many Illyri felt uneasy about annihilating beings that appeared to be self-aware, and so it was agreed that the Mechs would be sent into exile on a remote world. The Illyri watched their ships go, their vessels gradually growing smaller and smaller until they were lost among the stars.

But the Mechs were betrayed, for their ships self-destructed long before they reached their destination, and only a handful of Illyri knew of what had occurred. That, at least, was the story that had been told, but Meia, and now Alis, gave lie to it.

Ali was watching him impassively.

'Then I can tell you nothing either,' she said.

'That's not very helpful.'

'I'm sorry.'

'I don't think you are, not really.'

Alis seemed about to say something more, but stopped herself. Instead she asked him a question of her own.

'The human, Galton: why did he go back to the *Envion*? Why did he want to die?'

'He was in love with a woman named Cady. She was killed down on Torma. He couldn't live without her, or thought that he couldn't.'

'He was wrong to do what he did,' said Alis. 'He despaired. We should not despair. There must always be hope. There must always be faith in the Creator.'

'Galton was in shock,' said Paul. 'Under other circumstances perhaps we could have saved him, but we were in shock too. And sometimes people just break. Call it a design flaw. When you see the Creator, be sure to bring it up.'

'But you wear the Christian symbol. I've read about it. You believe.'

'I believe,' agreed Paul. 'But there are times – like the deaths on Torma and the suffering of my people under the Illyri back on Earth – when I wonder why I do. Maybe I just believe because I'm frightened.'

'Of what?'

'Of not having anything to believe in.'

Paul stood. He wouldn't wake Rizzo after all. He had a pretty good idea where the coffee was anyway.

Alis's hand touched his. He was surprised by how warm it was. He was fascinated by the reality of the Mechs. He wanted to know more about them, but for now he was content to have his theory about Alis confirmed.

'I am sorry that I can't tell you more about us,' said Alis. 'Truly. You knew of one, and now you know of two.'

'And there are more,' he said.

It wasn't a question, but a statement of fact. He didn't even need her to nod in agreement.

'Meia,' she said.

'What about her?'

'Meia is important.'

Her hand tightened on his, as though imploring him to act on Meia's behalf. But Meia was far away and Paul couldn't help her. Then again, when he'd last looked Meia didn't seem like the kind who needed much help. Meia was like a one-Mech army.

'Am I interrupting something?'

It was Thula. He was grinning at Paul. Alis released her grip.

'It's not what you think,' said Paul, and instantly realised that this was just the sort of thing someone would say if it was *exactly* what another person thought.

'Maybe if I become a lieutenant, attractive aliens will start throwing themselves at me, too,' mused Thula.

'If you don't wipe that grin off your mug, something heavy and sharp will be thrown at you,' warned Paul.

Thula managed to straighten his face, but it was obviously a struggle.

'I'm going to find coffee,' said Paul.

'Good,' said Thula. 'I'll stay here.'

Paul slipped by him, conscious that his face was red.

'Do that.'

'And I won't hold hands with anyone.'

'I'm warning you . . .'

Everyone was awake by the time Paul returned with coffee, porridge oats, and a pile of ready meals. The coffee was instant, but better than nothing. The galley provided hot water, and pretty soon all of the humans were eating. The Illyri consumed their own food from the supplies on the vessel – mostly rehydrated vegetables mixed with meat that smelled to Paul like pork that had gone off. Even Alis joined them, raising another question in Paul's mind about the workings of the Mech digestive system, although he wasn't sure that it was a question he actually wanted answered.

'Why does Thula keep grinning at you?' asked Steven.

'Thula finds jokes where there are none,' said Paul, but he took Thula aside when they had all finished eating, and spoke softly to him. When Thula returned he was no longer smiling, and he regarded Alis with renewed interest.

Steven was back in the pilot's chair, although there was little for him to do until they reached the first wormhole, and that wouldn't be for some hours yet. (Although far from Illyr, they followed the Illyri clock, which had a thirty-hour day.) The coordinates had been fed into the ship's computer, and its powerful engines were doing the rest. The *Nomad* also continually scanned for signs of pursuit or radio transmissions. Like everything else about it, the range of its scanners was greater than anything Paul had encountered before. They would receive more than adequate warning if any ships were in their vicinity, but so far the scanners had picked up nothing.

Paul walked to the conference room at the rear of the ship, where he found Peris and Tiray in conversation. It didn't appear to Paul to be anything particularly secret, just the talk of two Illyri with some knowledge of each other who were making the best of their time together to catch up on mutual acquaintances. Paul took a seat across from them, and the discussion petered out. Both Illyri waited for him to speak.

'Alis is a Mech,' said Paul.

Both Tiray and Peris looked surprised although, Paul supposed, for different reasons. He could see from Peris's face that the old soldier had no idea about Alis's true nature, while Tiray was probably astonished that Paul knew.

'She told you?' asked Tiray.

'I guessed,' Paul replied, and he couldn't help but feel a hint of pleasure as he saw Tiray's opinion of him change once again. 'My question is, why is she with you?'

'I sheltered her when the exile was announced. I knew what was about to occur. She was valuable to me. I trusted her.'

'So she's the only one?'

'Yes.'

'You're lying.'

Tiray didn't look happy to be called a liar, but Paul didn't care.

'You should pick your words more carefully, young human,' said Tiray. 'This is still an Illyri vessel, and the rules of both command and courtesy require you to guard your tongue.'

Paul ignored him.

'Here's what I think,' he said. 'You, and a handful of other senior Illyri, told the Mechs about what was planned for them. As a result, their ships weren't blown to pieces, and they made their way to safety. But you and your friends wanted to keep channels of communication open with them, so you held a few back and hid them among your staff.'

Tiray didn't answer.

'Tiray, we know about Meia,' said Peris. 'It was she who acted to help Governor Andrus's daughter back on Earth.'

Tiray nodded. His eyes were filled with sorrow.

'We couldn't save them all,' he said. 'We only found out about the devices on the ships at the last minute. By then, two of the transports had already left the galaxy. Their communication systems had been disabled. There was no way of contacting them. We did what was necessary to save the Mechs on board the final vessel.'

'Where are they?' asked Paul.

'I don't know.'

Paul was about to call him a liar again, but Tiray raised a hand to stop him.

'I'm telling you the truth. It was deemed better that we did not know, in case someone discovered what we had done and we were interrogated. Alis stayed with me, and I know of four other Mechs who remain hidden with sympathetic Illyri, but only one of the Mechs from that final ship eventually returned.'

'Meia,' said Paul.

'Yes, Meia. She is the only one who knows the location of the refuge.'

'How many were saved?' asked Peris.

'Five thousand.'

'Five *thousand*?' said Paul.

He was shocked. He had not thought that there might be so many.

And, again, a sadness enveloped Tiray.

'Only five thousand,' he said. 'The *Vianne*, the last vessel, was the smallest of the three ships. Each of the others held almost ten times as many. What happened was a crime, but one for which no one will ever be punished.'

'Why?' asked Paul.

'Because if we were to reveal our knowledge of the plot to destroy the Mechs, we might also be forced to reveal that we managed to save the five thousand. No proof exists of what occurred, apart from the Mechs who were saved, but they are safe only as long as their existence remains unknown.

'And even if, by some miracle, we were able to produce evidence of the plot without endangering the Mechs, those responsible for that slaughter are among the most powerful Illyri in the Empire. They are the elite of the Diplomatic Corps. Their role is to punish, not to be punished.'

Paul turned his attention to Peris.

'You were the last one to speak to Meia,' he said.

'Yes.'

'Who else knew about her?'

'No one. Well, aside from Lord Andrus, obviously. And Danis, I would think. Andrus trusted Danis more than anyone.'

Danis was the head of the Illyri Military in Britain and also Ani's father.

'And the Securitats didn't suspect Meia?' Paul asked.

'I don't know,' replied Peris. 'I don't think so. They hated her, Vena most of all. Vena ordered Meia's arrest in the last days on Earth, but I don't know if she'd discovered that Meia was a Mech. She was accused of treason and murder. If they had found out the truth, and then caught her, she would not have survived for long.'

Paul was troubled. A lot of those at Dundearg had seen Meia and witnessed her actions during the battle. They must have realised that she was no ordinary Illyri. If they were found by the Securitats, and tortured to reveal what they knew . . .

Perhaps all would be well. Meia was more intelligent than any of them, and hugely resourceful. She had kept herself hidden for a long time.

But it was as Alis had hinted to him: if one Mech could survive, then so could many. If Vena knew Meia's secret, she would not rest until she was found.

II
MEIA

CHAPTER 34

The Resistance had been following the movements of Lord Andrus, the Illyri governor of Europe, for weeks in the hope of establishing some kind of pattern. He left his base at Edinburgh Castle less frequently nowadays, which made targeting him that much harder, but as the figurehead of Illyri rule in the region, Lord Andrus was among those whom the Resistance held responsible for the repression in Scotland.

And so an assassin was dispatched.

The rifle was a prototype, but one that had already been tested for months in the Scottish Highlands. It was a combination of human workmanship and advanced Illyri technology, a killing device designed with one purpose in mind: to assassinate Lord Andrus. Its range was twice that of its nearest rival, and it fired a depleted uranium bullet capable of penetrating up to six inches of steel or cement while sacrificing only a fraction of its velocity. The rifle had been smuggled into the sniper's nest in parts over a period of weeks, then rebuilt. Now its sights were fixed on one of the lower courtyards of Edinburgh Castle, where Lord Andrus's private shuttle waited.

The sniper had been in place for six days, waiting for the opportunity that must surely come. He ate self-heating rations, and performed his ablutions in plastic bags. He lay beside his gun, its muzzle not even protruding an inch through the camouflaged hole in the brickwork for fear that an Illyri scan might reveal its presence. The only light came through that hole, filtered by gauze. At night, he lay entirely in blackness. He enjoyed brief periods of sleep, but he seemed to have a sixth sense for movement in the target area, and came instantly awake when a figure entered his killing zone. His nest was a cleverly disguised crawlspace, barely five feet wide and three feet high, above an existing attic in a building on the Royal Mile. It resembled a coffin of brick and wood, but the sniper was not one to suffer from claustrophobia. Neither did it ever enter his mind that he might survive his mission. Once the shooting began, they would seal off the area and come for him. It didn't matter. They would find only his body – at the thought, he flicked his tongue over the cyanide capsule in his tooth – and beside it a picture of the sniper with a woman and two teenage boys, all gone now, all dead.

Early on the seventh morning came a burst of activity. The governor's shuttle was being prepared for departure. Instinctively, the sniper controlled his breathing. He placed his right eye to the telescopic sight, and his finger under the guard, hovering barely milli-metres above the trigger. Figures appeared in his scope, but they wore the black of Securitats or the uniform of the castle guards. None was the one whom he sought.

More movement. A glimpse of red. The Nairene Sister. And if she was present then so too –

There! His finger touched the trigger. He prepared to release a breath, and with it would come the bullet, as though he himself were the weapon, and his mouth the muzzle.

A massive shock rippled through his body, turning his chest into a resonance chamber, and his heart burst before he could fire the shot. He briefly recognised the fact of his own dying, and welcomed it. He was only sorry that he had not managed to kill the target. It was his final thought as he was reunited at last with those whom he had lost.

In the attic space below, a hooded figure lowered a hand-held pulse weapon. Its skin was slightly scarred below the hairline, and beside and beneath the chin, as though it wore an imperfectly fitted mask. The features had an eerie blankness, as if an expensive showroom dummy had somehow come to life, a consequence of the ProGen skin that had been applied to form a face, and then kept in a state of suppleness by regularly passing a small electric current through the base material. With the application of a little make-up, the blank effect largely disappeared, but there had been no time to apply it that morning. Even a delay of seconds would have resulted in the death of Lord Andrus.

The figure descended through the levels of the old building, slipping out through a window at the back just as the first rays of sunlight touched the skyline, and it lost itself in the shadows. Had there been anyone to bear witness, they might have glimpsed what appeared to be a youthful Illyri female, smaller than average, with quick, lithe movements, wearing only thin, dark clothes despite the morning cold – for the sensations of cold and heat were simply not part of her programming. Curiously, though, she did feel a sense of regret at the sniper's death, for she knew something of his history, and the reasons why he had volunteered for a mission that he knew could end only one way for him. Such an emotion was unequivocally *not* part of her programming. Neither were loyalty, attraction, hatred, or love – for she was a biomechanical organism, a Mech – and yet these feelings had begun to manifest themselves in her. She was changing, developing.

In the Edinburgh chill, Meia shivered.

CHAPTER 35

They called it the Scourging of the Highlands. It was not the first such persecution of the Scots – Scotland's history was marked with many instances of similar brutality over the years – but it was terrible in the degree of its ruthlessness. Houses were razed, their inhabitants left to watch them burn. Entire villages were wiped from the map, leaving only craters where communities had once stood. For the first time since the early days of the Illyri Conquest, refugees travelled the roads of Scotland in convoys of cars and trucks, and sometimes even on foot if the Illyri had chosen to compound their punishment by depriving them of their vehicles. They headed for the cities and the towns where friends and relatives might be willing to put them up for a time until they could find new accommodation, new schools for their children, and new jobs if they were fortunate enough not to be blacklisted.

'Blacklisting' was another Illyri variation on an old conqueror's trick: those suspected of sympathising, if not actively conspiring, with the Resistance could be put on temporary 'Denial of Employment' lists, which made it illegal for anyone to offer them work, paid or unpaid. Initially the Scots had tried to get around the lists by allowing people to take up voluntary positions and paying them in food, fuel, or shelter. Those citizens who had lived through the Second World War in Europe, or had fled the Nazis when they took similar measures against Jews, and homosexuals, and gypsies, and union organisers, looked on the actions of the Illyri with bleak, angry eyes, reminded – as if any reminder was necessary – that history merely finds new ways to repeat old crimes. Swastikas began to appear on the walls of Illyri bases and the sides of their vehicles, and in one week in December alone, two Glasgow youths were shot dead by Illyri forces while engaged in such acts of defacement, and twenty others were injured, eight seriously. The result, hardly unexpectedly, was not a reduction but a sharp increase in the number of swastikas being painted, and an order from the Illyri rulers in Edinburgh that lethal force was not to be used against unarmed children. Since many Scottish youths routinely carried small knives, and even a stone could be considered a weapon, the order did nothing to reduce the number of shooting incidents.

The reason why the Illyri boot was being pressed so heavily to the Scottish throat could be summarised in just one word: Dundearg. At this Highland castle, now reduced to blackened ruins, a band of Resistance fighters had successfully annihilated the remnants of an Illyri strike force that had descended on the Highlands to rescue the high-ranking Illyri Grand Consul Gradus, and kill his Resistance captors. Instead, in a series of engagements, the Resistance left the remains of three Illyri heavy cruisers, two shuttles, and a still untold number of Illyri and conscripted Galatean corpses scattered across the landscape. Among the dead was Sedulus, the European head of the Securitats, the Illyri's hated security police.

The price of the victory at Dundearg, though, had proven high. Sedulus had a lover, Vena, who was also his underling, and upon his death she was promoted to his former position of Marshal. Vena was now responsible for avenging his loss, a bereavement that was both professional and deeply personal to her. This, perhaps, explained some of the relish with which she took to the task of punishing the Scots for Dundearg. Vena was unnaturally cruel; some said that she had not been born in the normal way, but had eaten her way out of her mother's womb.

But Vena had appointed another Illyri female, Cynna, to supervise in a hands-on fashion the crackdown on the Scots. If anything, Cynna was more vicious than her mistress, but lacked her intelligence. Still, it was useful for Vena to have someone like Cynna to do her dirty work. It meant that, where necessary, she could keep her hands clean, and pretend that the worst excesses of torture and killing had nothing to do with her. Cynna particularly favoured strangulation as a form of execution. She was uncommonly strong, even for an Illyri, and had left the marks of her fingers on countless necks.

But if the Illyri were guilty of revisiting the tactics of tyrants throughout history, so too were they repeating age-old mistakes and reaping the consequences. Not all of those who were enduring the Scourging – either as victims or onlookers – meekly accepted their fate. Many joined the Resistance in the Highlands, or swelled the membership of its cells in towns and cities north and south of the border. Some made their way to Ireland where, like the unfortunate British before them, the Illyri had found themselves locked in a state of perpetual guerilla warfare. Huge numbers of Illyri troops were kept busy by a comparatively small number of hostile units, although, unlike in the Irish Troubles of the previous century, those units now enjoyed the support of most of the population.

Throughout the world, similar hotbeds of resistance seemed to be mushrooming every day, and the ferocity of the fight was intense.

The problem for the Illyri was that they had never before attempted to conquer a race as advanced as humanity, so there was simply no model to follow. Partly by accident, partly by design, the Illyri based their colonisation on the successful empires and invaders of human history – the Romans, the Persians, even, to a degree, the Nazis – but ignored the greatest lesson to be learned from all of them: failure. Empires decayed, and invading forces could not survive indefinitely in hostile lands. The Illyri rule on Earth could not last, or so the Resistance whispered.

But there were those among the Illyri who did not want the mission on Earth to continue. They had other plans for humanity.

Darker plans.

The Resistance leaders at the battle of Dundearg quickly vanished in the aftermath, disappearing at dawn's light before Illyri reinforcements could arrive in numbers. They had not done so without trace, however, for they had left their DNA all over the castle, and Vena and her Securitats managed to identify most of those who had been present through the examination of minute samples of skin and hair, creating intricate facial reconstructions, even of those for whom they could find no other medical records. One of those identified was an Illyri deserter known to the Resistance as Fremd, or sometimes the Green Man. It was bad enough that an Illyri traitor should have been among the fighters at Dundearg, but Fremd was also a former Securitat, one long believed dead. Fremd had secret knowledge, knowledge that could endanger the whole Illyri mission on Earth. Fremd was dangerous, and much of Vena's efforts were focused on finding him. She wanted Fremd, dead or alive.

But Vena wanted Meia taken relatively unharmed. She had a selection of tools and blades ready and waiting for when Meia was captured, and hers would be a long, slow, painful trip to oblivion.

Vena's only regret was that she would not also be able to put Syl Hellais under a knife. But Vena's reach was long: someone else would take care of Syl for her, and her torments would be great.

She considered all this as she watched Cynna strangle the teenagers. They had been found painting a swastika on a garage door in Leith, which was bad enough, but one of them was armed with a pistol, and another had traces of explosive on his skin and clothes. Two girls, one boy. Cynna had saved the boy for last. When she turned to Vena, her eyes were bright with an excitement that was almost sexual.

'I want more,' said Cynna.

'And you will have more,' said Vena. 'As many as you want.'

CHAPTER 36

Trask sat on a bench by the old raven cages in the deserted grounds of Edinburgh Zoo, although deserted was a relative term when surrounded by over a thousand animals, any number of which only really began to find their mojo once darkness fell. He could hear an owl hooting nearby: probably Amber, the zoo's Eurasian eagle owl, a giant of a bird capable of taking a fox if it was hungry enough. Trask smiled, happy that he had remembered the bird's name. Once upon a time he could have named half of the animals here. Those names were probably still buried somewhere in the attic of his memory, along with the line-ups of various Hibs football teams from the eighties, and the girls that he'd kissed before he'd finally married and started a family.

When he let his guard down, he could recall other names too: the names of the lost, of the dead. Children, most of them, or little more than children, killed by the Illyri for trying to take back their world from the invaders. In truth, their faces were never far from his mind, and even if he had been inclined to forget them, they would have returned to him each time he passed the mother of one of them on the street, or met one of their fathers in a pub in St Leonard's, or the Grange, or Blackford. Some of those parents still blamed Trask for what had befallen their sons and daughters: to them he was the face of the Resistance, the one who had encouraged their children to rise up and fight.

In reality, though, Trask hadn't encouraged anyone to fight – quite the opposite, in fact. When kids came to him, their eyes bright and angry, looking to strike a blow for humanity, he would turn them away without exception and claim not to know what they were talking about. He didn't need any more deaths on his conscience, that was part of it, but he had also been in this game for long enough to know that you didn't take them the first time they asked, nor the second, and not even the third. Mostly, you didn't take the ones who asked at all. Instead you watched, and you waited. The really talented ones, the gifted ones, would show themselves with a look, a gesture, a minor act of insubordination, of rebellion. They were already fighting their war against the Illyri: they just hadn't formalised it yet.

And then there were others, like Paul Kerr, who were fashioned by the Illyri themselves, turned into warriors by the actions of the invaders. Trask had always known that Paul would make his mark in the Resistance. He'd known it before the boy entered his teens, had seen it in his eyes: the intelligence, the careful regard, the memory for detail, the capacity for leadership. But the Illyri had provided the finishing touches, taking some of the boy's sensitivity away and replacing it with a hint of coldness, a streak of ruthlessness. They'd done it by throwing his dad into the back of a Securitat transport, striking him with an electric baton, and then leaving him to die on the floor as his heart gave out from the shock. Trask had held Bob Kerr in his arms as the life departed from him, weeping over him, crying like a child. They'd been friends since they were boys and had started work in the zoo on the same day. Bob had ended up in charge of half-a-dozen mammals while Trask took care of the reptiles. They went to football matches together, to the pub together. They'd even holidayed together, because their wives got along with each other just as well as the husbands did. Hardly a day went by when he and Bob didn't at least talk on the phone, and even then they'd often make the effort to meet for a quick drink, or just to walk their dogs on Blackford Hill.

Now Bob was gone, and Katherine, Bob's widow, no longer spoke to Trask, whilst Trask's own missus had long since left him. It might even be true to say that Katherine Kerr hated Trask because he too had a cold, unthawed place in his heart. It had led him to make an exception to his own rule and approach Paul directly, offering him a chance to avenge his father's death by joining the Resistance. Paul had said yes, and in time his brother Steven had joined too, and so a train of events was set in motion that ended, finally, with their mother being deprived not only of her husband but her two boys, for they were now far away from Edinburgh, far away from anywhere that Trask could name. He looked up at the night sky. Even the most distant of the stars visible to him was not even close to wherever the Kerr boys might be. Now he could add their names to the list of the lost as well, and their fates to his conscience.

The owl grew quiet and Trask took a sip from the flask of whisky in his hand. The air had a damp chill to it. He felt the cold now in ways that he never had before. He was getting old, he realised. He could see it reflected in his daughters, Nessa and Jean. They were no longer girls, but young women. It was only a matter of time before they'd run off with fancy fellows, he guessed – well, it would be if they ever managed to find blokes that weren't scared to death of them. They were both attractive in their way, but Nessa was a big lass – not fat, but hard and muscular, and smart with it – while Jean had a fascination with knives that tended to make the lads nervous.

Trask glanced at his watch. She wouldn't be coming now. It had been many months since they'd last met, but he'd kept up their arrangement. They'd agreed to come to the zoo on the first and third Tuesdays of every month, three hours after sunset; more frequently if necessary, but always on those days. Then she had disappeared, hunted by the Illyri, but still he kept coming to the zoo, just in case. In a strange way, he kind of missed her. Oh, she scared him the way Nessa and Jean scared most of the menfolk of Edinburgh but, like them, she had character. Strange that she wasn't human. Stranger still, as it turned out, that she wasn't even Illyri either. She was – what was the word they used? – a 'Mech'. He'd have called her a robot, he supposed, but she wasn't quite that. A robot implied something mechanical, like the Tin Man in *The Wizard of Oz*, or that little R2D2 from *Star Wars*, a construct that would echo like an empty dustbin if you tapped it hard enough. But she had a layer of flesh and blood to her, and a sense of humour. She even liked him a little, Trask thought, and he didn't think that artificial beings could 'like'. He liked her in return. It was all very confusing.

He checked the scanner in his pocket, although it was primed to buzz and vibrate if it detected a signal. The device searched constantly for signs of Illyri surveillance. It couldn't do much about larger drones – which flew too high to pick up conversations anyway, and were used only to confirm positions and movements – but it was very good at detecting the various insects and arachnids that the Illyri had adapted for spying. Spiders, flies and even midges had been electronically enhanced by the Illyri to act as their eyes and ears, but they gave off minute signals that the scanner could detect. The zoo, though, appeared to be clear.

Trask took a final sip for the road and got to his feet. As he did so, he heard her voice speak directly behind him.

'It was good of you to come,' said Meia.

Trask smiled.

'I promised you that I would.'

'It's good, because it makes it easier for me to kill you.'

And his smile disappeared.

CHAPTER 37

Meia asked him if he had a weapon. Trask said no. She told him that, if she searched him and found he was lying, he would regret it.

'How?' he asked. 'It's not like you can kill me twice. Incidentally, you might like to tell me what I've done to deserve dying by your hand.'

She didn't reply. Instead, she asked him again – this time more forcefully – if he was carrying a weapon.

'No, but search away,' he said. He had still not turned to face her. 'I'm not fool enough to walk the streets of Edinburgh at night with a gun in my pocket.'

Trask heard her footfalls moving behind him. Moments later she took a seat on the next bench, folding her body on to it so that she could lean back and watch him. A scarf concealed most of her face, but he could see that she had changed, even before she let the material drop. Only her voice was the same. It was odd, knowing that it was her yet looking at the features of another. The cosmetics that she had applied lent her face some individuality, but it still looked unfinished.

'Was it hard?' he asked.

'There was . . . pain.'

That wasn't what Trask had meant, but he let it go. Anyway, if she was talking with him then she was one step removed from killing him, and he wanted to avoid that if at all possible.

'I thought robots couldn't feel pain.'

'I'm not a robot.'

'Mechs, then. Whatever. I mean, you're not – '

Trask paused. He wasn't sure what he wanted to say, or even if he should say it.

Meia finished the sentence for him. 'Alive?'

'Yes. I mean, no. I . . .'

He trailed off. It was wrong to say that Meia was not alive when she clearly had life of some kind. She had emotions too, but could an artificial life-form be programmed to feel or did it just imitate emotions, making all the right sounds and expressions but, in fact, experiencing nothing?

'Pain was not part of our design,' she said.

'Then why do you feel it?'

'I don't know.'

'Are you sure it was real?'

Meia smiled bleakly.

'Yes, it was real.'

They were silent for a time. Finally Trask spoke.

'That's very peculiar,' he said.

'Yes, it is. It's why we were marked for destruction. Our designers believed that there was a flaw in our programming, that our emotions were a – what is the word? – a "glitch".'

'And what do you believe?'

'I believe that I am alive, and all sentient beings have the capacity to develop. My feelings are real, because I am real.'

She looked at Trask. Her eyes were still the same as well, he realised; her eyes and her voice, and both were filled with a depth of emotion that could not be counterfeited. When Trask spoke again, he did so softly.

'Earlier, when I asked if it was hard, I meant losing your face, losing your identity.'

'My face is not my identity,' said Meia. 'My identity lies within. I have a soul.'

Bloody hell, thought Trask, we're on strange ground here, make no mistake about it.

'Do you believe in God?' Meia asked him.

'Sometimes,' said Trask. 'I lost my faith after your lot appeared, but sometimes it still surfaces.'

'Do you believe that you have a soul?'

'Yes, I suppose I do. But – and no offence meant here – I wasn't made in a laboratory, or built in a factory, or however you were put together.'

'You were created in the factory of the womb. You are an assemblage of cells, just as I am.'

'But your creators were the Illyri.'

'The Illyri simply put my cells together in the correct order. What I am made from came into being with the birth of the Universe, just as the materials of your body did. The Illyri did not make the matter of the Universe, and neither did humanity. We both come from elsewhere.'

Trask nodded. Very strange ground. Very strange ground indeed.

'Does this mean that you're not going to kill me after all?' he asked. Throughout their conversation, the little pulser in Meia's right hand had not wavered from its position. It had remained pointing at him throughout.

'No,' said Meia. 'It will take more than that to save you.'

'Why do you want to kill me?'

'I gave instructions. Lord Andrus was not to be touched.'

'With respect, you're in no position to give instructions to anyone.'

'You don't understand.'

'No, *you* don't understand. In case you haven't noticed, the Illyri are burning and killing their way through Scotland. We haven't seen oppression like this since the early days of the invasion. Your beloved Lord Andrus is in charge here, and the buck stops with him. He's a legitimate target – more than legitimate. We'll be doing humanity a favour if we wipe him from the face of the earth. Althea says he's not the same anyway; she says he's changed.'

Trask took a deep breath to calm himself. It didn't seem wise to shout at someone who had a weapon levelled at him, but for the first time Meia's resolve faltered.

'Althea?' she said, thrown. 'When did you speak to Althea?'

'This morning,' said Trask, and he gave a dull laugh, 'when she woke me up with a truly dreadful cup of tea. She's back, or did you miss that, Spymistress?'

Meia knew of the old affair between Trask and Syl's governess, yet nothing had been heard from Althea since she left for the Marque with Syl and Ani. In her own way Meia missed her, for while Althea had been quiet she had also been smart, and unfailingly loyal to those about whom she cared – and she'd cared about Meia. Not many among Lord Andrus's staff had.

'Where is she now?' she asked.

'At the castle. Watching and listening, as always. The killings would be far worse without the intelligence Althea provides, but of course you've missed all that too.'

'No,' said Meia, and her hand steadied on the weapon. 'I have seen it. I was in the Highlands. I watched burnings and murders. Where possible, I did what I could to stop them, even to the point of killing Securitats. But the Andrus I know would not act in this way. He is not as he once was: I admit as much. Perhaps what has happened to him can be undone, perhaps not. But I also owe him a debt of loyalty beyond anything you can comprehend, and for that reason, and that reason alone, he is not to be harmed. If another attempt is made on his life, I will make all involved pay dearly.'

Trask frowned, and any remaining affection for her vanished from his face.

'Was it you who killed the sniper?' he asked.

'His name was Benton and, yes, I killed him. He felt nothing, and he wanted to die anyway. It was an act of mercy.'

'I know his bloody name! I sent him to do it!'

'Which is why you're only a couple of breaths away from being killed in turn.'

Trask closed his eyes.

'Shoot, then. Just do it and stop babbling at me.'

'Open your eyes.'

Trask kept them closed for a few seconds more, then did as she told him.

'Why? So you can look into them as you shoot me?'

'No. So that, if I let you live, I'll know we're in agreement. Tell me, Trask: why did the Green Man tell you that he wanted a senior Diplomat captured and brought to him at Dundearg?'

Trask answered reluctantly.

'He said that the Illyri were developing some kind of new Chip. He spoke about biomechanics. He said that it could change the course of the conflict, and it was important that he got a look at it. We heard whispers, though. They spoke of something medical, an infection.'

'The Green Man lied to you, or perhaps he was just mistaken. Certain senior Diplomats, Consul Gradus included, were carrying something new in their skulls, but it wasn't an enhanced Chip.'

'What was it, then?'

'A life-form. An unknown organism. It may have infected Andrus – his own daughter sent me word that he was compromised before she was exiled.'

Trask's confusion was reflected on his face. 'But why? Was that the infection? Where does it come from?'

'I don't know, but I've been trying to find out. Lord Andrus may be able to provide some of those answers, but he can't if he's dead. Listen to me: I believe that these things, whatever they are, represent a threat to both the Illyri and humanity. There is much going on here that we do not understand. I need space to do what needs to be done, to uncover the truth. I cannot waste my time second-guessing the Resistance.'

Trask was thinking. He was a bright man. It was why Meia liked him, and why, if she had to, she would kill him before she left the zoo.

'Those rumours of people going missing,' he said, 'do they have something to do with this?'

Meia considered lying, but opted instead to tell the truth. She needed Trask. Only a handful of humans and Illyri knew precisely what had happened at Dundearg, and they were either being hunted, like Fremd and Maeve Buchanan, or were far from Earth, like Syl, Ani, and the Kerr brothers. Meia could not continue alone.

'At the Eden Project in Cornwall I witnessed countless bodies – both human and mammalian – being used as seeding beds for something, but back then I wasn't sure what it could be. Anyway, it's all gone now. I am the only one who saw it.'

'We have to warn people,' said Trask.

Meia was expecting this.

'Warn them about what?' she said. 'We know next to nothing. And if we reveal our suspicions now and cause a panic, the Diplomats and their Securitats will act, and what will follow will make the scouring of the Highlands seem like a gentle rebuke. It may even lead to the destruction of this planet.'

Trask rubbed his face with his hands. The action made his eyes water.

'We've had word from across the globe,' he said. 'The Corps is withdrawing its Diplomats on a daily basis and not replacing them.'

'I know.'

'Pretty soon there won't be a senior Diplomat left on Earth,' said Trask. 'We had started to hope.'

'Hope what?'

'That we'd won. That the Illyri were leaving.'

'They are leaving, but you have not won. We were all misled. The Conquest was only the first step. The true invasion has not yet begun.'

Trask noticed that the zoo had gone silent, as though something of what they were discussing, a hint of their fears and the consequences if they were correct about it, had communicated itself to the animals.

Meia lowered her weapon.

'Trask,' she said, 'I trust you. Now you have to trust me.'

CHAPTER 38

So Meia and Trask settled down to talk. They had no fear of being apprehended by the Illyri. Trask had entered the zoo unaccompanied, for that was his agreement with Meia: their working relationship was a matter for them alone, especially now that she was being hunted just as much, if not more, than the members of the Resistance. But the roads to and from the zoo were being monitored by his people and, as a sign of the faith that he had in them, his daughters were inside the zoo perimeter. They were under strict instructions not to approach the old raven cages, not unless half the Illyri forces in Scotland suddenly descended from the skies.

'I heard whispers that you made it to Iceland,' said Trask.

'They were true,' said Meia. 'The Highland Resistance arranged to move me between a series of fishing boats. The Green Man helped.'

'How is he?'

'Alive. Maeve too.'

'I'm glad.'

Trask took a swig from his hip flask. He didn't bother to offer it to Meia. She'd never accepted it in the past, and now that he knew she was a Mech, he understood why.

'I was surprised to hear that the Green Man was an Illyri,' said Trask. 'Shocked, even. Still doesn't make much sense to me.'

'We're not all bad.'

'Do you still think of yourself as one of them?'

'I'm not sure. Even before they began hunting me, I always felt like an outsider. But I had their skin, and their eyes, and I fought for their Conquest.'

'Complicated,' said Trask. 'It's a wonder you didn't blow a circuit.'

'Is that supposed to be a joke?'

'Maybe. What were you doing in Iceland?'

'I was curious to know why the Corps had sealed off the whole island nation.'

'And what did you find?'

'The ruins of a research facility at Dimmuborgir. Parts of it were still smouldering. I also discovered bodies in the volcanic caves. Lots of bodies. Hundreds of them. Teenagers mostly, but also older men and women. Some children too. All torn apart.'

Trask had another drink. It seemed appropriate.

'We'd lost contact with the Resistance in Iceland,' he said.

'That might explain why.'

'Any Illyri left?'

'A handful – mostly Securitats and a few junior Corps aides.'

'Did you manage to interrogate any of them?'

'One. His name was Suris. He was among those who torched the Illyri base there.'

'And what did he have to say about it?'

'He was little more than a janitor, but he said that humans were brought into that facility and didn't come out. Quarantine procedures were in place for them. He never saw the laboratories at the core.'

'He could have been lying.'

'No,' said Meia, 'he was not. Well, maybe at the start, but not by the end. He said the scientists left once they were certain that the facility was burning.'

Trask stared at his hands.

'I'd like to have had a few hours alone with the Illyri bastards who killed those people.'

'There are doubtless similar facilities elsewhere,' said Meia. 'If we could pull together all of the rumours about them, we might have a better picture of what was, or still is, happening. Not that it matters. As I said, I visited the Eden Project some time ago now. I believe what I saw inside the laboratories was evidence of attempted implantations. They were seeding human beings with an unknown alien species, but they kept failing.'

Trask wiped his face with the back of his arm and stared away into the middle distance. He blinked rapidly, opening his mouth as if to speak, but then shutting it again.

'If it's any consolation,' said Meia, 'the Illyri I found in Iceland are all dead now.'

'Well, that's something, I suppose.'

'It seemed like the least that I could do.'

'And yet the evidence is gone, up in smoke along with the entire Eden Project too,' said Trask. 'They claimed that the fire at Eden started accidentally, but I suppose I know better after what you've told me.'

Meia said nothing.

'What will they do with us?' Trask asked.

'I think that they will kill you all. Every human being. Every life-form on Earth.'

'Jesus.'

Meia turned to face him directly, and her unblinking eyes were unnerving.

'Trask, I need your help. I have to get off this planet.'

'Are you deserting the sinking ship too?'

'They will find me if I stay here, and if I am captured I can be of no help to you.'

'And you can be of more help to us billions of miles away?'

He could not keep the scepticism from his voice.

'Trask, you have no idea who I really am, or what I am capable of,' said Meia. 'All you have is my name. You can't even say that you recognise my face any longer. But I promise you, if you help me to escape from Earth, I will do everything I can to save your people and your world. Right now, Earth is about to become like Iceland: a sealed-off island where the Illyri can do as they please, and that means any help has to come from outside. Am I making myself clear?'

'Not really,' said Trask.

'You are a frustrating man.'

'I know. But it doesn't matter if I get what you say or not: I have to trust you. I don't have much choice, do I? What do you want me to do?'

'I want you to do what you do best: I want you to attack the Illyri, and I have one particular Illyri in mind . . .'

Later, when she was gone from the zoo, Trask remained seated on his bench, smoking and drinking. Eventually his daughters came looking for him, fearing that he might be dead, but they still did not approach him directly. Instead they spoke his name when they were sure that he was within earshot.

'Dad?' Nessa hissed. 'Dad, are you okay?'

He heard her voice and grinned. Even when she was trying to be quiet, Nessa was loud. He loved that about her: her confidence, her brashness. Just as with her size, it was how she had been made, and she luxuriated in it. Nessa was happier in her skin than anyone else he knew, and he was glad. That didn't mean she couldn't be hurt. She had her tender spots and insecurities, just like any other girl her age, but they were not the obvious ones. A boy could call her fat and she would not even blink. She'd take his head off, aye, but only to teach him a lesson about keeping his opinions to himself, and because she didn't like the way he'd said 'fat'.

Jean – she was a different matter. Lord, but he didn't know where she'd come from. She was quiet where her sister was loud, and always seeking the insult that she believed lay buried at the heart of any compliment. A rage burned inside her, a kind of madness, but he had no idea what its source might be. Jean had simply been born angry.

Trask blamed her mother.

'I'm fine,' he answered. 'Come out here where I can see you.'

The two girls emerged from the shadows and stood watching their father uncertainly. Trask patted either side of the bench beside him.

'Sit down for a moment. Sit down with your dad.'

They did as he asked, exchanging glances as they did so. Their father didn't even like them to sit in the same room as him as he watched his old movies – westerns, mostly, or gangster films. He claimed that they put him off because he knew they didn't appreciate them. The only time they sat together on a regular basis was at Resistance cell meetings.

And now Trask was putting his arms around their shoulders, pulling them to him. He kissed each of them softly on the head – Nessa first, then Jean. Something wet dripped on to Nessa's face. It was a teardrop. Their father was crying.

'What is it, Dad?' Nessa asked.

'The end of things,' he replied, and would say no more.

CHAPTER 39

Danis was surprised to receive the summons to the Archmage Syrene's presence in her chambers at Edinburgh Castle – surprised, but also resigned to whatever had been decided for him. He was tired of being a virtual prisoner in the castle, allowed to retain his rank but none of his power, and entirely cut off from Lord Andrus, who had been both his governor and his friend. Oh, Lord Andrus might still be a Military governor in name, but the real force behind the throne was Syrene, and Syrene's loyalties lay with the Diplomatic Corps. No, that wasn't entirely true: Syrene's loyalties, Danis knew, were to herself first, the Sisterhood second, and the Corps third. Everything else came fourth, although Danis felt it was unlikely that there was anything else, as far as Syrene was concerned, so it was a moot point.

Sickened, he had watched Andrus and Syrene walking arm-in-arm through the grounds like the lovers they undoubtedly were, even though they retained separate quarters. It didn't take her long to forget her late husband Gradus, thought Danis, yet she tricked my daughter into her damned Sisterhood out of revenge for his death, leaving my wife bitter with loss and grief, and me as a ghost haunting the castle walls. Then before they could even start sifting the ruins of Dundearg for Gradus's ashes, she was already warming the governor's bed.

Andrus was no longer the Illyri that Danis had once known and loved. He still spoke like Andrus and laughed like Andrus – in fact he laughed rather too much nowadays, like a giddy child – but there was a vacancy to his eyes. It was like peering through the windows of a room in which most of the lights had been extinguished. He always greeted Danis with great warmth if they happened to pass in a hallway, but it was a politician's greeting, and Danis was not entirely sure that Andrus really remembered who he was. In fact, Danis was not certain if Andrus any longer truly recalled who Andrus was. Danis was convinced that Andrus was either drugged or under some more sinister form of influence from Syrene, a suspicion confirmed for him by Andrus's refusal to be examined by anyone but Dr Hemet, the head of the Securitat's Scientific Development Division.

So Danis wandered the hallways and courtyards of Edinburgh Castle, his freedom of movement restricted for his 'safety', his head low, his body slumped, mourning the loss of his only daughter Ani to the bowels of the Marque. The whispered conversations that followed after him indicated that he had become estranged from his wife Fian, and they now occupied separate bedrooms. He was, to all intents and purposes, a broken figure, a cracked relic of an old order. It was no longer even clear why Andrus chose to keep him in Edinburgh. Even senior Diplomats on Earth, who had long disliked Danis, thought that he should be permitted to return to Illyr and live out his last days on the homeworld. They felt only pity for him now, and pity is a cheap emotion, easily spent. Poor Danis, they said. How could it ever have been that we feared an old scarecrow such as he?

But wiser heads had a different theory. It was Syrene's doing, they said. Although she had deprived Danis of a daughter, and caused Andrus to make him little more than a comfortable prisoner in an ancient castle, she did not trust the veteran soldier and was well aware of his influence among the Military. A human proverb came to mind: keep your friends close but your enemies closer still.

Meanwhile Danis shuffled along, seemingly heedless of it all, his gaze perhaps fixed on another place, another time, or indeed no place or time at all but only the welcome nothingness that death at last would bring.

Now the summons had come. What would it be, Danis mused, as he trudged slowly towards Syrene's chambers? Exile to some godforsaken world at the edge of a remote wormhole, there to succumb to an alien disease for which no cure existed because no one had any idea of the existence of the disease itself? They could put his organs in a jar after he died and examine slivers of them to determine the cause of his death, find an antidote, and add another alien virus to their growing list. Some laboratory assistant from the Scientific Development Division would joke that old Danis had finally done something useful in the end: he had died.

Or they could simply send him to one of the hellholes on Earth: Nigeria, perhaps, now overrun by radical Muslims who preached that the Illyri were created by the devil, not Allah, and it was the duty of all men of good faith to slaughter them at any and every opportunity. Or maybe Texas and New Mexico, where Christian preachers had come to the same conclusion, and were only a short step away from mounting full militia assaults on Illyri bases. Or one of the breakaway Russian republics, where religion, nationalism, and a hatred for both the alien invaders and the Russian president, who had allied himself to the Illyri in the hope of increasing his own power, had resulted in an all-out war that was reducing entire cities to rubble.

The situation on Earth had deteriorated catastrophically in a matter of months, and the Corps and the tamed Military were simply sitting by and watching it all happen. It was almost as though they wanted to see the planet tear itself apart, even if it meant the loss of Illyri lives along the way. Not that any senior Corps officials were at risk – most of them had already left. Only the Securitats remained, conducting their own dark campaign of secret and not-so-secret slaughter.

Danis was so lost in his thoughts that he found himself at Syrene's door before he even realised it. Two of her handmaidens guarded the entrance to her chambers – nasty little things, glowing in the reflected power of their mistress. One in particular, Cocile, gave Danis the creeps. She had a way of looking at him like he was a bug that had bitten her foot. On either side of the Novices stood two guards: Securitats, not Military. The old castle guard had been disbanded once Peris left, to be replaced by these killers of children. None of them spoke to him, or even acknowledged his presence. The door was simply opened by Cocile, and Danis stepped into the Archmage's chambers.

They were dark, as always. Syrene kept the windows covered, the drapes drawn. Danis knew that she disliked Edinburgh and did not wish to look upon it. She was standing at a table on which sat a bottle of cremos and two glasses. Her hands were clasped just below her stomach. She wore a vibrant red gown, and her head was bare.

'Thank you for coming, Danis,' she said.

'I was ordered to come, not requested,' he replied. He had long ago given up any but the barest pretence of civility towards Syrene.

'Nevertheless. May I offer you a drink?'

'Is it poisoned?'

She ignored him. He was so unimportant to her that she couldn't even pay him the compliment of mild irritation. His attempts to annoy Syrene seemed only to amuse her, which made him redouble his efforts.

Syrene poured herself a glass of the liquor and drank from it. She frowned. Her mouth opened. A small harsh rattle emerged from her throat.

And for an instant, Danis had hope.

Then Syrene smiled.

'It's a little young, that's all,' she said. 'It should have been put down for a few years longer. Why, did you think someone might have done you the favour of killing me?'

Danis did not answer. Insubordination was one thing, treason entirely another.

Syrene poured him a glass and handed it to him. He accepted. Too young or not, he wasn't about to turn down cremos from the Archmage's private cellar. She raised her glass in a toast, but Danis didn't join her in it. He just emptied half of his measure in one swallow. It wasn't harsh at all. Danis had drunk rotgut distilled by soldiers in fuel vats, so he knew harsh liquor when he tried it.

'What are we celebrating?' he asked.

'It is a dual celebration,' Syrene replied. 'One professional, one personal. We'll come to those in a moment. First, I have a small gift for you.'

She reached into the folds of her robes and produced a silver disk.

'A report on the progress of your daughter,' she said. 'There are some images too. As you will see, she is doing well and making friends. I thought you and your wife would like to have this.'

She handed the disk to Danis. After only the slightest hesitation, he accepted it. His daughter had been a source of frustration to him for her entire life, yet now he missed her more than he could ever have imagined. Althea had shared with him what she knew of Ani, and had reassured him that all was well with her, but it was no substitute for having her near.

'Thank you,' he said, and found that he meant the words.

'It is nothing, merely a mark of my esteem. Now, let us proceed to celebrations. The first is to do with you. I know that you have felt excluded by the recent turn of events. I am sorry for that, and Lord Andrus even more so. With that in mind, you are to be returned to active duty.'

'Really?' he said.

'I thought you would be more pleased.'

'Where are you sending me: Bogotá, Afghanistan, Chechnya?'

Syrene shook her head.

'You are not being sent anywhere. You are staying here. You are to be appointed Acting Governor of the United Kingdom and Ireland, with additional responsibility for all of Europe. You will be answerable to Junior Consul Steyr, who now has overall command of the continent, and of course to Marshal Vena and her Securitats, but neither will interfere as long as you maintain control. Congratulations, Governor.'

Danis almost dropped his glass in shock. Acting Governor? Steyr was bright but inexperienced, and not the worst of the Corps officials on Earth by any means. Vena, though, was a monster, and her workhorse Cynna was pure evil. The only consolation was that Vena was now based at the old Nazi fortress of Akershus in Oslo, Norway

– at least when she wasn't scouring the Highlands trying to track down the Resistance and the Mech, Meia.

'If I am to be Acting Governor, what is to happen to Lord Andrus?' he asked.

'Lord Andrus will soon be returning to Illyr, with me. Which brings us to the second cause for celebration.'

She smiled.

'Dearest?' she called.

The door to her chambers opened and Andrus entered. He shook Danis's hand with his usual false good cheer, and went to stand by Syrene's side. The Nairene gave him her hand and Andrus pressed it to his lips, then they smiled at each other.

'Lord Andrus and I are to be married,' said Syrene.

This time, Danis did drop his glass.

CHAPTER 40

Danis returned to his rooms. His wife was not present. He did not know where she was. Since Althea had returned, Fian had taken to walking the streets surrounding the Royal Mile with her, and the pair of them were as thick as thieves, reminding him, not without a twinge in his heart, of his daughter and her best friend, Syl. He had tried to convince them not to wander, but his wife would not listen, and Althea brushed his worries aside with a smile and nothing more. When the guards at the gate attempted to stop Fian from leaving, at his request, she shouted and screamed and made a scene so dreadful that, in the end, it was easier just to let her go with Althea despite the possible risk of kidnapping, attack, or even assassination. It was cold consolation that such risks were lessened now that the Securitats prowled Edinburgh in numbers.

Their relationship felt broken, or if not broken then certainly stretched to breaking point. Perhaps the report about Ani might help. Danis badly wanted to view it immediately, to see his daughter's face, but he decided to wait. He and Fian would watch it together.

Now that he was back in his own space, he tried to come to terms with what he had heard in Syrene's quarters. A governorship with immediate effect, for Syrene and Andrus planned to leave for Illyr the next morning.

And marriage! But he could understand the reason for that, at least in political terms: a formal alliance between the Sisterhood and the most respected Illyri Military official on Earth would deal a severe blow to those in the Military who still sought to curb the power of the Diplomatic Corps. As Syrene announced the news to Danis,

Andrus wore the happy but confused look of a man who had won a lottery but couldn't remember buying a ticket. If love entered into it, then it was not any love that Danis could understand.

His appointment to the governorship was more confusing still. Syrene knew that Danis was no friend of the Corps or the Sisterhood, and Steyr was too wet behind the ears to be able to control a wily old operator like him. Then again, Danis was a soldier, not a politician. Andrus had been both, which was a rare talent, but Danis was not sure that he could successfully rule as governor. He had no idea where to start. Maybe he would need Steyr's help after all, if only to keep Vena and her Securitats in check.

Britain was at a tipping point, and being governor of the region was potentially a dark command, a poisoned chalice. The actions of the Securitats in Scotland had led to an increase in Resistance activity that was spreading across the country. As governor, he would be required to hunt down those responsible and hand them over to the Securitats for interrogation, imprisonment, and possibly execution, for capital punishment by hanging or firing squad had recently been restored for all crimes involving Illyri fatalities. It applied to anyone over the age of fifteen, although the youngest person executed so far was eighteen, and until recently nobody had yet been executed in Britain or Ireland – not officially anyway. Reports suggested that the Securitats were not so particular about what they did in their basement cells, however, and the strangulated bodies of captured Resistance fighters were now being dumped in Glasgow's Craigton Cemetery on a regular basis.

Danis wondered if he could convince Steyr to suspend capital punishment. It was doing more harm than good. But, again, he came back to his unsettling belief that elements in the Corps and the Securitats *wanted* chaos and anarchy. Their violence made the humans respond more violently in turn, leading to even harsher measures being introduced against them, onwards and onwards in a great spiral of brutality. Danis could try to bring a halt to it, but he didn't have much hope of success. He concluded that he was being made governor because it was an impossible job. He was being punished with promotion.

A noise came from behind him. Perhaps his wife had returned, although he had not heard the door open. He turned. A hooded figure stood in the centre of his living room, the lower half of its face hidden by a scarf. In one hand it held a rough piece of electronic equipment, all tangled wires and circuitry; in the other, a pulser, which was pointing at him.

'Hello, General Danis,' said the visitor.

He recognised the voice immediately.

'Meia,' he said. 'I wondered when you'd show up. And that's *Governor* Danis to you . . .'

Meia took a chair across from Danis, after he had briefly explained the reason for his sudden promotion, and told her of the impending marriage between Andrus and Syrene. In response, she merely stared at him until it got uncomfortable.

'You can put the weapon away,' he said, breaking the tension. 'I don't know why you felt the need to bring it anyway.'

'It wasn't for you – not unless you forced me to use it.'

'Hardly likely. Given the current state of affairs, you almost count as a friend. Almost.'

She lowered the pulser, but did not get rid of it, holding it by her side instead. She pulled the scarf from her face. The features were not yet fully formed, but Danis could see a distinct visage starting to emerge. It was like looking at a face distorted by mist. It struck him as familiar, although he could not place it.

'I see you're changing your appearance.'

'It seemed wise.'

'It's a pity that your personality remains intact.'

'Likewise.'

He indicated the device in her hand. 'A surveillance blocker?'

'I assumed that they would be monitoring you.'

'I think they've given up. I'm no longer that interesting – or I thought I wasn't until I was notified of my governorship.'

'Congratulations. I'm sure your reign will be long and prosperous.'

'Doubtful. By the way, I didn't mention how surprised I am to find you here, which is what I believe one is supposed to say in these situations. I thought that the Securitats had discovered all of your rat runs under the castle.'

'I'm sure that they tried, but these stones are old and thick. They can hide a multitude of secrets.'

Danis sat back on his couch.

'Why are you here, Meia? If you want me to help you get away from Scotland, then I'll do what I can, but all flights off this island are being monitored: retinal scans, body searches, even tissue samples. Vena wants you very, very badly. The best thing for you might be to find somewhere deep beneath this castle, put yourself into "sleep" mode, and wait for her to die.'

'That wasn't my first plan.'

'I didn't think so. Again, what is it you want?'

'To tell you what I know, and what I suspect. And you, in turn, can confirm for me the location of various Illyri within the castle.'

Meia had not expected Syrene to be leaving Earth so soon. Her plan had called for more time, but now she would have only one night.

'You came to me about this, and not Lord Andrus? He loved you, you know. You were like a child to him.'

'Lord Andrus is not . . . *himself*, as you are no doubt aware.'

'That red bitch has drugged him, that's what I think.'

'No,' said Meia. 'She has done something far worse.'

And she told Danis of all that she had learned.

Far beyond the castle walls, Trask began gathering his people. He had fewer of them to call on than before because the Securitats were doing their work well: three Resistance members dead in the last week alone, and twice as many again imprisoned. For each operative that the Illyri captured, more were often betrayed, their identities obtained through torture or, when that failed, threats to wives, husbands and children. These were not idle threats either: Trask had seen the bodies, dumped at the outskirts of the city with their identity cards stuffed in their mouths. It helped with putting names to the corpses, because the Securitats' torturers quickly progressed to the face.

The Resistance would have lost more people if it weren't for its strict cell structure. Operatives at the lower level only knew three others. One of them, the most senior, then reported to another cell of four, and so on up the chain. It made it harder for traitors to infiltrate the Resistance, and protected the majority in the event of the capture of one or two.

But the Illyri were slowly and surely working their way up the command structure.

What if he himself were captured? What if he were killed? He was one of only a handful of men and women who knew what the Illyri might be planning for all life on his planet, and that knowledge would die with him. Yet Meia had warned him to remain silent, while Trask's instinct had been to broadcast the news as widely as possible, to force humanity to rise up against the Illyri. And what then? Meia was certain that it would simply accelerate whatever was about to occur, and there was nowhere for humanity to hide. The human race was trapped on Earth, just as assuredly as if it had been sealed under a glass dome. The Illyri could do with it as they wished.

And now Trask was gambling what was left of his Resistance force on a plan to aid Meia's escape: a series of near-simultaneous strikes against the Illyri, with the last of them the most daring and dangerous of all, just so a mechanical spy with vague promises of help could slip through the net. Still, Trask told himself, a vague promise of help was better than no hope of help at all.

When he was done, he returned to the zoo to wait for Meia. He arrived early and walked among the enclosures, silently watching the animals. He felt that he would not be returning here any time soon, and perhaps might never see it again.

Meia came. She looked different. That half-formed mannequin's face was gone. He could tell from the skin around her eyes, even though her headscarf hid her features from the cheekbones down. He also saw marks around the knuckles of her right hand, like surgical scars on her ProGen skin.

'You hurt yourself?' he asked.

'Upgrades, you might say.'

She gave him a time for the action to begin and made him detail the preparations he had already made, advising him to make changes where she believed it necessary. His head hurt by the end of it all.

'Is that it?' he said. 'You don't want me to carry you personally on to a ship and blow you a kiss as you leave? To be honest, I think I'll be happy to see you go after all this.'

'Not quite.'

She told him that a new governor would soon be in charge of Britain: Danis.

While Trask was still absorbing this information, Meia suddenly moved closer to him, and a tiny voice in his head said, *This is it. This is where she kills me. And after all we've been through together.*

But no blade pierced him, and no pulse blasted his organs. Meia simply hugged him, and after a moment he hugged her back.

'If they could see us now,' he said, and she laughed in his ear.

'I have one more favour to ask,' she said, her voice muffled by the material of the scarf. 'Well, two actually.'

'As if you haven't asked for enough already.'

'If I can help you, all this will seem like a small price.'

'And if you can't, then it won't matter anyway.'

'Exactly.'

Trask sighed heavily. 'So what else do you want?'

'Firstly, send Althea my regards. And tell her I'm sorry that I did not get to see her.'

'I will, but that's already two favours.'

Meia stared at him, unamused, until he relented.

'Sure, of course I'll tell her,' he said. 'But what next? A pint of blood? A kidney? My firstborn?'

'Simply that you take no action against Governor Danis,' she replied. 'No assassination attempts, no attacks on his staff, no RPGs aimed at ships entering or leaving the castle in the hope of a lucky strike on him. Danis is to be left unharmed, and I want the word spread discreetly to *all* Resistance leaders on this island. Treat Danis as you would your own father.'

'My father is long dead,' said Trask. He fumbled in his pockets for his cigarettes, opened the pack, and found it empty. It was one of those nights. He crushed the pack and stuffed it into his pocket again.

'And tell me,' he said, 'why would I do something so foolish as to try and convince the Resistance that their primary target on this island is not actually a target at all?'

'Because Danis knows,' said Meia. 'He *knows*.'

Danis was alone. He had not moved from his couch, not even when Meia slipped away and left him. He had been vaguely aware of the noise of a stone shifting, but he paid little attention to it.

He felt a range of emotions: bafflement, rage, shame. If Meia was right, his race was about to commit a crime without parallel in the history of civilisation: the sacrifice of an entire planet and every species that lived upon it to an alien parasite. Genocide, but more than genocide: mass extinction.

And the final twist: they had made him governor of a people that would soon cease to exist, and he would die with them, for Danis was certain that none of the Corps' enemies on Earth would be permitted to leave before the infestation began. In its final days, the planet would be returned to Military rule, and not a single Securitat or minor Corps functionary would be present for the destruction of all life upon it.

The door opened, and his wife appeared.

'I heard the news about Andrus and Syrene,' she said.

She gave no sign of approval or disapproval. Such matters no longer concerned her. Danis stood and took her hands in his.

'I've been waiting for you to return,' he said. 'I have something to show you.'

Danis made her join him on the couch. He waved his right hand, and a three-dimensional image of Ani appeared before them and began to move. They watched it together, and for a time they were at peace.

CHAPTER 41

The two black shuttles stood at the base of Beinn Dorain, a peak in Glen Auch, halfway between the Bridge of Orchy and Tyndrum in the Scottish Highlands. A steady rain fell on the squad of Securitats who had finished their cursory search of the mountain and come up with nothing. Cynna watched them unhappily.

'We were misled,' said her sergeant.

His name was Seft, and he wore a dark slicker over his uniform to protect him from the rain. It was not regulation attire, but Cynna did not concern herself with such details. Those under her command followed her orders to the letter, and that was enough. They were trigger-happy killers of men, women and children, and none of them ever lost a night's sleep over what they did.

The information they had received was believed to be cast-iron in its reliability and accuracy. It came from one of their most trusted informants, a bartender named Preston down in Merchiston who had fed them a number of Resistance members over recent months – minor operatives for the most part, although Cynna was convinced that bigger fish would follow if they were patient with him. So when the bartender told her that he had a lead on the Green Man, Cynna prepared her squad and flew at dawn to Glen Auch, where the Green Man was rumoured to be meeting with two other leaders of the Highland Resistance in a copse by the southern foot of the mountain.

But Preston, it seemed, had been misled. The terrain was grim and damp, and empty of any life worth the name as far as Cynna could tell. She would have to arrange a discreet interview with Preston upon her return to Edinburgh, in the course of which he would learn the importance of accuracy in his information.

Unfortunately, although Cynna did not yet know it, that interview was destined never to happen. Preston was dead, but he was persuaded to make that final call to his Illyri paymasters before he was disposed of – 'to atone for your sins', as Trask's voice had whispered to him in his last moments.

'Let's get out of here,' said Cynna. 'We've wasted enough time already.'

She was halfway to her shuttle when the first RPG struck it, entering through the open cabin door and exploding as it hit the interior. The heavy hull contained most of the blast, which was good news for the Securitats in the vicinity but bad news for the pilots inside. Another RPG struck the plating of the second shuttle, rocking it on its landing skids but leaving it otherwise unharmed. Cynna heard gunfire, and suddenly the ground was opening up around them as the Resistance fighters emerged from the pits in which they had hidden themselves, the holes concealed by squares of wood camouflaged with mats of turf. Her Securitats responded with full pulse blasts, but half of them had already been cut down before they could activate their weapons, and were lying dead or injured on the ground.

But the surviving Securitats' training kicked in. They laid down covering fire while the injured were helped to the remaining shuttle, which had already powered up its engines. Once they were off the ground, the shuttle's cannon and missile array could rain down fire on the Resistance fighters, and they would be torn apart. For now, though, the priority was to get everyone into the air.

'Quickly!' Cynna shouted as the last of her troops ran for the shuttle. 'Go! Go!'

She drew a bead on a dark-haired young woman carrying a semiautomatic rifle, and fired. The pulse took the woman full in the chest, knocking her off her feet and destroying her internal organs. Bullets whined around them, kicking sparks from the shuttle and dirt from the ground, but Cynna remained unharmed. Behind her, the shuttle rose a foot from the ground. What was left of her squad was now safely on board. It was time to leave. They would come back for the bodies of the dead later, and in force. An example would be made of the people of Tyndrum for what had happened here this morning: two – no, four – of theirs for every one of hers who had died. That seemed fair.

Cynna twisted her body and placed one foot on the skid. A hand reached down to pull her up, and then her body spasmed as two dart-like electrodes hooked on to her back. The pulses penetrated her body armour, shocking her repeatedly, like a series of punches landing so fast as to feel almost like one. Cynna fell back as the shuttle continued to ascend, landing on her side, her body still jerking, the wires from the darts trailing behind her along the ground. She bit her tongue as the pulses kept coming, and then suddenly, thankfully, they stopped. Now she was being dragged across the damp grass, and her head lolled as she was pulled under the ground.

The last thing she saw before the trapdoor closed was the shuttle exploding as the mine that had been attached to its underbelly did its work. The earth shook as the wreckage landed above her. Strong arms held her down, and she felt suddenly claustrophobic. This was what it was like to be buried alive.

Then the trapdoor opened again. A face looked down on her: an Illyri face.

'I hear that you've been looking for me,' said Fremd. 'I am the Green Man.'

The message came through to the Resistance in Edinburgh. They had Cynna. Now another call was made to the Securitats, this time by one of the Resistance's own agents, a woman named Hilary Simmons whose dangerous job it was to feed false information to the Illyri when possible. Simmons was old, and dying of cancer. If the Illyri discovered her game, then so be it. She knew no names, and her instructions came in the form of messages left under a stone in Princes Street Gardens. Let them do with her what they wanted. She didn't care.

'It was a trap,' she said, when her call was put through to one of Vena's lieutenants.

'We know that now, you old fool!' came the reply. 'That would have been of help an hour ago.'

'But there's more,' Simmons whispered. 'I heard them say that she wanted Cynna taken alive, and something about a facial scan.'

'What? Who? Who wanted Cynna captured alive?'

'Oh, what was the name again?' Simmons hummed and hawed. 'May-something? Meia. Does that sound right? They said Meia wanted Cynna taken alive.'

The second attack came in the form of a series of car bombs close to the old Glasgow School of Art on Renfrew Street, which was now the headquarters of the Securitats in Scotland, and at Holyrood Park and Calton Hill in Edinburgh. Nobody was injured, for a warning had been phoned in minutes before the attack, and the streets were cleared before the blasts occurred. But they caused traffic chaos, and tied up the Illyri and the police, diverting attention from the area around the castle where the final and most important assault was about to occur.

For as the Archmage Syrene and Lord Andrus, watched by Governor Danis, made their way to the big skimmer idling on the Esplanade, the skimmer that would take them and their retinue offworld for the first leg of their journey back to Illyr, the mortars began to fall in and around the castle. Vena herself should have been in charge of security at the skimmer, supervising as her Securitats prepared to check the identities of everyone intending to board, but Vena was otherwise engaged. She was already en route to Glen Auch to lead the search for Cynna, whose Chip had ceased to function.

The noise and confusion of the mortars distracted everyone. The two Securitats at the skimmer briefly left their posts, their weapons drawn, as though pulsers could be of any help against a low velocity explosive projectile. For a few crucial seconds, all eyes were directed away from the craft on the Esplanade . . .

Now Syrene and Andrus were trapped halfway to the skimmer, frozen briefly by an explosion from close to the gatehouse. Then Andrus's old instincts kicked in, aided by Danis's shouts. They were in real danger if they stayed out in the open, and they were closer to the skimmer than they were to any of the main buildings of the castle that might have provided some protection. He ushered the hand-maidens and a pair of his own junior aides to the skimmer, ignoring the protests of the Securitats at this breach of Vena's protocols, protests that were cut short anyway as more mortar shells landed, this time targeted with precision at the ditch between the gatehouse and the Esplanade. The cabin door closed and the skimmer ascended rapidly as the attackers ceased firing for a time before resuming their barrage.

Five minutes later, the two automatic mortars had been located, targeted, and destroyed by the Illyri from the air. The aiming had been done remotely, and no crews were directly involved, so no Resistance members were killed or captured. But the mortars had been among the most valuable of the Resistance's weapons, and their loss was a considerable blow.

'Tell me, Dad,' asked Nessa, as she and her father watched the smoke rise above the castle, and the shuttles circle the ruined mortars. 'What was all that for? Is it the beginning of something?'

'I hope so, darling,' said Trask. 'For all our sakes.'

CHAPTER 42

Vena walked through the killing site at Glen Auch, counting the bodies and examining the wreckage of the ruined shuttles, while around her a team swept the area for DNA samples, footprints, anything that might be used to track down those responsible and find Cynna. The message from Hilary Simmons had reached her. *Cynna. Meia. A facial scan.* Was it possible that Meia had hoped to create a ProGen face in Cynna's image, and use her new identity to try and escape from Earth? If so, that particular plan was now doomed to failure. Vena had already placed Cynna on a watch list. If someone claiming to be Cynna tried to use her authority to get on board any craft leaving Britain, she would immediately be arrested.

One of the search team called to her.

'Have you found something?' she asked.

'I think so – but not here.'

'What, then?'

'It's Cynna's Chip. It looks like it's been reactivated.'

'Where is she?'

'Just a few miles from here. The beacon says she's at Bridge of Orchy.'

Bridge of Orchy had once been a small but pretty village of mostly white buildings gathered around the historic Bridge of Orchy Hotel, but the hotel had been destroyed when its owner was found to be storing arms for the Resistance, and the surrounding houses burned. No one lived there now, and only the old bridge over the River Orchy still remained intact, built by British forces during the campaign to pacify the warlike Highland clans in the 18th century.

Vena's shuttle swept over the ruined hamlet, but could find no signs of life. She was not about to be ambushed the way that Cynna had, so she ordered seismic detectors to be dropped to determine if there was any activity below ground. The detectors found no trace of movement.

'Where's the signal coming from?' she asked.

'Under the bridge, Commander.'

The shape of the bridge, and its shadows, made it impossible to see what might lie beneath.

'It could be a trap,' she said. 'Send out a drone.'

The shuttle dispatched a small drone fitted with a camera front and back, and sensitive microphones. The drone began to transmit sound and images as soon as it left the shuttle. It went in low over the water, the splashing of the Orchy filling the cabin of the shuttle as the river itself was displayed for Vena. It drew closer to the bridge, then stopped. A shape moved in the darkness.

'Give me some light,' said Vena.

The drone shone a beam into the gloom beneath the bridge. It picked out Cynna's body, hanging by the neck from a rope, her feet almost touching the water flowing below. A hand-lettered sign was pinned to her uniform. It bore one word:

MURDERER

'Meia,' said Vena. 'Meia is responsible for this.'

But she was wrong.

Meia was long gone.

III
TOGETHER

CHAPTER 43

Syl Hellais was not in class.

'She's not feeling well,' explained Ani, when the register was taken. 'She stayed in bed.'

But Syl wasn't in her bed at all.

Instead her hair was wrapped in old sheeting and she was wearing Elda's faded, off-white robe as she slipped quickly through the Thirteenth Realm – home to the senior Novices and Half-Sisters – all the while studiously avoiding eye contact and keeping to the quieter corridors, carrying a mop and a bucket half-filled with soapy suds in case anyone doubted her disguise. She'd been here so often now that she knew her way around the network of hallways and service lanes, and she also knew that this was the best time to be here, when most of the pupils were in class. The occasional girl who passed her while running an errand or going to the loo paid no heed to the drudge she pretended to be.

Syl was more nervous than she'd been since starting her illicit investigation of the Marque, for in her pocket was the set of keys, shiny contraband wrapped snugly in a washcloth so that they wouldn't jangle in the quiet.

But it was time to be fearless. Swiftly, silently, Syl made her way to the rear of the Thirteenth Realm, to the large sliding doorway with the wide red eye of the Sisterhood emblazoned on it. It was through this entrance that the Sisters who taught the Novices flooded every morning. She had been as far as the door several times before, placing her palms flat against the cool metal, peering cautiously through the glass slats that showed yet another corridor disappearing tantalisingly around a bend beyond. But this one was different from the other hallways she'd been down so far, for this was the entrance to the Fourteenth Realm, and the end of the line for Novices. Beyond here, only full Sisters could venture. It even looked different for, on the other side of the door, the curved walls, ceiling and floor were not the stark rock face and grimy whitewash of the Twelfth and Thirteenth Realms. Instead they gleamed deepest red, the surfaces twinkling slightly as if dusted with crushed rubies, creating the impression of a healthy artery pumping life into the Marque's core.

Now Syl stood before the door once more, her heart a piston in her chest. She was panting slightly as she studied the keypad in the wall, with its silver hole awaiting a pin-like key. Next to it was a fat, rather old-fashioned looking button, browned with age, but she knew that pressing this would only summon a Sister to the door, for she'd made that mistake before, cowering and staring at her feet as the red-clad guardian peered at her through the opening.

'Why did you ring?'

'My apologies, Sister. I was cleaning and must have leaned against the button by accident,' she'd muttered, and the door had purred shut again.

Another time she'd pressed it on purpose and a different Sister had appeared, her face furious.

'What?'

'May I come in to clean, Sister?' Syl had said, and the quake in her voice had been real.

'Of course you can't! Where's your key? No one can come in unless they have a key.'

'Uh, then who cleans that side?' asked Syl.

'Are you new here? The Service Sisters, of course. They have keys! Speak to your superior and stop wasting my time.'

This time though, Syl did have keys. After another quick glance around, she slipped the bunch from her pocket. She held up the red-tipped one and took a deep breath.

'The woman that deliberates is lost,' she whispered, adding automatically, '*Cato*, by Joseph Addison' because her father had always thought it important to acknowledge the source of your quotes and aphorisms.

She slotted the pin into the keyhole. There was a welcoming beep and, with a hiss, the door slid open. Syl was in; it was as easy as that.

It smelled different here beyond the doors: fragrant, sweeter, the air almost sugary; thick and rich and exotic, like spiced wine.

It smelled of Syrene; it smelled of her father's breath after Syrene had infected him.

Syl swallowed down the urge to retch. Instead she looked around.

The ground beneath her feet was softer, a little springy, and when she touched the walls they had gentle give in them too, calling to mind spongy red seaweed, although her hand came away dry. Her fingers left temporary indentations when she pressed down, but the dark sparkle did not come off on her fingertips. It seemed ingrained, twinkling like a mineral catching the light down a mine. Natural stalactites pierced the red of the ceiling – there must have once been water here, thought Syl – and particularly striking rock formations had been allowed to jut out from the carved walls, a stark contrast to the soft red sparkle. The effect was lush and decadent, yet tasteful, and as she made her way down the wide passage, automatic light lit her way, dimming to a faint gleam again behind her once she'd passed.

It was like being inside a working model of a large, bloodless organ.

She passed doors now, three of them set into the burgundy walls, unmarked. She hurried on, unsure what to do, for what would she say if she opened one and was faced with a Nairene when she was prying where she shouldn't be?

A little farther on the passageway dipped steeply downwards, heading deeper under the ground, and the red on the walls melted from solid colour to coiling patterns, breaking off like the roots of a felled tree sprouting from a thick red stem. Between the red spirals the rock face now showed, polished smooth to best display strata of granite and quartz and shining stone that Syl didn't recognise.

Again thoughts of Syrene flooded her head, Syrene with those striking red filigree tattoos that spilled across her smooth, pious face, and coiled like snakes into her shaven hairline, tattoos that found an echo in these very walls. Perhaps the artwork on Syrene's skin was based on these markings, or perhaps her apparently legendary beauty was the inspiration for the decoration. Either way, it seemed like great vanity, and Syl felt as if she were an ant walking across the face of her enemy. Surely her presence must be felt here; surely she would soon be brushed away, crushed with no pity or feeling. And oh, that smell, the smell of her loss and sorrow . . .

Enough of this! I am Syl Hellais.

The words were spoken only in her head, as Syl once again shored up the mental defences that she hoped would protect her.

I am here to do a job, to find out what lies at the cold soul of the Nairene Sisterhood.

She walked with more purpose, growing headstrong and fierce deep inside, feeling the shields coming down like cast iron, feeling the barriers in her head clanging shut, weighted with lead, sealed with blood.

I have powers of which you have no knowledge.

She thought of her father, of Earth, of Paul and Steven, of Althea and Meia, of Fremd and Heather and Just Joe. She thought of all the death and destruction she'd seen, and for what? For what?

I have powers beyond your dreams, powers beyond your nightmares.

She thought of the thing she'd seen inside Grand Consul Gradus's head before it had torn him apart, of the mysterious parasite wrapped around his brainstem, and the irony didn't escape her now.

I'm within you, Syrene. I'm inside your nerve centre. And you don't know what I'm capable of.

And she saw again the human who died at her bidding, throwing himself on his own bayonet because she willed it, and for the first time she didn't squirm away from the memory. Instead she took strength from it, for had she not taken up arms now, and was she not fighting the war he declared was his own? She smiled grimly.

Even I don't know what I'm capable of . . .

The automatic lighting faded away now, for through the rock ran a seam of glowing stone which provided illumination as flattering as firelight. Trailing her fingers along it, Syl rounded a final bend and then stopped short, gasping, partly in fright but also partly in wonder. Before her the artery had exploded into a vast chamber that soared up from the deep, high into the dark night sky, the walls curlicued and twinkling and red, tendrils of burgundy and claret reaching as tall as church steeples, twisting into a honeycomb ceiling of jagged boulders and distant crystal domes, breaking up the stars. Around the sides of the chamber were ornate stone balconies and landings, beautifully carved and twisted from the rock. Rows of well-spaced doors opened off these high galleries, each shiny and black, each bearing a name plaque. There were even plants down here, blue-black fronds growing rich and lush, their greedy red and purple blooms reaching towards the faraway ceiling and its promise of the ultraviolet light that this curious Illyri flora lived for.

At its centre, the chamber was furnished with plump cushions of scarlet, vibrant purple sofas, and recliners fashioned from heavy tapestry and brocade. Ornately patterned red rugs covered the floor. And far above this opulent seating area, the wall was adorned with yet another red eye, staring down unblinkingly on those who lived in its name.

It was the beautiful, sterile heart of the Fourteenth Realm.

But right now that heart was beating. It was alive.

And everywhere was the Sisterhood.

CHAPTER 44

The red-clad Sister sitting nearest to Syl was watching her curiously. Syl looked back, keeping her features bland while inwardly stacking up the blocks and barriers in her head. *I am one of you*, she willed. *I am with you. Look at me, and see your own.* But she felt none of the probing she associated with Syrene or Oriel, for few shared their psychic abilities.

'Why are you just standing there? There is no time to lose,' said the Sister finally. 'The cleaning must be finished before the tutors return from class. It is imperative today of all days.'

'Yes, ma'am,' muttered Syl, ducking her head and bumbling past her.

Service Sisters were darting all around, scrubbing and shaking and puffing and spritzing, busy white corpuscles in the giant organ of velvet and blood. Syl's presence went unremarked upon as she joined their ranks, for they vastly outnumbered the smattering of red-robed Illyri who reclined on chairs and cushions, reading and making notes, or earnestly talking, occasionally lifting their feet automatically so the floor beneath them could be swept. From behind the trailing end of her headscarf Syl could make out Amera, the biology lecturer, chewing on her fingernail as she studied a screen in front of her. Syl slipped silently by, looking in the other direction, reading the plaques on the doors as she made her way through the chamber. Most bore names she knew or vaguely recognised from among the vast teaching staff who had made the education of would-be Sisters their life's work, and some were even her own tutors. Seeing them all together like this, Syl found herself newly in awe of the enormity of the Marque. If this was just the teachers, what then lay beyond in the other Realms on Avila Minor? Somewhere in this underground maze were Ezil and the other elders – the First Five. Somewhere there lingered the secret of the Sisterhood.

With fresh determination, she moved on.

In the centre of the room she passed a vaguely foreboding double door. It was unlabelled, but clearly these were the largest quarters of all, and easily accessible for an older Sister, one who might be less than steady on her ageing legs. They could only be Oriel's, and Syl's skin prickled under her robes as she went by. She hadn't seen Oriel since the incident in Elda's rooms. At first the head of these three Realms had been declared ill, and then it was said that she had been called away to important meetings, but Syl had not mourned her absence. Far too often thoughts of the old witch invaded her head, unbidden and unwanted, and she wondered if the Grandmage was close by, scrutinising her, trying to unlock her mind. Whenever it happened she felt physically ill and afterwards had a headache, but Syl saw nothing of the crone in the actual flesh. Fitfully she wondered if she imagined Oriel's presence, yet still she knew she must always remain vigilant.

Syl walked past two white-clad Sisters who were deep in conversation, and she heard Oriel's name. Trying to look inconspicuous, she stopped, bent down, and used the edge of her cloth to rub at a make-believe mark on the edge of a rug.

'She's due back around lunchtime, I believe.'

'Before the end of Novice classes? But there'll hardly be anyone to welcome her.'

'That's how she wants it. You know Grandmage Oriel.'

'Not well, thankfully.'

'I know what you mean.'

The pair laughed as they moved on towards the farthest reaches of the gallery. After a heartbeat, Syl followed.

They came to a wide door, sealed shut, and the smaller of the women held down a button beside it, set deep into the wall. The door slid open. They went through it, and after a few seconds Syl followed, unhindered, although her throat felt as if it would close with nerves. Before her wound another long corridor. A third Service Sister approached, but she went by with a mere nod of greeting, and Syl nodded back as casually as she could.

The pair that she'd followed stopped some way ahead and opened a door carved into the wall. As Syl watched, they took off their dirt-smeared white robes, revealing simple red vestments underneath, tossed the soiled garments into what appeared to be a cupboard, then opened a second and withdrew freshly laundered white clothing. They slipped these on with barely a break in their conversation, and then moved away. One of them glanced at Syl as they left, but didn't raise as much as an eyebrow of recognition, and Syl breathed out deeply.

I am one of you, she repeated over and over in her head. *We are the same.*

Quickly she went over to the cupboard and removed her own faded off-white robe, slipping on another from the fresh stock behind the second door before anyone saw her own telltale Novice under-garments. She took the keys from her pocket before she shoved the old robe that had once been Elda's into a large laundry basket behind the first door, and then, emboldened, she opened the third cupboard. Inside were piles of neatly pressed and folded headscarves. Syl could have clapped. There was no way she could risk removing her own makeshift one here, in the open, so she simply knotted the new scarf over the top. Already she felt that she blended in better.

The Sisters she was following had now disappeared from view and so Syl hurried on, passing doors and windows that revealed what lay beyond. Here was an exercise room of sorts, or perhaps a health centre, fitted with equipment and body function monitors. Inside, a lone Service Sister was languidly washing the floor, drawing slow, looping pictures on the stone with her mop. She yawned and scratched a cheek.

Further along there was a clutch of meditation rooms, all open and welcoming, their cushions plumped and ready, fragrance cubes in nooks by the door waiting to be lit. Haunting Illyri music played from inside one and Syl glimpsed the Sisters whom she had trailed. The taller of the pair was half-heartedly cleaning but the other had called up a screen and was leaning against the wall, washrags hanging forgotten at her side, laughing rudely at whatever it was she watched.

'Hush, Eya,' said the first. 'You'll get us in trouble.'

Syl tiptoed by.

The pathway rose upwards, a steep ascent, and another glass-fronted room appeared. Syl slowed as she passed, marvelling at the long, golden pool inside. It was clearly some sort of bathhouse for a fountain steamed at one end and a brace of Sisters reclined in the water, bubbles rising large as plates around them. Three Service Sisters waited on them at the side of the pool. The first held towels while another sprinkled shards of shining soap over the water. The third bent over a figure in the pool, expertly pumicing a proffered foot. As Syl stood and stared, one of the bathers looked up and glared at her. Quickly, she turned and left.

Now the corridor she was following split. Syl was about to take the wider path, which veered to the right, when she heard voices, and saw a reflection of red bounce off the walls around the bend ahead. Swiftly she skipped up the narrower passage to the left and scurried away, her heart thudding.

The route twisted and turned sharply for a while, then porthole windows opened up high in the walls, revealing the sky. There were no entrances or exits, so Syl guessed that she was travelling down a connecting tunnel to somewhere different, perhaps to a new Realm. Or rather an old Realm, for the walls around her were dark and shiny, rubbed that way with age, and the floor was grooved as if many feet had walked this way over the years, eroding a pathway into the rock. At points it was patched with flat stepping stones, also shaded with wear. The air felt thin and Syl shivered, for it was colder here. Wherever she was, it was very old indeed.

Syl knew that the oldest areas of the Marque predated even the arrival of the Sisterhood. It had never been entirely clear who carved out the original primitive tunnels, for they were without decoration and their creators had left no trace of themselves behind: no pots, no animal bones, no Illyri remains. The annals of the Sisterhood suggested that the moon's caves had originally provided a refuge for those seeking to escape some form of persecution back on Illyr, just as the first Sisters had done. This was disputed by some of the Sisterhood's own historians, who claimed that the age of the tunnels indicated they had been constructed *before* the invention of interplanetary travel. It was, it seemed, one of those mysteries destined to remain unsolved.

Finally Syl came to two descending staircases. Both had steep, worn steps carved from the rock, grey on the outer edges yet black in the middle, stained and worn down by aeons of footfalls. Syl took the steps to the left, for it seemed like the most sensible course of action: if she kept going left and then on her return she reversed this, and stayed to the right, she'd have less chance of becoming lost, or so she hoped. Down she went, spiralling and twisting, deeper and deeper into the moon. The light was dim, no more than flickering service bulbs, and the air smelled stale as she descended, fusty and forgotten. The stairs petered out into a narrow, uneven passageway, the walls rough-hewn but the edges of the rock cuts smoothed by time. It was very quiet, and her feet left vague prints in the dust on the floor as she tiptoed along, hearing herself breathing in the silence, hearing the blood thundering in her ears.

Ahead dual archways opened into the walls, and Syl stopped and peered inside. Each room was a mirror-image of the other, two large, gloomy caves, both with shelves piled on to boulders, each shelf stacked with higgledy-piggledy piles of books and documents, some held down by rocks, others fallen over and shuffled accidentally across the floor. Everywhere was grime and grit, and a small rock fall seemed to have flattened an old cabinet in the middle of the room on the left. Crushed exhibits spilled from it: frayed fabric, torn leathery parchment and chunks of sinewed brown matter that Syl preferred not to think about too much. Instead, she went into the room on the right and peered at the nearest pile of documents.

'Dammit,' she said, jumping slightly as her voice hissed back at her, *dammit, dammit, dammit.* The documents were in an unfamiliar language. No, not just an unfamiliar language but a completely foreign script: an alphabet she had never seen before, the jagged symbols set down in spiral form, utterly incomprehensible. She brushed the dirt from another document. While different, it too was completely alien in the truest sense of the word, clearly from another world entirely. The parchment felt almost sticky under her fingers, as if it was sucking at her skin, and she quickly pulled her hand away. She moved further into the room, blowing dust off here, wiping away grime there, but everything was much of the same: impenetrable, and clearly packed away here to be all but forgotten, an archive created by Sisters long-since dead.

Then she saw a garniad scurrying up a nearby wall, and she almost screamed. She only recognised it because they'd studied these armoured, spiderlike creatures in biology, staring into a glass case while inside a lone garniad tapped its hard legs angrily against the glass. She knew they had a nasty bite. The biology lecturer, Amera, had explained that garniads were the scourge of the Marque of old, but now their numbers were controlled.

'But beware,' Amera had said, 'for you will still find them in the most ancient parts of the Marque. Even when you become full Sisters, with wide access to our buildings here, I recommend you stay away from the disused tunnels, for a garniad sting hurts, and several garniad stings in tandem can be deadly, particularly to small children and the elderly.'

With a shiver, Syl took her leave. She headed up the corridor a little further just to be sure she'd missed nothing, but the light faded away around the next curve, and Syl could clearly make out the reason why: a massive roof collapse blocked the way ahead, boulders the size of cars piled from floor to crumpled ceiling. She'd heard how some older parts of the Marque had caved in a long time ago, and suddenly something occurred to her: hadn't Elda said her friend had been killed by a rockfall too? What was she called? Kosia yes, that was it: Kosia. Now Syl wondered where exactly Kosia had been when she had died, for the Realms where the Novices and Half-Sisters resided were relatively new and free of such dangers.

So first Kosia died, and then her apparent friend, the otherwise solitary Elda, was killed too, one in a rock fall, the other by suicidally leaving the Marque at night. The first death was no doubt categorised as an unfortunate accident, while the second had been covered up with lies about a young Novice who was unhappy, so was allowed to go home. And yet Syl had seen what had spilled from the cascid's belly: clearly Elda had been so much more than she seemed.

Could Kosia have been a spy too?

And rock falls would surely only take place in the oldest sections of the Marque, the deepest, darkest ones such as this. What would Kosia have been doing nosing around in the ancient Realms? As she looked at the barricade of boulders laced with frayed 'caution' tape, Syl felt she was finally getting somewhere, although where exactly that might be she could not say.

Anyway, this was the end of the line, for now. She must return to her quarters, for she had been away too long.

Syl retraced her steps, past the forgotten archives and up those wretched stairs again, being sure to keep her hands tight to her sides for fear of garniads. At the top she stopped to catch her breath, and found herself staring down the second set of steps. They were wider than the ones she'd just come from, and the light seemed brighter – or perhaps that was just her imagination.

Tomorrow she would be ill once more, she decided; tomorrow she would return.

CHAPTER 45

It was all very well that the universe appeared to be peppered with wormholes, thought Paul – at least relatively speaking – but their existence was useless without a minutely accurate map of their locations.

When the theory of wormholes – or Einstein-Rosen bridges, to give them their proper name among human scientists – was first proposed, the very idea of them was extraordinary enough without anyone giving thought to what they might actually look like. The reality, as it turned out, was that they were inconsistent in appearance, to the extent that many were not visible at all. True, the largest of them – but not necessarily the most stable – distorted the fabric of space, like a lens placed against the stars, but the smaller ones were virtually undetectable unless one was in their immediate vicinity, which, in terms of the size of the universe, meant less than a million miles away. Even then, one had to know where to look, and so a ship could pass within a stone's throw (again, in universal terms) of a wormhole without actually knowing that it was present.

Put simply, decided Paul, it was a little like trying to fit a pin through a previously existing pinhole in a sheet measuring millions and millions of square miles. No, make that a three-dimensional sheet, although he figured that all sheets were three-dimensional, so that particular analogy didn't work. Science had never been one of Paul's strong points in school.

He was standing in what had once been the captain's quarters on the *Nomad*. The small room contained a bed, a desk, and not much else. The artificial intelligence system kept a screen permanently activated over the bunk, displaying system details alongside real-time images from every section of the ship, allowing the captain to monitor all activity from his cabin. The screen could be dimmed with a sweep of a hand, but Paul had not found a way to deactivate it. Perhaps it couldn't be shut down. He had tried to find mission information on the system, but to no avail. He suspected that no such information existed, just in case the ship was captured.

Now, once again, he was lost in the middle of a section of the wormhole map, marvelling at the intricacy of it. This map was the basis for the Illyri Conquest. Without it, the Illyri would just have been a more advanced version of humanity, limited to their small corner of the universe, even with their combination of advanced fusion engines coupled with localised mining of hydrogen, helium and sulphur for fuel, like little filling stations dotted throughout galaxies. The knowledge of the wormholes had made them con-querors, but how had they come by it?

He traced a wormhole with his finger. It reminded him of something, but whatever it was danced away like a butterfly every time he tried to grasp it. For some reason, the image brought Syl to mind: the grace of her, the exoticism. With it came an overwhelming sense of hopelessness. He wanted to rescue her, but instead he was stuck on a strange ship about to enter a series of wormholes, a journey that would, if they survived, lead them to a cordoned-off system, and no one isolated an entire planetary system without both good cause and a means of protecting it from intruders.

Paul turned in a slow circle. Wormholes swirled around him like frayed threads in the fabric of the cosmos.

Threads. Filaments.

He had arrived in the cellars of Dundearg just in time to see Consul Gradus destroyed by what was inside him, but Syl had told him of the consul's transformation: the images of an insectoid organism attached to his brain stem, and his body's reaction to his captors' attempts to probe it. The filaments that the organism had spread throughout his system erupted from Gradus's skin until his entire form was masked by them, his every pore extruding a fine thread.

What if . . . ?

Paul closed his eyes, even the beauty of the wormholes now becoming a distraction to him. He recalled his Granddad Jim, whose pride and joy was his allotment. Unlike his neighbours, Granddad Jim did not grow vegetables on his little patch of land. Instead he bred roses, and the bane of his life was spider mites, tiny reddish creatures that spun their webs beneath the rose leaves and merrily wreaked havoc on his blooms. According to Granddad Jim, spider mites could be found almost everywhere in the world. They were hitchhikers, floating on wind currents to find new plants to colonise. They were also able to detect the coming of winter, which caused their systems to enter a period of dormancy called diapause, from which they only emerged when the weather improved. Paul had a vague memory of certain spiders being able to do something similar, and mud-dwelling fish too, shutting down their systems in order to survive the most inhospitable conditions.

From this, Paul made another mental leap. Before the coming of the Illyri, and the subject races that fought for them, most human scientific speculation had centred on the likelihood of the first alien life being discovered in the form of microbes. He had a strong memory of a dispute arising over the fragment of a meteor in which microscopic filaments had been found, with the scientist responsible for its discovery arguing that they represented some form of extra-terrestrial life, now long dead.

But what if – and there were those words again – a similar life-form were capable of surviving in space, semi-dormant but somehow aware, storing the details of its travels through the universe, information that could later be retrieved? Was such a thing even possible? How could a primitive organism retain such knowledge?

A primitive life-form could not, but an advanced extraterrestrial life-form could, perhaps the kind that could also latch on to an Illyri brain stem and experience the outside world through the responses of its host.

Paul opened his eyes. Rizzo stood before him.

'Are you okay?' she asked.

'Yes. No. Possibly.'

Rizzo cocked an eyebrow at him.

'Are you sure you should be in charge?'

'Yes. No. Possibly. What is it?'

'We've arrived at the first wormhole.'

CHAPTER 46

The following morning, Syl made her way to the top of the dual staircases once more and, without hesitating, down she went.

This second staircase was shorter, and definitely seemed brighter as Syl descended. The steps widened at the bottom into a corridor similar to the one she'd been in the day before, only this was certainly much cleaner, without the dusty, scuffed floors or the stale smell of the other. And it was in use, of that there was no doubt, for cleaning equipment had been left along the wall, and rags and mops hung from makeshift hooks. A tap stuck out of the rock face, dripping gently into a bucket placed beneath it to catch the droplets. Syl took a few tentative steps away from the stairwell and realised the air really did smell different here – familiar even, but in a good way. She breathed deeply, trying to place it, for it was a fragrance she knew. That was it: laundry. It smelled like detergent, and as she walked onwards the smell became stronger until she stood outside what was clearly a washing hub, wide and whirring, stacked with shiny machinery that buzzed and clicked as it cleaned and dried its multiple loads, red silk flashing within. She didn't go inside, for several Service Sisters were also buzzing around, busy and efficient, folding piles of vivid red robes.

The closest Illyri looked up and saw Syl, and confusion clouded her face.

'Excuse me, but who are you?' she said, and the others stopped what they were doing and stared at her. Plastering on her most winning smile, Syl immediately started her inner mantra again.

We are the same. I am one of you. I. One of you. The same.

'Never mind,' said the Sister, shaking her head, befuddled, as Syl turned and walked away as fast as she could without looking too conspicuous.

She passed rooms stacked with chairs, and piled with folded bedding. One was stocked with bedsteads, and another was filled to the ceiling with drum upon drum of fresh water. There were stores of soap and chemicals, and heaps of crisp towels, and several neat supply rooms lined with tools of the sort a handyman might put on his belt, only far sleeker and slighter, made for precision work.

Clearly the secrets of the Nairene Sisterhood were not going to be down here with the scullery maids and washerwomen of the order, so Syl quickened her pace, sticking to what appeared to be the main route upwards, passing chutes in the wall and service trolleys, and even what were apparently the lowliest of sleeping quarters, window-less, grey and grimly lit.

Onward she went, understanding that she was probably losing her bearings, but she felt relatively secure in her white robes as she brushed deferentially past red Nairenes, more and more of them the further she ascended, and yet they paid her no heed. She was swept along on occasional waves of Service Sisters too, and no one questioned her, or even looked at her. She tried to keep to routes that the red Sisters favoured, for surely it was along these that the truth of the order would be found. And yet she could not help but stare in wonder at all she saw.

Libraries as cavernous as any cathedral soared off to either side, so very many libraries, and there were scriptoriums reaching several storeys high, where Sisters squinted and scribbled or tapped earnestly at screens, many wearing white gloves to protect the rare and precious volumes they transcribed and translated. There were dining halls and gymnasiums, and giant greenhouses flourishing with life, and chambers full of silvery mirrors and lights. She saw a small orchestra practising, picking on ethereal string instruments, and she found the zoological department she thought had been a figment of some Novice's imagination. Through one window she thought that she briefly glimpsed a unicorn.

Strangest of all, however, was the stone-walled grotto she stumbled into at the point where several corridors came together in a star shape. It was dim in the grotto, while being unusually cold for the Marque, and candles glimmered on rough-hewn shelves and in crevices. At the heart of the space were four plinths of rock upon which rested a large, flat boulder, pockmarked and jagged at the edges, but otherwise resembling a medieval banqueting table. The boulder itself wasn't particularly strange; what was odd was that it was protected from curious hands by a large glass dome and, odder yet, as Sisters skirted around it, without fail they would kiss their fingertips, and then press them to the dome. A Service Sister was on hand, regularly stepping forward to rub away the smears they left on the clear surface. Just to be safe, Syl kissed her own fingers then trailed them curiously along the glass, but she didn't dare stop to investigate, for the rock was at a busy juncture and Sisters scurried by like ants, absently dropping their kisses as they went about their business.

As Syl left the grotto, there came a low, sweet chiming, growing louder and more insistent, and gradually the Sisters finished what they were doing and drifted in the direction of the numerous dining halls. What? It was already lunchtime?

Syl knew she shouldn't stretch her luck by tarrying any longer but, frankly, she was now spectacularly lost.

'Excuse me, Sister, but I seem to have lost my bearings. What Realm is this?' said Syl, awkwardly approaching a young Illyri in white robes just like her own.

We are the same, she thought. *The same.*

'Oh, I know, it's so easy to do. This is the Ninth. Where are you trying to get to?'

'The Twelfth Realm.'

'Really? You'd think after training there you'd remember that much at least, wouldn't you, but I still get confused too. Have you not got your cartograph?'

Syl looked at her feet, a little frightened. What was a cartograph?

I am one of you.

'No. I forgot it.'

We are the same.

The Sister chuckled. 'You're having quite a day! Well here, look at mine. My name's Lista, by the way. I'm from the Eighth. Who are you?'

'I'm, uh, Tanit. From the Seventh.'

'Really?' said Lista. 'I didn't know there were any of us in the Seventh.'

'No.' Syl laughed a little too hard. 'I mean that's where I just came from. I live in the Fifteenth.'

I am like you.

'Right. Okay then.'

Lista pulled her lanyard from under her robes. Attached to it, next to her keys, was a small black card. She squeezed the edge between her thumb and forefinger and immediately a labyrinth of lines spread across the surface. A blue light flashed in the centre. She held it in front of Syl, who did her best not to look surprised.

'So you're here,' she said, pointing at the blue light, 'and you need to be there.'

She spread her thumb and forefinger, and the image zoomed out.

'So if you just follow this route here – '

But Syl didn't hear what Lista said. Instead she stared at the card, overcome with longing. Why, it was a map, a map to the entire Marque! She had to have it. She watched Lista closely as the girl babbled on.

I am like you. We are the same.

'Lista, dearest, please may I borrow it? Just for a bit. I'm dreadfully late, and I'll be in terrible trouble if I get lost again. I'm all panicked, you see . . .'

Lista hesitated.

'But you know it's not allowed.'

Syl stared at her, smiling reassuringly while she manipulated Lista's thoughts. The girl looked at the card for a few moments, then shrugged.

'Well, if you promise you'll get it back to me as soon as you're finished with it.'

'Of course I will. Thank you, Lista.'

'Please, don't forget. I'm in the Eighth, remember.'

She handed over the cartograph.

'Good luck,' Lista said. 'See you later, Tanit.'

Syl froze, then realised Lista was talking to her.

'Yes, of course. See you later,' she managed.

In the privacy of a small side tunnel, Syl studied the cartograph. The blue light at the middle clearly showed the whereabouts of the card itself, for the shining dot remained static while the lines moved around it depending on which direction she faced. She could zoom in or zoom out, showing either greater or lesser detail accordingly. As Illyri technology went it was quite primitive, but also rather effective, like much of the electronics on the Marque.

Very soon, Syl had figured out where she was, for she was surprisingly close to the pathway she'd intended taking earlier. She'd gone through what appeared to be the old Third Realm, after veering briefly into the Second – the tumbledown section where she'd seen the garniad the day before – and she'd walked across the Fifteenth, where the laundries were housed, to end up here, in the Ninth. The route she'd followed curved back around on itself, but without the cartograph she'd never have guessed it. It was like those stories of explorers lost in the desert, walking in never-ending circles only minutes from an oasis until they fell down and died.

Only now, thought Syl as she headed back towards the Twelfth Realm, she was an explorer who had a map.

CHAPTER 47

Steven had killed the thrusters, so the ship remained stationary before the phenomenon. The wormhole appeared as a slightly elongated area of distortion, a fractured lens. The sight of a wormhole always made Paul nervous. He'd been through enough of them by now for the novelty to have worn off, but not the fear. He wondered if it was similar to claustrophobia, that reluctance to be trapped in an enclosed space, especially one with the potential for collapse. Illyri research into wormholes had concluded that they degraded over time, becoming less stable as they grew older. Unfortunately, while the wormhole map detailed the location of each one, it did not offer an estimate of age or stability. They could only conclude that, if a wormhole was included on the map, it was because it was safe to use.

Alis magnified a section of the cockpit display.

'This is our route,' she said, as a series of wormholes were illuminated in red. 'Once we're through this one, the next is just a few hours away. As long as we don't encounter any problems, it should take us six boosts to get to the Archaeon system.'

'How long altogether?' asked Paul.

'Arrival approximately seventy-eight hours since our departure from Torma.'

Paul, who had been leaning against the bulkhead, instinctively found himself running the fingers of his right hand along the interior of the *Nomad*, as though reassuring himself of its strength.

Will the ship be able to take six boosts? he wondered.

Even the strongest vessels in the Illyri fleet rarely made more than two boosts in succession without running a full system and maintenance diagnostic afterwards, and the *Nomad* had already made at least one boost to get to Torma. But there was no choice.

'Check all hatches and storage,' said Paul. 'I want everything tied down and sealed away.'

They were all used to the procedures: nobody wanted to have a limb broken or a skull fractured by a falling piece of equipment during a difficult jump. When Paul was satisfied that all was secure, he ordered everyone to take position, and finally strapped himself into the lead chair directly behind Steven and Alis.

'Okay,' he said, and his voice quavered ever so slightly. 'Take us in.'

After all the preparations and precautions, it was one of the easiest boosts that Paul could recall. He had a vague sense of stars elongating, creating lines of light in which spectrums danced; of an intense pressure against his temples that felt as though his eyeballs were being squeezed from his skull; and of a tingling at his fingertips and toes that verged on, but did not quite become, pain.

'Emerging,' said Steven. 'Boost complete.'

'Starting emergence procedures,' said Alis.

The most dangerous aspect of boosting was not moving through the wormhole itself, although that could be risky enough. No, it was in leaving the wormhole that the greatest threats often lay. Regularly trafficked wormholes had automated monitoring stations installed at their mouths, so that in the event of a problem – asteroids, for example – a warning drone could be sent through to advise against boosts until the danger had passed. But the last thing they wanted was for news of an unscheduled boost to reach the Illyri, so Steven and Alis had made adjustments to their route in order to avoid any such stations.

The trick in emerging from an unmonitored wormhole was to halt the ship at the very periphery of its mouth, and then slip back into the hole if any obstacle was present, a solution that was far from foolproof. Paul gritted his teeth and dug his fingers into the armrest of his chair, only relaxing when Alis gave the all-clear moments later. And then it was over, and they emerged into an area of space that looked not entirely dissimilar to the one they had just left.

Paul checked over his shoulder to make sure that everyone was okay. Thula slowly opened his left eye, then his right, as though unconvinced that he could still be in one piece. Thula hated jumps.

'Was it just me,' he said, 'or was that not as horrible as usual?'

'It's the ship,' said Steven. He couldn't keep the admiration and excitement from his voice. 'A wormhole could be collapsing around us, and we wouldn't even notice.'

Paul didn't particularly want to test that theory, but it gave him some reassurance about the boosts to come.

'All credit to the pilots too,' he said. 'Well done.'

A burst of only semi-ironic applause came from Thula and Rizzo, who suggested that Paul should start awarding medals with his own face on them. Paul ignored her, and signalled to Peris that he wished to speak with him. Tiray stood to join them, but Paul was growing tired of Tiray assuming that he could automatically include himself in any conversation he chose.

'No, you can stay where you are, Councillor,' said Paul. 'I'd like to speak with Peris alone.'

Tiray didn't look happy about this, but remained in his seat. Peris followed Paul to the captain's quarters. He said nothing, but he was increasingly impressed by Paul's assumption of command. It was a good thing that he was no longer involved with the Resistance on Earth, for he would have become a powerful enemy. On the other hand, Peris was also aware that, while one could take the man out of the Resistance, one could not take the Resistance out of the man. Paul Kerr was still no friend to the Illyri, and the issue of the weapons in the hold remained.

'You don't like Tiray much, do you?' said Peris.

'I don't like or dislike him. I don't even know him well enough to care if something were to happen to him.'

'But?'

'I don't trust him. He hasn't told us everything that he knows.'

'He's a politician. He probably hasn't even told himself everything that he knows. So, what's on your mind, Lieutenant?'

'This ship.'

'Yes?'

'Do you think it has a flight recorder? We called them black boxes back on Earth?'

'Actually, the technical human term for them is "cockpit voice recorders". Ours are a little more advanced, but, yes, this ship will have one.'

'Can it be turned off?'

'I don't know. I suppose it can. The ship's systems have been programmed to erase all traces of its past, so the recorder might also have been deactivated. My guess, though, is that it probably wasn't. It would be more sensible simply to secure the recorder. Everything about this ship suggests secrecy, but also a degree of complacency, such as the absence of security codes on its main operating systems, and of DNA locks on that weaponry you found. The erasing of its flight records was designed to discourage only a casual search. In reality, whoever designed this ship and sent it on its mission never anticipated that it might be boarded or, even if it was, that it wouldn't be retaken almost immediately.'

'And the recorder would start up at what point?'

'Well, from the ship's first activation, I should think.'

'So if we found the recorder, we could learn where it was built?'

Oh, you bright young man.

'Yes, I believe so. But, as I said, if anything on this ship is going to be properly secured, it will be the recorder, and I don't have the kind of expertise or intelligence to get past its firewalls. And, with absolute respect, neither do you.'

'But Alis does.'

'Alis works for Tiray.'

'Actually,' said Paul, 'I don't think that's entirely true. Alis's true loyalties lie elsewhere.'

'With the Mechs?'

'Yes. I think I can persuade her to access the recorder without necessarily informing Tiray of what she might find.'

'And why would she do that?'

'This ship is like the Mechs: where there's one, there can be two, and then many more than two. This kind of technology could change the course of a war.'

Peris considered what Paul had said.

'You're suggesting that this ship, and the one we destroyed, are part of a fleet?'

'Don't pretend that you haven't considered the possibility. Why build just two ships when you have half the wealth of an empire to spend, and investing in a fleet might just win you the other half as well? Unless we're all very much mistaken, forces aligned with the Diplomatic Corps created this ship. The Corps wants to rule the empire. To do that, it needs to wipe out the Military. At the moment, the Military's firepower outweighs the Corps', but not by much. Enough ships like this could tip the balance.'

'But you still haven't explained why Alis might be willing to keep secrets from Tiray.'

'It's only a matter of time before the Corps finds out about the Mechs. Meia is the weak link. She was exposed at Dundearg, and people will be talking. Five thousand powerful, self-aware machines who know that one hundred thousand more like them were destroyed on the orders of the Diplomatic Corps won't be allowed to survive once the Corps takes over the Illyri empire.

'You told me yourself: Tiray is a politician. Right now, the Corps is after him because they know he's curious about Archaeon, but the fact that they didn't just blow his ship to pieces means they don't necessarily regard him as an enemy, not yet. Suppose Tiray gets to Archeaon, discovers whatever the Corps and its allies may be hiding there, and decides that it might be in his best interests, and that of the Civilians, to side with them against the Military? All politicians have one aim: to survive. I'm pretty sure Alis is well aware of those. She's not just working with Tiray. She's watching him.'

'You're very cynical for one so young,' said Peris.

'You may be rubbing off on me.'

Peris acknowledged the gibe with a laugh.

'And where do you fit into all this?' he asked.

'Personally, I'd be quite happy to see the Illyri empire tear itself apart in another civil war,' Paul replied. 'If you're killing one another, then you're doing humanity a favour, and saving us the trouble of killing you instead. But if the Corps were to win, an already bad situation for humanity would become much worse.'

'You're talking about that thing found in Gradus's head, and the experiments Meia saw?'

Paul nodded. 'None of it suggests the Corps' plans for humankind are gentle,' he said. 'I've also been wondering if that organism might be linked to the technology used to build this ship?'

'In what way? By imparting knowledge?'

'Or enhancing brain functions, maybe. It's all just guesswork and speculation, but it makes a kind of sense.'

'So the Corps provides hosts for these life-forms, whatever they might be, and in return the Diplomats get smarter,' said Peris. 'But what's in it for the organism?'

Bodies split open like bags of fertiliser. Host animals on Earth torn apart in the process of failed implantations.

Paul made the final leaps before replying. An advanced species is found – humanity – that is potentially capable of acting as host for the organism, just as the Illyri were, but for some reason the implantation doesn't take, like a body rejecting a transplant organ. Humans are just different enough from the Illyri to make them unsuitable as hosts. And if human beings are no good as hosts, then what other function can they usefully serve?

Bodies split open. Fertiliser.

'Humanity,' said Paul, and his mouth dried up on the word. 'The Corps is going to give them the Earth.'

CHAPTER 48

Alis needed little persuading to seek out the flight recorder and try to recover its data. She didn't even object when Paul suggested that she keep her task secret from Tiray, which confirmed all that he believed about the nature of their relationship. The only difficulty lay in ensuring that Tiray's suspicions were not aroused. It was left to Peris to spin a tale for the politician, which he did by wrapping the lie in a kind of truth: Alis, Tiray was told, was looking for the recorder in order to disable it, because if they did somehow manage to investigate the Archaeon system and escape undetected, it might be politic – and Peris used the word quite deliberately – to leave as little trace as possible of their presence. Tiray appeared to swallow the story, but Paul quietly assigned Rizzo to keep a close eye on him, just in case he took it into his head to do some snooping.

In fact, it was Steven who seemed most upset by Alis's new role. Perhaps inspired in part by Thula's earlier knowing grins, he had decided that Paul was attracted to Alis, and now he might have a rival for her affections in the form of his own brother. Back on Earth, Paul thought that his brother might have had a crush on Syl's friend Ani, but it appeared to have passed. His feelings for Alis, though, seemed destined to make his life very complicated.

'You have to tell him,' Paul informed Alis, although he was forced to inform her lower body only, as her upper half was lost somewhere below floor level.

'Found it!' she cried, and emerged holding a silver block.

'Well done,' said Paul. 'You still have to tell him.'

'Tell who what?' said Alis. It was clear that she had tuned out Paul entirely while she was engaged in her search, leading Paul to doubt that her programming extended to multitasking, however sophisticated it might be in other ways.

'You have to tell my brother that you're a Mech.'

Her joy at finding the recorder disappeared.

'Why?'

'Because he's shooting daggers at me while staring dog-eyed at you.'

'I don't understand anything of what you've just said. Do you mean that your brother has been throwing knives at you?'

Paul permitted himself a deep sigh. He was certain that Napoleon Bonaparte, or Alexander the Great, or any other great military commander in history, had never found himself having this sort of conversation. Being in charge wasn't all that it was cracked up to be.

'No, it means that he's sending hostile looks in my direction while at the same time gazing at you in a lovesick manner. There: is that clear enough?'

Alis looked at the block in her hand as though she wanted to use it on someone's head, but wasn't sure whose head should be first.

'But why is he angry with you?'

'He thinks that I'm attracted to you.'

'Are you?' Alis asked, uncertainly.

'No, of course not.'

Paul knew that he was in trouble as soon as he heard the words leave his mouth. They had sounded so much more reasonable, and so much less hurtful, in his head. If he could have laid his hands on the Illyri responsible for programming Alis, he would happily have throttled him. Or her.

Yet Alis did not respond with anger but with a kind of confused sadness.

'Am I so repellent?' she asked.

'No.'

'Is it because I am—?'

Paul interrupted her.

'A Mech? No, absolutely not.'

But even as he said it, he wondered if he might not be lying, at least a little.

'It's because,' he continued, 'there's someone else.'

'A human?'

Paul sank back against the hull.

'No, as it happens. An Illyri.'

If possible, Alis looked even more confused.

'But you're human!'

'Hang on a minute, you just implied that I might not be attracted to you because you're a Mech. It never even crossed your mind that it might be because you look like an Illyri.'

That still didn't sound right, but by this point Paul had largely given up caring. He felt like he'd blundered into a minefield, and all he could do was hope to escape from it without losing a limb.

'Who is she?' said Alis.

'Syl Hellais,' said Paul.

'Lord Andrus's daughter?'

'Yes, the very same. That's how I came into contact with Meia. What has Steven told you about us, and how we came to be here? You've had all that time together in the cockpit. It must have come up.'

'Very little,' said Alis. 'He just said that both of you were in trouble on Earth, and it was either conscription or a Punishment Battalion. You chose conscription.'

Paul experienced a surge of pride at his brother's discretion. Even in his attraction for Alis, he had kept his mouth closed about their circumstances.

'Choice didn't enter into it,' said Paul.

And he told Alis most of their story, leaving out only those details that he believed she didn't need to know because they might harm others. He told her nothing about the Resistance beyond the barest facts of its existence, and left out entirely any mention of Fremd, the Green Man, whose suspicions and knowledge had led to the discovery of the organism in Gradus's skull.

'Peris took a great chance by intervening on your behalf,' said Alis when he was done.

'He did so because Meia asked him to.'

'It doesn't matter,' said Alis. 'You're in his debt.'

Paul hadn't looked at it like that before. It made him uncomfortable because it was true.

'Now you know our story,' he said. 'It doesn't change anything, though. You still need to talk to Steven.'

Alis's face contorted into an expression of pure misery.

'I am afraid,' she said.

'Of what?'

'That he may not want to be around me any more. That he may hate me.'

'I think,' said Paul, with only slightly more confidence than he felt, 'that you may be underestimating my brother.'

Alis spoke to Steven in the captain's quarters, while the *Nomad*'s autopilot brought the ship closer and closer to the next wormhole. Paul left them in private, his eyes fixed on the stars, his thoughts with them in the void. He must have lost track of the minutes, for it seemed to be a long time before Steven emerged to return to the pilot's chair. He did so without even glancing in his brother's direction, the expression on his face entirely unreadable, but Paul saw that Steven's lips were red and swollen, and his skin was flushed with pleasure.

Alis rejoined Steven as the *Nomad* neared the second wormhole, and the drills and procedures began again: checking, stowing, securing. This time, Paul felt only the slightest of pressure on his skull as they boosted, but he had the impression that this boost took longer than the last.

'Emerging,' said Steven.

'Commencing procedures,' said Alis. 'We have—'

Something struck the *Nomad*, causing it to list suddenly to starboard. Warning lights flashed, and Paul heard the emergency signal howl.

'Meteor strike!' shouted Alis. 'We've got more incoming.'

An image of the *Nomad* appeared on the display before her. It was surrounded by fast-moving irregular shapes, some of them almost as big as the ship itself. It reminded Paul of the old *Asteroids* video game, but this time for real. The tail of the meteor cloud was long, extending for miles, but the storm itself was not deep. It extended into space like a great but irregular stone snake. Meteors blinked out of existence as they entered the wormhole. To go back into it would be just as dangerous as remaining where they were: sharing wormhole space with meteors would be lethal enough, but at the other end the rocks would shoot out like missiles. The chances of the *Nomad* being hit were very high.

Afterwards, Paul would be torn between hugging his brother and banging the boy's head against the *Nomad*'s hull, but only once his terror had faded to the point where he could stop shaking. Like Paul, Steven had spotted that the cloud was shallow, but his next thought was not the same as his brother's, for Steven believed that he could steer them through it.

And that was what he did. It took no more than a minute, and Paul spent most of it with his eyes closed, but it was the longest minute of his life, and he experienced the moment of his dying at least ten times during it. When he did open his eyes, he saw meteors flashing past them or, worse, towards them at speed, which caused him to squeeze his eyes shut again.

'We're through,' said Steven, mercifully.

Paul's jaw ached from gritting his teeth, and he badly needed a toilet break. Even when he allowed his eyes to open again, he found himself anticipating the sight of another onrushing meteor.

'I hate you,' Thula told Steven. 'I'm only glad that you're still alive so I can kill you myself.'

Paul managed to speak. The words came out as a series of croaks, but they could at least be understood.

'Damage assessment?' he managed.

'We've taken a hit to port, but no breach,' said Alis. 'We'll have a dent, though.'

Paul released his belt and rose unsteadily to his feet. He walked over to the pilot's chair and stood behind his brother, breathing deeply. Then he punched Steven on the arm.

'Ow! What was that for?'

'Well done,' said Paul. 'Just don't ever do it again.'

He turned to Alis. He hadn't spoken to her since her little chat – if that was what it could be called – with his brother.

'How are you doing with that recorder?'

'Nothing yet. I haven't figured out the security algorithms. I may have to access it directly.'

Paul didn't know what that meant, and told her so.

'It means that, instead of using the ship's systems, I could use my own.'

'What, like plugging yourself into it?' said Steven. 'Is that dangerous?'

'It shouldn't be. Its power source is pretty low-level. It's just a data storage device.'

'Okay, do it,' said Paul.

'Wait a minute—' Steven interrupted, but Paul silenced him with a look.

'Remember who's in charge here,' he said.

Steven, sensibly, held his tongue.

'Do it,' Paul continued, 'but wait until we've made the final boost.'

'Are you afraid I'll blow a fuse?' asked Alis.

'Do you have fuses?'

'No,' said Alis. 'I'm slightly more complicated than that.'

And, oh boy, don't I know it, Paul thought.

The next three boosts came in such close succession that everyone remained strapped in their seats for the duration. Rizzo slept through them all. Thula vomited during the fifth boost, as did Tiray. Even Peris looked queasy. The body reacted poorly to so many boosts in such a short time. It was like spending too long on a theme park ride. The only consolation was that the boosts were uneventful. No more meteors, and no problems beyond a shaky trip on the fourth. It would take them twelve hours to reach the final wormhole that led into the Archaeon system, so Paul instructed Steven to rest. He, Thula and Peris alternated watches as the ship ploughed silently on. Each dozed a

little, but as the final hour approached they all found themselves
awake. Alis continued to work on the flight recorder, although she
admitted that its firewalls continued to frustrate her, and she was
pessimistic about accessing the information that Paul wanted. He left
her and consulted with Peris and Thula about their situation.

'Thoughts?' said Paul.

'Our pursuers may well have found the debris on Torma by now,'
said Peris. 'They'll be trying to figure out what happened.'

'It won't take them long to discover that they're missing a ship,'
said Thula.

'But they won't yet understand why,' said Peris.

'Will its flight recorder have registered the strike that blew up the
other Nomad vessel?' asked Paul.

'Maybe. But they'll have to find it first.'

'They'll find it,' said Paul. 'And they may well make an educated
guess about where we're heading in their ship. We won't have long
to investigate Archaeon.'

'They'll probably have to take the same route that we did,' said
Peris. 'It's unlikely that they'll want to use monitored wormholes, not
if they're using unregistered ships.'

'So what have we got?' asked Paul. 'Half a day?'

'A little more,' conceded Peris. 'But that's assuming we're not
arrested or blown to pieces the moment we emerge from the Archaeon
wormhole.'

'You know,' said Thula, 'you're a glass is half-empty kind of guy.'

'We're in a stolen craft, being hunted by unknown agents of the
Empire, and about to enter a prohibited system with no idea what's
waiting for us there,' said Peris. 'Under those circumstances, thinking
the glass is only half-empty makes me an optimist.'

Thula thought about this.

'You have a point,' he said.

'Wake the others,' said Paul. 'It's time.'

CHAPTER 49

When Syl got back to her quarters, Ani was waiting for her.
'Syl, where have you been? You have to get that stupid book back to Onwyn right now.

Syl had been in the changing rooms at the gym, hiding her white garments in her locker, but Ani didn't need those details, not right now. It was enough that Ani knew she'd been exploring.

'What's the big hurry?'

'I don't know. She said it's overdue, but mine isn't and she wants that one too. I've got mine here. I just don't know where yours is, though.'

Syl bent down next to the small cupboard in the kitchen and fished out the now rather scuffed copy of *The Interplanetary Pioneers* from underneath it.

'Should I take yours, too?' she said.

'Yes please. I don't want to face that old bat again. She seemed a bit nuts.'

A new voice cut in.

'Old bat? What's a "bat"?'

They both turned, and in the doorway stood Dessa.

'Hi, Dessa,' said Ani, blushing, and looking rather pleased. 'Come in. We were just talking about Onwyn. She's freaking out because she wants these books back.'

Dessa laughed. 'So I take it "old bat" means "crazy old fool" then. What books?'

Ani showed her.

'They're missing the last chapter though,' she said.

'Really?' said Dessa, absently flicking to the end of one volume.

'Yes, both copies are. It's very odd.'

'I'd probably better take them now,' said Syl.

Dessa handed the book to her. 'I'll walk with you.'

If Syl was taken aback, Ani was startled.

'Dessa, do you not want to stay?' she said. 'I can make us a drink.'

'No thank you, Ani. I actually just dropped by to see how Syl was. You said she was sick.' She turned to Syl, her purple eyes wide with concern. 'How are you feeling now?'

'Uh, better I guess.'

'Oh good. It's funny how these things can come and go. Anyway, should we walk? Or would you prefer it if I dropped the books back for you if you're not up to it?'

'No, I'll take them,' said Syl, suddenly fearing that if Dessa had them she'd spirit them away and deny all knowledge, landing Syl in a mountain of trouble. She couldn't figure out why Dessa – a Gifted Novice, and one of Tanit's gang, no less – seemed so intent upon be-friending her. Syl walked quickly from the room, and Dessa followed.

'Hey, wait up. Syl, you still don't trust me? After everything . . . ?'

It was like the older girl read her mind, and now she trailed her fingers delicately down Syl's arm.

'Oh, Syl! How can you not see that I just want to be your friend? I like you. I like your fire and your strength, and also' – she pulled Syl to a halt, forcing her to face her, and looking at her was like drowning in sad, amethyst pools – 'I think you're lonely. Very lonely. I know what that's like.'

To her shame, Syl felt tears in her eyes. She looked away quickly. Dessa still held her arm, caressing it with her thumb.

'Dear Syl, you sweet creature. I'm here for you.'

Dessa said no more. She merely slipped her hand through the crook of Syl's elbow and together they walked to the library, as if they were the best of friends. The Novices they passed stepped aside as they always did when they saw blue robes, and then looked at the pair again in surprise: a Gifted third-year strolling arm-in-arm with an unpopular Novice, smiling beatifically.

Syl felt unmoored, a little like she was floating. Maybe she really was ill after all, but then she'd had quite a day already. She found herself leaning on Dessa's arm.

Inside the library she held out the books to Onwyn, who snatched them from her, glaring.

'About time,' she grumbled. She appeared about to say more, but then she noticed Dessa standing beside Syl, and she nodded at her in greeting, acknowledging of one of Syrene's chosen few.

'A word?' said Onwyn to Syl. 'Alone?'

'Of course, Sister,' said Syl, and Dessa squeezed her arm sympathetically.

'I'll be outside,' she said.

Syl waited, but Onwyn was focused on the two books she had just been given. Silently she flicked to the back of the first, and frowned, before repeating the exercise with the second. Then she placed the books on her desk and reached out her hand to Syl. It felt small and bony against Syl's own, dry and fragile as a dead bird in her palm, but when the old librarian lifted her eyes to meet Syl's, her gaze was steady and strong.

'You looked up Archaeon on the system,' she said, and it was a statement, not a question.

Syl opened her mouth to reply, but Onwyn shook her head, pressing Syl's fingers.

'Hush, child. Keep silent, and hope that silence cannot be used against you. Be cautious, and hear my words, for nothing is as it appears to be. Nothing.'

Her eyes bored into Syl's until she was forced to look away under their intensity, but Onwyn spoke on.

'You must take care, Syl Hellais. My books have been defaced, and the last Novice who was curious about Archaeon was crushed to death in a rock fall in the Second Realm.'

'Kosia?' said Syl, hoping she'd hidden her disquiet for she'd passed through the deserted corridors of the Second only hours earlier.

'Kosia. So you have heard her name. A terrible accident, they said, but no one ever explained why she was in the Second Realm, and how a mere Novice came to be there in the first place. It is a dangerous area – stay away from it. *Nothing is as it appears to be.*'

'What do you mean?'

Onwyn shook her head, and let go of Syl's hand.

'Simply that you should tread with care. Now go. I have work to do.'

'But— '

'I said go.'

She turned away. Their conversation was over.

Dessa giggled companionably as Syl came out of the library, dazed.

'What did she want?'

Syl thought quickly. 'She accused me of damaging that book.'

'Why would you do that? The silly old, er, bat,' Dessa said.

'Oh, she's not so bad,' said Syl, half to herself.

'Was it worth all that fuss though?'

'What?'

'The book. Was it any good?'

'Actually it was, but, like Ani said, the last chapter was torn out.'

'How annoying for you. Shall I see if I can get you another copy?'

Syl stopped. 'From where?'

'The Half-Sisters' library, obviously.'

Syl stared at Dessa. 'How could you do that? It's off-limits.'

'Don't make me say it, please. I hate to bring it up because I know it makes me sound like a bit of a doorknob, but these blue robes do convey special privileges, you know. I may still be a Novice, but I am in third year and, as one of the Gifted, that means I can use the Half-Sisters' library whenever I choose. In fact, it's positively encouraged.'

'And you'd get the book for me?' said Syl, mouth agape.

'I said I would, didn't I? Now what's it called?'

Minutes later, Dessa was back in Syl's quarters, a familiar-looking volume tucked under her arm. Ani glanced up and smiled to see the older girl again, but Dessa brushed past her with a dismissive little wave and knocked on Syl's door. Inside, Syl was studying the carto-graph, and the interruption startled her. Quickly, she tucked the device in her drawer.

'Yes?'

'It's me, Dessa.' The older girl opened the door and peered inside. 'I've got it!'

'Already?'

Dessa came in, pushing the door closed behind her with her foot, and placed the book on Syl's bedside table.

'Far as I can tell, it's all there.'

Syl longed to open it, but she couldn't, not with Dessa still present.

'Thank you. I really appreciate it,' she said, and she meant it too.

Grinning, Dessa climbed on to the bed next to Syl and made herself comfortable.

'Anytime. If there's anything else you want, just name it. I know the Novice library can run a bit dry.'

Syl almost laughed, for it would take her a thousand lifetimes to read all that was in the Novice library. Dessa didn't seem to notice her amusement. Instead she gave Syl a friendly pat on the knee.

'So tell me a bit about yourself, Syl Hellais the Earthborn.'

'What do you want to know?'

'Everything, of course! We're friends now, aren't we? You came here from an entirely different planet, and I'm fascinated by other worlds. You of all people must understand that.' She inclined her head towards *The Interplanetary Pioneers*. 'So what is it like then, on Earth? What are humans like? Did you know any?'

'A few.'

Dessa's eyes widened.

'Really? Did you know them well?'

Syl thought of Paul, and smiled. 'I knew some pretty well.'

'What? Did they work for you?'

'No, they didn't. They were my friends.'

'You were friends with humans? Wow! But aren't the humans fighting us? Don't they want us dead?'

'It's not as simple as that. We invaded their planet, don't you see?

They're just protecting their home. But once you get to know them, some of them are really nice. Kind. Gentle. Loving.'

'Loving?'

Syl blushed.

'Ah! You're going red. What aren't you telling me, Syl?' Dessa grinned wickedly. 'Was there someone special?'

Syl bit her lip and shook her head. What was she thinking? Dessa was one of *them*, one of Tanit's crew, one of Syrene's darlings, but then Dessa had also intervened on her behalf when the Gifted were bullying Elda; Dessa had risked Tanit's wrath to befriend Syl; Dessa had got Syl the book she wanted from a library that was off-bounds to mere Novices, which must be against all the rules. And she said she would get Syl more illicit reading matter – all Syl had to do was ask.

'Oh come on, Syl. You can't leave me hanging.'

Syl shrugged. What could the harm be?

'Well, there was this boy . . .'

Only after her visitor had left did it occur to Syl that Dessa could have asked Ani those same questions. Ani would probably have been more forthcoming, too. What had she done in sharing with Dessa in this way? But really, did it matter? It had felt good to talk, and it wasn't like her life history was a great secret to the Sisterhood anyway.

Shrugging it off, Syl reached for the book that Dessa had left her. She was sure that this book represented one small but crucial part of the puzzle she was trying to solve. There was a secret here. Clearly others thought so too, or else why go to the trouble of defacing the other copies? She flicked quickly through it until she reached the final chapter. And there it was:

The New World

It had no name when we arrived, this azure jewel of a planet, floating in space like a precious nugget. It was the first celestial body we came to with any significant life on it at all, and what life it was, vast and abundant, with herds of gentle quadrupeds grazing as far as the eye could see. Creatures ancient and obscure roamed the green and luscious plains. Pristine seas teemed with sleek, gilled beasts that swam and dived.

On our in-flight system, the blue planet was logged as FE17, as is the nature of scientific labelling; later it would become known as Archaeon, and would be declared a restricted zone.

But for now, for us, it was alive with creatures great and small, creatures we could walk up to and touch, for they were as curious about us as we were about them and they knew no natural fear. For a glorious moment in time, verdant Archaeon was ours to explore, and what a wonder it was to behold . . .

CHAPTER 50

This was set to be the worst boost ever, thought Paul, as he strapped himself into his chair. He and Thula had broken out some of the weaponry seized from the raiders, and all the humans, as well as Peris and Alis, were now fully armed. Rizzo was dubious about taking possession of one of the new pulse rifles, even if they weren't DNA locked. She was happier with a shotgun, but she consented to add a pulse pistol to her belt, just in case. Only Tiray remained unarmed. He told Thula that he had never yet held a pulse weapon, and didn't see any reason to start now.

'Not being killed would be a good reason,' said Thula, but Tiray simply ignored him.

None of the weapons, though, would be of much help to them when they first emerged from the wormhole. The Illyri wouldn't effectively seal off an entire system and then leave it unprotected. All of the ship's defensive systems were activated, and Alis had linked herself to them, leaving Steven to take care of piloting the *Nomad* through the wormhole and do his best to get them out of trouble if – or when – they encountered any. Paul had also patched Tiray into the communications console in the faint hope that, if they were threatened with destruction by superior forces, the presence of the politician on board might help them. But not for the first time, Paul wondered just what they had let themselves in for by allying themselves, however uncertainly, with Tiray. All he knew was that if the Illyri had gone to such trouble to hide something in the Archaeon system, then it was probably worth finding out just what it was. He tried not to consider the possibility that finding out might be the last thing they ever did, and that the knowledge wouldn't be much use to them if they were dead.

Steven waited for the order. Paul gave it.

'Take us in,' he said, and as the wormhole swallowed them Paul began to pray.

The first thing that struck Paul as they emerged was that the planet looked a lot like Earth: it had oceans and visible continents, although it was much, much smaller than his homeworld. It was about the same size as Mercury, he reckoned.

'Planet identified as system homeworld, Archaeon,' said Alis.

Archaeon: classified as I-3, according to the ship's display, support- ing significant biodiversity – large mammals, reptiles, ocean life – but no advanced species comparable to Illyri or humans. It loomed before them, the wormhole practically on its doorstep. Small satellites circled it, but as he watched four of them detached themselves from orbit and moved towards the newly arrived ship.

'No life signs,' said Alis. 'They're drones.'

As the drones approached, Paul saw that they were more oval than circular, with a central core that glowed as they neared the *Nomad*. A series of red warning flashes appeared on the cockpit display.

'They're weaponised,' said Steven. 'We're being scanned. Advise, Lieutenant.'

'Hold your course,' said Paul. 'No evasive action.'

The four drones surrounded the *Nomad*.

'Drone targeting systems are activating,' said Steven. A slight edge of panic crept into his voice. 'If we're going to do something about them, now would be a good time. Do we arm?'

'No. We wait.'

Nobody spoke. Nobody even moved, as though the slightest action might bring the drones down upon them. Paul found that he was clutching to the cross around his neck. If they open fire we won't know much about it, he thought. We'll just go straight from existence to non-existence without any stops in between. We won't feel a thing. Well, not much anyway.

Alis broke the silence, although she still spoke softly.

'They're communicating with the ship's core operating system,' she said.

'And what is the operating system doing?' asked Paul.

'It's answering back. I think it's a clearance protocol.'

The warning flashes on the display turned green.

'Targeting off,' said Steven. 'They're withdrawing.'

They watched with relief as the drones returned to their stationary orbits around the planet. Paul let out the breath he had been holding since the drones locked in on them.

'What just happened?' said Thula.

'You didn't die,' Paul told him.

'Well, all of this not dying is bad for my nerves,' Thula replied.

The cockpit display changed.

'We're being offered a guidance route down to the planet's surface,' said Steven.

'It's automated,' said Alis. 'I'm picking up no further communication.'

'Take the route,' said Paul. Any deviation might cause the drones to reconsider their attitude to the *Nomad*.

Steven adjusted their setting, realigning the *Nomad* to bring them in on the correct approach path.

'Breaching atmosphere in five – four – three – two – one!'

The *Nomad* shuddered as it entered Archeaon's atmosphere. They passed through thick banks of cloud. Lightning sparked angrily in their depths. Then they were out of the clouds, the detail of the landscape below gradually becoming apparent. They glimpsed forests and grey-green meadows; also a lake that seemed to be awash with some form of algae. Closer now, closer. They saw the fields below filled with movement, like dark grass being pulled back and forth by competing winds.

'Oh my God,' said Rizzo.

They saw hell.

★ ★ ★

At first, Paul mistook them for anemones somehow stranded far from the ocean, as though a great catastrophe had suddenly and fatally drained a seabed, leaving behind to die the life that it once contained. The anemone directly below the cockpit window was big, perhaps three or four feet in height, with thin reddish tentacles that twisted and stretched as they reached towards the sky. Its column, the anemone's support structure, was flatter than those of its smaller counterparts on Earth, and seemed to pulse softly with some life of its own. It was only as they drew closer to the surface that Paul understood that what he was looking at was not quite an anemone, and what supported it was most certainly not a column.

The organism appeared to have erupted from the body of some form of mammal, four-legged and pale, with a flat, spade-like head that was embedded in thick shoulder muscles without any obvious neck in between. The entire left side of its body had been ripped open from within, and its innards exposed. The animal was still alive, although barely: its death agonies were almost at an end. It lifted its face, revealing soft, dark eyes, and its body shuddered for a final time. Its head dropped back to the ground, and a long green tongue lolled from its open mouth as it died.

The anemone contracted as the life left its host, its tentacles curling in upon themselves until it was barely half its previous size. And then, simultaneously, they spread themselves again, and Paul glimpsed a dark opening at the parasite's heart. A great cloud of reddish spores rose from its insides and was carried into the air.

'Craft incoming,' said Steven.

He altered their flight path as, from the south, a zeppelin appeared. Paul had seen computer images of the helium zeppelins that were used on Illyr for the transportation of goods and people. This one was smaller than the Illyri craft – too small to be anything but automated – yet clearly modelled on the same design. The zeppelin moved in over the anemone and a hatch opened in its belly. The trajectory of the spores altered as they were sucked into the zeppelin, the little vessel remaining in place as cloud after cloud of dust was expelled by the creature below. They left the zeppelin to its work and continued their exploration in near silence, stunned by the sight of a living world that had been transformed into a slaughterhouse.

They passed over more of the anemone-like creatures, some pumping their spores into waiting zeppelins, others dead or dormant amid the skeletons of long-deceased animals. Small herds of the mammalian hosts were dotted here and there, nibbling nervously on vegetation. As they watched, one of the mammals fell to the ground and began thrashing, its mouth wide as it moaned in pain. Immediately the rest of the herd separated from the unfortunate animal, retreating into the low bush in an effort to put as much distance as possible between themselves and their dying fellow. The mammal's body swelled, and the crew of the *Nomad* could see the shape of the parasite within pressing against its insides. Then the animal burst, and from the bloody wound of its dying emerged the tentacles of the organism that had gestated inside it.

'There,' said Alis. 'To the north.'

Paul turned in that direction, grateful to take his eyes from the terrible birth below, even if only for a few seconds. A series of low white buildings lay on the horizon, and above them loomed a cooling tower and a round containment structure. Water vapor poured from the opening in the tower.

'That looks like a nuclear reactor,' said Peris.

They made one low pass over it, but saw no signs of operatives or movement outside the facility. The lower structures around it were windowless, but appeared to be ventilated. As they came by for a second pass a door opened in one of the units, and from it emerged a herd of the mammals, although these were clearly smaller and younger than the others they had seen so far. A pair of small drones drove them away from the facility with the aid of electric prods, until the animals commenced grazing, their tails swinging contentedly behind them. Paul wondered how long that would last: probably only, he guessed, until the first of them collapsed to the ground and began dying.

They continued north, following the curvature of the planet. They discovered four smaller nuclear facilities, but the only life-forms they saw were hosts and parasites. Meanwhile the zeppelins continued harvesting spores. In every case, once the parasites below had exhausted themselves, the zeppelins headed in the same direction: west.

'Follow that one,' Paul ordered, as a zeppelin finished its work and, its cargo hold apparently full, rose higher in the air and turned west.

They stayed on its tail. It was gradually joined by others until the *Nomad* flew above a flock of silver zeppelins, like children's balloons floating in unison. After a time, the zeppelins commenced their descent as they approached a fenced area with a trio of massive landing bays at its heart. Two were currently occupied by big cargo transporters, while the third lay empty. The zeppelins began an orderly docking, each attaching itself to a raised outlet on the hull of the first transporter. Unloading their cargo of spores took only minutes, after which each zeppelin ascended to begin its work again. Only the final zeppelin did not dock with the others, but moved instead to the second transporter.

'You see that?' said Steven.

'Looks like the first transporter has eaten its fill of spores,' said Paul. 'Might be an idea to give it a little room.'

Steven took them up and away from the bays. A thought struck Paul as they ascended.

'Alis, how familiar are you with this ship's systems?'

'I am . . . *intimate* with them,' she replied, and Paul knew what she meant, given that she had plugged herself into the flight recorder and, by extension, the *Nomad* itself.

'Does it have, I don't know, any kind of tracking devices, something that we could use to monitor the progress of that transporter?'

Alis considered the question.

'There are cluster transmitters,' she said. 'One of those might work.'

Cluster transmitters were used by Illyri craft to leave signals for other vessels, like electronic messages in floating bottles. They were linked to one another, forming a chain of markers.

'How quickly can you program one?'

'In minutes. What do you want it to do?'

'To drop a transmitter every time that transporter below enters or leaves a wormhole.'

'Consider it done.'

Alis left the co-pilot's chair and moved to a console at the back of the cockpit. She laid her right hand palm up on the console, and pulled back a flap of skin from her wrist, revealing a tiny connector port. Using a cable attached to the console, she plugged herself into the *Nomad*'s systems again.

'Man, that's weird,' said Thula.

'What, a woman taking a piece of outside equipment inside her?' said Rizzo.

'Yeah.'

'How do you think *you* were conceived?'

'I came down from heaven, like an angel.'

'I'm sure your mother would be fascinated to hear your theory of conception,' said Rizzo.

In the bay below, the metal docking restraints that held the transporter in place unlocked, leaving the ship free to fly.

'Departure imminent,' said Steven.

'Almost done,' said Alis.

Her left hand gripped the cable and pulled it free. She nodded at Paul.

'Done.'

'Activate it.'

A round device, resembling a clump of white bubbles, shot from the *Nomad* and attached itself to the hull of the transporter just as it began to rise from the bay. They watched it ascend slowly, then turn and head for the wormhole.

'Steven, continue the exploration,' Paul ordered. 'If there's anything else we need to know about this planet, I want you to find it. Rizzo, stay with him as a second pair of eyes. The rest of you, meet me in the briefing room in ten minutes.'

Paul left them. Peris and Tiray appeared to want to join him, but Paul shook his head. He wanted a little time alone before he spoke to them.

He needed to plan.

CHAPTER 51

'So, you think you're one of us now?'

Syl stiffened. She was alone in the locker room, for she was skipping her applied diplomacy class. She'd been about to open her locker, to put on the robes of a Service Sister again, to risk another foray beyond the Fourteenth Realm, only this time with the help of Lista's cartograph. Now Syl looked over her shoulder as Tanit materialised behind her. She must have followed her in. The door clicked shut, and Sarea and Nemein stepped out of the shadows too. Without taking her eyes off them, Syl quietly posted the cartograph through the slot in her locker, then turned to face them.

'Skulking again?' said Tanit.

'No more than you are.'

Tanit stepped close and reared over her. 'You have no importance at all, and yet you think you can compare your actions with mine?'

'We both breathe the same air, don't we?'

'Only because I allow you to, though you show no gratitude.'

'Well, thank you,' said Syl sarcastically, and Tanit sneered.

'You think you're so damned clever, and yet you're stupid enough to believe you can befriend the Lady Uludess, one of Archmage Syrene's chosen? You – one who means nothing!'

'Dessa?' Syl forced out a laugh. 'Well, I mean enough for you to think I'm a threat, obviously.'

'You mean *nothing*,' Tanit reiterated. 'And you mean less than nothing in your own right. The only thing that grants your protection, Syl Hellais, is the seed that made you, and even that was misplaced in the womb of a mother who rejected the Sisterhood.'

'At least you've heard of my father and mother. I have no clue as to your parentage.'

Tanit grabbed Syl's face between her fingers. They were as scorching as coals.

'That's because you've never been to Illyr. You're Earthborn, a mongrel. Without that stain your father made in your filthy gene pool, the Archmage Syrene would have had you thrown to the cascids long ago.'

'But would she have her trained monkeys crush my bones first, or is that part optional?' Syl surprised even herself with her boldness. It was a worthwhile risk though, for the cloud of fear that moved over Tanit's face was answer enough to any lingering questions Syl might have had about Elda's fate.

'What are you talking about, you cretin?' said Tanit, but her recovery came too late. Whatever they did to Syl now would be almost worth it, for her darkest suspicions had been confirmed.

'I think you know. And if you've already forgotten about Elda, I'm sure Sarea will remind you.'

Tanit shoved her face close to Syl's, a vein in her temple pulsing with rage. Her breath was hot and smelled of lightning, of ozone, sharp and pungent as the sparks on a bumper car ride. Syl's skin prickled under the heat and she felt redness rising across her cheeks, as if she was standing too close to a flame. Tanit clearly longed to burn the girl properly and fire flashed in her golden eyes, but then she glanced away.

'Actually, after that little outburst, I think perhaps Sarea should remind you of who you're dealing with. Sarea?'

Sarea stepped forward obediently.

'Just something small, please, dear,' instructed Tanit, and she looked back at Syl, watching her intently, licking her lips in anticipation. Instantly Syl felt an unseen vice tighten around her ring finger. She winced, grabbing her own hand in reflex, and Tanit smiled and nodded encouragingly.

Sarea laughed quietly, but Nemein let out a wail.

'I want a turn too,' she complained, but Tanit raised a hand to silence her.

'In a moment,' she said.

Gradually the pain in Syl's finger intensified, but it was almost secondary for Syl was doing battle with her own mind, determined not to reveal her powers, determined not to fight back.

Build walls. Block out the pain. Block. Shield.

She counselled herself to let it happen, not to put an end to it, not turn Sarea's power back on herself, for she felt the other girl's strength moving within her as if it was her own power to control too. Perhaps she could do it, but no, not now. Not now! It was too soon.

Walls. Bricks. Shields. Block out the pain.

Block. Out. The. Pain.

Pain!

There was a fierce crack and Syl opened her mouth to scream, yet her howl of agony was drowned out by another. It was Sarea, clutching her own hand wildly, staring at it in horror, for the bone of her ring finger had burst through the skin, and blood spurted from the wound.

Sarea, panicking at the pain and the sight of her own blood, whimpered as she grasped at anything for help. She reached for Tanit, but the pack leader stepped smartly out of her way, her lips twisting in distaste. Sarea lost her balance, and tumbled against Syl as she crashed to the ground. Syl was knocked backwards on to one of the slatted benches beside the showers, and her skull thudded against the wall so hard that silver lights danced before her eyes. Woozy, feeling like things were happening in slow motion, she looked down at her hand where it flopped in her lap. At least it had to be her hand, she reasoned, because it was attached to her arm, wasn't it? But she struggled to recognise this blue, swollen thing, with the ring finger hanging at an entirely new angle, twisted at the knuckle, dislocated from the joint, although the skin was smooth and unbroken. And, oh, the pain!

The pain!

Then there was nothing but darkness.

CHAPTER 52

Paul was seated at the head of the table when the others entered the briefing room, and they took chairs at either side of him, Tiray and Alis to his right, Thula and Peris to his left. They all appeared to be in varying states of shock, but Tiray most of all. Whatever he might have expected to find on Archaeon, it was not this.

Paul waited for them to get as comfortable as possible before sharing with them his knowledge of the implantation of alien organisms into senior Corps officials. Peris already knew, but there was no point in hiding the knowledge from the rest of them, not after what they'd just witnessed on Archaeon. He gave them a moment to absorb the information, then asked for their impressions of what they had seen.

Alis replied first.

'The planet appears to have been transformed into a facility for the production and harvesting of those spores,' she said. 'It's an enclosed system. Host mammals are birthed and raised in holding pens, then released. The parasitic organisms that will ultimately kill them are either implanted shortly after birth, or simply find their way into their hosts through their presence in the atmosphere. Those harvester zeppelins can't collect all of the spores. Some get away. Nevertheless, the former seems most likely. Why leave it to chance when the process could be guaranteed by implantation?

'And it's fully automated to avoid the risk of infection, or unwanted implantation. Although, given what we now know about Consul Gradus and his final moments – which suggests an apparent series of controlled implantations of these creatures into senior Diplomats – the relationship between the host and the organism is not the same as it is between the organism and those unfortunate creatures down on Archaeon.'

'Is it even the same organism?' asked Tiray.

Paul tried to remember everything that Syl had told him of Consul Gradus's agonising transformation, and the death of the Illyri laboratory assistant who was involved in examining him. Gradus's body had changed, producing tendrils – presumably similar to those sprouting out of the organisms on Archaeon – before shooting clouds of spores from his mouth. These, in turn, had infected the laboratory assistant, whose body had swollen as he, too, was turned into nothing more than a storage sack for spores.

'Suppose it is the same organism, but reacts in different ways according to the host in which it is implanted, or the circumstances in which it finds itself,' said Paul. 'In Gradus and the chosen Illyri it becomes a passenger, experiencing the outside world through them but not harming them unless it's threatened. But, in the case of the animals on Archaeon, it takes a more primitive form, and uses the host purely as a means to reproduce.'

Alis cocked a perfect Illyri eyebrow at him.

'That's an interesting theory,' she said.

'I'm no scientist,' Paul admitted.

'Sometimes imagination is a useful starting point.'

'Forgive me for interrupting a beautiful moment,' said Thula, 'but they are only spores. They are like pollen. How can a grain of pollen make such decisions?'

'It doesn't,' said Peris. 'It's simply hardwired into its DNA.'

Thula looked dubious, but didn't argue.

'Thula has a point, although not the one that he actually made,' said Alis.

'Thank you,' said Thula. 'I think.'

'Spores are subject to random influences,' said Alis. 'Wind, water, animals, flying creatures: they need something to transport them so they can reproduce, but they usually can't control the means. They're at its mercy.

'Now let's say that, at some time in the past, the Illyri discovered the existence of these organisms, maybe through infection or some other form of contact. Assuming that these organisms have a kind of intelligence in their mature form, an accommodation was reached: the Illyri would find suitable hosts for them in which to reproduce, and in return these organisms would give the Illyri certain enhancements. Both sides win.'

'And the hosts lose,' said Thula.

'Yes, the hosts lose.'

'It would be useful to harvest some of those spores ourselves,' said Paul. 'And perhaps samples from the mature organism and the host creatures.'

'Useful, but dangerous,' said Tiray.

'Are there any suitable storage facilities on board?' asked Paul.

'We don't have isolation chambers, if that's what you mean,' said Alis. 'We could put the samples in jars and seal them. I could go down and collect them. I don't believe that the organism will be able to implant in a non-biological host.'

Paul shook his head.

'No, it's too risky. Archaeon's atmosphere is probably rich with those spores. They'd be on your clothing, your skin, your hair. Even full sterilisation might not be enough to get rid of them all.'

He stood, walked to one of the windows of the briefing room, and looked down as the landscape passed beneath them. Peris joined him.

'This planet is just the beginning, isn't it?' said Paul.

'I think so. Whatever these organisms are, they're not going to be content simply to reproduce indefinitely in a backwater of the universe.'

'The Illyri are going to give the Earth to them,' said Paul. 'Ultimately, that's where those cargo transporters will end up.'

'I fear you may be right. What do you want us to do, Lieutenant?'

Paul continued to gaze upon Archaeon. Thankfully, the *Nomad* was flying too high to reveal the sufferings of the host animals, but the sight of zeppelins passing to and fro beneath them was a constant reminder to Paul of what was occurring on the surface.

'Alis?' said Paul. 'Confirm ordnance status.'

'Three heavy cannon – two laser, one pulse. Twelve torpedoes. Four proximity mines.' Proximity mines could be released from a ship and left to float in space until a pursuing craft came close enough to set them off.

'Can those mines be converted from proximity to timed detonation?'

'Yes, Lieutenant.'

'Destructive power?'

'Catastrophic. I believe that one of them could take out a destroyer.'

'I don't want to take out a destroyer. I want to blow up a nuclear reactor.'

'Then I think one of them will serve your purpose perfectly well.'

Tiray leaned forward in his chair.

'Did I hear you right? You intend to destroy the reactor?'

'Do you have an objection?'

'All Illyri-built structures on the surface are almost certainly linked to that reactor,' said Tiray. 'You'll irradiate the entire planet.'

'That's my intention.'

'But what of the indigenous species?'

'The last time I checked, the outlook for the indigenous species was bleak. It seemed to involve dying painfully.'

'And what you're suggesting is somehow better?'

'Councilor Tiray, the Illyri have turned Archaeon into a breeding ground for a hostile alien organism, one that I am certain is going to be used against my own people. The first step in fighting back is to bring to an end what is happening on the planet.'

'Not all Illyri!' Tiray protested. 'I had no part in this. Neither did Peris, or Alis. Most Illyri have no idea of what is being done in their name. If they did, they would surely object. They would not permit it!'

'That's very reassuring to hear,' said Paul. 'Unfortunately, it comes a little late. Who knows how many of those transporters with their cargos of spores have already left Archaeon?'

'If you destroy that planet, you will be guilty of the annihilation of species that may exist nowhere else in the universe,' said Tiray. 'It is the equivalent of genocide.'

'And when those transporters reach Earth?' shouted Paul. 'What then? *That*, Councillor, will be genocide, and I am not about to let it happen. Alis, how long to convert one of those mines?'

'A few hours. Less, if I work fast.'

'Do it.'

'Alis' – Tiray's voice carried a note of warning – 'I order you not to assist the lieutenant with what he is planning.'

'I am sorry, Councillor. I agree with you that the destruction of Archaeon is regrettable, but that process of destruction commenced as soon as the Illyri gave it to the organisms as a breeding facility. From that moment, Archaeon was doomed. We are merely finishing what the Illyri started.'

'You speak of the Illyri as though we were another race,' said Tiray.

'You *are* another race. I am not Illyri. I am Mech.'

'But – ' Tiray looked distraught. 'I saved you. I treated you like my own child.'

'And I will always be grateful to you for it,' said Alis. 'But I am not a child, and I am not yours to command.'

She stood and left the briefing room. Tiray let her go. He sat staring at the table, his expression a potent mixture of sadness and anger.

One by one the others left until only Tiray and Paul remained.

'This will change nothing,' said Tiray.

'Maybe not, but it's a start.'

'If these organisms are intelligent, perhaps they can be reasoned with. Your planet, your people, may not have to be sacrificed.'

'And what will you offer them instead?' asked Paul. 'Another Archaeon, or some other unfortunate world that the Illyri can hand over without too much guilt because whatever lives on it can't speak out against what will happen? No, the time for reasoning is over. The bargain has already been struck, Councillor. Someone on Illyr made a deal with the devil.'

Tiray's reply dripped with scorn.

'The devil! I've read about your beliefs. I see the charm you wear around your neck. You're no better than a deluded Mech, worshipping ghosts in the sky. I do not believe in a "devil". I believe only in what I can see.'

'You've seen Archaeon,' said Paul. 'How can you look at it, at the evil of it, and not believe in demons?'

Tiray rose from his chair.

'How can you look at it,' he asked Paul, 'and believe in a god?'

Paul had no answer.

Chapter 53

Syl awoke in an unfamiliar bed in a room that wasn't her own: it was bright white, over-lit, and smelled of chemicals. It took a moment for the throbbing ache in her hand to make sense, for her thoughts were clouded with medication and the memory of what had happened in the changing rooms felt like a tall story someone else had told her.

A blurred face loomed over the bed.

'Althea?' Syl said, confused, and the word croaked out from her dry lips like a cough.

'You're awake,' said Althea. 'How are you feeling?'

'Fine. Can I . . . ?' She tried to sit up, but gentle hands pushed her back.

'Stay where you are. You had a nasty bump on the head. And your hand, your poor hand – what happened, Syl Hellais?'

'I don't know.' She was struggling to focus on Althea – her eyes felt like they were full of grit. 'Where am I? How did I get here?'

'You're in the sick bay. The medics brought you here. You were found unconscious in the changing rooms at the gymnasium.'

It hadn't been her imagination then. But where had Althea come from? Syl covered her eyes, wondering what was wrong with her vision. She needed to see clearly; she needed to think straight. When she looked again, Althea seemed to be shrouded in a cloud of red.

'Sarea. What happened to Sarea?' said Syl.

'Why do you want to know about Sarea?'

'She was in the changing rooms. Her hand – the bone came through. She fell. Where is she?'

'She was with you?'

'Yes. She was, and Tanit, and Nemein too.'

'Yet you were found alone. Why don't you tell me what happened?'

'She was hurting me. Sarea was hurting me. Hurting my hand. Then she was injured – oh God, it went right through her skin. There was so much blood . . .'

'As I said, you were found alone. Listen to me: tell me what you remember from the very beginning. Tell me everything.'

'But how can I have been alone? Where's Sarea? What happened to Tanit?'

'Well, Tanit is hardly likely to be visiting you, is she, Syl Hellais?'

It was an odd response and Syl felt a stirring of unease. Why was Althea using her proper name? To Althea, she had always been Syl, and only Syl. She shook her head and it thrummed uncomfortably, as if her brain were rattling in her skull, but Althea was still blurred and strange, and now she seemed to be wearing the red robes of the Sisterhood. Then Syl became aware of something else, something stabbing into her mind, a sharp pain as if someone was poking at her cerebrum with a stick. The stick was bony though, resembling a broad finger. It was age-spotted, wrinkled, covered in thin flesh –

'Oriel!'

The old witch gave a laugh as she came into focus, and droplets of her spittle speckled Syl's cheek. Syl turned her face away in disgust, but Oriel just cackled again as she sat down beside Syl's bed.

'Oh, how quickly you forget your manners when you're not performing. To you, I am Grandmage Oriel. Never forget who I am, Earth-child. Never forget *what* I am.'

Syl thought quickly, furious with herself. Of course Althea wasn't here, but for the sweetest moment she had thought that her governess had returned to care for her. She realised how lost she was, and a deep sadness sucked at her guts. She yearned to let go of all this anxiety, but it consumed her. There was fear, too, at how easily Oriel had tricked her. How much did Oriel know? What had Syl told her, or inadvertently revealed? What did Oriel already know of what happened in the changing room? Syl's best bet would surely be to play dumb.

'My sincere apologies, Grandmage,' she said. 'I don't quite feel myself. I'm sure you understand.'

'And there she goes again. Always a performer, just like her mother.'

'Grandmage?'

Oriel glared at Syl now, her every feature contorted with disgust.

'Enough with the games. You revolt me. Spoilt little madam with your nursemaid and your darling daddy sheltering you, making you think you're special. You came here believing that you could tear us apart, but we are so much older than you can ever know, so much wiser. Yet still you persist, like a piece of grit in the shoe of a giant.'

'*Tolluntur in altum, ut lapsu graviore ruant,*' said Syl, glaring back.

'What?'

'The bigger they are, the harder they fall, basically,' said Syl. 'It's Latin. The poet Claudian, I think.'

Oriel smiled triumphantly. 'So you admit it: you wish to see the Sisterhood fall. This is treason!'

'I admit nothing of the sort. I was merely referring to giants, and quoting a poet from Earth. And how can it be treason if you are simply librarians?'

'Enough! Your prattle is exhausting. I know you were in the changing room I know exactly who you were with. Yes, you were found alone but that is only because Tanit – your elder and better, lest you forget it – had the good sense to clean up your mess and remove Sarea to a safe location before she called Sister Thona, and of course Sister Thona summoned me. So now explain to me what happened to Sarea. Tell me what you did to her, you wicked child.'

'I did nothing. I swear I did nothing!'

With surprising speed, Oriel slapped Syl hard across the cheek, hard enough to turn her head on her neck and bring tears to her eyes.

'How then did her finger break so badly that the bone tore through the skin?' Oriel said. 'I saw her injury with my own eyes, Earthborn.'

'But it wasn't me that did it! I don't know what happened to Sarea. It just, I don't know, happened. Honestly.'

With a face of cold stone, Oriel snatched Syl's injured hand and squeezed, hard. Syl yowled with pain and tried to writhe away, but the old woman was unnervingly strong, and Syl was weak with medication.

'She hurt me, but I didn't hurt her back. I didn't!'

Syl's dislocated joint had been popped back into place by the medics, but now Oriel yanked it backwards again, baring her teeth, threatening to wrench the bone from the socket. Syl squealed, and felt sure she would pass out: blackness started to cloud her vision.

'I didn't do it!'

Oriel let go, looking quite pleased with the outcome.

'I suspect you truly believe what you're saying. However, I don't believe it. Do you care to hear what Sarea says?'

Syl breathed out heavily, which Oriel took as assent.

'Sarea thinks that she somehow injured herself. Poor Sarea is devastated because she fears that she lost control of her formidable and very unique powers and turned them on herself, like the recoil of a weapon injuring a shooter. That truly brilliant Novice is all but broken, thanks to you. She's terrified to practise her skills again for fear of damaging herself. She is undergoing intensive counselling as we speak. You may have ruined her.'

'But it really wasn't me that did it,' said Syl again, cradling her injured hand in her healthy one for fear that Oriel would strike again. Yet Sarea doubted herself? Good, thought Syl. She stared back sullenly at Oriel.

'I feel you blocking me,' said the Grandmage. 'I feel your wall of hatred. I will find out what's behind it though – you mark my words. I will find out what powers you hide, for there is something foul within you, of this I am sure.'

'Just like there's something foul within the Sisterhood?'

Oriel's eyes glowed red then, or perhaps it was just the light catching and reflecting her robes. When she opened her mouth to speak she pushed her face into Syl's, and her breath was sickly sweet and spicy.

'I will tear your secret out of you. I will wrench it from within you myself. I will strip you bare and leave you empty, until all that remains is the husk of what was once Syl Hellais. You'll be a shadow of what went before, just like what remains of your ridiculous father, that smiling idiot, that empty shell.'

Syl's lip quivered with impotent fury. 'What did you do to my father?'

Oriel really did laugh now, sounding for the first time like her pleasure was real.

'Syrene's dancing puppet, you mean?' came the old witch's reply. 'When it comes to your father, Earthborn, we've barely even started. Oh yes. Syrene will return soon. When she does, perhaps she will fill you in.'

Chuckling with cruel amusement, Oriel arose and swept from the room.

CHAPTER 54

Syl stayed in the infirmary for several more days, her door locked, her medication administered by a silent nursing drone, clicking around on silver wheels. A taciturn doctor dressed in Sisterly red saw to Syl's hand and prodded her head, and her food came mashed on a tray. She had a small collection of bland books – mainly sycophantic volumes covering the history of the Sisterhood, so she had little trouble guessing who had chosen them for her – and no other distractions. The only visitor she received was Oriel. The Grandmage would sit beside her bed for hours at a time, watching her, probing at her mind, and Syl would concentrate on irrelevant things, summoning gentle memories from her days of innocence. She allowed Oriel into her head far enough to witness her tamest thoughts – the sweet faces of daffodils, a castle cat stalking a teasing robin, a kilt blowing up and revealing neon underwear, she and Ani hanging out of the castle windows watching an enormous red moon rise over Scotland – and still she felt Oriel picking and digging. She could no longer pretend to Oriel that she had no abilities at all, but she could conceal the true extent of them. There was a great difference between the kind of learned mental discipline that Syl was exhibiting – the capacity to block out pain, to create images of walls and barriers in one's mind to prevent others from divining one's thoughts – and the reality of her powers and of what she was capable of doing with them: clouding, compelling.

Killing.

She let Oriel see Paul, for the Sisterhood knew of her affection for him, and so she taunted the old witch with rosy, lingering recollections of a shared kiss, of tongues slipping pinkly over each other, and Paul's skinny, muscled body, lean and pale as he dived like an eager seal through the freezing waters of the loch. She could feel the revulsion spilling out of Oriel like mud, and it seemed to distract the Nairene, to make her recoil. Encouraged, Syl thought about humans, many humans: humans stuffing their faces with cake, laughing with their mouths open so it spilled down their chests. She thought of them burping and farting and copulating. She thought about their eyes, about the lids that creased oddly to cover them, and their stocky, compact bodies, until Oriel's repulsion became like a hard tumour in Syl's head. The Grandmage probed no further.

Yet still, her stark surroundings ground Syl down. The relentless brightness of her small ward – a sterile cell with no windows, and a small toilet cubicle – was only divided into time periods by the arrival of her meals. In between she slept heavily, exhausted by her mental jousting with Oriel. Often she considered the task that she'd set herself, and she despaired. Sometimes it felt that just surrendering to the allure of the Sisterhood was the only real option, the only way that she'd ever know peace again . . .

Until Syl awoke from a nap to find three different red–clad females waiting silently beside her bed. The two at the back bowed their heads in respect as the third stepped forward regally, her eyes never leaving Syl's. She was younger than Oriel, and strangely beautiful, her face laced with filigree tattoos, her scarlet lips plump to the point of bursting, like overripe fruit.

'Syrene,' said Syl.

Syrene studied Syl, her features bland, and Syl stared back, part horrified but also mesmerised. The tension grew too great and the young Illyri looked away.

'Is it just Syrene? The Grandmage Oriel warned me that, even when hurt, you remain insolent,' said Syrene. 'How are your injuries, Syl Hellais? I brought you flowers.'

She lifted a bouquet of tangled blooms above Syl's bed, and thick, wet pollen drooled from their outsized stamens on to her sheets. The smell filled the room: avatis blossoms, the very flowers Syl had first seen in Syrene's rooms on Earth before she'd been sent away. Syrene was toying with her.

Smiling, Syrene reached out to touch Syl's head and Syl flinched, shifting away, for the Archmage's fingers had burned her before, searing pathways into her mind, yet this time those inquisitive fingers stopped short, and the hand was withdrawn. Syrene observed Syl haughtily, and the twin eyes tattooed on her cheeks seemed to glare too, so that momentarily Syrene resembled a bug, a spider with multiple eyes. Then, with a dismissive flick, the Archmage dropped the blossoms on to Syl's exposed neck. As they made contact the heads of each flower closed and a cloud of foul-smelling gas huffed into Syl's face: the flower's defence mechanism. She coughed, while Syrene looked on disdainfully.

'What a strange way to thank me for my exquisite gift. And still you do not even have the courtesy to greet me properly,' she said.

'I greet you, Your Eminence. I thank you.'

'That's better. And do you not also welcome me back to my home? I have been gone a long time, and you are my guest at the Marque, are you not?'

'I welcome you home, Archmage,' sighed Syl.

'I trust you have been treated well by my Sisters. I stressed that they were to look after you as if you were my own daughter.'

Behind Syrene the two younger Sisters looked up, sniggering audibly. They seemed familiar, and Syrene followed the direction of Syl's eyes as she took them in, frowning.

'You remember my handmaiden, Cocile, I presume? And my scribe, Layne. You met on Earth, of course, although then they were dressed in the yellow robes of Novices.'

Syrene was enjoying Syl's confusion. How could Novices have progressed to the full rank of the Sisterhood so quickly?

'Obviously they are anything but Novices,' said Syrene. 'The seemingly lowly status denoted by the robes of the Novitiate works in our favour. Donning yellow gowns when appropriate means that my best and brightest Sisters are frequently underestimated. Is that not so, Cocile?'

'Indeed, Your Eminence,' said Cocile.

Now Syl remembered these two, but it was little comfort that last time she'd seen them had been back in Edinburgh, when Meia had knocked them both unconscious to gain access to Syrene's quarters in order to rescue Syl. There was no Meia here to protect her now, and Syl watched Syrene unhappily. The pollen on her chest was itching dreadfully and the smell in her nostrils was of putrefying flesh, but she was loath to push the flowers aside and let Syrene know of her discomfort.

'Now we are returned to the Marque, however briefly,' continued Syrene, 'and they can once again be who they truly are. Although we did become very familiar with your home on Earth, Syl Hellais. Very familiar indeed. Your father sends his greetings.'

'My father? How is he?'

'He is well. So accommodating. I believe he would do anything for me. Anything at all.'

Syl grabbed the flowers and sat up, placing them on the sheets on her lap. Noticing the red hives that had already swollen across Syl's neck, Syrene smiled properly for the first time, but she said nothing. This was all just a game to her.

'What have you done to my father?' said Syl.

'What could you possibly mean? He is better than I've ever seen him. So happy. Yes, wouldn't you say he's happy, Cocile?'

'Ecstatic, Your Eminence.'

'Ecstatic – an excellent choice of words. I think perhaps being relieved of the burden of a disruptive, disobedient teenage daughter may have given him a new zest for life. He is a changed figure. And so very warm and loving. So . . . sensuous.'

Syl pretended to study the flowers on her lap while rage swelled like a toxic balloon in her chest.

'I don't understand what you mean, Your Eminence,' she finally managed, lifting her eyes and trying to read the Archmage's face. For a second she considered probing her mind too, or at least attempting to, but that would be foolhardy: the Red Witch was a skilled psychic, a veteran of the craft, and it had been all Syl could do to hide her own growing talents from the Nairene Sisterhood. She must bide her time, keeping her gifts a secret for when they could be best used.

'Perhaps I have said too much. Suffice to say Andrus – Lord Andrus – has become a valued companion,' said Syrene. 'Anyway, it is my belief that you will soon see your father once more. Does that please you?'

'When can I see him, Your Eminence?'

'Oh, I'm sure we can come up with something. Just make sure you understand that we're on the same side, Syl Hellais – that is, if you are on the same side as your esteemed father?'

'My father? The same father who sired me? Of course I am. I'll always be on his side.'

If Syrene noticed the subtlety of her message, she didn't show it.

'Good. You need to get well soon, for there is much to be done. The sooner you leave the infirmary, the better.'

Syl looked at her bandaged hand.

'I think I'm probably well enough to leave now, Your Eminence.'

Syrene clapped her hands as if nothing pleased her more.

'Wonderful,' she said, 'for we have a ball to prepare for: the Genesis Ball. And you are to attend, Syl Hellais. Nothing will please me more than knowing the daughter of Lord Andrus will dance at the Genesis Ball.'

'I am invited to the Genesis Ball, Archmage?' Syl was sure it must be a joke.

'Indeed – the invitation is mine to give. As the only daughter of my respected comrade and beloved friend Lord Andrus, I shall expect you to attend in honour of your father, and as a symbol of the growing closeness between our families. I insist on it.'

It was exactly what Syl had wanted, but coming from the Archmage, weighted as it was with innuendo and hints of impropriety, the notion now galled her.

'Is that where I shall see my father?' she said tightly.

'Oh no, indeed you shall not. The great Military leader Lord Andrus would not return to Illyr for something as inconsequential as a debutantes' ball. What does he care for the making of suitable matches among the Sisterhood? Oriel is quite capable of overseeing that matter alone. I shall be returning to Earth, for there is work to be done. When you see our dear Lord Andrus again, it will be for something of far greater import than that, something much more wonderful entirely. You can be sure of that much, at least.'

'Really? What?'

Syrene gave Syl a pointed look, and Syl felt a cracking pain under her skull, as if she'd been struck sharply with a hammer. She put her fingers to her head, and Syrene nodded slightly. It had been a warning.

'May I ask the nature of the occasion that will allow me to see my father, Your Eminence?' said Syl instead.

Syrene let out a high, tinkling laugh, and her voice splintered around the room like breaking glass.

'That, my child, is still a secret, for his proposal is not yet public knowledge. Oops, I have let it slip, have I not? How silly. But, as his only progeny, I imagine it is safe to entrust our wonderful news to you. In due course, Lord Andrus and I shall be wed.'

'What?' Syl felt like she'd been punched.

'You *are* happy for us?'

Even while Syrene smiled, there was chill in her voice and a blatant threat in her eyes. Syl swallowed down her rage, and her tears, and nodded, not trusting herself to speak. Her father, her beloved father, was to marry this creature?

'Excellent,' said Syrene, although Syl had given no answer. 'And naturally, it will be an occasion of great joy, and you will be expected to celebrate with us. But for now we must prepare for the Genesis Ball, for other alliances need to be assured, too. So come, for it is time for you to stop lounging around in bed like a spoilt princess. Rise, my . . . stepdaughter.'

She swept out of the room without another word.

Seconds later the doctor hurried in, a nurse at her heels. With no formalities, she instructed Syl to clear out, and clicked her fingers at the nurse, who immediately yanked the young Illyri from the bed. Syl stood semi-clad and pale, holding her bandaged limb gingerly, for the sudden movement had left it throbbing.

'Is my hand mended?'

'Your hand is fine,' said the doctor, and she narrowed her eyes spitefully.

'It doesn't feel fine.'

'Take the bandage off,' the doctor instructed. Nervously, the nurse stepped forward and unwrapped Syl's hand. The skin was puckered from being covered up, but otherwise it was smooth and undamaged, the fingers straight and strong.

'But it still hurts.'

'Wiggle your fingers,' said the doctor. Syl did as she was told, carefully, and felt her eyes water as the unused joints cracked and ground.

'It was dislocated,' continued the doctor. 'We fixed the injury. We left the pain.'

'Why would you do that?'

The nurse was looking at her feet, but the doctor grinned.

'To teach you a lesson, Syl Hellais, Earthborn, daughter of the Lady Orianne. Now go, before I teach you another one.'

CHAPTER 55

Thula offered to help Alis with the conversion of the mine. He was strong, and had hands that didn't shake, although Alis was a Mech, and weakness and trembling weren't concerns for her. Still, the mine was large and heavy, and fitting a timer to it required the removal of panels and the deactivation of its proximity sensors, which involved holding back wires and replacing circuits. Alis was grateful for Thula's assistance, and the work was completed in about two hours.

While Alis and Thula worked, Paul and Steven made a number of passes over the reactor, scanning it from various angles in order to build up a more detailed three-dimensional picture of it. The model was now rotating in the air before them. Peris stroked his chin and peered at it from every possible perspective. Rizzo simply poked it with her finger and said, 'Bang.'

'Does it matter where we set the mine?' asked Steven.

'You're asking the wrong person,' said Paul. 'I've never blown up anything bigger than a truck. Those reactor walls are four feet of concrete and steel. I don't just want to damage them a little. I want the explosion to make Chernobyl look like a mild case of wind.'

Alis appeared on the other side of the model, Thula behind her.

'I think I can guarantee that as long as the mine is set beside, or even near, the containment structure, then you will not want to be anywhere near it when it blows,' said Alis.

'Is there a safe distance?' asked Rizzo.

'Far away,' said Alis.

'Right,' said Rizzo.

'And even then, I'd prefer to be farther yet.'

'I didn't know you were programmed to be funny,' said Rizzo.

'I wasn't.'

'Oh.'

'We'll set it for thirty minutes,' said Paul. 'That'll give us time to clear the atmosphere and watch the fireworks from orbit.'

'I have more good news for you,' said Alis. 'Councillor Tiray was right, those secondary reactors are linked to the primary facility. When the big one goes, there's a good chance that it'll cause a system breakdown in the others. At the very least, they'll cease to function, but I would anticipate a series of ancillary blasts.'

At that moment, a beeping came from the main cockpit, and the display produced an image of the Archaeon wormhole. A ship was emerging from it.

'A cargo transporter returning?' asked Paul.

Steven moved to the console and enlarged the image of the ship.

'No, and it's not a known fleet craft. It's not giving out a signal.'

'Hell,' said Paul. 'They've found us.'

They worked fast. It would take the new arrival a while to reach Archaeon and breach its atmosphere, but its long range scanners would reveal the presence of the *Nomad* before it even entered the planet's orbit. They could try to hide from it by staying on the opposite side, allowing the planet to shield them, but they could only do that for so long before they would be forced to expose themselves in order to attempt an escape. The craft was much larger than the *Nomad*, and its firepower was undoubtedly greater. Taking into account all of those factors, Paul instructed Steven to land their craft close to the reactor's containment dome in the hope that their smaller ship might be camouflaged by the machinery and buildings of the facility. In the event that they were discovered, their proximity to the reactor might also buy them some bargaining power: any attempt to destroy the *Nomad* from above risked damaging the reactor and irradiating Archaeon. Negotiation would be the only way to secure the *Nomad*'s surrender, although that gave Paul little consolation. He had no doubt that, once surrender was achieved and the *Nomad* secured, everyone on board the ship, with the possible exception of Tiray, would be killed.

Of course, it was possible that the unknown voyager had been scheduled to arrive at Archaeon in any case, and knew nothing of the *Nomad*'s presence, but Paul doubted it. Here was another ship cloaked to make it appear like little more than a flying scrapheap, but scrapheaps did not emerge unscathed from wormholes. No, the craft was there because it had either followed their trail, or guessed their destination. Tiray was its target, and if their pursuers were aware that the wormhole map was in his possession then it wouldn't have taken massive powers of deduction to conclude that he might eventually make his way to the secluded Archaeon system.

Paul watched the big ship approach the planet. He was frightened. He had been frightened almost from the moment that he had been forced to join the Brigades, just as he had lived in a state of near constant fear during his time with the Resistance: fear of discovery, of betrayal, of torture; fear that something terrible might befall his mother, or his brother, or his friends because of a mistake that he had made. Paul was old beyond his years. He had fought and killed. He had suffered injury and privation. If he hadn't been born to lead, then the very act of surviving had moulded him that way.

Yet the young lieutenant still felt himself to be a fraud because he was afraid, and there was no one to whom he could admit his weakness, not even his brother. Lives depended on him: not just the lives of those on board the *Nomad*, but perhaps the fate of every living thing on his home planet, and he did not believe himself worthy or capable of accepting that burden. But Paul Kerr, now nearly eighteen, had not yet come to understand the truth about fear: that bravery and courage did not depend upon the absence of fear, but the control of it.

And so he silently prayed, although he did not know for what, exactly. It was enough to recite the words of childhood prayers like a mantra in the hope that, somewhere beyond, his god – any god – might be listening.

'They're not following the same approach path that we did,' said Steven. 'They're ignoring the guidance.'

Paul watched the display. Instead of coming in on a route that would bring them almost directly over the reactor, the ship had turned northeast in its approach. Time: they had just been given a little more of it, and a little might be all that they needed. His fear vanished so quickly that he did not even recognise its passing, and it was replaced by the desire to act.

'Alis!' Paul shouted. 'Status!'

'We're primed,' said Thula, from the open bay in which Alis was making the final adjustments to the mine. 'She just needs a timing, and then we're ready to go.'

Paul returned his attention to Steven.

'I want a calculation,' he said. 'Based upon that ship's trajectory, calculate the point at which it will be here' – he indicated an area on the planet's surface roughly corresponding to its north pole – 'and the time it will take them to reach the reactor, allowing for their acceleration once they spot us. I don't expect it to be exact, but I do need a ballpark, and I need it fast. Alis?'

'Yes, Lieutenant?'

'Your assessment of "far away" as a safe distance from the blast is a little inexact. Give me something better.'

'At full acceleration, I believe we will need to be at least fifty miles from the site when the initial explosion occurs.'

'Thank you. Did you hear that, Steven?'

'Yes. Got it. I've made a rough estimate on the other ship, given that I don't have any idea of its engine capacity, and can only base it on our own. If they were to find out where we were at that point, it would take between eight and twelve minutes for them to reach us, but I'm kind of pulling that figure from my backside.'

Paul glanced behind him. Tiray was slumped in a chair, his arms folded, a scowl on his face. He looked like a sulky child. Rizzo was seated at a secondary console, and had activated the weapons systems. If they were forced to make a quick exit Steven would need all of his concentration to pilot the *Nomad*, and Rizzo was a fine gunner. Peris was standing only a few feet from Paul, and watching him closely. Already he knew what the young officer was thinking.

'It's dangerous,' he said. 'You will only have a small window of opportunity, and your brother's calculations are, by his own curiously phrased admission, far from precise.'

'Do you know what one of our instructors told us during Brigade training? He said that, in any military situation, a bad decision is better than no decision at all.'

'That was *my* class. I told you that.'

'So is it true?'

'Yes, although the right decision is always preferable.'

'If you have a better idea, I'd love to hear it.'

'If I had a better idea, I'd tell you.'

'Then we're agreed.'

'Hey,' said Steven. 'Any chance you could share the big idea with the rest of us?'

'I will, just as soon as I've given Thula the timing for the mine. That okay with you, Rizzo?'

Rizzo shrugged.

'We're still going to blow up something, right?' she asked.

'Yes.'

'Then that's all I need to know,' she replied, and returned to checking the heavy cannon and torpedoes.

Peris stepped closer to Paul.

'She's an interesting young woman,' he whispered.

'Yes.'

'When I say "interesting", I mean "terrifying".'

'I know. Aren't you glad she's on our side?'

'To be honest, I'm not sure. And she's only on "our" side for now.'

'What do you mean?'

'I mean that, deep down, she is not on my side, or Tiray's. In the end, Rizzo, Thula, and your brother, they are all on *your* side. Alis I cannot speak for, but I suspect that her loyalties, beyond those to her own kind, now also lie with you.'

'Because seventy five per cent of them are human?'

'Yes, there's that, but also because they trust you.'

'And you? Where do you stand?'

'As I said, I trust you too, at least until the time comes when you have to choose between your loyalty to your own kind and your loyalty to the Brigades.'

'I have no loyalty to the Brigades beyond keeping alive those under my command. You know that.'

Peris nodded.

'At least you are honest. You always have been. Should I summon Alis and Thula?'

'Please.'

Peris prepared to turn away, but Paul called his name. He spoke his next words softly, so that only he and Peris could hear them.

'I will not kill you unless you force me to,' he said.

'And I make the same promise to you,' Peris replied. 'You are already a fine soldier, Paul. May we both live long enough to see you become an even better one.'

Paul watched him go. Once again, he was disturbed by his affection for the Illyri warrior. Shaking off the feeling, he moved deeper into the main cockpit and enlarged the planetary display.

'Steven,' he said, 'prime the engines. On my mark, I want you to follow this course, and I want you to stay low . . .'

Chapter 56

Each of them had a role to play. Steven monitored the progress of the recently arrived ship, checking for any deviation in its course, any sign that the presence of the *Nomad* might have been discovered. Rizzo stayed on the cannon, tracking the ship even though it was out of range, ready to fire should it suddenly present itself as an immediate threat and come into her sights. Thula and Alis made a final check on the mine, even, to Paul's dismay, briefly activating the timer to make sure that it worked. Paul didn't want to hear the words 'activate' and 'mine' used while the device was still on board the *Nomad*. Peris prepped the ship for a fast getaway, conducting the same checks required prior to a boost. Tiray was enlisted to assist with stowing away any loose items, but he helped only reluctantly, despite the fact that a falling helmet could concuss him just as easily as any of them.

Paul tried to keep an eye on everything at once. Most of his attention lay with Steven and the other ship cruising only half a mile above the planet's surface. The *Nomad* was like a small fish hiding from a great shark, knowing that its refuge was only temporary and it would inevitably be found; it could only hope its speed and agility would be enough to save it from the predator's jaws.

When all was ready, and Paul was certain that no more could be done, they waited, silently watching the display, monitoring the slow, careful movements of the hostile ship as it scanned the landscape for traces of intrusion.

'Give me a count,' said Paul. 'Fifteen-second intervals.'

'Five minutes, at present velocity,' said Steven.

'Understood. Alis, prepare for release on my command.'

'Yes, Lieutenant.'

Alis moved into position, Thula shadowing her. By now Thula was growing familiar with the Mech. He didn't understand quite what she had done with the timer and the mine, for Thula's particular strengths did not lie in electronics and circuitry, but he was an astute observer of body language, and was able to get out of Alis's way an instant before she moved, and intervene to lift, or hold before she even had to ask.

'Four forty-five,' said Steven.

Something on the display caught his attention: a minute change in the hunter's course and velocity. He stayed with it until he was certain that it was no cause for alarm.

'Four-thirty.'

Paul moved to join Alis and Thula in the area of the *Nomad* above the weapons bay, which contained the mines and torpedoes. The mine could not be released while the *Nomad* was on the ground, but their heat signature would draw the hunter to them the moment that they lifted off. Yes, the deployment of weaponry could be controlled from the cockpit, but Alis had elected to carry out her part in the plan at the bay, so that she could focus on it more completely. The Mech did not want any distractions when dropping the mine, and she was once again plugged directly into the ship's systems. In case of any problems, she had also left open part of the decking, exposing the manual release lever.

The plan at least had the virtue of being simple. At Paul's signal, Steven would start the *Nomad*'s engines and lift the craft vertically until it was thirty or forty feet above the surface of the planet. The bay doors would then open, and the mine would drop (and 'mine' and 'drop' were two more words that made Paul uncomfortable when used in the same sentence). Once the mine was in place, the *Nomad* would beat a retreat west, on a course parallel to the ground and making no apparent attempt to ascend. Paul wanted the pursuing craft to stay low, and to head directly for the reactor. The *Nomad* was the bait in their trap, and to make it even more attractive to those hunting them, he had told Steven to adopt an uneven, halting movement, as though their ship might have been damaged in the course of the many boosts that had brought it to Archaeon.

He gave one further order, one that caused even Peris to object: the doors were to remain open after the mine was released and until they had cleared the planet's atmosphere, assuming they lived that long. It was not standard operating procedure; it was, in fact, actively against all protocols, but this way the bay would remain sealed off from the rest of the ship. It would be exposed to the atmosphere of Archaeon while the mine was being dropped into position, and Paul did not want to risk any of those spores taking up residence on the *Nomad*. His plan was that they would briefly re-enter Archaeon's atmosphere after leaving it, and the heat of re-entry would burn everything in the open bay. They would be forced to dump all remaining mines and torpedoes before they tried to escape the planet, because heat and explosives did not mix, and Paul did not want to avoid being destroyed by their pursuers only to have the *Nomad* blown up by its own ordnance.

'Three-thirty,' said Steven. 'Three-fifteen. Wait, they're changing course! Heading towards us. Definitely heading towards us. Three minutes.'

'Someone has put two and two together,' said Peris.

'All right,' said Paul. 'Alis, prepare for release. Steven, get us up in the air.'

The ship shuddered and vibrated as its engines kicked into life. They felt it ascend slowly, Steven exercising extreme caution because he had wedged them into the smallest space available among the various components of the reactor. Nevertheless, the *Nomad* still rocked slightly, and they were forced to grab hold of whatever they could in order to steady themselves. Only Tiray misjudged it, crashing against the hull of the ship and striking his head. He sank to his knees, holding his injured scalp. A thin stream of blood trickled from it, but no one had time to see to him. He was conscious for now, so he couldn't be too badly hurt, and Paul was secretly relieved that the politician was out of commission, if only for a while. He did not trust him, and had Tiray decided to interfere with Steven or Alis at this delicate time, then he could have doomed them all.

'We're clear,' said Steven.

'Hold her steady!' Paul ordered. 'Alis, release the mine.'

They felt the bay doors open. Thula was poised above the manual release, ready to pull on it if necessary, but the mine dropped cleanly. Paul couldn't help but tense for an explosion as the device descended, but Alis had done her work well. The mine would detonate, but only at the appointed time.

'Steven, start moving, and get ready to give us full throttle at my command.'

Steven did as he had been instructed, taking the *Nomad* away from the reactor while making it appear to limp like a wounded animal. He kept a close watch on the display as their pursuers accelerated to intercept them.

'God, it's fast,' said Steven. 'Forget what I said earlier. They'll be at the reactor in fewer than five minutes.'

By now Alis and Thula were back with them. Paul gestured to her to take the co-pilot's chair.

'Is that going to give us enough time?' he asked.

'It will be close,' said Alis. 'There are too many unknown factors to calculate with certainty. We don't have any idea of the size of the reactor, or what kind of chain reaction an explosion might provoke. I can guarantee this: as long as it stays on its present course, that ship will be in the blast radius when the mine goes off, even if the reactor itself doesn't blow. The question is, will we?'

Paul made his decision.

'Steven, perhaps it might be a good idea to accelerate a little. Do it gradually, but do it.'

'With pleasure,' said Steven.

He carefully increased their velocity, but kept the acceleration jittery. 'They're matching us,' he said.

'Thula, get Tiray secured in a chair,' said Paul. 'Peris, lock yourself down.'

Thula lifted the woozy Tiray bodily from the floor, folded him into a chair, and strapped him in. Peris took the chair beside Tiray. Rizzo was already belted.

'They're coming into range,' she said. 'In range . . . now!'

At that instant, the ship was rocked by a blast from its port side.

'They're firing on us!' shouted Steven.

'It's got to be a warning shot,' Paul replied. He was surprised by how calm he sounded. 'Rizzo, fire in response. We don't want them to suspect that we're drawing them in.'

Rizzo gave them a blast with the pulse cannon, her face lighting up with pleasure as she got to shoot at something at last.

'Lieutenant, they're trying to communicate with us,' said Alis.

'Ignore them,' said Paul. 'Whatever they have to say, we don't need to hear it. Time to detonation?'

'One minute.'

'Time until that ship is dead meat?'

'Fifteen seconds.'

'Steven, you heard it. Fifteen seconds. At sixteen, you put your foot down and get us out of here.'

Another shot from the pursuing craft came across their bows, this time closer than the first. There would not be a third warning. If the bigger ship had pulse weapons – and there was no reason to assume it did not – it could fire a disabling blast at the *Nomad*, assuming their pursuers were willing to risk the *Nomad* crashing to the surface of Archaeon, and possibly killing everyone on board.

'Five seconds,' said Steven. 'Four. Three. Two. One!'

Paul dived for a seat and strapped himself in just as Steven gave the *Nomad* full throttle. He was pressed back by the force of the acceleration, and he felt the vessel begin to rise slowly. They might have been on the cusp of a nuclear explosion, but Steven was still not about to risk ruining everything by making a sudden ascent.

'They're staying in pursuit. Altering course again, but we've still got a good lead on them.'

'Rizzo, open fire,' ordered Paul. 'All cannon! Just keep them occupied.'

Rizzo didn't need to be told twice. She already had all three of the rotating heavy cannon directed behind them. She flipped a tab, and fired.

As she did so, the mine exploded, and seconds later the reactor itself. Even with the blast behind them, the cabin was bathed with white light so blinding that they had to cover their eyes with their hands. The *Nomad* shook with the force of the explosion, and had they not been strapped into their seats they would all have had their brains dashed out against the body of the ship. When Paul opened his eyes, he saw the planetary display flickering before him, the pursuing ship still on their tail.

And then the ship was gone, lost in a wave that swept from the core of what had once been the reactor, and the display vanished with it. Now the *Nomad* was shuddering again, but this time because it was breaching the planet's atmosphere, shaking off Archaeon's gravitational pull and entering the silence of space.

The display reconstituted itself. It revealed an overview of the planet, and a series of explosions emanating from the facilities linked to the reactor. Archaeon had just become a different kind of hell.

Rizzo broke the silence.

'Wow, we did that. Epic.'

CHAPTER 57

Syl and Ani were summoned to the Thirteenth Realm, the home of the Half-Sisters, along with the only other Gifted first-year Novice, Mila.

They were led into a lecture hall filled to capacity with older Novices in a wash of sea-green robes – the Half-Sisters. Some wore gowns piped with the blue of the Gifted, psychics who may have been older but were not as talented as Tanit and her crew.

This was because it was only relatively recently that the Sisterhood had learned it could actively manipulate the abilities of those rare individuals in possession of psychic powers. With each intake, more resources were poured into developing the skills of young psychics during the narrow window of puberty, for their powers would stabilise once they reached maturity. In addition, it had transpired that the coming-of-age implantation of neural Chips could actually suppress – or, indeed, eliminate entirely – any such fledgling abilities, although this news had come too late for many of the older, and possibly psychically gifted, Half-Sisters. Chips were subsequently banned for all future psychics. By this twist of fate, Tanit and her fellow Gifted were the most powerful psychics yet by some distance, putting the Half-Sisters to shame.

And there they were now, lounging in the front row like a fetid smear of deceptively lovely blue. Syl's skin crawled at the sight of Sarea.

Before the assembly stood two Sisters in red, clearly waiting to begin. They looked up as the door opened and, as all faces turned to see the newcomers, the room went deathly quiet. The three Novices froze where they were, uncertain, then Syl realised they weren't looking at Ani or Mila, but instead at her, standing out in yellow, the only ordinary Novice in the room. She stood her ground, staring back defiantly, and gradually everyone turned away again, muttering muted objections and occasionally glancing back at Syl.

'Mila,' called a voice from within the knot of blue. It was Xaron. 'Mila, Ani, over here.'

Ani plucked at Syl's sleeve and, reluctantly but with no better offer, Syl followed. Tanit glared at Syl, but Dessa smiled in delight and shuffled over, making room for Syl at the very end of the bench, while Ani and Mila were squeezed in at the middle.

'I heard you might be coming to the ball,' Dessa whispered. 'This couldn't be working out better.'

Syl felt a wave of gratitude, even affection, for the older girl. She couldn't decide if this was good or bad, but didn't have time to think about it for the meeting was beginning.

'Present today are those of the unordained Novitiate who have been hand-selected by our order for a great honour,' declared one of the Sisters in red, her pronouncement bringing the room to silence once more. It was the Applied Diplomacy lecturer, Priety, upright and proper, but for once she smiled, for they all knew what was coming.

'By the grace of her eminence Archmage Syrene, you are hereby invited to represent the Nairene Sisterhood at the Genesis Ball.'

The applause rang loud as bells.

'As you are doubtless aware, the purpose of the Genesis Ball is to introduce eligible Sisters, as well as selected Half-Sisters and Novices, to Illyri society. Since you will be ambassadors for our order, you will be dressed in the finest attire we can offer, and your behaviour will, of course, be exemplary at all times. But then, why would it be anything else, for do we not embody all that is great about the Illyri?'

There was more applause and a smattering of raucous cheers. At this, Priety frowned her disapproval and immediately the shouting ceased.

'Today I shall be covering rules and expectations, just to be sure that we all understand what is required of us. Then appointments will be made for dress fittings. In the interim, there will be deportment and dancing tuition, along with Applied Diplomacy refresher classes.'

She paused and smiled, but no one felt the need to applaud this.

'Finally, while we attend to these pressing matters, you will all be excused from your normal duties and classes . . .'

Even her glare couldn't shut off the spontaneous clapping and cheering that exploded through the room.

'. . . in order that you may study current affairs and matters of leadership and politics, so that you may speak knowledgeably . . .' She trailed off, shrugging with feigned indifference as her voice was drowned out.

Syl found herself being taken through the Thirteenth Realm again, and then into the rarefied Fourteenth, where no Novice was supposed to go unaccompanied, ushered onwards for the first of several fittings with the skilled seamstresses of the Sisterhood. With her were Ani and Mila. Mila hooked her arm through Ani's possessively and ignored Syl, but without the backing of her sister Xaron, or the other Gifted, Mila seemed subdued, and even a little jumpy.

'Wow!' said Ani as they passed the red curlicued walls that caught the light, twinkling gently, as if they were down a mine of precious gemstones. And she gasped again as they moved through the cavernous, towering living quarters of the Fourteenth Realm. Syl nodded and played along, but her chest thumped with worry that one of the white-robed Service Sisters would spot her. Yes, her wild bronze hair had been hidden in a headscarf on her previous incursions and yes, she'd barely spoken to anyone, apart from Lista, yet still fear clutched at her guts.

As they moved onwards and away from the areas she'd been in before, she paid close attention to the route they were taking and also to the space they were in, although most doors they passed remained shut. The further they moved from the Twelfth and Thirteenth Realms, the more the Red Sisters stared at the interlopers, some with small smiles as if they knew that this trio of shy Cinderellas had been invited to the ball, and some in bafflement. They whispered and sometimes pointed, and again Syl garnered the most attention in her yellow garb. She looked at her feet and walked on with her head bent, for it seemed to guarantee her more anonymity that way, especially as she intended coming back to explore just as soon as she could.

Finally they were led through a door and into the Seventh Realm, and Syl almost laughed for here was where she'd initially told Lista she lived: here! Now she understood Lista's bemusement, for it was immediately apparent that things were different in this Realm. The Seventh was carved deep into the old stone of Avila Minor, and here the seamstresses worked in tight, brightly lit caverns overflowing with bolts of jewel-coloured fabric and spools of vibrant silk. Jars of trinkets and baubles lined the walls and spilled across the floors. The hallways were spiked with hooks upon which hung newly crafted garments and just-cut pattern-pieces, as well as completed robes and finery, wrapped in clear sleeves and labelled for collection, or delivery, or adjustment. Large, ornate cases displayed what were clearly museum pieces, including faded, threadbare red robes in the styles of yesteryear, and jewelled gowns as ancient and fragile as cobwebs.

Wide-eyed, Syl, Ani and Mila were ushered into three large interlinked caves. The one on the left was heaped to the ceiling with what appeared to be jars of butterfly wings, buttons and sparkling crystals, separated by colour and design. On the right, furs, silks and hides were stacked beside rolls of iridescent cloth, and cloth that glowed, and cloth that seemed to have pictures moving across it: ferns caught in a breeze, clouds rumbling across a horizon, flowers nodding in the sunlight.

Everything overflowed into the cave in the centre, where a clutch of energetic seamstresses stood waiting for them. All wore custom-made red robes, the sleeves cut short so that they wouldn't interfere with their work, and various implements and pins dangled from their skirts.

At the core of the group a lone Sister sat on the only chair in the room and, although she appeared substantially younger than the others, she was clearly in charge. Her hair was shaved short, shorter even than was customary among full Sisters, but wings, frayed strands of ribbons, tiny beads, glitter, and threads of silver had caught – or been placed – on the stubble covering her skull, so that she seemed to wear a close-fitting cap crafted from torn insects and the sparkling ghosts of frivolity past.

'That's Sister Illan, the chief Nairene designer, but you are to call her "Your Elegance",' whispered their escort, before scurrying outside to wait.

Sister Illan watched closely as they walked towards her, and nodded almost dismissively at their polite greetings. Mila and Ani, in their rich blue robes, were beckoned forward and a lackey instructed them to twirl before the designer. Illan eyed them shrewdly, making notes and quick sketches on a screen before her. Next they were told to remove their robes, and they stood there shy and exposed in their under-garments while the seamstresses whispered among themselves. Finally Illan spoke.

'The only stipulation from the Archmage Syrene is that each deb-utante should wear the colour that denotes her station. This is customary. So you two will be in blue, obviously; beautiful, Gifted blue.'

She smiled, almost warmly, and Ani and Mila smiled eagerly back:

'Thank you, Your Elegance,' said Ani.

'Yes, thank you,' nodded Mila.

'Come,' Illan said, standing up and leading them over to an arrangement of blue cloth. She turned and studied the pair one last time, prodding Mila's shoulders hard so that the Novice stood up straight, and then pinching Ani on the cheek.

'A lovely face,' she declared, looking closely at Ani. 'A great pity you're not taller, but you're quite enchanting nonetheless.'

Mila wriggled, clearly hoping for a compliment of her own, but the designer was unforthcoming.

'I think I have just the thing for you,' was all Illan said to her, and she picked up a length of dark blue velvet, pushing the fabric into Mila's hands.

'Just stand up straight and it will look very well on you,' she told

Mila, who visibly wilted. 'We can trim it with stones, I would say, yes, Sister Rundl?'

'Indeed, Your Elegance,' said one of the seamstresses, stepping forward to take charge of Mila. 'Sapphires?'

'Oh dear me, no. The lapis lazuli or similar will suffice,' said Illan, clearly bored of the notion, and Sister Rundl herded the dejected-looking Mila and her uninspiring blue fabric away.

'But for you, pretty one with the silver hair,' said Illan, stroking Ani's mane, 'I think we need something extra special.'

She touched several fabrics, shaking her head, then wandered deeper into the section of the cave filled with textiles until she could no longer be seen. They all waited silently, Syl forgotten near the door, and Ani half-naked and blushing in the bright light. Finally, Illan reappeared looking very pleased with herself.

'This,' she said, and held up an indigo waterfall. At least that's what it appeared to be, for even as it settled and finally fell still, the marks on the sheer fabric flowed over each other, eddying and tumbling and sending up plumes of foam. With a flourish, Illan draped the fabric over Ani's shoulders so that she appeared to be emerging like a mermaid from a pool of restless water, her hair echoing the silver spray. The seamstresses all applauded.

'Perfect,' said the designer. 'Do you like it?'

'I do, Your Elegance. Very much.'

'Good. It suits you, but then I suspect most things would.'

She pointed to one of her team.

'Xela – I'd like you to take this one, for the finest fabrics need the finest needles.'

'Of course, Sister Illan,' said Xela as she came forward to take Ani away. 'I shall not let you down.'

With the fabric still flooding around her neck, Ani was led from the cavern. Now Illan turned to Syl, and frowned.

'I thought I'd imagined you, but no, you're still here. And still in yellow.'

'I am, Your Elegance,' said Syl, and she couldn't help but glance greedily at the lush fabrics piled behind the designer. She'd never admit it, but she too wanted to be beautiful for the ball.

'So the rumour is true then . . . But why, pray tell, is a mere yellow Novice going to the Genesis Ball?'

Syl said nothing, and Illan sighed heavily.

'It is not for me to question the powers that be,' she said dramatically, upon which the others laughed loudly, as if this was precisely what Illan enjoyed doing most of all. 'If I must make a costume of yellow, then so be it.'

'Thank you, Your Elegance,' said Syl, and she felt ashamed.

'Oh, I'm sure I can force myself to, although I hope Syrene does not intend to make a habit of it. I loathe yellow, and yet it is my second time working in it this year. I suppose at least this time I have a whole, live Novice to work on, not pieces of a dead one!'

Everyone laughed again, and Illan looked affronted when Syl didn't join in.

'I apologise, Your Elegance, but I don't understand,' said Syl.

'Nor should you, but if Novices will get themselves crushed by falling walls . . . Anyway, take those robes off. Let's see what we're working with.'

For Syl, Illan quickly selected a bolt of pale yellow fabric that changed hue as the light hit it. Nobody seemed particularly impressed by it, or bothered with her – least of all the unnamed seamstress who was assigned to her – but secretly Syl loved it. The material felt shivery as it slipped over her skin, soft and cool, but more importantly the changing colours put her in mind of the almost forgotten light and shadow of the burning Earth-sun as it tipped over the golden dunes of the Namib Desert in southern Africa. Her father had taken her there once when she was merely a child and, with Syl squashed safely between his knees aboard a flat toboggan, together they'd sailed down the mountains of shifting, soft sand, screaming in delight. Lord Andrus's staff had looked away to hide their smiles.

'And decoration, Sister Illan?' said the seamstress in a bored voice.

'Oh, I'm sure amber will do. Don't waste the precious gems on a yellow Novice.'

And Syl went away to be measured and fitted.

★ ★ ★

In the run-up to the Genesis Ball, Syl made several more visits to the
Seventh Realm of the Marque, where her yellow dress was cut and
styled until it fell over her in soft, vaguely clinging curves, the long
sleeves cut into trailing, pointed cuffs that floated beneath her arms
like wings. A low-slung belt of amber and leather was crafted to cinch
it together, and Syl felt like a warrior princess. Not that anyone
seemed to care what she thought or felt, but still Illan and her staff
took pride in their work – in all their work – an so even Mila's comparatively dull velvet material was fashioned into something lovely
and Romanesque, with rough blue stones and chunks of raw quartz
decorating the hem and neckline.

But Ani's dress was the most beautiful by far, the cut simple and
elegant, rippling close to her skin at the front and showing off her neat
figure to best effect, while from behind the fabric fell free as a cloak,
like water cascading wildly down her back, with the hem splashing
behind her as if she were trailing rapids. Sapphires caught the material
together like droplets of impossibly blue water, and Syl sighed in envy
when she saw her friend at the final fitting. Privately, she felt glad that
Paul would not be there to see how very beautiful Ani could be, as
wild and wanton as an ocean beside Syl's gentle, placid sand.

In between the fittings, the deportment classes, dancing lessons,
and the seemingly endless Applied Diplomacy lectures, Syl also managed a few more illicit forays into the Marque, with Lista's cartograph
tucked in the pocket of her white robes alongside the contraband
keys, and her telltale hair wrapped securely in a Service Sister
headscarf. Each time she went, she tried to explore somewhere new,
but the libraries and other structures of Avila Minor were vast, greater
in scope than she'd ever imagined, burrowing deep into the ground
with Realms often interlinked by countless passageways and tunnels,
so that sometimes she ended up where she'd started. Still, she felt she
was getting a sense of the place, and her fear of being caught
diminished too, for with the number of Sisters scurrying about and
the countless places they might be going to, one more wench in
domestic whites went unnoticed in the throng. Yet still she was

cautious, for she feared Oriel: Syl's disguise would be no match for the old witch, and she had little desire to become cascid fodder.

Back in her quarters she made a rough map of where she'd been, and a list of the different realms she'd entered and what they contained. For instance, most of the hydroponic farming of food, as well as the general organisation of the complex logistics required for running an operation as vast as the Marque – from fresh air to running water – seemed to take place in the Tenth and Eleventh Realms, which were roughly central to the entire community. Both of these also had large landing areas for incoming craft.

She had made it as far as the doors to what was apparently the Sixteenth Realm, but this area was locked and required special permission to access, though from what she'd heard – and secretly overheard – the Sixteenth housed all manner of creatures that flew and crawled and slithered on their bellies from both the homeworld and other worlds. Cleaning in the Sixteenth was a particularly noxious duty, which the Service Sisters universally loathed. The Sixteenth was in turn linked to the Ninth, which provided some overflow facilities, and that was where Syl had seen what looked remarkably like a unicorn on her first visit.

And in every Realm she entered she found libraries, vast and daunting, epic repositories of everything that the Illyri knew or had encountered. For such a claustrophobic place, Syl found it ironic that you could be locked in here forever and still discover everything there was to know in the universe.

As for Syl's injuries, by now the pain in her hand had all but subsided, and it seemed everyone had accepted the story of how she'd hurt herself when she'd supposedly fallen in the changing rooms. Even Ani didn't question it, but her studious avoidance of the topic suggested to Syl that she suspected more, yet preferred not to know, and she certainly didn't ask. This hurt Syl, but it also made her more comfortable about keeping her forbidden forays into the rest of the Marque a secret from her best friend. If Ani noticed her prolonged absences, she didn't mention them either. Often she wandered off and looked for Tanit, then artfully feigned surprise when she stumbled across the older girl. Sometimes, Syl wondered if Ani was a little in love with her, for her cheeks turned pink in the older Novice's presence, and increasingly it seemed that all Ani wanted to do was impress Tanit. But Tanit never exposed her ruse, and instead always smiled and welcomed Ani with apparent delight, making space for her by her side as she would a sweet foundling, or a pretty little pet.

Meanwhile Nemein smiled indulgently, for she was convinced that the starstruck first year had no chance of usurping her own place in the hierarchy, and selective kindness painted her in a good light.

As for Sarea, she said nothing, for she had become intermittently brooding and sullen following the incident with Syl. The damaged finger on her previously flawless hands had healed slightly crooked, and now bent unnaturally at the knuckle. This imperfection bothered her, but she rebuffed offers from the medical team to attempt to straighten it.

'No,' she informed Thona and the rest of the Gifted, 'I shall keep it as a reminder that once I was weak and careless, that my own powers are so great even I myself am at risk. And I shall never let that happen again. Never! I shall practise until I am unstoppable.'

When Oriel was told this, she nodded encouragingly, and pride pulsed through her cold heart, for such devotion to the cause would please Syrene greatly. Indeed, it would please everyone – and every-thing – that mattered.

And meanwhile, in the privacy of her bedroom, Syl obsessively sharpened her own psychic talents, honing her skills every spare moment she could find, for she felt a change coming, like the shift in the air before a thunderstorm, and she knew, she must be prepared.

CHAPTER 58

It was only in the aftermath, following a brief re-entry to the planet's atmosphere to scour the ship of spores, and the boost through the Archaeon wormhole, that the enormity of what he had done struck Paul. The *Nomad*'s display showed a series of blast points on the surface, the largest of them where the reactor had once stood. Alis had adjusted the 3-D image of the planet to track the spread of radiation, and with each second that went by another area of Archaeon turned from green to red. It was hard to conceive of anything surviving the catastrophe that they – that Paul – had inflicted on the ecosystem below.

Was he any better than the Illyri after all? They had sacrificed Archaeon to the unknown organisms for reasons known only to a handful of them. Now Paul had finished off the planet, justifying his actions on the grounds that they were necessary to save his own world. But who was he to make that decision? Who was he to decide that one world, or one species, was more worthy of survival than another? He had done the wrong thing for the right reason, or what he believed to be the right reason, but this did not change the fact that he was responsible for a terrible act of destruction.

And then there was the craft that had been swallowed up in the first explosion. He had never contemplated negotiating with its commander, never considered any possibility other than drawing it into a trap from which it could not escape. He had given no chance to those on board. It didn't matter to him now that, if the situation had been reversed, they would probably have shown him and his crew no mercy either: he didn't want to be the same as the worst of the Illyri. He wanted to be better than all of them.

With another boost imminent, Paul sat in the captain's quarters, his eyes empty, his heart filled with a guilt that threatened to overwhelm him entirely.

Alis appeared at the door, but she had to say his name twice before he took notice of her.

'What is it?'

'We're at the next wormhole, but I think we should delay the boost until we've run a diagnostics check on the ship. She's been through a lot. We don't want to enter another wormhole and have her come apart around us. I was surprised she made it out of the Archaeon system without a problem.'

There wouldn't be much that they could do if the *Nomad* was badly damaged, thought Paul. They were far from any maintenance facility, and the ship appeared to be carrying only the minimum of spare parts. Whoever had sent it after Tiray had not reckoned on it having to perform more than a couple of jumps before it returned home with its prize.

'How long will it take?'

'Not more than an hour, if I patch myself in directly.'

'Please do it.'

'Yes, Lieutenant.'

Alis did not move.

'Was there something else?' Paul asked.

He could see her trying to formulate the words she wished to speak. He could hear them already, although they remained yet unspoken: *You did what you had to do, you had no choice . . .*

'Do you feel guilt?' she asked at last.

'Yes,' he replied. 'I do.'

'Good. You should.'

He felt his anger rising. He did not need this artificial being, this imitation of a living creature, criticising him. She had no right. If anyone were going to torment him, it would be himself.

If Alis saw the effect her words were having on him, she took no notice. Instead she continued to speak.

'I am glad that you are in pain. I am pleased that you feel ashamed of what you have done – what *we* have done, for I assisted you every step of the way. If you did not experience these emotions, you would be less of a sentient being. For someone to unleash such destruction and not feel the burden of it would be a sign of sickness, of madness. We committed a wrong to prevent a greater wrong. We did what was necessary, and it cannot be undone, but we will bear the mark of it upon our souls, and we will answer for it to the Creator.'

'And what will the "Creator" say,' asked Paul, 'when we face him?'

'Who can tell?' replied Alis. 'But I believe this: there is no sin so great that it cannot be forgiven, and the Creator will consider the intention as much as the act in making his judgement. Anyway, I will inform you of the results of the diagnostic as soon as I have collated the data.'

He managed something like a smile.

'Thank you, Alis.'

'You're welcome. Oh, and you used the word *him* of the Creator. Why did you do that?'

Good grief, thought Paul. Next thing you know she'll be trying to sell me a Bible.

'Because I always have,' he said. 'Because my church always referred to our god as male.'

'You think of the Creator as male because you are male, and your church exists through the rule of men. Your holy books talk of man being created in your god's image, but I think instead that you have imagined him in yours. It's odd, don't you think?'

'Is it? I've never really thought about it.'

'It's odd to believe in an entity that gave birth to planets, galaxies, every form of life, and yet conceive of it as male.'

'Do you see this Creator as a woman, then?'

'I do not "see" the Creator at all. The Creator simply is.'

'Alis,' said Paul, smiling, 'you are an unusual individual, and I don't say that simply because you're a Mech. Go and start the diagnostics. I'll join you in a moment.'

He watched her leave. His dark mood had been broken by her

words – it was not gone, but it was eased somewhat. A figure emerged from the shadows and intercepted Alis. It was Steven. His brother reached for the Mech, and touched her gently on the cheek with his right hand. She bowed her head and placed it against Steven's shoulder, so that her face was turned in Paul's direction. She saw him watching them, but she did not try to move away from his brother.

Paul simply turned his back and left them in peace for a time.

The diagnostic check, when complete, revealed weaknesses in two of the exterior panels, either as a result of the impact of the asteroid on the ship or the proximity of the shots it had received across its bows on Archaeon. They were not a source of immediate concern, according to Alis, but they would need to be checked after each jump. She also advised routing their way back to Illyr via the most stable wormholes. Steven calculated that could be done in four boosts, but it would take them days.

Paul consulted with Peris.

'Will they still be looking for us?' he asked.

Peris thought for a couple of seconds, then pulled up from the *Nomad*'s memory an image of the ship that had hunted them on Archaeon. He pointed at two structures, one on either side of the main body.

'They're hangars, but our final scan just before it was destroyed suggests they were empty,' said Peris. 'This was a small mothership, and I'd say that the *Nomad* once rested in one of those bays, and the ship we destroyed at Torma was transported in the other. For now, it seems our most direct pursuers are no more. It's possible that the mothership may have sent a message informing others of its intention to investigate a possible intrusion into the Archaeon system. If so, it will have taken some time for the message to be received, and still more for a response to be decided upon. We're safe, for now, but the question remains: what happens when we draw closer to Illyr? Whoever created this ship won't want it to be discovered.'

'We'll send out a distress call on a Military channel as soon as we near a beacon,' said Paul. 'We'll let our own forces escort us in, but my orders are to reveal nothing – *nothing* – about the true nature of this ship. As far as any Military or Corps vessel may be concerned, this is a Nomad ship, seized by us following an attack by unknown forces at Torma.'

'That story won't hold up under close examination, and there will be a full inquiry. The Military does not take lightly the loss of a destroyer – even one attached to the Brigades.'

'Our story doesn't have to be watertight,' said Paul. 'It just has to be believed for long enough to get us to the Illyr system without someone deciding to annihilate us in order to destroy evidence of this ship's existence. Once we're back at Illyr, you can see about getting in touch with senior Military commanders that you trust, and we can start telling the truth.'

The thought of explaining what they had found on Archaeon seemed to cause Peris's shoulders to sag.

'I have instructed Alis to place all recordings and images from Archaeon on a secure drive,' said Peris. 'We will present evidence of a secret facility on the planet, apparently designed to allow an unknown alien species to breed. But the rest – the implantations of a similar species in the bodies of Corps officials, and a possible plot to contaminate the Earth with these organisms – well, that can only be speculation for the moment.

'And Paul, you don't need me to tell you how dangerous it is for us to be in possession of this information. Our best hope is that nobody on Illyr yet knows that we have been to Archaeon. It will give me time to make the correct approaches. While we can say with some certainty that this is a Corps operation, the Military is not as hostile to the Corps as it once was. There was a time when I could have trusted every senior officer without hesitation, but that time is gone. The Sisterhood has its claws in the Military, and who knows how many officers have suspect loyalties? We must move carefully.'

Paul understood. Part of him wanted to broadcast what they had discovered on every available channel, to blast it with loudspeakers from every rooftop in every city on Earth, but he accepted that Peris was right to be cautious. Yet if Peris and his allies did not act fast enough, then Paul would take matters into his own hands, if he could. If those spores were ultimately destined for Earth, then a clock was ticking on his planet's future. He thought of his mum, and his friends, and of Trask, Nessa, Jean, and Just Joe. He thought of Heather and little Alice. And he thought of Fremd – the Green Man, yet no more human than Syl was. He sighed heavily.

'What about Tiray?' he asked after a few moments' silence.

'I've spoken with him. He appears as disturbed as we are by what he saw on Archaeon. He agrees that the proper authorities need to be informed, but he will not say what he believes those authorities to be. He's keeping his own counsel.'

'Again: can he be trusted? And no cynical asides about politicians, please: I'd like a straight answer.'

'From what I know of him, I would say, yes, we can trust him.'

'Keep an eye on him anyway.'

'I will. Now, may I ask you a question?'

'Go ahead.'

'You have weapons. You have a fast ship, one with no identifiers, which makes it hard to hunt. You have a loyal crew. You could run, and perhaps find your way back to Earth using the wormhole map. But instead you seem willing, even eager, to go to Illyr. Why?'

'Because,' said Paul, 'the Marque orbits Illyr, and Syl is on the Marque.'

'You want to try to see her?' asked Peris. 'But no male can set foot on Avila Minor. To do so is an instant sentence of life imprisonment, assuming the Marque's security systems don't deal with you first. From what I hear they don't have a stun setting. They're designed only to kill.'

Paul laid a hand on Peris's upper arm.

'I'm not going to try to see her,' Paul assured him.

Peris looked relieved, but only until Paul spoke again.

'I'm going to rescue her.'

CHAPTER 59

The special classes for the gifted Blue Novices were not suspended, nor would they ever be. Every day they met and, when they'd finished the inevitable excited discussion of the coming ball, describing their gowns to each other in swooning detail, Ani honed her psychic skills. With the encouragement of the other Gifted and her tutors, she felt herself making progress. While her clouding dexterity developed slowly, still some way behind Dessa's talent, her ability to toy with minds, to make others think they were seeing something that wasn't there, was causing even Thona to pause and look again at what she'd initially thought to be merely a silly Earthborn Novice with wan gifts.

It was the day that two Tanits appeared in class that sealed it.

Tanit had arrived sometime earlier with Nemein, Dessa and Sarea, smiling broadly, and was now quietly watching Sarea warming up by pulverising the carcass of a small mammal. The mercifully long-dead creature bucked and reared on the table in front of Sarea as she twitched its slack muscles and defunct organs with her mind. Nemein was helping, which meant she would name a body part – 'Liver!' 'Sternum!' 'Eyeball' 'Ass!', upon which she and Dessa fell about laughing – and then Sarea would attempt to isolate and crush the chosen internal structure. She wasn't laughing though; she rarely did nowadays. Instead her eyes were steely, her features set, her jaw a foreboding line of determination. The only thing that seemed to give her joy at all was pleasing Tanit, and causing damage. A flicker of satisfaction briefly lit her fine features as she broke the animal's ribs one by one, each with a satisfying crack, as if she were running her finger along the keys of a piano.

That's when Tanit stalked in, looking livid.

'Sarea! Nemein! Dessa!' she spat. Instantly the rabbit-creature fell still as her three friends spun around and stared at their leader, slack-jawed. 'I told you to wait for me outside the dining hall. Where were you?'

'But . . . but . . . Tanit?' Sarea turned around slowly and stared at Ani, sitting on the chair behind her, exactly where she'd seen Tanit only a split-second before, her legs crossed neatly at the ankle, her hands folded meekly in her lap, just as Tanit's had been. She and Nemein looked between Tanit and Ani again, clearly baffled, but now Dessa started to laugh.

'Oh dear. Oh goodness, I can't believe I fell for that.'

Tanit strode towards the chuckling Dessa, and grabbed her face between her fingers.

'You laugh at me, Uludess? You? At ME?'

'No! Not at you, Tanit – never! I was laughing because of what Ani just did. She clouded! She became you. She was so convincing . . .'

Thona materialised next to them then, and immediately Tanit let go of Dessa's face, but there were telltale pink fingerprints on her cheeks: in her rage she had scorched Dessa's flesh.

'What is the meaning of this?' said Thona.

'It's Ani,' said Tanit, turning and staring at the younger girl. 'Apparently she pretended to be me.'

'You did what, Ani Cienda?' Thona asked, her voice thick with incredulity.

'I clouded, Sister Thona. I made them think I was Tanit.'

'Why? You know that it is against the rules to practise unsanctioned on one another. Explain yourself.'

Ani looked mortified. 'Well, it's just that if the others are expecting me to cloud I can never fool them. I wanted to see if I could do it when they weren't expecting me to.'

'You little lowlife,' said Sarea. 'Who do you think you are?'

'How dare you impersonate Tanit?' interrupted Nemein, elbowing

Sarea aside. 'You! A mere first year, pretending to be Tanit. I'll deal with you.'

'Step back, Nemein,' said Thona loudly. 'I am in charge here, and I shall take the necessary action, thank you.'

She turned to Ani, who was shrinking into herself on the chair, pale but defiant. 'Ani, come. We must report this incident to Grandmage Oriel immediately. She will be most interested to hear of it.'

'But it's not fair,' said Ani, her voice catching. 'How can I improve when you're always all blocking me? How can I demonstrate what I'm capable of when you won't let me? It's not like I did any harm. In the real world, out of this classroom, no one's going to be blocking me. They won't even know I'm doing anything.'

'Ani, come!' said Thona.

'No,' said Tanit, 'Ani's right. Of course she is. We've had so much practice blocking clouders, thanks to Dessa. And we're always primed to block Ani before she begins. It's not fair on her: she barely gets a chance.'

'But she pretended to be you, Tanit,' said Sarea.

'Of all people,' added Nemein unnecessarily.

Thona stepped to one side and folded her arms, watching her students curiously to see how this would pan out.

'I'm aware of that, thank you very much,' said Tanit. 'It was audacious of her, granted, and I'm a little affronted by her cheek' — she looked at Ani sternly as she said this, and Ani turned away, her ears reddening — 'yet I also think it was a stroke of genius. After all, she made those I am closest to believe she was me. Does that not show remarkable skill, which has only been revealed now that she allowed herself to spread her wings? Wings we'd clipped, I might add. I'm rather proud of her, actually. And I suspect this skill could be put to very good use. I, for one, will find it most helpful.'

'How so?' said Sarea, pouting.

'Well, I've always wished I could be in two places at once. Now I can be, or at least I can appear to be. How can that not be a blessing? Think about it, my beloved bone-crusher. Just imagine what you could get up to in private if everyone thought you were elsewhere.'

'You mean like this?' said Sarea, her voice harsh, and the rabbit-creature behind her was instantly torn in two. Dessa, who was closest, squealed as a smattering of yellow gore splashed across her robes.

Tanit smiled. 'Oh, Sarea, don't feel bad. I suspect I also would have been fooled had she pretended to be you. She'll just have to promise never to impersonate any of us again without our permission. All right, Ani?'

Ani looked up eagerly.

'Because if she does, then we may decide to use our skills on her without her knowledge, too.'

Tanit stepped passed Nemein and looked down at Ani, her face a benign mask, but only Ani felt the burning heat rising from the base of her spine.

'You do understand, don't you, my dearest Ani? Please say you do. After all, I have grown so very fond of you.'

'Yes I do, Tanit. I'm truly sorry.'

The burning faded away, and Ani wondered if she'd imagined it as Tanit bent down and embraced her, folding Ani against her hard, deadly body.

'It's okay, darling,' Tanit whispered, 'I couldn't stay angry with you, because you know I just love you to bits. And I certainly want you on my side – that was some mind trick!'

And this time the warmth Ani felt rising inside her was definitely not pain, but pure pleasure.

'Everyone, back to work,' said Thona, moving forward again, nodding in satisfaction. 'You sorted it out among yourselves, which is just the sort of teamwork we like to see. Thank you, Tanit – you proved yourself to be a wise moderator, yet again. Ani, you can stay here. I shall of course report everything that has transpired to Grandmage Oriel immediately, but I suspect she will feel as I do on the matter: that valuable lessons have been learned. While I am gone, continue to practise, please.'

The rest of the class passed in a blur of shaky pleasure for Ani. Sarea and Nemein seemed willing to forgive her at Tanit's command,

and Dessa kept grinning at her and squeezing her elbow conspiratorially.

'Wait till you tell Syl – she'll be so pleased,' she whispered under her breath.

Ani wondered aloud if she dared.

'Of course you must,' said Dessa. 'It's important that she feels included.'

Later that day Ani felt the warm glow fading as she faced her oldest friend in their quarters, and she found herself growing angry and wishing that she hadn't taken Dessa's advice.

'But I have genuine talent,' she protested as Syl stared at her balefully.

'And they know that now – and they know what to expect from you, too,' said Syl. 'Don't you see? If you show them all your cards, there's no way you can win the game.'

'Really, Syl? Is it necessary to be quite so trite and annoying?'

'I'm just saying that maybe you should be more careful, Ani. We don't know what we're up against yet.'

'I think what you mean is that *you* don't know what you're up against. I know precisely what I'm doing.'

'Do you really?' snarled Syl.

'Yes. They're my *friends*. They support and encourage me. But you – you just want to flatten me.'

'It's not like that. I just don't want you to be used by them.'

'What? Anymore than I was used by your precious Meia? If she hadn't taken advantage of me like she did, forcing me to cloud the minds of guards, then none of this would ever have happened.'

'But she was using you for good! She was saving Paul and Steven from execution.'

'No, saving them was just incidental to her. She was playing her games, and we were the pawns. I can't see how you don't see that!'

'Her aims were pure, Ani, whatever her methods. But we know the aims of the Sisterhood to be much darker than that.'

'Do we really? I thought we wanted to find out what was going on, but it seems to me that you made up your mind long before we even got here.'

'Oh Ani, have you really forgotten?'

Ani was enraged now. 'I've forgotten *nothing*, Syl. I remember every moment of it. I dream about it at night. But by day I want to move on – to make the most of myself and my talents – and you don't. You won't.'

Her voice assumed a self-righteous tone. 'Sometimes I think you're just jealous of my abilities, because here I'm seen as the special one, not you.'

'Oh really?' exploded Syl. 'Is that what you think of me, Ani Cienda? Here, then—'

She tore into the kitchen and took a plate from the cupboard. Ani watched, mystified, as Syl slammed the plate down in front of her and put her hand on it.

'Go on,' she said, 'make me burn.'

'Syl?'

'Just do it. Please.'

Ani shuffled in her seat, her lips set in a stubborn line.

'Now, Ani. I'm begging you. Make the plate hot. Or can't you do it?'

'Fine!' said Ani. She sat up straight and glared at Syl, her eyes steely. 'But remember, you asked.'

Syl felt the plate beneath her hand grow warm. She stared back at Ani, her features blank. The plate turned cold. She watched her oldest friend squint with concentration, and the veins in her temples stood out, but still the plate was cold. Finally, a trickle of blood spilled from Ani's nostril.

'No!' she said, distressed, trying to cover her nose, and her eyes filled with horror as blood flowed faster on to her robes, becoming a dramatic spurt that had her grabbing for a discarded towel and holding it over her face.

'Maybe,' said Syl softly, 'just maybe, Ani, other people have skills too.'

Ani looked at her over the towel, her eyes wide with hurt. After some time she pulled it away, smearing blood across her cheeks.

'You have skills, Syl? And you didn't tell me?'

Now Syl felt angry with herself. This was her secret, her trump card, and in her anger and pride she'd behaved rashly. At least Ani had only seen the surface and not what lay far beneath: the horror.

'Well, not really skills,' she said, looking down so that her hair covered her face, fumbling for words, finding the right lie. 'But I can sort of block people a bit, you know. Just a bit.'

Ani sniffed loudly once more, and then she found her smile, and she reached for her friend's hand.

'But that's wonderful, Syl! You have skills! I always hoped you might if you just opened yourself up to them. What else can you do?'

'Nothing much. That's it, really.'

'Oh Syl, why don't we tell them? You may have other hidden gifts too! I'm sure with practice and the right teaching you could enhance your skills. You may find that you're capable of much more than you think. I mean, look how far I've come. Look what I did today! Imagine what we could do together.'

In her peripheral vision Syl could see the cold plate spotted with Ani's blood, and she felt wretched. This was so like Ani: to be delighted that Syl might be able to join her in her rarefied world, eager to include her and build her up. If Ani only knew the half of it . . .

'No Ani, I can't do that. Please don't say anything. I'm here to investigate the Sisterhood, remember, not to help them. And I could never be on the same side as Syrene, or Tanit and Sarea. They're something else. They're not like me, and I don't believe that they're like you either. And we still don't know what the Sisterhood plans to do with you all, do we?'

Ani snatched her hand away. 'I guess it's too much for you to believe they're just making us into the best we can possibly be?'

'Ani, I think that's too much for anyone to believe. If Elda was still among us, I know she'd back me up. But please, as my best friend – as my only friend in this wretched place – keep this to yourself, okay? You have to hide this from them. You have to conceal it behind a cloud.'

Ani tutted.

'Oh, if you insist. But I'm really not convinced they were involved in whatever happened to Elda. It doesn't make sense, and if you only saw how kind Tanit can be . . .'

She remembered again how Tanit had embraced her and said that she loved her, and she felt a pleasurable shiver at the memory – and yet it was so very complicated loving two people who seemed bent on destroying each other. Syl and Tanit were like different sides of the same coin: so close, yet never really seeing each other. It drove Ani demented with distress.

'But Dessa is your friend too, isn't she?' Ani continued, casting around for positives. 'She was so excited for me today, and for you to hear about it.'

'Yeah, well, Dessa doesn't seem that bad.'

'None of them are, really. Sarea and Nemein are a bit difficult, but once they like you they'll do anything for you. Maybe you'll get to know them all better at the ball.'

Syl looked at her friend and nodded, but inside she felt terribly sad.

'Well, you never know what may happen at the ball, Ani. You just never know.'

CHAPTER 60

Three red shuttles were waiting to take the debutantes to the ball, each bearing the great red eye of the Sisterhood. The first one would hold Oriel, muted and sullen in classical dress robes, loath to leave her rock, and with her a few more senior Sisters that Syl did not know. Alongside them would travel a brace of younger full Sisters clearly destined for marriage, if the Sisterhood had its way. They were dressed in every manner of sumptuous finery, in shades of a deep and glorious sunset – red, but also gold, bronze, orange, purple, magenta, soft pink and luminous black – uniformly trimmed with the signature scarlet of the Nairenes. All had glossy hair worn short and studded with gems, feathers and sharp stars of cold metal. Each also wore a ring featuring a solitary outsized ruby, a gift from the Order that had just been presented to them, and they were admiring them happily, all bright eyes, flashing nails, and brittle, sparkling smiles. Together they were exquisite, and terrifying.

The second ship would take the Half-Sisters, ebbing and flowing like a tropical sea in their water-coloured gowns, with their own flotsam of jade dragonfly wings, emerald crystals, and blown glass beads of lightest green. The Gifted Half-Sisters were recognisable in the throng by the sapphires strung through their hair, and the royal blue silk that wove patterns on their lagoon-green hemlines.

The last ship, the smallest of the three, was reserved for the gifted Novices, resplendent in rich blue, who were to be chaperoned by Thona and Cale, as well as a handful of seamstresses, jewellers and hairstylists, all in red work robes, brought along just in case their expertise was required.

And then there was Syl, the lone figure in yellow. She stood by herself at the back of the third group, watching guardedly as Ani shimmied and bobbed ahead of her, giggling with the other Gifted, hopping delicately from one foot to the other with excitement. She was clutching hands with Tanit to her left and Iria on her right, but it was Tanit to whom she cleaved closest.

It wasn't Ani's fault that Syl stood alone, for she had been steered to Tanit's side by Thona – 'The Gifted always stand together,' Thona said – while Cale sent Syl to the rear of the party, vaguely apologetic yet firm.

One of the stylists had arranged rows of crystals under Ani's eyes, curling them upwards and twisting them into her hairline, and they caught the light, throwing sparkling shards across her cheeks and brow, only adding to her radiance. From her hair tumbled ribbons of blue. In contrast, Syl felt dull and wrong, and she knew Cale was right to move her out of the way, for she stood out like a smear of cheap yellow mustard plopped on to the tablecloth at a grand banquet. Perhaps it was the flowing cape that had arrived with her gown, which had seemed so elegant as she dressed in her room, but out here, all this splendour made her feel like an entrant in a sack race. Even her treasured leather and amber belt now seemed coarse and crude, as if she'd dressed for another function entirely. Her only other adornment was a tortoiseshell clasp in her hair, a dated trinket that a stylist had clipped in place almost as an afterthought. For Syl there were no jewels, no gems, no family heirlooms set aside. However, around her neck she wore Elda's locket, hidden on its long cord. Absently, she now took it out and fiddled with it for want of something better to do with her hands.

No, it wasn't Ani's fault that they were separated. Syl knew that. Still, yet again she felt Ani didn't need to look quite as happy as she did.

Because of where she stood in line Syl was last to board the final craft, so she was seated right at the back again on a single chair, far from the windows, pressed up against various boxes and packing cases loaded on by the stylists. She was only grateful that she'd brought a book, but she didn't have much chance to read because, soon after takeoff, Dessa slid over and plopped herself down on the floor at Syl's feet.

'Hey, pretty,' she said.

'Oh please,' replied Syl, looking down at the older girl, whose purple eyes were made even more striking by the amethyst shimmer of her elegantly cut gown. 'You look beautiful, Dessa.'

'So do you.'

'I look stupid. I stick out like a sore thumb – a sore thumb with jaundice.'

Dessa laughed. 'You're so silly. You look great. I like your belt. So how are you feeling about this, your first trip to Illyr? Excited?'

Syl thought about it. How did she feel?

'Excited? Sort of, I think. And nervous too.'

'Why? There's nothing to be nervous of at all. It's just a fabulous, grand party.'

'Where I won't know anyone.'

'You know me. And Ani.'

Syl looked over to where Ani was messing about on a screen with Mila, and Dessa followed her eyes. She patted Syl affectionately on the arm.

'Oh, don't worry about her, Syl; I'll stick with you. We'll stick together, you and I.'

'I don't think Tanit and the others will approve of that, some-how.'

Dessa huffed and rolled her eyes. 'Just you wait: the moment we arrive they'll all be racing off in search of the best-looking Illyri to dance with. The last thing they'll be worried about is me. Or you, for that matter. We might have some adventures of our own. We might even meet some nice handsome suitors.'

She grinned, but Syl shook her head. She thought of adventures she'd had before; she thought of Paul.

'I don't think I want to meet anyone, Dessa. Not now.'

'You're still thinking about that human – Paul?'

To her surprise, Syl felt her eyes getting wet.

'I guess. I miss him, Dessa, especially when I'm feeling lonely. And I miss my home. I miss my dad.'

Dessa stared hard at Syl, then bit her lip. 'I miss my dad too.'

'What? Why? Where is he? Is he okay?'

Dessa looked down, her hair closing like curtains over her face.

'He's dead, Syl. Killed in the Conquest.'

Syl felt queasy, and she reached out a hand and touched Dessa's wrist uncertainly. 'Oh Dessa, I never knew. I'm so sorry. What happened? Who killed him?'

'A traitor. An enemy of the Illyri. My father was a soldier on Earth, actually.'

Syl gasped. Questions spilled out – where, when, how – but Dessa simply mumbled a choked response from under her hair. 'I don't want to talk about it now. I don't want to cry again.'

Syl was at a loss for words, so she just twiddled her hair uncomfortably. Eventually the older girl looked up at her, seemingly in control of her emotions once more.

'Why don't you tell me about your time on Earth, Syl?'

Seeing Syl's hesitation, Dessa face crumpled as if she might start sobbing. 'Please,' she begged. 'It'll distract me. Tell me about your adventures. Tell me what happened to you in Scotland. Now you know that my father served on Earth, you must understand how I need to know everything about it, about the last place he saw.'

'Well, it's rather complicated. I'm not sure.'

'Syl, please. Your father is still alive. Mine is dead. Humour me.'

And Syl had to concede that Dessa was right. Slowly, reluctantly, she filled the rest of the long journey to the planet below with stories of Earth, and Dessa sat up straight and alert, her sadness forgotten, eyes bright with interest, and quick with questions and clarifications, until they finally docked on the homeworld.

As they disembarked, Dessa touched Syl on the elbow.

'Did you know someone called Vena?' she said, and Syl thought she'd faint dead away with shock right there.

'Vena?' she repeated, and she could hear the horror in her own voice.

Dessa grinned. 'Ah, you do then. And it doesn't sound as if you like her very much either. Don't worry, neither do I. Nobody does. She's my mother's little sister, but she's an utter demon. They haven't spoken in years.'

Syl had a million questions, but none that would form coherently. She followed Dessa from the craft as if she were an automaton, vaguely aware of the handsome young fellow in the black dress uniform of the Diplomatic Corps taking her cloak, and of another serving them each a tumbler of cremos from a tray. Syl slugged it back, and he immediately handed her another, smiling.

'Welcome to the Genesis Ball,' he said. 'And it certainly looks like some of you came ready to party.'

CHAPTER 61

Syl was drunk. She knew she must be. Her head was swimming, her tongue felt loose in her mouth, and she kept seeing things.

At first they'd feasted, a great banquet at which Syl had properly gorged herself. The tables were set against a wall of water through which darted tropical fish-like creatures, small and nimble, and Syl found she could trail her fingers through the liquid, the swimmers rushing from her hand, yet still the water stayed in place. It reminded her of an old story she'd heard on Earth, something about a sea parting: this must be how it had looked.

On the far side of the water she could make out swirls of the landscape beyond: a desert, a green island, a storm, or was it a yellow crashing sea, and a green boat? She rubbed her eyes, but the ripples rendered everything indistinct.

During the banquet she was greeted repeatedly, and she saw Oriel scowling as she was forced to direct yet another curious Illyri adult in Syl's direction. Fingers pointed at her, and she heard her father's name mentioned repeatedly, heard herself described as Lord Andrus's daughter as she was swept from conversation to conversation. She felt proud as people complimented her on her parentage time and time again − her father's brilliance as a commander, her mother's beauty and wisdom − as if she'd had any say as to the womb she came from, or the Illyri leader that sired her.

'Your mother is an inspiration to us all,' whispered one female Securitat of high rank, before kissing Syl fondly on the cheek and congratulating her.

'My mother is dead,' replied Syl, confused. It took her a moment to realise that it was not the Lady Orianne who was being praised, but Syrene. Syl had hoped that the Archmage was merely tormenting her when she spoke of a union with Lord Andrus, but now the look on the Securitat's face confirmed her worst fears. Word had spread, and already Syl had a new mother.

Just as the Securitat began to reply, Cale appeared and pushed someone new on Syl, and Dessa handed her more cremos, and she drank deeply. Everything started to blur, and she was grateful for it.

And then she danced, smiling wildly as she was introduced to officer after officer, Dessa at her side, Dessa steering her, Dessa showing her how things worked and how things were done. Occasionally Ani would spin past, beautiful and laughing, twirling in the arms of a male, and then a female, and then Tanit who bent down and kissed the younger Novice, kissed her full on the mouth, and Ani responded, twining her wrists around Tanit's slim neck, and Syl felt dizzy and wondered if she'd imagined it. When she tried to focus, Ani was gone.

Now Dessa was before her once more, pressing another drink upon her, guiding another slick Illyri male into her orbit, a young Romeo who held her so close that she felt bits of his body hard against her groin, bits she'd rather pretend weren't there, and then he licked her ear, and Dessa laughed as Syl pushed him away. Another drink appeared in her hand. She spun some more and found herself in other arms, and it all began to seem hilarious. She shouted to Dessa over the music, answering more questions about Earth, for hiding what had happened didn't seem to matter now, not if her father was marrying the Archmage, not when she was here with her friend, with Dessa, drinking another draught as the layers of hurt and anger deep inside were sloughed away, drinking until she felt warm and fuzzy at the edges, until those who pressed too close made her giggle even more.

She saw Ani again, and Tanit, and wondered if she had imagined that deep kiss. Ani's eyes were bright as stars and her cheeks were pink with pleasure, and Tanit looped her close, Ani clutching like a limpet to her side. Ani waved and it was like watching a film-reel of someone else's dream. Even Tanit smiled. The unfamiliar Illyri music swirled around them, a vortex of sound that seemed to beat deep inside Syl, setting her heart off on a different rhythm, and she didn't feel like herself, and her feet didn't feel like they were touching the floor.

A voice spoke next to her ear, a shout that came through like a whisper.

'Come Syl, let's get some air.'

Dessa took her by the arm and led her away from the dancing, back towards the near-empty banqueting hall with its wall of elegant water, but they were stopped by Oriel. She materialised before them, solid and red while everything else shimmered.

'Where are you going?' she said.

'We just wanted a little peace, Grandmage,' replied Dessa, sweet as sugar, and Oriel looked at her for several long seconds. Then she nodded, and watched them closely as they slipped by her. Syl felt the familiar tendrils of the old witch trying to probe her mind.

'She hates me,' she muttered drunkenly to Dessa.

'Now why would anyone hate you, Syl Hellais?'

'Your aunt hates me. Your aunt Vena.'

'Hush. We'll talk about that in a minute. Let's get out of here.'

They reached the wall of water.

'It's a protective barrier. But do you see what's on the other side?' Dessa asked. Syl shook her head, for the image outside was dark now, and blurred by the flow.

'Would you like to?'

Without waiting for an answer, Dessa stepped into the liquid and yanked Syl with her. Syl gasped as the icy water swamped her body, tasting its saltiness as it splashed into her mouth. A fish slithered over her arm, and then just as suddenly they were through the water, standing dripping on an outside terrace, their finery limp and bedraggled.

Before them curved a shallow, elegant staircase, and from the bottom of those steps stretched a desertscape, peppered with little round islands of green. The last rays of the departing sun sent purple beams into the slate sky, vibrant as searchlights, but Syl barely noticed it for she was pulling at her sodden dress, which sagged shapelessly. She feared that it was ruined.

But then something caught her attention out of the corner of her eye. There was movement out there, and across the sand Syl saw living forms pause and turn towards them, moving ponderously, as though considering their options. They were strange crab-like creatures, vaguely reminiscent of the cascids of Avila Minor, and now she could hear their pincers clicking out of time with the muffled beat of the music that thumped from beyond the wall of water.

And all the while Dessa was laughing, its pitch slightly hysterical to Syl's ears. She was watching Syl closely, not seeing the desert, not aware of the sand crabs.

'Dessa!' said Syl, glancing back at the creatures as they moved nearer. They seemed to be quickening their pace. All had multiple eyes on stalk-like antennae, which turned greedily towards the two females standing exposed on the terrace. The crabs moved slowly, raptly, across the desert floor towards the glimmering building – and the temptingly soft flesh that waited on its wide veranda. The only obstacle in their way was the lazy sweep of a grand staircase.

'Dessa, we need to go back inside. Now! Those' – what were they anyway? – '*things* are coming. Look!'

'Tell me about Earth, Syl,' said Dessa, not looking. 'Tell me what happened in those last days in Scotland.'

Syl felt fear rising in her chest. The creatures came closer and she stepped backwards towards the wall of water, watching them over Dessa's shoulder.

'Dessa!' she cried. 'We must leave.'

'First tell me about Vena, Earthborn. Tell me about Sedulus.'

'Sedulus? What are you talking about? Dessa! Come on, let's go!'

She stepped back, pushing against the water, but it froze instantly as she did so, becoming impenetrable: a wall of thick ice, cold and unyielding.

'Dessa! What's happening? I can't get past.'

'Of course you can't. It's a one-way system or the ostraca would simply walk through and destroy all who are inside. Imagine it: beauty and life so close to ugliness and death.'

Syl grabbed Dessa and shook her, looking into her face desperately.

'Why did you bring us out here then? How can we get back in?'

Dessa shoved Syl away, and her eyes were no longer mournful or beguiling. Not remotely.

'I'll show you how we get back in when you tell me what you did to my father, and how you got him killed.'

'Dessa, you're scaring me. I don't know what you're talking about! Who is your father? I didn't get anyone killed.'

Even as she said it, Syl knew it wasn't true. Many had died, some because of her actions. Briefly an image of a human impaling himself on his own bayonet came to mind, but it vanished almost immediately, for the creatures behind Dessa were massing, shuffling closer.

'Are you actually stupid, Syl Hellais? Vena said you were clever when she contacted me, and yet still you never figured it out.'

'Figured what out?'

'That I am Uludess, daughter of Sedulus: my name is just an anagram of his. How did you not see that? Vena contacted me after my father died – yes, she is my aunt, though I detest her, for she bewitched my father and stole him away from her own sister. But nonetheless, Vena said you were to blame for what befell him. She said you must pay the price.'

Syl pressed hard against the wall of ice, feeling frost against her back, the fabric of her dress freezing to it as Dessa's saliva flew in her face. The creatures moved behind Dessa, emboldened and curious, close enough now that she could see the lights from the party reflected in their myriad eyes.

'But I did nothing,' she protested.

'You can't deny it, Syl. This ends tonight, with you either torn apart by desert animals or dead by my hand, for I will avenge my father.'

Syl felt a tickling inside her head again, at the very front of her skull. Oriel? Was it Oriel? It was as if someone were trying to find her. Ani? Could it be? She opened up her mind and mentally screamed out her message. *Help me! Save me!*

She tried to pull away from Dessa, but her gown was now frozen fast into the ice, and Dessa stepped back, laughing as she watched Syl's face fall. Water began trickling over Syl's shoulders, solidifying into icicles around her arms, locking her in place against the wall.

'Dessa, please,' she said, frantic. Water dribbled on to her cheeks, the droplets freezing as they touched her. 'Those things will kill you too.'

Dessa stepped forward and pressed her forehead against Syl's.

'I can leave whenever I want, but you're staying right here. I suspect the ostraca are hungry, for they feed at dusk.'

As Dessa spoke, water splashed on to her, running down her face, and suddenly Syl understood. This was trickery, an illusion that felt as real as reality itself, for Dessa was a clouder: she could make her victims see things that weren't there, feel things that weren't happening, just like Ani could. The plate hadn't really turned hot, and the water wasn't really turning to ice on contact – after all, it wasn't freezing as it slopped on to Dessa.

As if to prove the point, Iria stepped through the water and, for a moment, Dessa suffered a lapse in concentration. Immediately Syl felt the ice at her back turn to sludge. However, she didn't move, not wanting to give anything away, not now that Iria was there too. More of the Gifted might well follow, for they moved as a pack, and Syl wasn't strong enough to take on all of them.

'Iria!' cried Dessa. 'What are you doing here?'

'I was worried. Oriel said I should keep an eye on you – you and the Earth bitch. I felt you were in danger. I felt you call. And I don't trust *her*.'

'But I didn't call,' said Dessa, as Iria threw Syl a glance of pure venom, but Syl didn't respond. Instead she watched the creatures behind Dessa for they, at least, were most certainly real, and getting nearer. The first of them reached the bottom of the steps and contemplated the tableau above on the patio, its multiple eyes cold and hungry.

'I'm just dealing with an outstanding debt,' continued Dessa.

'Are you going to leave her for the ostraca?' Iria smiled at the notion.

'Indeed I am, for it's not me who is in danger tonight, is it, Syl Hellais? It's not me who's about to die.'

'Oh good,' said Iria. 'But perhaps we should go now. They are a little too close for—'

Syl stepped backwards, and the wall of water drank her in with ease, plummeting over her like a crashing wave, but she never saw the fish that slid past her, and she never saw the look of bewilderment on Dessa's face as her prey slipped away. All Syl saw was red, thick as clotting blood, her mind darkening with rage. As she made her escape, she willed the water frozen in her wake, but this was no deception. Dessa's power was one of illusion, but Syl's was real.

Outside, Iria screamed a warning, for Syl's sudden movement had jolted the first ostraca into action. It scurried forward, and Iria stepped towards the frozen water, grabbing Dessa's sleeve as she did so, pulling her along. Together they hurtled into the barrier, sending shards of ice twinkling into the air as they slid stunned to the ground. The ostraca rushed forward in a swarm, pincers clicking rapturously, the sound of a hundred hands clapping.

Inside the banqueting hall, Syl sank to the floor, dripping wet and shaking, tears streaming down her cheeks. Briefly she witnessed the blurred figures outside beating against the ice, and then the ostraca reached them. Syl turned away from their feeding, and the ice began to melt. When she looked again, the wall of water was ribboned with dark Illyri blood, the complex technological arrangement that had created the feature drawing the blood upwards, and the fish that once swam in it tumbled from the rivulets, suffocated by blood and ice.

Syl crept under the nearest row of tables and – hidden by opulent tablecloths – crawled away, just as the screaming started.

Chapter 62

Syl stayed under the farthest table for as long as she dared, aware of boots rushing by and sounds of panic as the music suddenly stopped and bright lights were switched on. There were shots fired as the blood-frenzied ostracas were dealt with, and questions barked as to why the security beams had been switched off, and she could hear sobbing and wailing, and instructions being shouted. She was shaking uncontrollably, but she couldn't tell if it was from cold or from shock, or perhaps it was the effects of the alcohol and the Illyri air. Whatever, she didn't trust her legs to hold her up.

Finally, she slid from her hiding place and slunk through the almost-deserted ballroom to the cloakroom to fetch her wrap. The few folk who still milled around in here, far from the chaos at the wall, were too busy talking amongst themselves to be concerned with a bedraggled nobody, for the Illyri rumour mill had already started. Theories were fast becoming facts, and facts were becoming conspiracies; the very unfortunate death of two drunk, foolish Novices would never be seen as just an accident.

'What happened to you?' said the young officer in black and gold who had taken her cloak earlier, but he was distracted, peering over her shoulder to see what was happening.

'I got wet trying to help.'

'I see,' he said, handing over her yellow wrap without even looking at her. 'It's a tragedy, a real tragedy.'

Syl said nothing. She simply pulled the billowing layers around herself, grateful now that this old-fashioned cape was hers.

★ ★ ★

The return to Avila Minor was an unhappy one, for everywhere were stony-faced Sisters and Novices weeping; nobody paid any heed to Syl as she huddled in her cloak at the back of the third ship. As close friends of the deceased, Ani and the other Gifted had been instructed to travel with Oriel, and a smattering of the younger red Sisters had been forced to take their places in this less opulent transport. They were surly and bitter, angry that their matchmaking chances had been thwarted by the stupidity of a pair of Novices. They ignored all those around them, Syl included, heedful only of their own perceived misfortune.

Syl was thankful for the solitude.

The arrival at the Marque was uneventful, and Syl was able to hang her wet dress away in her closet before Ani returned to their quarters. Yet Ani did not come back that day, or the next. When she finally did, Syl had another shock: Ani was leaving her. Thona had instructed her to fetch her things and move into Dessa's old room immediately. Henceforth, the Blue Novices would be kept together – together, and apart from the rest.

Following the twin tragedy at the Genesis Ball, the Marque went into a period of official mourning for the lost members of the Sisterhood. Everyone, from the Novices to the Gifted to the full Sisters, and even the Grandmage Oriel herself, was issued with robes of navy blue, the colour of grieving amongst the Nairenes. An ordinance of complete silence was imposed for a period of a week, which could only be broken to give an essential instruction, and all classes were halted. No words were spoken, no music played, no songs were hummed, and the only sounds were footfalls, the hushed turning of pages, and the silvery clinking of eating utensils, punctuated by the occasional cough or sob.

Syl simply stayed in her room for the first three days, staring out of the high window, missing the company of Ani but also mourning Dessa, loathing Dessa, deeply hurt that Dessa had tricked her, furious with herself for being tricked, alternating between desperate sadness and white-hot rage. She fretted over the stories Dessa had told her, about what was true and what was not, but ultimately it made no difference. She wondered if there was another way she could have handled things, if she could have prevented two more deaths instead of taking two more lives. Finally, resigned, she wrote their names on her heart, beside the other deaths that she had caused, both directly and indirectly.

What am I? she wondered. *What have I become?*

When she did eventually emerge from her silent quarters, she briefly considered using the ubiquitous navy robes to her advantage to explore the Marque once more, but her scheme was thwarted because all Realms were locked down for the period of mourning, and a constant guard was kept on the door to the Fourteenth.

Finally, inevitably, Syl was summoned by Oriel and cross-questioned about her part in the tragedy at the Genesis Ball, but she stuck to her story: she'd gone to the bathroom to be sick, she explained, for she'd overindulged in the free-flowing cremos, and when she returned Dessa, her new friend, was already dead. Syl even cried, and the tears were real.

Oriel watched her guardedly and her mind prodded at Syl's, but her efforts were half-hearted.

'I do not believe you, Syl Hellais,' she said finally, 'but you remain under the protection of Syrene. I can understand her reasoning, even while I loathe it, and distrust you. However, that protection is now more powerful still since you are to become her stepdaughter.'

Syl seemed about to object to the use of the word, but Oriel immediately silenced any dissent.

'You fool!' she said. 'Do you still delude yourself that your feelings matter, that you have any sway here? Invitations have already been sent – it is as good as done. And I am reliably informed that the Archmage will deal with you in her own time, that she will bring you around just as she did your father, but for now nothing must cast a cloud over their coming nuptials. It seems that I must tolerate your presence in my hallways and classrooms for a while yet, but I take solace from the knowledge that it shall not be for much longer.'

She dismissed Syl with a flick of her wrist.

★ ★ ★

The next day the mourning period was lifted and classes resumed, although the Gifted did not reappear, for they were having classes alone. Two days later, Oriel called a general meeting of all Novices – Gifted, Half-Sisters and yellow Novices alike – and they gathered nervously, wondering what was about to befall them. The fact that Oriel was smiling was of little comfort; it was like watching the grimace of a predator. Syl spotted Ani up ahead, carried on a wave of Half-Sisters, but she couldn't attract her attention.

Oriel stood to speak, and silence fell.

'My dear Nairenes in training,' she said. 'After the devastating loss of our friends Uludess and Iria, it gives me much pleasure to make an announcement that should lift your spirits and swiftly move you all from grief to celebration.'

Hundreds of eyes stared back at her expectantly.

'I am pleased to announce that, following the period of mourning for her late husband, Consul Gradus, our beloved Archmage Syrene is finally to marry another.'

An excited whisper went through the hall. Who, they wondered. Who?

'The lucky recipient of the Archmage's attention is none other than Lord Andrus, respected and esteemed leader of the Military, and soon to be a father figure to you all.'

There was a stunned silence, followed by cheering, and the odd face turned towards Syl, for some vaguely recalled that the unpopular Earthborn child was Lord Andrus's daughter, but it hadn't mattered, not back then. Yet the only eyes that Syl would meet were Ani's, for her friend had finally found her from across the room, and they looked at each other for a long time. Finally, Ani gave a troubled little grin, and Syl managed a tiny smile in response.

Oriel let the hubbub die down.

'And lastly,' she said, 'I'm delighted to announce that you will all attend the wedding too, for the Nairene Sisterhood will host this grand event at the glorious palace of Erebos. Preparations will begin immediately. Long life to the couple! Long life to the Sisterhood!'

CHAPTER 63

Paul set up a roster of watches for the journey to Illyr, with a particular focus on the weapons system. Without mines or torpedoes, they were solely reliant on the guns, and in the event of an attack Paul did not want their lives to be lost because someone fell asleep at the controls. He, Peris, Thula and Rizzo alternated four-hour shifts, while Alis took responsibility for most of the piloting, allowing Steven to rest or take an occasional shift on the guns. Mostly, though, Steven preferred to stay in the cockpit with Alis, sometimes even sleeping in his chair when his period of duty ended. Thula found it all very amusing.

'If they have children,' he asked Paul, 'just how biomechanical will they be?'

'I don't think they've got that far yet,' said Paul. 'At least, I very much hope not.'

It was, he had to admit, an unusual situation, one that he could say with some confidence had not arisen before. Officially, relationships between Illyri and artificial beings were expressly forbidden. Peris had conceded – under pressure from Thula – that unions between Mechs and Illyri had occurred in the past, even though they were generally discreet. However, he could recall no Illyri, male or female, having done more than admit to them in private, and then only among their closest friends.

But the growing intimacy between Steven and Alis, human and Mech, was the first of its kind – unless Meia had been engaging in some unusual behaviour of her own back on Earth. What Paul saw developing between them was a source of concern to him. Alis might have looked like a young Illyri, but Peris, after talking with Tiray, reckoned that she had been 'activated' at least twenty-five years earlier. And aside from Thula's observations about the difficulties any physical relationship might present, there was also the matter of ageing to consider. What if, by some miracle, they did remain together? Steven would grow old, but Alis's outward appearance would never change, not unless she took it upon herself to alter her ProGen skin to make herself look older and, frankly, Paul couldn't imagine anyone – human, Illyri, or Mech – making that sacrifice.

But Paul also wondered to what degree Alis was using his brother to explore her own emotional capacities. Alis had probably been kept sheltered in Tiray's service, protected from unnecessary contact with others for fear that her true nature might be discovered. It seemed incredible that she had managed to remain undetected for so long, but the deception could not have gone on indefinitely. Eventually, someone would have started to wonder why Councillor Tiray's assistant never seemed to age. Perhaps some kind of cosmetic adjustments could have been made to her face to create the impression of ageing, but that's all it would have been: an imitation. Now, far from Illyr, and forced into the company of a young human who was clearly attracted to her, she had been presented with an opportunity to develop new emotions to add to the ghosts that the Illyri believed already haunted her machine: affection, compassion.

Love.

It seemed to Paul that the relationship between Steven and Alis could only end one way, and it would not be well. But he said nothing, and kept his thoughts to himself. No good could come of interfering, and circumstances would decide their future, not him. It was, in the end, ridiculous to worry about his brother settling into a long-term relationship with Alis when the chances of survival for all of them appeared slim.

Again and again, thoughts of Steven and Alis brought him back to Syl. He had tried not to think of her too much during those long months in the Brigades because – although he hated to admit it – it broke his heart. But distance, and the apparent hopelessness of their situation, had given him some perspective on his feelings for her. He realised that he loved Syl and did not want to resign himself to a life without her. Securing her release from the Marque had been a remote possibility for most of his time in service, but now events had taken an unexpected turn, to put it mildly, and he found himself on the way to the Illyr system, a galaxy from which non-Illyri were almost entirely excluded, especially those who served with the human Brigades. What had seemed virtually impossible just days earlier was now a reality: he would be within reach of Syl, and he had to seize that chance. Another such opportunity might never come along.

Paul did not even consider that Syl might refuse to leave if the chance presented itself. Yet it was all very well for him to talk of releasing Syl from her imprisonment on the Marque, but quite another thing to figure out a way that it might be achieved. Even Peris, who had a great deal of affection for Syl and did not want to see her trapped on Avila Minor any more than Paul did, could not conceive of a way to free her. The Marque had become less like a great storehouse of knowledge and more like a fortress as the Sisterhood strengthened their position in Illyri society. It would take a fleet of ships to mount a full assault, and they did not have a fleet at their command: they had only one vessel, and in all probability, the Marque's defence system would blow it to pieces before they even managed to knocked on the door.

So Paul fretted about a solution while the crew followed the routine that he had set. They watched, they slept, they ate. They made their boosts, and Alis ran a diagnostics check before and after each one. The weaknesses in the hull remained, but they did not appear to be growing more serious. Not for the first time, they were all thankful for the *Nomad*'s advanced design, no matter who – or what – might have been responsible for it.

Only after they emerged from the third wormhole did they start to encounter other craft – cargo vessels, largely, although smaller ships were scattered among them, mostly headed for the final wormhole, so that the *Nomad* became part of a stream of traffic. But clearly, too, their emergence as an unregistered vessel had attracted attention, for they were not long out when the *Nomad* was hailed and asked to identify itself. They were fortunate that the first contact came in the form of a Military patrol and not a vessel of the Diplomatic Corps or, worse, their Securitats. Once Peris had identified himself, and Tiray's presence on board was confirmed, the first patrol ship was joined by a second, then a third, so that the *Nomad* entered the final wormhole at the heart of an arrowhead of craft. This was the Melos Passage, so named because it was not one single wormhole but four interconnected gateways, all funnelling into the Illyri home system, and its shape corresponded to Melos, one of the symbols of the Illyri alphabet. Their escort even enabled them to skip the queue, for a backlog of craft waited to make the boost that would bring them close to Illyr.

It was Tiray who asked the reason for the huge number of ships.

'It's the marriage ceremony, Councillor,' came the reply from the commander of the main escort ship.

'Marriage?' said Tiray. 'What marriage?'

'Between Lord Andrus and the Archmage Syrene. The notification arrived only days ago, and they came through Melos yesterday. The ceremony is tomorrow morning. You'll be just in time for it.'

Before they entered the wormhole, Steven turned and regarded his brother carefully. Paul nodded his understanding, for they shared the same thought: if Lord Andrus was marrying again, then surely his only daughter would have to be present, and if males were forbidden to enter the Marque, then the ceremony would have to be held elsewhere.

Paul's grip tightened on his chair as they boosted, but for once it was not out of fear.

Hear me, Syl: I am coming for you.

Chapter 64

They were not escorted directly to Illyr, which caused Paul some dismay when he heard the news coming over the communications system. Instead, the *Nomad* was brought to the massive Military base known as Melos Station, close to the mouth of the wormhole.

'It's good news,' Peris assured him. 'We're safer with the Military than we are at one of the shared docking stations closer to Illyr.'

It didn't sound like good news to Paul. He could be of no help to Syl trapped at the edge of the Illyri system.

'But what about Syl?' he asked bluntly. 'How am I supposed to get to her from here?'

Peris looked at him in amusement.

'If there is to be a wedding,' he said, 'then it can't be held on the Marque, for obvious reasons.'

'I know that,' interrupted Paul. 'No males on the Marque. They probably have a sign to let everyone know.'

Peris sighed, the way the old will when the young don't want to wait to learn.

'But it won't be held on Illyr either,' he finished.

'Why?'

'Call it bad memories. The Sisterhood isn't one great mass of females, all in agreement with one another, all thinking the same thoughts. As far as I know, the majority of the younger ones, led by Syrene, are actively intent on forging links with the Corps – and now, clearly, the Military – through marriage. Syrene leads those among the senior Sisters who serve as advisers to the Corps, both openly and more secretly. But the bulk of the older Sisters prefer to keep their distance from Illyr, physically as well as emotionally, because they've studied their history books, and they remember the reasons why the Sisterhood was forced to flee to the Marque to begin with.'

'They're afraid of another conflict,' said Paul.

'And with good reason, perhaps, if this ship we're on is anything to go by. But it's even simpler than that: back on Illyr the Sisterhood was once persecuted, and most of its adherents murdered, and the scars have never healed. But Syrene is clever – too clever to risk alienating some of the most influential voices on the Marque by excluding them from the ceremony. No, if my guess is right, the wedding will take place at Erebos.'

The name was unfamiliar to Paul. It wasn't any planet or moon that he knew of in the Illyri system.

'What's Erebos?'

'Erebos was the favourite palace of Meus, the Unifier of Worlds. It's said to be the most beautiful building in the known universe – if you like that kind of thing. It's used on only the greatest civic occasions: the truce to end the Civil War was signed there, and it's where presidents are inaugurated. If the Military and the Sisterhood are to form their most important bond in Illyri history, then they will do so at Erebos.'

'And where's Erebos?'

Peris leaned across Paul and pointed through one of the portside windows, where a small blue-grey world was spinning in the void, three tiny moons of descending size set against it like a row of pearls. It looked close enough to touch.

'*There* is Erebos.'

Now the Military station loomed before them. It reminded Paul of a Christmas bauble stripped from a great tree. It was shaped like a cut diamond, but one of silver, with a central ring from which protruded numerous needlelike docking ports, most of which were currently occupied by vessels, varying in size from massive carriers and destroyers to small patrol ships like their escorts. Paul assumed that the station was heavily defended, although he could see no obvious weapons ports.

Together they had agreed a story to present to the inevitable Military inquiry into the destruction of the *Envion*, and the loss of everyone else on board. It was mostly true, detailing everything from the events on Torma, and the species of silicon-based life discovered there, which was no minor matter; the escape in the shuttle from the drilling platform; the discovery of the *Envion*, already crippled; the fight on board; the capture of the Nomad vessel; and the voyage to the Illyr system. What they left out were their suspicions about the possible identity and motives of the attackers; the advanced nature of the captured ship; and any mention at all of their visit to Archaeon. The delay in returning to Illyr could be explained by their fear of further pursuit and their desire to protect Tiray, which led to their decision to use unmonitored wormholes, although Paul had been careful to check with Alis that the ship's flight recorder remained inoperative, and no record existed of their actual routing.

Once that was decided, it was time to address their immediate plans upon arrival at the base.

'Councillor,' said Peris, 'it would be my advice to announce that this is now your personal ship, and any attempt by the Military to seize it would be viewed as a criminal act. As far as the Military is concerned, you're arriving in a rattling old Nomad craft. The conclusion of the authorities will probably be that you've lost your senses if you want to retain it for your personal use, but I can't see them objecting.'

Tiray agreed. He knew that they all remained at risk because of what they had seen and done on Archaeon, and he might well be glad of an escape route if the Military station proved more hostile than they might have hoped.

'I'll request a routine exterior maintenance check to address the weaknesses in the hull,' Peris continued. 'It should just be a matter of strengthening the panels and securing the seals. I'll also advise that, under your orders, the ship's ordnance should be resupplied: that means torpedoes and mines. Alis, you'll supervise the operation, assisted by Rizzo.'

'Not Thula?'

She sounded disappointed.

'Missing me already?' asked Thula.

'Only your strength,' said Alis. 'Not your personality.'

If Paul didn't know better, he might have suspected that Alis's attraction to human males extended further than his brother. He also experienced a twinge of annoyance that Peris was now the one giving orders. Paul's time in charge was over. He was now just another Brigade lieutenant, and on a Military station it was Illyri officers, even ones at instructor level like Peris, who were in command.

'No, I want Thula and Paul to stay with Councillor Tiray as his personal security, with his approval.'

To Paul's surprise, Tiray raised no objection. The politician guessed the reason for Paul's change of expression.

'I am aware, Lieutenant, that you may not like or trust me, but I am a realist,' said Tiray. 'There is a conspiracy infecting my society, and I now have more knowledge of it than is appropriate for my continued good health. If a move is made against me, then it will come from within the Illyri, and perhaps even from someone close to me, for I have to admit that I am no longer certain of the loyalties of even some of those whom I have called colleagues and friends. Under these circumstances, I will accept the protection of humans above Illyri.'

He shifted his attention back to Peris.

'And I am aware of the nature of the weapons seized at Torma,' he said. 'For now, it suits me to pretend that I know nothing of them. Please don't give me cause to lament it.'

For a moment, Paul regretted not finding a way to lock Tiray up in a closet from the first moment they'd found him. The politician had sharp ears and eyes, far sharper than Paul had believed. But he, like Peris, understood what was being offered here. A deal was being made. Paul and Thula would not be permitted to carry weapons that could be used against Illyri, even on a Military base like Melos Station. They were soldiers of the Brigades, and though the Illyri were content to use them as troops, they had the same feelings towards them that Paul had towards Tiray: no affection, and no trust, so there was no question of them arming themselves with pistols and shotguns. They could, though, carry Illyri weaponry, because it would be assumed that such armaments were DNA-locked to prevent them being used against their makers. To anyone looking on, the humans would be armed with pulse weapons only for show, like small boys playing with toy guns.

'I will have safe quarters assigned to Councillor Tiray, and you will escort him to them,' said Peris. 'Nobody is to enter unless they are with me. If I approach with others, and I am being forced to do so against my will, I will use your first name, Paul, not your rank. You will then have my full permission to turn your weapons on those with me. Keep them set on a low level though. I don't want people killed on that station if I can avoid it.'

They were almost at their docking port now. Their escorts split away, leaving Steven to keep pace with the slow revolution of the station until he brought them safely against the buffers, and the station locked on to them.

'How long will we need to keep the Councillor secure?' asked Paul.

'Until the wedding,' said Peris. He looked for confirmation to Tiray, who nodded.

'Through Peris, I can arrange to have messages sent to those whom I still trust. They will all be attending the ceremony at Erebos. But so too will senior members of the Corps and the Securitats, and we will be surrounded by enemies.'

Tiray left them and headed for the bathroom to make himself look somewhat respectable for his arrival at Melos Station.

'And there's one other problem,' said Peris, when Tiray was gone.

'I think we have enough already,' said Thula, 'but thank you for offering.'

Peris ignored him.

'No weapons of any kind are permitted on Erebos,' he said. 'Not for anyone. Once you get there, you're going to be completely unarmed.'

CHAPTER 65

On their arrival, they were met by the base commander, Hadix, and a platoon of the station's own security force. Their surprise at finding four Brigade soldiers on board what appeared to be a captured Nomad ship, along with one previously missing Councillor and his aide, was lessened somewhat by Peris's presence. It was immediately clear that he and Hadix went back a long way, and their relationship was good. Peris's request that Councillor Tiray be given private quarters, and that the Brigade should act as his personal security detail for the duration of his visit, was instantly accepted, although first Paul and Thula had to consent to a body search in case they were carrying unapproved weapons. Their pulse rifles were given only a casual glance, for Peris had been correct: it was simply assumed that the humans were wearing them out of habit and not usefulness.

Paul and Thula accompanied Tiray to his quarters, where he washed and then lay down to rest, informing Paul that he did not wish to be disturbed for a few hours. Paul joined Thula on guard outside. Now that they were away from the cramped interior of the *Nomad*, Paul realised how badly he and Thula smelled, and how tattered and filthy their uniforms were.

'You need a shower,' he told Thula.

'I do,' Thula admitted. 'You, on the other hand, smell like a fresh flower. How do you manage to stay so neat and clean when I am a filthy embarrassment to the Brigades?'

'That's sarcasm, right?'

'Yes, that *is* sarcasm.'

They leaned against the wall, their hands hovering near their pulse weapons. Although he had slept fitfully on the trip back to Illyr, Paul was still teetering on the edge of exhaustion. Then again, he was a soldier, and all soldiers learned to eat and sleep when they could, and tolerated the fact that, by and large, they would never eat or sleep quite as well as they would have liked.

After two long hours, Peris appeared. He wore a fresh uniform, and bore the look of a man who had recently enjoyed a long shower and a hot meal.

'Is he settled?' he asked Paul.

'Seems to be. He left orders that he wasn't to be disturbed for a while. He wants to bathe and sleep, and he'll eat later.'

'I'm sure you'd like to do the same,' said Peris. 'Unfortunately, I can only offer you the chance to shower and take some nourishment. Sleep will have to wait.'

Peris joined Paul on guard while Thula was allowed to go to the showers and the mess. Paul and Peris exchanged some small talk, but that was all, as Peris had warned them to watch what they said while on the base, for they did not know who might be listening.

Thula was gone for only a short time. When he came back, Paul took his turn in the shower, requisitioned a set of Illyri Military overalls that were slightly too large for him, and ate a meal of Illyri food at the officer's mess, where the quality was a little better than that served to the lower ranks. It still contained too many unidenti-fiable elements for Paul's liking, but he was hungry enough not to care. They had spent the last week living on coffee, porridge oats, ready-to-eat meals, and pale, noodle-like carbohydrates that tasted like salty bootlaces. Whatever he was eating now, it was fresh and, given the Illyri concerns about good health, probably not actively bad for him.

'Well, look at you,' said Thula, when Paul returned. 'How pretty you are!'

Peris gave him an odd look, but said nothing.

'Shut up,' said Paul.

'Yes, sir.'

Peris left them, but not before he found two chairs for them.

'Try not to fall asleep,' he warned, 'or at least not at the same time,' and then he was gone.

Thula magicked up a coin from somewhere on his person.

'Toss you for it,' he said.

'Heads.'

'It's tails.'

'Damn.'

Thula sat, rested his head against the wall behind him, and closed his eyes. Within seconds, he was fast asleep.

Paul allowed Thula an hour, and then they switched positions. Paul was woken by the intercom beside his ear. Tiray's voice emerged from it, requesting that food be brought to him.

'What if they poison it?' whispered Thula.

'You have eaten the food here, right?' said Paul. 'It tastes like it's been poisoned already.'

Peris subsequently arrived with a tray, and stayed taking instructions from Tiray for almost an hour, getting details of those whom the politician wished to contact. When Peris eventually emerged, he did not speak to Paul or Thula and they did not disturb his thoughts, for he had a lot of names to remember, and a lot of messages to transmit via a secure channel.

Some time later, Steven and Rizzo arrived to relieve them so that they could get some proper rest.

'Who's minding the ship?' asked Thula.

'Alis,' said Steven. 'It's secure.'

'And how is your girlfriend?' Thula enquired.

Steven tried to ignore him, but Thula persisted.

'You're a little young for her, aren't you?'

Steven kept his gaze fixed on the wall ahead, refusing even to look at Thula, but he managed to force the word 'No' through gritted teeth.

'I think she would be better off with a man like me,' said Thula. 'I'm more mature and' – he reached into the pack on his belt, and produced a small plastic bottle – 'I will always carry oil, just in case she gets rusty.'

That was too much for Steven. He made a leap at Thula, swinging his fists wildly, but Thula kept him at bay with his long arms, laughing all the time. It was left to Paul to drag his brother away, Steven still swearing at Thula.

'Let it go!' Paul told him. 'Can't you see he's just trying to get a rise out of you?'

Steven managed to calm himself, but his face was very red. Thula apologised, though he didn't look as though he meant it. His grin was too wide for that. Paul gave him a shove to send him on his way before following.

'Did you really have to bait him like that?' he asked Thula, once they were out of earshot.

'I was just having fun with him.'

'He's still young, and not just in years. Last time he thought he was in love, it wasn't reciprocated. This is all new for him. And it's hard. The first time is always rough.'

'Spoken like a man who's had his heart broken.'

'Me? No, not really. But you don't actually fancy Alis, do you?'

'No! I prefer mine—'

Thula stopped himself. He was about to say 'human' but he was conscious both of Peris's warning that their conversations might be monitored, and of Paul's own tenderness for a non-human, for Syl. Paul had told Thula of her when they were going through basic training together, and for a long time he had been one of the few who knew of the depth of Paul's feelings for the young Illyri female. Since then Paul had taken Rizzo and Alis into his confidence too, but nobody else needed to know, and certainly no one on board a secure Military base in the Illyri home system.

'I prefer mine a little older-looking,' Thula concluded instead.

Paul knew what he had done, and was grateful for it, but that didn't mean he couldn't bait Thula in turn.

'How old?' he asked. 'Like, grandmother old?'

'No,' said Thula, with great dignity. 'That isn't what I said.'

'You said old.'

'I said *older*.'

'What, older than grandmothers? You mean *great*-grandmothers? My God, what's wrong with you?'

'You're deliberately misunderstanding me.'

'No, I'm not. I heard it.'

'That is not what you heard.'

'You said it. You can't take it back now.'

Thula aimed a boot at Paul's rear end, but Paul was too quick for him.

'Attempting to strike a superior officer!' Paul shouted, but he was laughing as he said it. 'I could have you court-martialled!'

A pair of passing Illyri soldiers regarded them curiously, unsure of what was going on.

'If you stay still long enough,' said Thula, 'I'll give you a reason to have me shot.'

They were both still smiling as they reached the quarters assigned to them. The room contained two bunks, two lockers, two chairs, and not much else. The packs containing their personal belongings were already there, probably left by Peris. Paul searched in his pack until he found a notepad and pen. He wrote on the first sheet of paper, and showed it to Thula.

I think Syl will be at the wedding ceremony tomorrow. I'm going to try to find her and take her away from the Sisterhood.

Thula wrote his reply in turn.

How?

The Nomad. *If I can get us on board, I can make a jump through the Melos wormhole. Four ways out.*

Who else knows?

Steven. Peris knows that I want to help Syl escape, but not how. Maybe he suspects though.

Dangerous.

I'm not asking for your help.

Paul made it clear by his expression that he didn't mean the words harshly. He was only trying to protect Thula.

Yes, you are.

Okay, maybe I am, but I don't expect you to risk your life for this.

I'm in. Rizzo too, Thula added. *She'll follow you, especially if it means she can shoot things.*

Paul felt his eyes well up with gratitude. He did not really believe that he could attempt a rescue without Thula standing by him, and he had hoped that his friend would agree to help, but he could not be certain. He gripped Thula's left arm in thanks.

Get your hand off me, Thula wrote.

And Paul thumped him.

Chapter 66

Nothing is as it appears to be.

Syl could still hear the words spoken by Onwyn, could almost feel the old librarian's skin against hers, her thin, bony hand clasped in Syl's palm, fragile yet substantial with life. If nothing was as it appeared, did Onwyn also include Kosia's death in her summation, poor Kosia who – like Syl, like Elda – had been researching Archaeon? The more Syl thought about it, the more she became convinced that the discovery of Kosia's body in the Second Realm had been no accident. If she had been discovered, then killing her and making it look like an unfortunate cave-in would serve to keep others away, and reinforce the Second's reputation for dangerous instability. Syl didn't like it, not one bit, but clearly the Second Realm was where she needed to be.

And although she now knew that Archaeon was a planet, she still did not understand why the Sisterhood seemed so anxious to delete details of its existence. So it was a habitable world, with some form of life. What of it? It was not as if it was the only such world. Why was it important enough to kill for – for it surely seemed that Elda had died because of Archaeon, or why else would she have scratched its name on a locket and entrusted it to Syl to spirit off Avila Minor and take to her mother? Did Elda's mother know of her daughter's double life, she wondered? Would she be shocked, disappointed, or proud? For now, though, it was left to Syl to take this clue left by Elda and make some sense of it.

The imminent wedding of her father and Syrene gave Syl an opportunity to explore that she would never get again, for it plunged the Marque into a state of excitement and distraction. All but the most essential of personnel were leaving for Erebos, since the Sisterhood was in charge of the arrangements for the day, from catering to security. The Novices and Half-Sisters were to act as hosts and servers at the wedding, and they had set off before dawn, clad in crisp, new robes, to prepare for the guests. However, as the future stepdaughter of the Archmage, Syl was exempt from these duties. Instead she was expected to put on appropriate finery along with her happiest smile, and then stand behind her father as he wed the creature that had destroyed him.

Syl was left entirely alone to get ready. Her yellow dress from the Genesis Ball had been laundered and now hung in her wardrobe, the stones on the belt polished to a sheen, but she could hardly bear to look at it.

Instead, shortly after breakfast, Syl slipped into her stolen white robes and made her way into the underbelly of the Marque. There was little need for further subterfuge. Only a skeleton staff of maintenance crew seemed to be around, and they were too preoccupied with keeping all systems functioning to pay a passing Service Sister much heed.

So it was that she reached the entrance to the Second Realm entirely without incident. She made her way down the old staircase until she reached the section where the tunnel was sealed off by heaps of rocks, but zooming closer on Lista's cartograph revealed a way around it: a narrow access tunnel in the back of one of the deserted libraries behind her, for the rocks and cautionary tape were a deterrent and nothing more. This old Realm was too honeycombed to ever be entirely secure.

Within the dank tunnel there was some light, even without activating a glowstick, for the disused space was home to microorganisms that grew in the walls and gleamed in the darkness. It wasn't much illumination, but it was enough to see by. However, Syl soon encountered another problem: the tunnel was so narrow that she had to turn sideways to work her way along it, and at one point it constricted so much that she found herself unable to go forwards or backwards, and was convinced that she would remain stuck forever.

This, she thought, is why they didn't block it off, because it's use-less. The rocks pressed against her back, pinning her in place, but then she remembered the creeping garniads and, after some rather panicked flailing, she managed to wriggle free, ripping her robe and leaving a nasty scrape along her hipbone. Shaken, she moved onwards.

Eventually the old access tunnel rejoined the main one, and she made good progress until she rounded a corner and saw that the way was again blocked by a rock fall. Boulders, stones and pebbles were piled from floor to ceiling without any way around them, and the cartograph appeared to be getting no readings at all. Even the path she was on didn't show, and only the blue light blinked forlornly on the device. She studied the rocks, thinking of Kosia, of her broken remains being pulled from a pile such as this. Onwyn's words echoed back at her.

Nothing is as it appears . . .

Syl tested the rocks, but they seemed solid enough. She tried the walls alongside, but they were firm too. She supposed that she could work her way back and try to find another sub-tunnel, but the prospect of squeezing herself through that tight space again terrified her. She forced herself to think logically.

Assumption 1: Kosia had died here while trying to discover the Realm's secrets. If Kosia had been right, and the Second was being used to hide something, then some among the Sisterhood would probably want access to it.

Assumption 2: If access was required, then the tunnel could not really be sealed off, unless the collapse was recent, although it couldn't be as the wispy webs of garniads floated in the spaces between the rocks, and the dust was thick enough for her to write her name in.

Conclusion: There had to be a way past.

She began working her way along the wall of stones again, touching each one, testing it carefully, wary of being bitten, until she came to a small, indented area to the left, close to the tunnel wall, where the garniad webs were at their thickest. She stood before it and peered in, using her glowstick to illuminate the webs. She could see no movement. Still, she didn't want to be attacked. One sting would hurt, but Amera had said multiple stings could flood the Illyri system with enough venom to stop a heart from beating, and this looked like a very big nest. Still, if there was a means to gain access beyond the rock collapse, it might well be behind the web.

Had Kosia come to the same conclusion? What if she, too, had put her hand into the web, found a lever, and triggered a further collapse in a trap set by the Sisterhood, a trap only for the bold? But Syl had come this far, and she wanted to know the truth. Frankly, she had nothing to lose. Everything that mattered to her seemed lost anyway. She closed her eyes, inserted her hand into the web, and waited for the first bite. None came. Instead she felt a rounded button against her fingers. She pressed down hard, holding her finger in place, and after several seconds a section of the wall to her left slid open, revealing a small tunnel that curved around the rocks. She withdrew her hand and the doorway stayed open for long enough to permit her to slip through, after which it closed behind her once more. Syl checked the rock wall on the other side. Yes, there was a gap in the stones, but this time without any webs to hide the presence of the button. The experience of getting out would, she hoped, be less nerve-racking than getting in.

The tunnel beyond was far cleaner than the one behind, and lights were set in its roof because the walls had been cleared of micro-organisms. Syl saw moisture on the stones, and smelled disinfectant, just as she heard a low whirring from ahead of her. She thought about retreating back into the little tunnel doorway, but there was no time. From around the corner appeared a small circular drone, hovering midway between floor and roof. A series of nozzles on its frame sprayed liquid evenly along the tunnel and, in this case, over Syl. She closed her eyes and mouth, and covered her face with her hands, as the disinfectant covered her from head to toe. It wasn't toxic, and it did not burn: it seemed just strong enough to kill bacteria. The drone stopped at the rocks, beeped once, then returned the way it had come, still spraying disinfectant as it went. Syl followed it until she came to a clear glass window set into the tunnel wall, and there she stopped.

She had found the First Five.

CHAPTER 67

Through the glass, four of the ancient Sisters were seated as though at points of a compass, facing north, south, east, and west respectively. The fifth, and by far the eldest, sat in the centre, slumped on a chair set higher than the others, her head resting against its heavy padding.

'Mage Ezil,' murmured Syl: it had to be.

So she was not dead, although perhaps she might wish to be. Wires connected the bodies of the Sisters to an array of monitors. Feeding pipes were fixed to their mouths, and catheters and rectal tubes took care of waste products. The face of the Sister facing Syl was deathly pale, and her eyes were like marbles floating just below the surface of curdled milk, clouded by cataracts – they stared sightlessly ahead, not registering Syl's presence. The Sister's body was concealed beneath a white medical gown, and tattooed hands rested on her thighs. Silver nursing droids set on rubberised tracks waited patiently nearby, their multiple arms ending in pincers, needles and blades, ready to intervene at any sign of a medical emergency. No other Sisters were to be seen.

But it was none of this that made Syl's stomach turn, and it was not the sight of these shaven-headed old females seated like statues that made her raise her hands to her mouth and choke back the urge to be violently ill.

No, it was this:

The skull of each Sister was smothered in a mass of red tendrils that came together to form a series of fleshy cables. The thinner cables connected each of the Sisters in the outer circle to one other, snaking between their heads, pulsating and wet as if alive. Four thicker, tangled cords extended inwards like the spokes of a wheel, coming together at the top of Ezil's head, their red coils concealing her forehead entirely. The tendrils curled and twisted, sometimes sliding free and probing at the air around them before diving back down greedily towards their host, so that the old Mage's skull was like the hair of Medusa, the serpent-haired gorgons of mythology.

And stretching upwards out of that central entanglement was a single link of a deeper red, an umbilical cord running from Ezil's skull and ending in the belly of a creature of which Syl had seen the likes only once before: wrapped around the brain stem of Grand Consul Gradus. However, that organism had appeared little bigger than a prawn, or the larva of some insect. This one, though, was much larger, about the size of a morbidly obese child, and it was held up by a web of tendrils that formed a hammock underneath the high roof of the cave.

The creature's body was transparent, misted slightly like a steamy window, and through its outer membrane Syl could make out a central dark heart pumping blood through the vessels, supported by a series of earthworm-like lateral hearts. She could see the swelling and contraction of what might have been lungs, and the pinkish-yellow mass of its brain above two dark eyes. The rest of its head consisted entirely of sucking tentacles, most of which extended through the web and connected it still further to the Sisters below. It had no legs but instead had smaller, gripping tentacles on its lower body, and these were covered with short hairs and sharp barbs.

Syl looked to her right, to where a closed door led into the room beyond. She wanted to get nearer to them now that she was starting to overcome her initial shock and revulsion. She wanted to *see*.

The door opened automatically as she approached, revealing a sub-chamber in which hung medical scrubs and facemasks. A voice spoke automatically from a hidden speaker, reminding all personnel to adhere to safety procedures before entering. A diagram on the wall made clear what those procedures might be: put on scrubs and mask; enter decontamination shower; proceed. Syl slipped into scrubs and a mask, and entered the shower room through a sliding glass door. Her body was enveloped in a sterilisation mist, a buzzer sounded the all-clear, and she was admitted into the main chamber.

She could smell it even through her mask and the sterilisation fluid: decay, bodily waste, and something worse, like the stink of a slaughter-house. She moved closer to the Sisters, most of her attention fixed on the organism above them, although – just like the elderly Nairenes – it did not seem to register Syl's presence. She made a full circle of the Sisters, casting anxious glances at the net above her head, fearful that one of those tendrils might reach down for her as well. Finally, she ducked beneath the outer cable and approached Ezil on her raised dais, her head level with the Mage's hands.

Cautiously she reached out and touched Ezil's wrist.

It was as though Syl had put her hand to an electric cable. Her body arched, and her fingers seemed glued to Ezil's pale, withered flesh. At the same time, a series of images exploded in her head.

The flight of the original First Five to Avila Minor; the early days in the tunnels and caves; the construction of the Marque; the ongoing exploration of the moon . . .

And the discovery of the meteor: the very same as the boulder she had seen in its glass dome showered with endless kisses.

Syl saw it all as though she were present at every important moment. She saw a Nairene scientist tell Ezil of the discovery of organisms inside the meteor that they'd unearthed on the moon, and heard the order to place the rock in quarantine, but by then it was too late. Four Sisters had already been infected, Ezil among them, contaminated by ancient parasites, entities almost as old as the Universe itself, things with no name, for there had been nothing to give them a name when they came into being.

The Others, Syl thought.

They had wandered the universe for billions and billions of years, carried on debris, buffeted by solar winds, each organism capable of independent existence but linked to the rest, sharing their discoveries, recording, remembering, mapping solar systems, galaxies.

Wormholes.

And all the time the creatures sought suitable worlds, planets with life that could be corrupted and used as breeding stock, the parasitic spores exploding from the ruined bodies of their hosts, their high kinetic energy making them capable of escaping even the gravitational pull of planets.

But sometimes the Others would lie dormant, letting life evolve, waiting to be discovered, just as they had on Avila Minor.

Yet the Others had never encountered a species as advanced as the Illyri, or a being as clever as Ezil – or as Ezil thought herself to be. A deal was struck. The Others relied on chance to discover host worlds and host entities, but the Universe was largely devoid of life.

Spare us, Ezil argued, *and we will find worlds for you. Make the Illyri great, and in return you will have life.*

So the Others formed a symbiotic relationship with the Illyri, the most lethal of them embedding in the First Five, and slowly they shared their knowledge of the Universe with the Sisterhood. Thus the Illyri Conquest began.

But the price that the Sisterhood had paid. Oh, the price . . .

Syl felt not only Ezil's suffering, but the agony of her four Sisters as well: Atis, Loneil, Ineh and Tola, names that she had seen written and heard whispered. In the lore of the Sisterhood they had retreated deep into the Marque many decades earlier to immerse themselves entirely in the pursuit of knowledge. They had assumed the status of myths, of near-goddesses. Instead they had given themselves over as hostages to an entity far more intelligent and ravenous than they could ever have imagined.

Their pain was not just physical: it was emotional and mental too. Even as the tendrils of the organism extended itself through them, controlling them, feeding off their energy, sustaining them as it slowly sucked them dry, still they had the capacity to feel sorrow, regret, guilt. Ezil had believed that she could hold off these parasites by striking a bargain she had no intention of fulfilling on her side, promising them other worlds, other species, but all the while plotting the destruction of these ancient terrors. Slowly, she had been forced to make sacrifices: a primitive animal here, an entire species there.

But they are hungry, so hungry.

Until finally whole worlds were sacrificed.

Archaeon.

The word echoed in Syl's head. She heard it spoken in Ezil's voice even though the Mage's lips had not moved.

We gave them Archaeon.

Her corruption had been slow but inevitable, for there are no small evils: each one is simply a step on the road to ultimate damnation.

And Earth will follow.

Suddenly another consciousness intruded into Syl's revelation, one that was ancient, and malevolent, and hungry. It was both one and many, a great shadow that swept across her mind, and hidden in the shadow were billions of mouths, and each mouth was filled with a billion teeth.

The Other had become aware of her presence.

The contact between Syl and Ezil was broken, although whether by the Mage or herself, Syl could not tell. She was propelled backwards, falling against the cable of tendrils that linked Atis and Tola. The cable did not tear, but the impact caused Atis to tumble from her chair, and sent a shock wave through the rest. Loneil's eyes rolled blankly in their sockets. Ineh's lips moved soundlessly, Atis's head started to shake uncontrollably, and Syl thought that she heard Tola whimper.

Then their voices spoke in Syl's head: first one, then two, until finally all were screaming so loudly inside her that she thought she must go mad.

Kill me.

Kill us.

Please, kill us!

The medical droids bustled forward, alerted to the emergency by the shrill beeping of the monitors. A rustling noise came from above Syl's head as the organism moved for the first time in its fleshy web, the smaller filaments around its mouth twitching, its black eyes rolling in their sockets. Tendrils extruded from its body and slipped through the gaps in the lattice, searching for the source of the disturbance. Puffs of red dust appeared from tiny openings in its body: spores.

But Syl was already running.

Oriel was watching the latest shuttle to Erebos rise from the Marque when she felt a painful tightening at the base of her brain. The Other inside her head began bombarding her system with alarmed pulses, along with images transmitted to it by the dominant organism, deep in the Second Realm. Oriel caught a glimpse of a figure in white medical scrubs, her back to the Other, intent upon escape. A door opened. A mask was cast aside. A face was reflected in glass.

Syl Hellais.

CHAPTER 68

Syl didn't realise that she was crying until her vision began to blur. The sound of the First Five begging to be killed echoed in her head even as the voices themselves began to fade, the horrors of the chamber left farther and farther behind as she ran. As she fled she was listening: her greatest fear was that the creature, the Other, might somehow find its way out and pursue her. The decontamination chamber was too narrow to admit it, but suppose it broke the glass and escaped through the window? It didn't look like it could move very fast, which was something, but the thought of being trapped in the tunnel with it was horrifying.

She reached the rock wall and found the button embedded in the stones. She pressed it, but nothing happened.

'Please, please!' she cried aloud, banging at the button, wanting to be gone from this place. She was sorry that she had ever started to explore it, sorry for her curiosity, sorry for everything.

She wanted to *unknow*, but her mind felt wide open now, exposed, like a coconut split by a machete. Everything came spilling in as if she were a satellite dish. As she stood there, she was picking up the thoughts and signals of all life in this vile Realm: she could feel the furious probing of the Other, and the whispering tendrils of despair from the Sisters tickling like gossamer in the corners of her mind. She was intensely sensitised, aware even of the garniads living in the rocks. She sensed them deep in the crevices and felt their consciousness, something entirely alien to her, a dark mess of base appetites and nothing more. In their way, they were like the Others, but without the intelligence. She could almost taste the bugs, so deep inside them was she.

And they were clearly aware of her: she could feel them coming as if drawn by some primal instinct.

But there was another coming too: she felt it, and swooned with fear.

Reeling, she thumped the button again with her right fist, but something crawled over her hand. She froze. It was a garniad. It had to be. Its hard legs danced over her skin, and then it was probing at her thumb. She didn't want to be stung, not even once, for each sting would emit a chemical signal drawing more of its kind to the source of prey. In that way, even large animals could be overwhelmed by enough of the bugs.

There was a crash in the room behind her.

'Please, not that,' she whispered.

Keeping her right hand completely still, the garniad balanced delicately upon it, Syl lifted her left and held her finger down on the button this time.

One . . . two . . . three . . . four . . .

On five, the mechanism rumbled, and the doorway opened. As slowly as she dared she slipped through the gap, twisting as she went so that her hand was the only part of her that remained in the hallway. Fingers outstretched, she waited, watching the garniad, barely breathing as the entrance began to creak closed. At the last possible moment, a fraction of a second before the door would crush her wrist, she yanked her hand back through the gap, knocking the creature off against the wall and hoping the door would do the rest as it clanged shut. The garniad toppled to the ground, where it lay like a dung beetle on its back, waving its legs indignantly. Syl looked at it and found herself giggling with hysterical relief as she watched it right itself: relief that she hadn't been stung, but mostly at putting the rock wall between her and all that lay behind it.

She turned to go, and the laughter died. Oriel was standing in the tunnel, her hands clasped before her.

'I never trusted you, Syl Hellais,' she said. 'There was always something dishonest about you. Now you've been poking your nose in places that don't concern you, but it's the last thing you'll ever do.'

With her consciousness laid bare, Syl felt the loathing behind the words like needles in her head, yet her initial shock at seeing Oriel was already giving way to rage.

'You *knew*?' said Syl. 'You knew about that – that *monster* back there, about the First Five and how they're suffering, and you did nothing? You're a Nairene. They're your Sisters! How could you let them go through that? How could you stand by and let that monster torture them? They want to *die*.'

'But you didn't kill them either,' said Oriel. 'They cried out to you, and you didn't lift a finger to help them. You just ran away. You're like a child that finds an animal with a broken back, but won't put it out of its misery. Instead you whine and moan and beg someone else to do the dirty work for you.

'Except, in this case, the dirty work is keeping them alive. You think that it doesn't trouble me, knowing what they're going through? You think I don't wish that I could put an end to it? But they have sacrificed themselves so the rest of us can flourish.'

'No,' said Syl. 'The First Five thought they could outwit those creatures, but they didn't realise how terrible they are, how *hungry* they are. And they're never going to stop: entire worlds won't be enough for them. They live to feed and to breed. The First Five showed me. I saw it all.'

Syl stopped. She stared at Oriel. Now, for the first time, she truly understood.

'But none of this is news to you, is it?' said Syl, quieter now. 'It's not the First Five who have sacrificed themselves to those monsters. *You've* sacrificed them: you, and Syrene, and the other senior Sisters. You're not the ones trapped back there with that creature. You're not the ones wishing for death, yet forced to stay alive. Everything you've just said to me is a lie. You don't feel any pity for them at all.'

If the truth of Syl's words troubled Oriel, she gave no sign of it.

'You're young and ignorant,' said Oriel. 'But that won't save you.'

'Just like it didn't save Elda or Kosia?'

'You have been a little snoop, haven't you?'

'But I'm right. You killed them, or had them killed.'

'Either. Both. It hardly matters now. I will give you some credit, though: you hid your powers well. Yes, Syl Hellais, I felt your strength when Ezil reacted to your presence. I felt it through her, for then you were not blocking me. Until then I didn't think it was possible for one so young to conceal herself from me, but you managed to do it. You have such potential. We thought it was Ani who represented the best hope among the latest first-year Novices, but *you* – you're truly exceptional. If Syrene knew what you could do, then she might well want to spare you.'

Oriel advanced a step.

'But we can't have that,' she concluded. 'You're dangerous. As far as I'm concerned, the benefits of keeping you alive are far outweighed by the drawbacks. And now I know to be true what I had begun to suspect: you are responsible for the murder of those promising young Novices. For whatever reason, you conspired to maroon them out on the veranda and leave them as prey for the ostraca. For what you did to them, there must be recompense. For that alone, you must die.'

Oriel reached out with her right hand as though grasping an apple in her palm, and tightened her grip, turning her fingers to claws. Syl experienced a sensation of pressure on her heart, and then stabs of pain as Oriel tested the walls of it with her fingernails.

'So much life,' said Oriel. 'And soon it will be gone.'

Syl closed her mind to the old Sister. She searched the darkness. She felt for the garniads again, reaching into their awareness. The pressure on her heart increased. She heard a gasp of pain – but it came not from herself, but from Oriel.

When she looked again, the first of the garniads had found Oriel and stung her on the ankle. Its legs gripped its prey as the venomous barb from its underbelly entered the flesh. The second and third of the creatures were already crawling up Oriel's left leg, stinging as they went, and more were pouring from the cracks in the tunnel and from the rock wall behind Syl, carving a path around her and then coming together again as they flowed towards the old Sister. Oriel tried to slap them away from her skin, but their grip was fast, and their response to any attack was simply to sting again.

'I killed only because I had no choice,' said Syl, 'but *you* are a torturer and a murderer. So feel it. Feel some of the First Five's pain.'

But Oriel did not hear her, for she was lost in her own agonies. Within seconds her entire body was covered head to foot in bugs, and the tunnel filled with her screams until the first of the garniads found her mouth. Briefly, Syl felt Oriel's pain as her panic clawed its way into her own psyche, but it was over almost as soon as it began.

When Syl stepped over the Grandmage, she was already dead.

Nobody else challenged Syl as she made her way to her quarters, and as she walked she felt things she hadn't felt before, hearing the thoughts and silent whispers of others in her head. She found that she was able to repel them more easily, as if the intrusions were rubber balls, bouncing in then knocked out again at her will. And she felt strong, stronger than she'd ever been in all her young life.

Back in her bedroom she changed into her yellow ballgown and filled a small backpack with a few essential belongings. She would not be returning to the Marque, whatever happened. She would try to find a way to escape from Erebos. If she could not, then she would go down fighting.

Only when she reached the door of the nearest waiting shuttle did a Nairene pilot emerge and ask her business.

'My name is Syl Hellais,' she said. 'My father is marrying the Archmage. I wish to be taken to Erebos for the ceremony.'

The Sister examined the electronic manifest.

'You're not scheduled to depart until later today,' she said.

'I should like to be there when my father arrives,' said Syl. 'I think my stepmother might appreciate the gesture too.'

The mention of Syrene was all that it took to overcome any opposition. Syl didn't even have to use her mind to manipulate her – or she didn't think she had. Such manipulation was becoming so natural to her that sometimes she didn't even notice.

CHAPTER 69

Paul could not help but gasp as the palace at Erebos came into sight.

'My God, just look at it,' he said. 'It's huge.'

They had left Melos Station early that morning in order to be present for the marriage of the Archmage and Lord Andrus. Tiray appeared tense. Peris was silent and watchful.

'It's beautiful,' said Rizzo, who was seated across from Paul on the *Nomad*. Her response surprised him almost as much as the size of the palace. Rizzo was not usually one for appreciating the aesthetics of anything that didn't fire a projectile.

Erebos was not a single building but a series of interconnected structures joined by covered walkways and galleries, and encircled by great walls some twenty feet thick, linked to the main buildings by arched bridges that radiated inwards. The centrepiece of Erebos was the Grand Hall, constructed entirely from crystal, both tough enough to withstand a direct hit from a small missile yet pure enough to be entirely transparent, with no distortive effect. In total, the palace covered over a hundred million square feet of buildings and gardens, with the Great Hall alone accounting for one tenth of that space, making it larger than the entire Palace of Versailles in France. The scale of it, the opulence, was breathtaking, even from high above the moon's surface.

The *Nomad* was not permitted to land at Erebos. To ensure that no breaches of the weapons code occurred, all ships were required to dock at one of a series of eight floating platforms, each capable of accommodating twenty vessels. From these a steady stream of small shuttles ferried guests down to the surface. Each VIP was entitled to bring two guests with them; they could be family members who had not received personal invitations, or guards. Most, Tiray assured Paul, would be bringing guards. Despite the thaw in relations between the Military and the Corps, old enmities still ran deep.

Paul would be heading down to Erebos as one-half of Tiray's security team, but Thula would not be able to form the other.

'It's because I'm black, isn't it?'

'Unfortunately it is,' Tiray conceded. 'No non-Illyri has ever set foot on Erebos. The authorities would never permit it. With his visor down to cover his eyes, Paul is just about tall enough to pass for a pale-skinned Illyri. The same cannot be said of you.'

'It's racism.'

'On so many levels,' said Tiray.

'You'll need more than one guard,' said Peris. 'I'll take Thula's place.'

'Agreed.'

Paul deeply regretted the absence of Thula. But on the other hand, he didn't need to attract any attention to himself on Erebos, not if he was to find Syl and somehow manage to get her off the moon without being apprehended, and Thula certainly caught the eye. There was also the small matter of Syrene and Lord Andrus: Paul had stood before both of them down on Earth, and each had good cause to remember his face. The less anyone suspected, the better. On the other hand, if he had to fight his way off Erebos, even unarmed, he wasn't sure that he could rely on Peris to help him, especially if Paul had to hurt, or even kill, Illyri to escape.

He was sure he had been in worse situations. He just couldn't recall what they might have been.

But he reminded himself that it was not very long ago when any hope of rescuing Syl had seemed faint and distant, and now he was about to be in the same building as her: a huge one, admittedly, but if she was there, he would find her.

Peris traced the direction of his thoughts.

'What are you going to say to her when you see her?' he asked.

Run, thought Paul, but he contented himself with telling Peris that he was sure he would come up with something appropriate when the time came.

The *Nomad* docked without incident. Tiray, as a figure of some importance, was bustled towards the nearest available shuttle, Peris and Paul behind him, Paul's visored face not attracting a first glance, never mind a second one. The shuttle had fifty seats, most of which were already occupied when they arrived. Tiray greeted many of the other guests by name, shaking hands and patting backs like the career politician that he was.

Paul's attention, though, drifted to the cockpit, where the pilot and co-pilot were making the final checks. They were both female and wore uniforms that were strangely familiar yet unlike any he had seen before – red and ornate, with short decorative cloaks held in place by a bright clasp bearing an engraved eye.

'They're Nairene Sisters,' Paul whispered to Peris.

'The Sisterhood is in charge of all arrangements for the ceremony,' Peris replied. 'Transport, food, lodging, security – everything is in their hands. Syrene apparently insisted, and Lord Andrus did not object.'

Paul wasn't yet sure if this was a good or bad thing. He was inclined towards bad. Most things involving the Sisterhood seemed to be, in his limited experience.

The shuttle door closed. A recorded announcement advised everyone to take their seats and secure their belts. A small vibration rocked the ship as the docking gantry disengaged, and then they were descending rapidly to Erebos.

The glass roof over the reception hall was supported by massive trees in full bloom, their crowns stretching across the dome high above. The trees were genetically modified, spliced with the DNA of the bioluminescent organisms found on the Marque, so that the hall was filled with a faint green glow.

The Sisterhood was out in force. Red-garbed Nairenes stood at every doorway, mingled among the crowds gathering in the anterooms for food and refreshment, and walked in the grounds or on the battlements, always in pairs and always with a slight smile on their faces, as though they had recently experimented with a mild but pleasing drug. Flitting among them like smaller birds of a different plumage were Novices in various stages of their training: pale yellows, sea greens, and the occasional flash of rich blue, like a kingfisher darting through reeds. They served food on polished trays, offered glasses of the finest cremos, and guided to their quarters those guests who were sufficiently grand to be offered their own private areas in which to wash, dress, or rest before the ceremony.

'What colour robes will Syl be wearing?' Paul asked Peris.

'Yellow, I imagine. That's what the Novices wear.'

Paul carefully examined the face of every passing Novice in yellow, but could find no trace of Syl. Then it occurred to him that Syl was unlikely to be reduced to the status of a servant if it was her own father who was getting married. She was Lord Andrus's only daughter, not Cinderella. She would be elsewhere. She might even be dressed in finery for the wedding. At the thought, his confidence briefly wavered: perhaps she would even be helping Syrene to prepare, a devoted stepdaughter-in-waiting. Perhaps things had changed, for so much had happened and it had been so long. He looked at the refined, composed Novices, so unlike the awkward Syl he remembered striding across the Highlands in a tatty farmhand's shirt, with dirty hands and the wind whipping at her copper hair, who'd become tongue-tied when he'd touched her. Might she have changed?

Peris nudged him, and Paul jumped.

'Your best chance of seeing her is at the ceremony, and the celebration to follow,' said Peris. 'For now, try to keep your mind on Tiray. I can already tell that some here are no friends of his. Look to your right.'

Casually, Paul risked a glance. He saw a knot of five older Illyri wearing white robes, their fingers heavy with bejewelled rings: Senior Consuls. Beside them stood two more Illyri – one male, one female – wearing the black of the Securitats. All of them were watching Tiray carefully, and none of them looked very pleased to see him.

Tiray seemed not to notice them and his own expression of good cheer never faltered, but Paul saw his eyes flick once in their direction, then pass on.

Through Peris, Tiray had made arrangements to meet with three Illyri at Erebos: the first was a senior Military commander named Joris; the second was the leader of the Civilians in the government, a younger politician called Hanan; and the final, and most surprising, was Kellar, a Junior Consul in the Diplomatic Corps related by marriage to the late Consul Gradus. These three were among the most influential of the Illyri who shared Tiray's concerns about the future of their race, and were most disturbed by the growing power of the Corps and its Nairene allies. Others present on Erebos for the wedding undoubtedly felt the same way, but they would follow Tiray's lead.

The meeting with Kellar would be the hardest to manage, and the most risky, especially if Tiray was already being watched by the Securitats. But the palace was even older than Edinburgh Castle, and had been a hotbed of plots and intrigue for many centuries. It had more secret passages and hiding holes than it was possible to count – and the Illyri, with their fondness for secrecy, kept adding to that number at every opportunity. It was a wonder that the whole complex didn't collapse into a big crater in the ground caused by all of the digging that was going on beneath it.

Hanan, the Civilian, was the first on the schedule. The meeting would be held in his quarters, since he was senior in position to Tiray. Then they had to get to Joris, too, before the wedding ceremony began.

Paul and Peris kept an eye out for any sign that they were being followed as they made their way to Hanan's rooms, but they detected no trace of Securitats. On the other hand, Sisters prowled everywhere, watching all, hearing all, but Tiray had no concerns about being seen with Hanan: they were both Civilians, and it was only natural that Tiray would take this opportunity to pay his respects to his superior.

The corridor in which Hanan's rooms lay was quiet when they reached it. Hanan's name was displayed on a screen by one of the doors. Paul pressed the buzzer beneath it, but the door did not open and the screen display did not change to show the face of Hanan or one of his assistants.

'He was expecting you, Councillor Tiray?' said Peris.

'Of course he was. You brought his reply to me yourself.'

'I didn't read it, though. You could not have misunderstood it?'

'No, it was clear. Try him again.'

Paul hit the buzzer a second time. Still nothing happened. He looked to Peris for a decision. On the off chance that it might work, Peris swept his hand across the door's sensor. The door opened silently, sliding into the wall. The room beyond was brightly lit and furnished with Illyri antiques, all of which looked more old than comfortable.

'Speaker Hanan?' Tiray called. 'May we come in?'

No reply came. Paul sniffed the air. He could smell cooked meat.

'Stay with the Councillor,' Peris instructed Paul.

Peris entered the room, his right hand instinctively reaching for a weapon, and freezing by his side as he remembered that he was unarmed. Paul and Tiray watched him slip into a side room. Neither of them spoke. The corridor remained empty. Paul wondered where the surveillance cameras were. None were visible, but he thought it unlikely that a place like Erebos would not have such a system.

Peris appeared again, moving with care, being careful not to touch anything.

'You'd better get in here,' he said. 'And close and lock that door behind you.'

Tiray entered first, Paul behind him. He made sure that the door could not be opened from outside, then joined Peris and Tiray. They were standing at the entrance to a huge bedroom, dominated by the biggest bed Paul had ever seen, suspended from the ceiling by thick chains. Beyond it was an open doorway leading into a tiled bathroom. The smell of charred meat was stronger here – unpleasantly so.

'In there,' said Peris. 'But I warn you, Councillor, it's bad.'

Tiray ignored him. He probably shouldn't have. Paul saw him freeze at the entrance to the bathroom. He stayed there, unmoving, for four or five seconds, then turned away and vomited on the bed. Paul passed him and looked for himself.

This room was almost as large as the bedroom, with two massive sunken baths in the floor. No water filled either of them, but they were not empty: three burned and blackened bodies lay in each, two in the first and one in the second. The white enamel inner surfaces had blackened and melted with the heat of the flames, and the room smelled of strong, roasted meat, but Paul could see no sign of the fire that had done this, and the alarms and sprinklers had not been set off by it.

Paul turned away. Peris found a napkin in the main sitting room and handed it to Tiray so that he could wipe his nose and mouth.

'What do you think?' Peris asked Paul while, Tiray recovered himself.

'It looks like they were forced into the empty baths, then something was poured on them – an accelerant or fuel – and then set alight. But any flames should have set off the alarms, unless they were deactivated.'

'They weren't. I've checked. And those bodies aren't just burned: they're incinerated almost to ash. That takes an incredible amount of heat.'

'We have to inform the Sisters,' said Tiray. His skin had a grey tinge beneath the gold.

'But this may be linked to you, Councillor,' said Peris. 'You were to meet with Hanan, and now he and his staff are dead. We have to warn Joris and Kellar before we do anything else.'

'But the Sisters – they must be told!' said Tiray. 'Security here is their responsibility.'

'Councillor Tiray,' said Peris gently. 'Think about what you've just said. If the Sisterhood is running this show, nothing happens here without their knowledge. *Nothing.*'

Tiray seemed at a loss for words. If Peris was right, they had all walked straight into a trap.

'We must leave,' he said. 'We have to get off Erebos.'

'And we will,' said Peris. 'Just as soon as we've located Joris and Kellar. Kellar is nothing to me, but I know Joris. She is a good soldier. I will not abandon her.'

Tiray nodded. He was already ashamed of his moment of panic.

'I'm sorry,' he said. 'You're right. Of course you are. Let's find them, and any others who may be on our side. The wedding be damned. They can't stop us all from leaving.'

But Paul was not so sure.

CHAPTER 70

The Lady Joris had travelled without security, for she had no concerns for her safety. She was among the longest-serving Military commanders but her relations with the Diplomatic Corps had always been good, by and large. Like Lord Andrus, who had been in the year below her at the academy, Joris was both a soldier and a politician, as skilled at negotiation as at fighting. She had long given the appearance of being the voice of reason in arguments between the Military and the Corps, moving between both camps, soothing ruffled feathers, negotiating compromises. In reality, though, her loyalty was entirely to the Illyri Empire and its Military, which she viewed as best equipped to protect the race and expand the Illyri Conquest.

However, in recent months her spies among the Corps and its sympathisers had come to her with alarming whispers of unregistered Corps facilities on conquered worlds, and there had been a troubling message from Earth, purportedly sent by a former Securitat named Fremd who had turned traitor. It spoke of a possible alien contaminant, an unknown extraterrestrial organism that had been introduced into the Illyri race. So Councillor Tiray had been dispatched to establish what he could of the truth behind the tales, and now he had returned. It was Joris's dearest hope that Tiray had discovered evidence linking the Corps and the Sisterhood to these crimes against their race, thus giving Joris a reason to prevent this abomination of a wedding ceremony, for it would firmly tie the Military to the Sisterhood.

A bell tolled lightly in her quarters. Joris's long-standing partner, Raya, who was accompanying her as a guest at the wedding, had been resting on the bed, but now she sat up. She knew something of her lover's worries, and of her plots and plans.

'Is it Tiray?' she asked.

'If it is, he's earlier than expected.'

Joris activated the camera. Two Novices in blue robes stood outside her door.

'Witches-in-training,' she said to Raya. 'What can these little brats want?'

She hit the unlock button. The door opened.

One of the Novices was holding a tray. On it stood a bowl of candied fruits, and a bottle of very dusty, and very old, cremos.

'With the compliments of the Marque,' said the Novices. They spoke in unison, and Joris saw that they bore a startling resemblance to each other, even though the one on the left was taller, and leaner.

'If the Sisterhood had done its homework, it would know that I don't drink intoxicants,' said Joris. 'Neither does the Lady Raya.'

The two Novices ignored her. They slipped past in perfect step, and set the tray on a table.

'Wait a minute,' said Joris. 'I didn't give you permission to come in here. I want your names. Now.'

'I am Xaron,' said the elder. 'And this is my sister, Mila.'

Mila smiled, and made a gesture with her left hand. The door behind Joris closed, and the display turned to 'Locked'.

'What do you think you're doing?' asked Joris, as the Sisters took each other's hands, staring at her. Raya stood in alarm and moved to join her, but then she stopped as something dripped on to her beautiful gown. She raised her right hand to her nose. It came back stained with blood.

'Joris, I'm bleeding,' she said.

The drops turned to a steady flow, covering her mouth and spilling over the front of her dress. Tears of blood started to weep from the corners of her eyes, and thin ribbons of it flowed from her ears. She opened her mouth to speak again, but a gush of fluid took the place of words, and bloodstains spread upon her clothing. She sank to her knees, uncomprehending, and sat back on her heels, her arms hanging loosely by her body, the light already leaving her eyes as she started to die. Joris could do nothing to help her, for tiny explosions of pain were erupting throughout her own body, their intensity increasing until all she could do was scream and scream, each cry punctuated by a fountain of blood.

And Xaron held Mila's right hand in her left, the better to concentrate their power as slowly, meticulously, like children pricking balloons, they burst every blood vessel in Joris's body.

CHAPTER 71

Junior Consul Kellar might have been young, but he was no fool. He knew that the Corps would be merciless with him if it discovered the extent of his treachery, but he was not to be swayed, even though one of his closest friends and allies had already died under mysterious circumstances. Radis had been found dead in the bathroom of his home. It was said that he had fallen and struck his head on a tiled corner. Apparently one of the tiles had shattered somehow, and pierced the base of his skull.

Kellar did not believe a word of it.

Kellar himself was of mixed Military and Diplomatic parentage, but he had married into a stalwart Diplomatic Corps family when he wed his childhood sweetheart, Velaine, who happened to be Consul Gradus's favourite niece. Yet Kellar was naturally inquisitive – nosey, as his laughing wife would call it – and gradually he had become aware of some mystery surrounding Gradus and his wife, the formidable Archmage Syrene. His curiosity piqued, he began to dig deeper until, through careful observation – and ultimately some illegal activity, including the electronic monitoring of meetings and the payment of bribes to aides – he realised that whatever was afoot, it was clearly designed to renew the hostilities of the Civil War.

Kellar's upbringing gave him a unique perspective on the enmity between Military and Corps: he had heard of the horrors of the Civil War from both sides, and was determined to do all in his power to prevent a second such war from erupting.

His weakness, if it could be called that, was his goodness.

Now the young consul stood on the steps that led down from his apartments on Erebos to the grass below. Guests walked on the grounds or sat beneath great trees to sip cremos in the glow of their luminescent branches, and a soft breeze carried the scents of flowers and blossoms. All appeared idyllic, but Kellar could see only shadows, and smell the poison that seeped through it all. He watched the Sisters moving along the walls and among the crowds, and they seemed to give form to all that was wrong with the Illyri. His wife's late uncle Gradus had even married the most public and powerful of them all: Syrene. Her fingerprints were all over the plots that Kellar had discovered.

Velaine had considered joining her husband for this most unusual of occasions, but memories of her dead uncle had stopped her. The pace at which the widow Syrene had secured herself a new husband seemed disrespectful, Velaine complained privately, and Kellar had been quietly relieved when she'd opted to stay on Illyr with their two children. Radis's strange death had shown that Kellar was engaged in dangerous business, and he was glad Velaine was safe at home. Instead, two guards had accompanied him; one stood outside the door to his rooms, and another waited at the bottom of the stairs. Still, even sandwiched between them as he was, he felt on edge, and he yearned for the comfort of his wife.

Suddenly figures below were standing up, and fingers pointed excitedly to the sky. A gold and red shuttle appeared, escorted by a pair of smaller skimmers in similar raiment trailing contrails of red smoke. Lord Andrus and Syrene were arriving for their wedding ceremony.

Kellar heard the door to his apartments open, although the buzzer had not sounded. He walked back inside and called out, 'Hello, who's there?'

A woman appeared from the hallway. It was Velaine. Kellar stumbled in shock at the sight of his wife.

'My darling, what are you doing here?' he asked, as he stepped towards her, his arms outstretched. He loved Velaine, and even his concern at her presence on Erebos at this difficult time could not overcome his affection for her.

'I couldn't stay away,' she said. 'I'm sorry. I wanted to see you.'

He hugged her to him, and her arms encircled his body.

'Where are the children?' he said.

'The children?' she said absently. 'I left them on Illyr.'

Kellar was startled.

'With whom?' he asked. 'Are they safe?'

'Of course. They're with your parents,' was her reply.

Wait, thought Kellar: something is wrong here, for only his mother was still alive.

'Did you say my *parents*?'

She held him tighter, clutching him like a vine, pressing herself against him, but it was not sexual. She cooed into his shoulder. It was oddly unsettling. And she *smelled* different. He was so used to Velaine's scent that he could detect it even beneath any perfume that she wore.

Soft lips kissed his neck, then she looked into his face, her curious breath filling his nostrils. It stank of corruption and disease. He drew back, but she held him grimly.

'I missed you,' said the thing that was not his wife.

He tried to pull away, but her grip on him was strong and she was stretching for his mouth greedily. Her lips parted, the tongue thick and wet. Over her shoulder he saw movement in the hallway. A female appeared dressed in the vestments of a more advanced Nairene Novice, a Half-Sister, but these sea-green robes were piped with bright blue, a combination he'd never seen before.

Her name was Bela, although Kellar would never learn it. She was adept at clouding but she sensed that Kellar had spotted the deception.

'Nemein,' she said. 'He knows.'

'It's all right,' said Nemein. 'It's started.'

She released her hold on Kellar and moved away from him. Now he could see her true form: thin and vicious, with features that spoke of hunger, and appetites that could not be filled. She was not beautiful. She was not his wife.

Kellar felt pain in his armpits. He touched his left hand to the skin beneath his right arm and felt lumps growing there.

'What have you done to me?' he said.

He raised his right hand before him. As he watched, his skin swelled, and the first of the tumours appeared, turning from red to black in the space of a heartbeat. He felt them spreading across his body, and his vision blurred as they reached his face, his cheeks distending, his eyelids bulging.

'Cancer,' said Nemein. 'Don't fret, it's almost over.'

Kellar tried to speak, but his tongue was inflamed. He reached for the Novice who had done this to him, but she skipped beyond his grasp, and he did not have the strength to leap forward and grab her. The disease continued its destruction of his body, flipping cells from white to black, until at last it reached his brain and, mercifully, the pain ended. Kellar hit the floor hard, and died without making another sound.

'I'm sorry,' said Bela. She looked appalled, but Kellar's corpse was not the source of her frustration. 'I thought I could fool him for longer.'

Nemein smiled.

'It was more than enough,' she said. 'In fact, you're almost as good as Dessa was. Anyway, I just needed to hold him for it to happen that quickly. Come though, we have more to do. You'll have plenty of opportunities to perfect your skill.'

Bela brightened at the compliment, and at the thought of more killing.

CHAPTER 72

Syl watched the descent of the shuttle carrying Lord Andrus and his bride-to-be. She was surprised at how cold she felt inside. This was her father: the man who had raised her after the death of her mother, who had indulged her, protected her, loved her, and from whom she had been separated by the vindictiveness of Syrene. Under ordinary circumstances Syl would have run to greet him, falling into his arms, burying her face in his chest, and congratulating him on at last finding a new partner in life after all his years alone.

But these were not ordinary circumstances. Her father was no longer the same. The Others had inhabited him – *infested* him – and Syrene was responsible, the same woman who would soon be called his wife. There was nothing for Syl to celebrate here.

She wondered if Oriel's body had been discovered yet. She felt no regret at what she had done to her, at taking yet another life. During the shuttle flight, she had examined her absence of guilt in a scientific way, as though she were her own subject beneath a microscope. Oriel would have killed her had Syl not murdered her first, and she would have rejoiced in the act. Syl had sensed Oriel's purpose in those final moments, could feel the hate pouring from her. But she had not taken pleasure in killing Oriel. It had simply been necessary. And she could have made the old witch suffer a great deal had she wished it, by holding the garniads back just a little and prolonging the pain, but she chose not to. From this she took cold comfort.

With any luck, it would be some time before the body was found, particularly as the Marque was as empty of life as it was ever likely to be. Still, it was only a matter of time before Oriel's death was discovered, and then connected to Syl, for her fingerprints and DNA would be all over the Second Realm. They would soon be looking for her, and in her elegant dress, she stood out in this sea of robes.

A figure in white vestments and a headscarf passed Syl as she stood at the window. Syl kept her face turned away, but the Service Sister glimpsed her reflection, and Syl saw her reaction reflected in turn. The girl stopped short and stared.

'Tanit? Is that you?'

For a split second, Syl almost forgot the name she'd given as her own.

'Hello, Lista,' she said, turning.

'Wow! What are you wearing? What a beautiful dress. Are you not working today?'

'No,' said Syl, thinking quickly. 'I have a family connection to the wedding party so I don't have to work – but I wish I did.'

'Goodness! Why would you want to do that?'

'Because I feel exposed in this dress. It's too tight, and I'm used to having my hair covered.'

'You're so weird. I'd die to have a dress like that.'

There was longing in her eyes, and her hands smoothed her plain robes absently.

'Well, why don't we swap? Just for a bit.'

Lista hesitated.

'We could exchange clothes, for fun,' Syl urged, 'and then meet here in a few hours to change back.'

'I don't trust you, Tanit. You never returned my cartograph, and no one in the Service Sisters had heard of you when I tried to find you. I got a right telling off when I applied for a new one.'

Syl thought fast, and in her head she willed Lista to comply.

'Oh Lista, I'm sorry,' she said, and she meant that part at least. 'I lied that day because I didn't want you to know who I really am. That's why I was in Service robes. When people hear I'm related to the Archmage Syrene by blood, they always act differently around me, like they have to wait on me . . .'

As she spoke, the girl's features softened. Her mind felt pink and doughy beneath Syl's probing. The combination of Syl's will, and Syrene's name, was making Lista malleable.

'Please?' added Syl.

Lista grinned. A doorway to a storage closet was set into the wall farther along the corridor, and she pulled Syl towards it. They squeezed inside where they quickly exchanged clothes. As they spilled out again, Lista was giggling.

'How do I look?' she said, twirling bashfully.

'Beautiful,' Syl replied. Tenderly she smoothed the girl's hair down, for it was mussed from her headscarf, which now covered Syl's own hair. She felt guilty, hoping the girl wouldn't be in dreadful trouble once the deception was discovered.

'It'll be fun to be waited on for once,' said Lista.

'It'll be nice to go unnoticed,' said Syl.

They smiled and then hugged each other.

'See you back here in, what, three hours?' said Lista.

Syl nodded, and Lista skipped away.

Syl went in the other direction. She rounded a corner, preparing to lose herself among the mingling guests, and almost collided with a figure in blue. Quickly she turned her face away as Sarea rudely shoved past, scowled at the obstruction, and then moved purposefully on. The doorway to one of the private VIP quarters stood open in the corridor behind her. Syl was certain that it was from there that Sarea had come. She was tempted to follow her old nemesis, but she was curious to discover what the Novice had been up to in this section of the palace. She padded noiselessly to the door and peered in.

Two bodies lay on the floor. One wore the formal dress of a Military officer, the other a Civilian's robes. Their throats had been crushed, as though a great weight had been dropped on their necks and then removed. Syl stared at them for a moment longer before checking the name on the room's display panel. It read 'Formia Deshan', but it meant nothing to Syl. She moved on, hurrying to catch up with Sarea. She spotted her just as she was joined by two more Gifted – Xaron and Mila. A fourth appeared: Nemein, that plague rat, and with her was a Half-Sister whom Syl didn't recognise, but the blue piping on her hem and cuffs gave her special status away.

Guests were heading for the Grand Hall to take their seats for the ceremony, but the Gifted moved against the flow. In the middle of the tide of Illyri, like a rock around which everyone was forced to pass, stood a final Blue Novice. Tanit was waiting for her Sisters to join her. Close beside her, smiling happily, stood Ani in her own robes of blue. Syl ducked her head, moving carefully now, not daring to use any of her own psychic abilities for fear that it might draw her friend's attention to her. Or Tanit's. Instead she relied upon the crowds, and the Service robes, to hide her.

The five Gifted gathered around Tanit and Ani. Some words were exchanged, and then Tanit bent and whispered into Ani's ear. Ani flushed, staring up at Tanit with delight, and nodded vehemently. Tanit kissed her cheek, and Ani turned to leave. Syl watched her go and, as she walked, Ani morphed before her eyes, fluidly becoming a second Tanit. The Gifted watched, and Tanit nodded in satisfaction. Then together they moved off.

And Syl followed.

Tiray was gazing down at Kellar's body. The Junior Consul's features were barely recognisable beneath the tumours that had sprouted like dark, dire flowers from his flesh. Tiray was unable to speak, so great was his shock and sorrow, but what could he have said anyway? There was nothing to say, nothing that would bring Kellar back to life, or explain how he had died.

'That's it,' said Paul. 'We're getting off this rock now.'

He activated the communicator in his helmet in order to contact Steven and Alis, but heard only static.

'Peris,' he said. 'I can't get through.'

'Let me try.'

Peris spoke aloud, relying on his Chip to make the connection.

'Peris to *Nomad*. Come in, *Nomad*.'

He got nothing.

'Something is blocking our transmissions,' said Peris.

'Then we'll just have to convince a couple of Sisters to take us back to our ship in one of their nice shuttles,' said Paul.

'And how are you going to do that without a gun?' asked Peris.

'I can be very persuasive,' Paul replied. 'And if that doesn't work, I'll knock them unconscious and you can fly us up there yourself.'

He gripped Tiray's arm.

'Councillor, we have to go. If you stay here, you're going to end up as dead as your friends. We all are.'

Tiray didn't move. His eyes were closed, and his lips moved soundlessly. If Paul hadn't known better, he might have said that Tiray was praying.

'Councillor—'

But now there was movement behind them, and Paul caught glimpses of rich blue, like birds gently alighting. He turned to find five young Illyri females blocking the exit from the room, all dressed in royal blue robes.

'Who are you?' he asked.

'My name is Tanit,' said the eldest of them. 'And these are my Sisters.'

And Paul's skin began to prickle as the first of the heat blisters appeared on it.

They had left Bela in the corridor to guard the door. The Half-Sister watched curiously as Syl approached, and Syl felt Bela's consciousness probing her own.

Lista. My name is Lista.

Bela's brow furrowed. She looked confused, and then confusion gave way to concern. She opened her mouth in warning, but Syl stilled her tongue. Then, with little more than a passing thought, Syl forced Bela to run head first into the nearest wall.

Paul's left hand felt as though it were being held over an open fire. He tried to move, but he was frozen in place. He could not even open his mouth to scream. Beside him Tiray was gurgling, his face growing redder and redder as he struggled to breathe. Peris, meanwhile, was watching in horror as the fingertips of his right hand turned inwards upon themselves and seemed to melt towards the knuckles.

The burning was spreading to Paul's forearm when suddenly it began to ease. The Nairene who had been staring so fixedly at him, the one who was strangely beautiful, even as she tortured him, tilted her head in puzzlement.

'This one is not Illyri,' she said. 'This one is . . . human!'

Her words seemed to have an effect on the two Nairenes at either side of her, and on the pair who stood behind them, hand in hand, their features almost identical, though one was shorter and broader.

'A human?' said the Nairene on the right, the one whose attention had been focused on Peris. 'But Tanit, it's not possible.'

The brief break in their concentration gave Paul the chance that he needed. His right hand shot out, the punch connecting squarely with the nose of the one called Tanit, the one who had been burning him, and he felt it break beneath the impact. Peris reacted seconds later, swinging his uninjured hand at the nearest of the young females, but he was right-handed by nature, and the blow from his left missed its target by inches. Paul tried to press home his advantage, but suddenly he found himself flying through the air, and his back hit a wall with enough force to stun him briefly. He went down on his knees, his helmet sliding to the floor, unable to see anything but flashes of pain for a few moments.

When he recovered himself, he looked up to see a vision of rage before him: Tanit, with the lower half of her face bathed in her blood, and her robes spattered with it. Tiray lay on the floor behind her, his body arching as he choked to death. Peris knelt beside him. The malady that was infecting the old soldier was a flesh-eating disease: already it had consumed his right arm up to the elbow.

But Paul could not help them. He could not even help himself. Like a puppet having its strings manipulated, he felt his left arm being raised, and the fingertips of his hand spread before him.

'I'll make you sorry you were ever born,' said Tanit.

And Paul's hand ignited in a white-hot flame.

CHAPTER 73

Whoever, or whatever, Syl had expected to see as she entered the room, it was not Paul Kerr. She was so astonished at the sight of him, his left hand raised before him like a fiery emblem, that it took her a few seconds to react. When she did, it was with a fury that matched the heat of Tanit's own anger.

Tanit was so lost in her own wrath and pain, and in the pleasure she was deriving from torturing the human male, that at first she did not feel her feet leave the floor. The sensation of levitation was one that she sometimes associated with the deepest of psychic trances, and only when the soles of her shoes were already inches from the carpet did she recognise the involvement of some outside force. But by then Syl was already flinging her across the room, and she landed painfully on an antique sideboard, sending flowers and ornaments scattering.

The fire on Paul's flesh went out, but the agony remained. His hand was charred black, the damaged skin split in places, like a volcanic landscape cut by rivulets of red lava. Tears ran down his cheeks, so that the room became a blur to him. Through it he saw another Nairene dressed in white robes, eyes wild, a headscarf slipping from a familiar bronze mane of hair. He blinked, and his vision cleared a little.

'Syl?' he said.

But Syl did not hear him, for she was beyond the reach of words or reason.

Syl was a being of pure rage.

★ ★ ★

Mila and Xaron turned to find Syl standing behind them. In their surprise at her appearance they released their grip on each other's hands. Together their power was squared, not doubled, but apart they were vulnerable. Xaron – older, more experienced – was the immediate threat. Syl felt Xaron's mind probing her and the pinpricks of her power as she tried to inflict pain all over Syl's body. But Syl pictured her own skin as steel armour through which Xaron could not penetrate. She allowed Xaron time to react, letting her increase the intensity of her efforts while she waited for Mila to join in – reaching for her sister's hand, for her sister's strength. Syl felt them come together, and she allowed them to go deeper and deeper into their killing trance so that they were lost in the single-mindedness of it. That's when she intervened, turning the force of their own potency against them like a series of double-pointed darts hurled back against their source.

Xaron's eyes widened with hurt as invisible needles pierced deep into her body. She turned to Mila, panicked, stretching for her with her free hand, hoping that together they might save themselves, but Mila was already past salvation, and her fingers slipped from Xaron's. She fell to the floor, her eyes sightless and her legs twitching as the last of her life left her body. Xaron joined her, but by then Syl had moved on to deal with the others. Xaron's last thought was that Syl could not even be bothered to watch her die.

By now Paul was on his feet, even as Nemein and Sarea prepared to tackle Syl. They were circling her, trying to divide her attention and weaken her ability to strike at either one of them. Syl concentrated on staying out of Nemein's reach. She didn't think that Nemein, walking virus that she was, was strong enough to infect her without touching, and even then she'd have to hold on for a while in order to break through Syl's defences. But Sarea was different. Something inside her was broken in the worst possible way. She was a sadist, a creature entirely without mercy, and that gave her fearsome power. Already Syl could feel pressure at her neck, her temples, her kidneys and her heart, as Sarea's mind squeezed.

But Sarea's love of inflicting pain was also her weakness. She could not control it properly. Once unleashed, it was like a torrent. So Syl did as she had with Xaron and Mila: she let Sarea's power come, taunting her to be stronger . . .

Come on! You've wanted to do this for so long. Hurt me. Kill me!

She saw Sarea smile, and watched as the muscles in her neck grew tighter and her fists began to clench. Syl felt as though her skull was being crushed in a vice, and her lungs were struggling to get enough air. Something popped painfully in her chest – Sarea had cracked one of her ribs – but at the same time Syl felt her urging the Nemein to keep her distance.

Stay away from her. She's mine.

Yes, I'm yours. Do it. Do it, you evil bitch!

Sarea's power was ratcheted up to ten. Syl's skull was seconds away from fracturing. Just as it seemed that it must surely break, Syl shot one simple image into Sarea's head, clouding her mind, and then stepped aside.

Before Sarea stood Nemein, but to Sarea she was Syl. Nemein, defenceless and unready, took the full force of Sarea's desire to crush and break. Syl heard a sound like the snapping of dry twigs, and Nemein's body crumpled into a lifeless heap.

And Syl's only thought was that, like Oriel's, Nemein's death was quicker than she deserved.

She looked down to see Peris lying at her feet, his right arm almost entirely eaten away, although there was no blood. He was deep in shock, and barely seemed to register Syl's presence. Beside him lay the body of another Illyri, but he was clearly dead, his neck twisted at an impossible angle.

Sarea was staring at Nemein's corpse. Now she spun towards Syl.

'Look what you made me do!' she screamed.

Syl thought of Elda, and the two bodies she had recently found with their throats crushed. Sarea was like a rabid animal – what Syl was about to do to her was almost a kindness.

She willed Sarea into the air, but nothing happened. Absorbing all of that pain, all of that hate, had weakened Syl momentarily, but a moment was all that the Blue Novice needed. Syl felt Sarea trying to hurt her again, and was too drained to resist. An intense pain exploded in her skull, and death reached out a hand to her.

The pain eased. Sarea shook her head, as though trying to dislodge an insect from her ear.

'I always knew you were cruel,' said a familiar voice, and Ani emerged from the hall outside. 'But I never realised how unworthy of those robes you are.'

The distraction was all that Syl needed, and Sarea's body hit the old stone wall of the palace with enough force to kill her instantly. Momentarily Syl felt weak, sapped of all energy, and she was sure that her legs must surely crumble beneath her, but instead her body shuddered, and a charge ran through her as her strength returned. She was momentarily amazed by the force of it: strangely, she felt even more powerful than before, but there was no time to consider it, for she had more pressing concerns.

She looked at Ani, but her friend had turned away, staring slack-jawed at the carnage around her. Syl wanted to say something, to explain, but as she opened her mouth to speak she felt heat on her left arm: the sleeve of her robe was on fire. She smelled burning hair, and realised that one side of her head was aflame too.

'No,' she said, and the flames went out.

'Oh, now I understand,' said another voice. It was Tanit. She was standing by the window, and beside her was Paul, his arms outstretched, his feet barely touching the floor, held in place by the force of Tanit's will.

'So this is the one you have feelings for,' she sneered. She sounded both amused and disgusted. 'Yes, Earth-whore, Dessa told me about your perversions. You should be ashamed.'

'Let him go,' said Syl.

Tanit did not. Instead she tried to burn Syl again, but this time the fire was extinguished before it was barely more than a spark.

'You hid yourself well,' said Tanit, her voice smooth and soft. 'We never suspected that you had that kind of power.'

'I didn't know the extent of it either – until now.'

'The Sisterhood will forgive you for what you have done here,' said Tanit. 'With your abilities, they would probably forgive you if you killed Syrene herself.'

'I may yet do that,' said Syl. 'But for now, I'm giving you a final warning: let him go.'

Tanit shook her head. She still believed that she could sway Syl.

'Join us,' she said. 'Join *me*. Me, and Ani. We could do so much for the Sisterhood, for all Illyri. We're the future. We will change society. We will alter it with our minds. Tell her, Ani. Tell her that I'm speaking the truth.'

Ani stood to one side, equidistant from both Tanit and Syl, like the third point in an awkward triangle. Tears ran down her cheeks, and Syl was horrified to hear her reply.

'She's right, Syl,' said Ani. 'We can change things for the better. It doesn't have to be the way it was on Earth. Together we can make the Corps and the Military do our will. We can prevent war. The Sisterhood would be the real power, and it would be a power for good.'

'Ani,' said Syl, 'look around you! There is no *good*! They're killing Illyri. They're wiping out anyone who disagrees with them, anyone who is a threat.'

'Them? They're enemies,' said Tanit. 'They would have hurt us had we not dealt with them first.'

Syl ignored her, and fixed her gaze on Ani.

'I've seen things, Ani, in the depths of the Marque. I've seen the First Five. They're alive, but there's a creature, a consciousness, holding them prisoner. They want to die. They started out believing they could control it, but now it controls them. They've sacrificed entire worlds to it – that's what happened to Archaeon – and Earth will be next. They thought they were doing good, but they made a terrible mistake. All that is wrong with the Empire, all that has poisoned it, has its roots in the Marque.'

'She's lying!' Tanit cried. Syl looked at her, and saw that she genuinely did not know anything about what Syl had witnessed.

'It's true, Tanit,' said Syl. 'They've used you too.'

But Tanit was not to be reasoned with.

'You're the poison!' she shouted. 'You're the mistake! And if I can't burn you, then I'll burn the thing you love.'

Paul screamed as puffs of smoke rose from all over his body, and the skin on his face and uninjured hand began to blister. Syl focused on Tanit, but the last of the Blue Novices was stronger than the others, so much stronger, and Paul's shrieks rose in pitch as he fell to the ground, desperately rolling as if he could put the flames out.

The smoke stopped rising. Like Sarea before her, Tanit felt Ani's influence as a buzzing in her head, a clouding of her consciousness.

'Stay out of this,' she hissed at Ani. 'Trust me, you're picking the wrong side.'

But Syl, forced to watch Paul suffer again, barely heard Tanit speak. Her feelings for him fuelled her own fire. He must have come here to find her, and she would not let him die for her. She focused all of her energy on Tanit, all of the power that she had drawn from the dead Novices whose bodies lay scattered across the room. For the first time since the carnage had begun, Syl felt tired of killing. She wanted it to end, but Tanit would not allow it.

And so Tanit, too, would have to die.

I have become a monster, thought Syl. *I am as bad as the rest of you, but so be it.*

Tanit gaped dumbstruck at the index finger of her left hand. It was burning. The fire turned from red to orange, and from yellow to white as its intensity increased. Tanit gritted her teeth and tried to douse the flame, but to no avail. Her hand moved upwards towards her forehead, her burning finger pausing an inch from her skin, her entire body shaking. She stared at Syl in disbelief, and found the strength to say her final words.

'They'll destroy you for this.'

Then Tanit's fingertip touched her forehead, and she burst into flames.

CHAPTER 74

Syl emerged as if from a trance. Tanit was no more, reduced to a mound of blackened flesh, and Syl was surrounded by the dead. Only Ani, Paul and Peris remained alive.

When she had time to think and consider her actions, Syl would try to analyse her feelings and state of mind during the carnage in Kellar's apartments. At first, it seemed to her that there was another Syl, a darker Syl, who had somehow taken over, and that she – the good Syl – was powerless to stop her. But, in silence and solitude, she was forced to admit that this was not the case: the true Syl, the one who could bend others to her will, even to the extent of forcing them to kill, or to take their own lives, was a combination of the two. And the most terrifying thing of all for Syl was that she still had no real understanding of her own nature, or of the extent of her power.

But all that was for another time. For now, what mattered was Paul. She ran to him, and he held her with one arm, keeping his injured hand away from her body.

'How did you get here?' she asked, her lips resting against his forehead, her mouth brushing his blistered skin.

'It's complicated,' said Paul.

Wincing, he hugged her.

'I've come to take you away,' he said, and he was grateful that she made no objection, and even more so that she did not ask him if he had a plan. His plan, insofar as it went, was to get back to the *Nomad*, point it towards the wormhole, and hope for the best. But without her intervention, he realised, he would be dead. Somehow, the rescuer had become the rescued.

'They'll be looking for me,' Syl told him. 'Not just for this. I killed a Sister in the Marque. I had to. I—'

Paul let go of her, and then placed his hand tenderly on her cheek. Her hair tickled his wrist.

'Not now,' he said. 'We can talk about it once we're safely off Erebos.'

He went to Peris and tried to lift him up, but the Illyri would not stand.

'How could they have known?' said Peris, as much to himself as to the others. 'They killed them all, but how could they have known?'

'Peris, we don't have time to hang around,' said Paul.

Peris was pale, and bathed in sweat. Only now did he seem to notice Paul.

'I'm not leaving,' he said.

'You have to. They'll want you dead.'

Peris shook his head. He was in agony, but still determined.

'Someone must stay. If we all run, there will be no one left to bear witness against them.'

Paul bent beside Peris. He was overcome by admiration for him, unclouded by anything but pure affection, and felt a fleeting stab of shame that he'd ever doubted him.

'I can't stay,' said Paul.

'I know. If you did, I'd damn you for a fool. Take Syl and Ani away. Look after them. Look after each other. And Paul' – Peris clasped the young human by the back of the head, pulling his face closer – 'find a way to fight them.'

Paul swallowed hard. He was sure that he was seeing Peris for the last time.

'I will.'

'Go! Go on, get out of here while you still can.'

Paul took Syl's hand and turned to go, but she pulled him back.

'Ani?' she said. Her best friend was crouched on the floor by Tanit's remains, her face in her hands, her body shaking with silent sobs. On hearing her name, she looked up, and her face was twisted with grief.

'How could you, Syl? How could you kill her? I loved her!'

'Ani, please, let's just go. We can talk about it later.'

Ani stood.

'No! I'm not coming with you. What if you decide to kill me? You've already murdered so many of us.'

'I had no choice. Look at the bodies! Look what they did to Peris! Think what Tanit was going to do to Paul.'

Paul interrupted: 'Ani, there's a trail of their victims in this damned palace. I've seen them, all slaughtered. Anyone who might get in the Sisterhood's way is being assassinated.'

Ani stared at him.

'Where's Steven?' she said finally.

'He's in a ship waiting to take us away. Come on, we must go.'

Ani stood, but then she shook her head and went to kneel by Peris.

'If what you say is true, Paul, then it's important I stay here with Peris. Together we will be witnesses. Together we will try to change things.'

She reached out and took Peris's undamaged hand. The old soldier looked up at her and opened his mouth, but his pain stole away any words.

'Please, Ani,' Syl begged. 'Come with me. You're my best friend.'

Ani turned and looked at Syl coldly.

'You!' she said. 'You lied to me about your gifts, Syl. You killed without mercy. And Tanit is gone – gone, forever. You can't even *begin* to understand what you've done to me. All my friends are dead, killed by your hand. No, I can't call you my friend, not now, not after what you've done.'

Syl tried to speak, but Ani silenced her with a glare.

'Don't!' she said. 'I will stay here and, if things are as you say they are, I will do my best to bring such evil to an end. You seem determined to forget that the Sisterhood was founded with a noble purpose, but I shall make it my mission to reclaim that purpose, however long it takes. In time I may even come to forgive you, but I will never trust you, Syl Hellais. Frankly, I'll be happy if I never lay eyes on you again.'

Ani took a deep breath, and it caught ragged in her throat as she continued: 'Yet we're both on the side of what is good and right, and so I wish you luck.'

Syl could barely see Ani, for her own tears obliterated her vision, but she saw enough to know that Ani had turned her back on her, and when she reached out desperately with her mind it was like running into broken glass.

'Ani,' she whispered. 'Ani, please . . .'

Ani's spine was rigid, and Paul pulled at Syl's hand.

'We have to go,' he said. She nodded.

Together, they ran.

The first step was to get to the shuttle landing pads. Once there, they could force a crew to take them up to the *Nomad*. Paul could see that shuttles continued to land and depart: with luck, they could just lose themselves in the traffic.

Guests were still making their way to the Grand Hall for the ceremony. Nairenes moved among them, but there was no sign of any more Blue Novices, and nobody appeared to be paying them very much attention at all. He looked at Syl and saw that, beneath her hastily rewound headscarf, her face was a rictus of concentration, her eyes puffy and red, but dry. She was doing her best to *make* both of them unnoticeable.

A covered glass tunnel connected the main palace complex with the landing pads. They were almost halfway down it, the crowds all gone now, when a voice spoke Syl's name. Syl stopped, and a great weariness swept over her. She should have known that escape would not be so easy.

She turned to face Syrene. The Archmage waited at a junction in the tunnel, about twenty feet from where Syl and Paul stood. She was flanked by her personal handmaidens, Cocile and Layne.

Other figures joined them now: Securitats, the very ones that had regarded Tiray with such hostility earlier that day. They appeared to be unarmed – clearly the laws about weapons on Erebos even applied to the Securitats – but they outnumbered Paul and Syl.

Paul heard footsteps behind him. He glanced over his shoulder and saw three more Securitats cutting off their route to the landing pads. They were surrounded.

It was then that Lord Andrus stepped into the tunnel.

Syl almost ran to her father. She had not been permitted to communicate with him since her departure for the Marque, and even though she had convinced herself that he was no longer the parent she had known, seeing him in the flesh forced everything but love from her mind, especially now, when she felt so raw and exposed.

'Father,' she said.

He smiled at her and extended his arms, inviting her into his embrace.

'Syl,' he replied. 'My beloved daughter. Come to me.'

Her feet moved of her own volition. Only Paul's grip on her hand prevented her from going further. He squeezed her fingers.

'Be careful,' he said, remembering Peris's warning about Andrus. 'He's different now.'

But he didn't look different. He was still the one who had held her as a child, who had indulged her as a teenager, who had shown her images of the late Lady Orianne, telling Syl stories of the mother she had never known, bringing her back to life by sharing his memories of her with their daughter.

Lord Andrus spoke her name again, but now his tone had an edge to it. He continued to smile, but his eyes had the glassiness of a doll's.

'Syl, come here. Do as I tell you.'

And in that moment Syl had the answer to Peris's question: Syrene's pet killers had known whom to target because her father – or the thing that now infected him – had revealed all his secrets to his wife-to-be. Trying desperately not to weep, Syl stepped back to join Paul, clutching his hand tighter.

Lord Andrus's smile faded, but it was Syrene who spoke next.

'We're disappointed in you, Syl. We had high hopes for you.'

But she didn't sound disappointed. Instead, Syl thought that she was almost impressed. Tentatively, Syl allowed her mind to probe Syrene's feelings. Yes, there it was: surprise. Syl had surprised her.

She knows, Syl thought. She knows about what I did to Oriel. She knows that I've seen the First Five. And she also knows what I can do with my mind. Like the others, she always believed that Ani was the one with the power, but she was wrong.

Surprise. I feel it. I sense it.

Surprise —

And fear.

Syrene swatted away Syl's probings, but she reacted just a second too late. She had exposed herself to the young female.

Now her eyes flicked briefly towards Paul.

'You should have stayed far from here, boy,' she told him. 'You'll die on Erebos now. If it's any consolation to you, at least you'll be dying for love.'

She returned her attention to Syl.

'You will attend our wedding,' she said. 'You shall smile throughout. When the ceremony is over, you will be returned to the Marque. And then, well, we shall see . . .'

Syrene ordered the Securitats behind them to seize Paul. Two of them were male, one female. The males grabbed Paul, one of them disabling him instantly by digging his gloved fingers into Paul's wounded hand. The female tried to hold Syl — for males were not permitted to touch Nairene Sisters, even a prisoner such as she — but by now it was a simple matter for Syl to cloud the Securitat's mind, and suddenly the Securitat was groping at one of the males holding Paul.

Then Syl felt Syrene's thoughts enter her mind, filling her brain with a painful, high-pitched shriek even as she tried to focus on the Securitat.

'Cocile, Layne: deal with her,' Syrene told her handmaidens, and the pair stepped forward.

What happened next convinced Syl that she had started to hallucinate. Layne fell behind and, just as Cocile neared Syl, Layne leapt in the air and landed a blow that knocked Cocile unconscious. The male Securitats holding Paul had no time to react before Layne was on them. Syl heard the snapping of vertebrae, and they were gone. The shrieking in Syl's head ceased, and she saw the female Securitat punching herself hard enough in the face to knock herself unconscious. A second later, the Securitat was on the ground.

Now Layne spun and extended her right hand in a closed fist. The flesh above the third finger burst, and a thin muzzle extended itself. The first of the pulses from it struck the Securitat closest to Syrene, and the second clipped the Archmage herself, sending her stumbling backwards in pain. The tunnel began to vibrate around them, and Syl looked up to see an unfamiliar ship coming in fast. It was the *Nomad*. Its heavy cannon swivelled, and moments later the far end of the tunnel disintegrated in shards of metal and glass.

'Run!' said Layne, and Paul and Syl raced to the gap while Syrene's servant covered their retreat, walking slowly backwards as her right arm bucked with the force of the pulse blasts.

The *Nomad* landed and the cabin door opened, the gangway automatically lowering. Thula appeared in the gap and helped Syl on board first, then Paul. Layne came last, still firing. When they were all safely inside, the *Nomad* turned in the direction of the landing pads, where a dozen shuttles stood waiting. Alis raked the pads with the heavy cannon, watching with satisfaction as Nairenes scattered and shuttles exploded. It would be some time before the pads could be used again.

'And there,' said Layne, pointing at an array of dishes and antennae straight ahead. The cannon spoke again, and the array was blasted to pieces.

'Good luck raising the alarm now,' said Steven.

The *Nomad* commenced a steep ascent, Steven giving the ship full throttle so that Paul and Syl barely had time to get into their seats before the G-force pushed them back against the padding. They left the moon's atmosphere less than a minute later, emerging into the vastness of space, Melos Station to their port side, the Melos wormhole to starboard.

Layne rose from her seat, found the ship's medical kit, and tried to examine Paul's hand. He pulled it away.

'Who are you?' Paul asked her. '*What* are you?'

'That's no way to speak to your rescuer,' said Alis from the cockpit. 'The correct words are "Thank you, Meia".'

'*Meia?*' said Syl.

And she reached out and embraced the Mech who had, once again, brought her to safety.

CHAPTER 75

While Meia treated Paul's burns, she told them as much as she could of how she had come to be on Erebos: the selection of a new identity (which, not entirely regrettably, had involved disposing of the real Layne, whose remains were now rotting deep below Edinburgh Castle); the journey from Earth, and her arrival on the moon with Syrene's party; and her discovery, through careful listening on the long voyage, of the plan to use the Blue Novices, the most adept generation yet of the Gifted, to dispose of enemies of both the Sisterhood and the Corps, with the wedding ceremony as cover for the killings.

Unfortunately, Meia had been too late to prevent the attacks, but she was present when the bodies of Tanit and the others were discovered, and had just enough time to speak to Peris and inform him of her identity before he was taken away for medical attention and questioning. It was he who had told her of Syl and Paul's flight, and also of the presence of the *Nomad* in orbit. As a Mech, the communications blackout imposed by the Sisterhood had no effect on her: Meia was her own communications system. Alis had homed in on Meia's signal, and when she saw the figures in the connector tunnel she knew exactly what to do.

Now Syl and Paul began to talk at once, trying to share what they had discovered both with each other and with Meia. But their conversation was cut short by a warning from Alis.

'Incoming craft from the wormhole,' she said. 'I'm picking up Corps chatter.'

'That's unfortunate,' said Meia, from Layne's mouth.

She had hoped that the destruction of the array might have bought them more time. She pulled up a screen and watched the approach of six ships, one much larger than the others.

'Wait, that's not any known ship,' she said. 'None of those craft have fleet identifiers, Corps or otherwise.'

She increased the size of the image.

'It's as big as a battleship, but I don't read any armaments. It's like a huge tanker.'

'We have visual,' said Paul.

Six ships appeared as growing white specks through the cockpit window. As they watched, two of them, including the tanker, peeled off and headed towards Melos Station. The others maintained their course towards the wormhole, increasing speed with astonishing rapidity, seeking to intercept the *Nomad*. They looked sleek and deadly, like silver daggers against the blackness of space.

'They're trying to cut us off!' said Alis.

'No Corps ship has that kind of acceleration,' said Meia.

'The Corps has been busy while you were on Earth,' said Steven. 'But at least we know what we're up against.'

He increased the *Nomad*'s velocity in order to reach the wormhole before their pursuers. Again, the four silver ships increased their pace, but the *Nomad* had enough of a lead on them to reach the wormhole before they did.

'They'll follow us,' said Meia.

'And there's one for each of the wormhole's mouths,' said Steven. 'No matter which way we go, we'll have a ship on our tail.'

More lights appeared on the long-range scanner. All were headed towards the wormhole. Eight dots now converged upon them.

'Actually, make that at least two on our tail, no matter which wormhole we take,' said Steven.

'Do you have any thoughts, Lieutenant?' said Alis.

Paul was already at a console. He pulled up the wormhole map and began to plot a course. When he was finished, he swiped his hand through the air to send the course over to Steven's cockpit display.

'You've got to be kidding me,' said Steven, when he saw the route.

'We have no choice,' said Paul. 'We need to stay away from the main wormholes. We'll be okay leaving Melos because they won't have had time to raise the alarm yet, but after that we'll be in trouble. We have to try to shake them off, and the best way to do that is through a lot of rapid boosts using unmonitored wormholes.'

'But this route brings us right to—'

'I know,' said Paul. 'With a little luck, we'll be free and clear before we're forced to make that last boost.'

'And if we're not?'

'Let's not think about it.'

He turned away, glancing quickly towards Syl, who quietly nodded her agreement. Her eyes were swollen, her hair was tangled, and her face was ghostly pale and blotchy. But, right now, Paul was sure he'd never see anything so welcome, and so beloved, for the rest of his days. He gave her a weak smile, then turned again to the control of his ship.

Steven and Alis were staring at the final wormhole on the list, and the word that marked the system beyond it: *Derith*. Unknown. The end of the line was a system from which nothing had ever returned.

'Prepare for first boost,' said Paul.

'What can I do?' said Syl.

'Nothing at the moment. Just strap yourself in.'

The others did as he ordered, all except Meia. She was watching the progress on screen of the two vessels heading for Melos Station.

'Too fast,' she said.

'What?' said Paul.

'That big ship: it's approaching Melos Station too quickly.'

They saw cannon flashes and the trails of torpedoes as the batteries on the base opened up. The smaller escort craft veered away, leaving the larger one to continue on its path. Not only was it heading too quickly towards the base, it was accelerating. Torpedoes flared against its hull, and the cannon fire rocked it, but none of the base's defences appeared able to stop it.

They all watched – on Meia's display, on the cockpit screens – as the huge ship struck the base, its bow cleaving through the walls of

Melos Station, shattering docking arms and causing the ships moored against them to ignite silently.

And then the ship exploded, taking with it Melos Station and the thousands who served on it. A blinding white flash filled the windows, forcing them all to turn away, and the *Nomad* was buffeted by the shock waves from the explosion.

When they looked again, Melos Station was gone, and only the wreckage of it remained.

'So many,' said Syl. 'So many dead . . .'

All on board were similarly frozen by what they had witnessed.

'It's war,' said Meia. 'Civil war.'

'Wormhole imminent!' said Alis. 'We're boosting.'

They belted themselves into their seats, spots of light still dancing before their eyes from the destruction of Melos Station, and then they were in the wormhole.

Eight ships followed, and three stayed with them.

They destroyed the first as soon as it exited the wormhole: a *Nomad* mine attached itself to their pursuer's hull and blew it to pieces while its crew were probably still shaking off the effects of the boost.

A stroke of luck left the second pursuer at their mercy, for it was disabled by a meteor in the Lodal system, and Rizzo calmly picked it off with their heavy cannon.

But the third stayed on their tail, and they played a game of cat and mouse with it for thirty-six hours. The fact that they had entered the wormhole first gave them a slight advantage, for it meant that the final Corps ship had to exit carefully, always anticipating an attack yet reluctant to allow the *Nomad* to gain a further lead on it. They attempted mines and ambushes. They made an effort to outrun it, with the engines at full throttle, but it kept pace with them all the way. They tried hiding, and alternative routes to the next wormhole, but the pilots of the hunting ship were masterful, and slowly it gained on them, aided by the absence of the kind of disguising layer of armour that slowed the *Nomad* ever so slightly. Gradually it ate away at their initial lead. Their pursuers also conserved their ammunition, firing when a chance presented itself but otherwise seemingly content to wait for the *Nomad* and its crew to tire or exhaust their own armaments.

And the *Nomad* was failing: the ship had made too many boosts, and the repairs made at Melos Station were patches and little more. The *Nomad* could not continue running forever.

So the pursuit continued, until they came to the last wormhole.

'What's it doing?' asked Rizzo.

'Waiting,' said Paul.

The final ship remained just within visual range, but out of reach of their cannon. No communication had been received from it, no request to halt and surrender. Like a predator chasing wounded prey, it had simply shadowed them until they were too worn out and exhausted to run any more. Now it had cornered them, or so it believed, for behind lay only the final wormhole, and nothing that entered it ever came out again.

Derith. Illyri for unknown.

The Derith Wormhole.

'We have activity,' said Steven.

Three small dots appeared on the display.

'Torpedoes,' said Alis. 'We're being targeted!'

The torpedoes sped towards them. One they could possibly avoid; two, with a miracle.

But three torpedoes would doom them.

'Prepare to boost,' yelled Paul.

'Are you sure?' said Steven.

Paul spun towards him.

'That wasn't a suggestion, *Private*!'

'Yes, Lieutenant! Commencing sequence. Boosting in ten – nine – eight – seven – six – '

The torpedoes kept coming. Closer now, converging on the *Nomad* from three different directions, their inbuilt intelligence systems adjusting course to ensure that no manoeuvre would permit their prey to escape them.

'Five – four – '

Paul strapped himself in. Everything was secured. Around him, the others were doing the same.

'Three – two – one.'

Paul gripped Syl's hand, closed his eyes, and prayed.

Hold together. Please, hold together.

And save us from whatever waits on the other side.

'Boosting,' said Steven.

And the Derith Wormhole swallowed them.

They emerged into the blackness of an unknown system. There was no collapsing star, no asteroid belt, no planet right at the wormhole's mouth with its atmosphere waiting to burn up anything that emerged at speed. There was only space, and the flickering of distant stars.

Then, slowly, space came alive; nothingness transforming into something, something that was all around them.

'My God,' said Syl. 'It's a ship.'